# the last
# night
# out

**Catherine O'Connell** divides her time between Chicago and Aspen, and sits on the board of Aspen Words, a literary centre whose aim is to support writers and reach out to readers. She is also a member of Mystery Writers of America and Sisters in Crime. Catherine has appeared on ABC, NBC, CBS, the Cox network and numerous radio shows including WGN Radio's *Sunday Papers with Rick Kogan.*

@cathyinaspen   catherineoconnell.net

*Also by Catherine O'Connell*


*The High Society Mysteries*

Well Bred and Dead
Well Read and Dead

# the last
# night
# out

## CATHERINE O'CONNELL

**BLACK**THORN

First published in Great Britain, the USA and Canada in 2019
by Black Thorn, an imprint of Canongate Books Ltd,
14 High Street, Edinburgh EH1 1TE

Distributed in the USA by Publishers Group West and in Canada by
Publishers Group Canada

First published in 2018 by Severn House Publishers Ltd,
Eardley House, 4 Uxbridge Street, London W8 7SY

blackthornbooks.com

1

*British Library Cataloguing in Publication Data*
A catalogue record for this book is available on request from the British
Library.

ISBN  978 1 78689 484 7

Typeset by Palimpsest Book Production Ltd, Falkirk,
Stirlingshire, Scotland.
Printed and bound in Great Britain by Clays Ltd, Elcograf S.p.A.

For my three siblings, Tom, Jane and Barney.
The best gift an author can have is a loving and eccentric family,
and I have been blessed with both.

# Present Day

sit alone in the music tent, in the back, away from any others. Rain pellets the pavilion's roof, dulling the atonal chords of the Schoenberg piano concerto. The dissonant music brings to mind how imperfection can be beautiful. A young cellist rushes in late and squirms into his seat in the orchestra. The change in the conductor's demeanor is barely perceptible, but it is clear he has taken note of the musician's tardiness. Is this a career-changing mistake on the cellist's part? It could well be. Music is a competitive field.

I wonder how many outcomes have hinged on such cringe-worthy moments: how many lives have been indelibly changed as a result of one misstep? Whether by choice or by deflection, the consequences of the alternate path can be dire. I ponder how my life might have turned out if not for my great misstep. Quite differently, I am certain.

There is comfort in knowing I was not directly responsible for Angela's death. Though over a quarter-century has passed since that night, it still creeps into my thoughts with undue frequency. And when I think of how my life turned out in the aftermath, there is always a twinge of guilt.

The rain ceases pounding just as the music comes to a rousing finish. The orchestra stands to thunderous applause, the tardy cellist rising alongside the others. Something about his lateness has appealed to me, and the realization comes in a flash. It is not too late to tell the story. It is never too late to out the truth. I slip from the tent ahead of the crowd and hurry across the parking lot to my car. As I drive home, with the peaks of the majestic Rockies rising to either side of me, I am already composing the words. By the time I arrive home, they are ready to fall into place.

So, if you will, travel back with me to a warm humid Chicago night in June of 1988. Changes were in play, but no one had any idea how profound they were. Disco was gasping its last breath, both men and women wore their hair long on the sides and short on top, jeans were stonewashed and high-waisted. Cher and people who lived in trailers were the only ones with tattoos. Gays were just coming out of the closet, while AIDS was already an epidemic. Computers were a novelty to anyone outside business, email barely existed, texting was science fiction, and if anyone had a cell phone, it was nearly the size of a shoe. The hottest phone technology was redial. As women, we were the first full generation of career seekers, monetarily and sexually liberated at last. But with our roles still being challenged in a man's world, we often settled for a lot less.

That's a snapshot of Chicago when this story begins. While I can bear witness to my role, you, the reader, must allow for the liberties I will take in assuming voice for the others. Though there may be some inaccuracies in my interpretation of what took place, I suspect in the end my story will ring true.

Margaret Mary Trueheart
July 10, 2013

# ONE

## 14 Days Until the Wedding

*Saturday, June 11, 1988*

I awoke to the sound of the phone ringing and with a sick, sinking feeling that I wasn't alone. As I lay on my side staring at the wall, there was no denying the heat of another body radiating beneath my designer sheets. I remembered that Flynn was out of town. A frantic replay of the night before brought up nothing more than scattered images. I was definitely still drunk.

The phone rang six times before the call went to the answering machine in the living room, and the sound of my voice echoed down the hall. *Hi, this is Maggie. You know what to do and when to do it.* The line went to a dial tone. The phone started ringing again. Once again the sound of my voice was followed by a hang-up. When it happened a third time, I realized the caller wasn't giving up. I rolled reluctantly onto my back to reach for the phone and my hand froze midair. It was the carpenter. The blue work shirt sans work shirt. He was grinning at me, his grin carving dimpled parentheses into his tanned cheeks. Nausea surged from my head to the toes of my all-too-naked body.

'Looks like someone sure wants to talk to you,' he said. Tapping a conspiratorial finger against his lips in a pledge of silence, he plucked the phone from its cradle and held it out to me, the cord cutting a swirling path through his matted chest hair. Horrified, I snatched the phone from him and cupped the mouthpiece next to my face, fearful my visitor might do something to make his presence known such as cough or speak or, God forbid, let loose the noisy emission so common to the male species in the morning hours.

'Hello,' croaked a voice hardly recognizable as my own.

'Maggie, oh Maggie, it's me, Suzanne.' Her words oozed with relief. 'Thank God you made it home OK.'

*That*, I thought, *is a matter of opinion*. My eyes settled back on my guest. He had made himself quite at home on his side of my bed, his curly head cradled in his hands, his elbows open like wings. He was still wearing a shit-eating grin, not quite the shy New Hampshire carpenter of the night before.

'Of course I made it home OK,' I lied. My eyes flashed to the clock. The digital readout told me it was seven forty-eight. Not super early, but still an uncivilized time for a phone call on a Saturday morning after a late Friday night, even from an early riser like Suzanne. In a lame attempt to sound flip, I asked, 'So what's up with calling at the break of dawn?'

There was a brief hesitation and then, 'I don't know how else to say this, Maggie. It's Angie. She's dead.'

The words cracked through my addled brain like a tamer's whip, causing me to bolt upright in the bed, my bare breasts exposed as the sheets fell away. I tugged the sheets back to my chin with delinquent modesty. That horse had already left the barn. 'This is a joke, right?' But even as the question fell from my lips, I knew its futility. Suzanne Lundgren was the least likely person on the planet to pull a prank of any kind, much less one so dark.

'I wish it were a joke.' The distress in her voice was evident. 'Kelly just called from the police station. Angie's been murdered. They found her body in Lincoln Park earlier this morning.'

'Kelly?' This didn't make sense. Scores of questions were forming in my head, but in my compromised state, the logical ones weren't surfacing. Instead of asking about Angie, I said, 'What does Kelly have to do with this?'

'Evidently, she was out for her morning run and she came across the crime scene,' Suzanne replied. 'She's at Area Three headquarters. They took her there to ask her questions about Angie, I guess.'

'But this is impossible. We were just together . . .' I glanced back at the clock. '. . . what, five, six hours ago? Didn't you take her home?'

This time Suzanne lost it, her words coming in breathy gasps. 'Maggie. Of course I took her home. After we left you, I poured her into a cab and took her straight to her house. I made the driver sit and wait until she went inside. I watched her close the door.'

Fragments of the night started coming back in a jigsaw-like jumble: Angie on the dance floor in black pants and a low-cut red top, her thick black hair sheeting her face in a dark curtain, her ample hips swaying teasingly over a pair of red stilettos. Angie propped against the neon bar, her tongue in an empty shot glass. Angie trying to stand up straight on Jello legs.

'Listen, I can't really talk anymore. I've told you all I know,' Suzanne said, her voice constricted in pain. 'Kelly promised to call as soon as she gets home with the rest of the details. In the meantime, will you call Carol Anne? I just can't do it.'

'Yes, of course,' I whispered. The line went dead.

Staring at the phone in my hand as if it was a foreign object, I fought to come to terms what had just happened. Surely I wasn't facing the finality of a friend's death. This had to be some kind of weird nightmare. Just like this stranger staring at me. He was part of the nightmare too. I would close my eyes and the world would go back to yesterday's normal. Angie would be alive, and I would be alone in my bed, and the worst thing anyone would suffer was the mother of all hangovers.

I pressed my eyes shut.

But when I reopened them he was still there, his presence nearly as disturbing as Angie's murder. His smile had disappeared, and his face was filled with genuine concern. He reached up and gently brushed my cheek. 'Is everything all right?'

'There was an accident,' I said, too dazed for tears, unwilling to share my personal grief with this stranger. 'You have to go now.'

Choosing to ignore my request, he reached out and stroked my face, brushing the back of his hand the length of my jawline. I fought back an involuntary shiver. There was a certain power in his hands, and I remembered being obsessed with them last night. They were large and strong with well-defined joints and hard-earned calluses that testified to hours of honest, physical labor. Hands so unlike Flynn's. Flynn's hands were silky and smooth with long tapered fingers and cuticle-free nails, hands that might carry a golf club or tennis racket, hands from an entirely different social strata.

'You are so beautiful,' he was saying, his caress migrating to the sensitive skin of my neck. 'So beautiful.'

Missing pieces began to emerge from the vodka cloud. Dancing to Cyndi Lauper at The Overhang, climbing into a white truck, the two of us bathed in yellow beneath the street-lamp outside my building. Still much of the jigsaw remained empty. With the dreamlike trance of the alcohol fading, and the protective cover of night gone, I was naked in the naked morning light. Eve staring at the apple. I thought of Flynn and my heart plummeted to the pit of my stomach. Then I thought about Angie, and my heart fell further still.

Apparently oblivious to my conflict, the carpenter brought his face to mine and kissed me lightly on the lips. 'No,' I protested, pulling away. Paying no attention to my attempted virtue, he slipped a hand to the small of my back and pulled me closer. So close I could feel the heat rising off the flat surface of his torso. He pressed his lips to my chin, to my nose, to my mouth. 'No,' I repeated, trying to summon some conviction as his lips continued their pilgrimage to behind my ear.

In a perfect world, the good me would have been repulsed by his very presence. In a perfect world, the good me would have slapped him hard and leapt from the bed. In a really perfect world, this man wouldn't have been there in the first place.

It's an imperfect world.

This was wrong, all wrong. How could I betray my fiancé like this? How could I even think of sex when I should be mourning the death of a friend? But something primal had sparked deep within me, overwhelming grief and guilt and sadness, taking my rational self as prisoner. My body was willing itself in his direction. I didn't even want to pretend to put up a fight. I wanted to be held by him, to bury my face in his chest, to allow him to bury himself in me.

I kissed him back hesitantly at first, and then in earnest, opening my mouth to accept his. He pushed me to the mattress and in no time we were rolling on my bed, our bodies pressed together. The movements grew more intense, and we were just shy of the inevitable when an unwelcome glimmer flickered in the recesses of my brain. I grabbed him by the hips and stopped him short of entering me. His breath came in desperate gasps as his coffee-colored eyes met mine.

'I don't suppose I used my diaphragm last night?' I panted.

His empty look answered the question. I sighed and pushed him from me. If there was any time to stop this insanity, the moment had presented itself. But sanity was not to prevail. I was a woman possessed.

I reached into the nightstand and pulled out my diaphragm, quickly slipping the trusted dome where it needed to be at the given moment, exorcising thoughts of where it should have been the night before. And then, as if there had been no break in activity, he was alongside me again. There was no sense of time, no awareness of the past, no fear of the future. The present was the only thing to consider, a very compelling present. I surrendered to him, leaving this consciousness for that arena where there is nothing else save you, and another body, and millions upon millions of greedy nerve endings vying for attention.

# TWO

When I awoke an hour later the carpenter was sleeping soundly beside me, one arm draped across my shoulder. I had sobered up somewhat, though the residual alcohol in my system would still have qualified me for a DUI. The raging hormones that had rendered me certifiable earlier had retreated, and the morning's events hit home squarely. I stared at my ceiling and tried to digest the new reality. I was a whore and Angie was dead.

Careful not to wake my guest, I extricated myself from under his arm and went into the bathroom. One look in the mirror served to confirm my self-assessment. My hair was matted tufts of auburn poking in all directions like a clown's wig, my green eyes were ringed in the ghoulish black of yesterday's mascara, and my face was raw with whisker burn. I painfully peeled off the contact lenses I had neglected to take out the night before and threw them in the trash. Then I sat down on the toilet and buried my head in my hands, trying to deal with the monster headache pulsing in my right temple. An image of Angie lying on a slab caused me to whimper aloud, filling my bloodshot eyes with tears. I thought about her parents and brothers, people I had known the better part of my life. If the loss of Angie was painful for me, it would be insufferable for them. I sat like that for a while before my thoughts jumped back to the stranger sleeping in my bed. What in hell had I been thinking? What if Flynn came back to town early? I had to get him out of my house. Right away. I grabbed my terry-cloth bathrobe from the hook and drew it around me, cinching it tightly at the waist.

He had awakened and dressed and was sitting at my kitchen table, flipping through a copy of the *Chicagoan*, his curls brushing the wire rims of his glasses. He looked up and his lips curved in an intimate smile, carving those dimpled parentheses back into his cheeks. He tipped his head down the hall towards the open bathroom door.

'Do you mind?' he asked.

'Mind what?'

'If I use your bathroom.'

As the door closed behind him, my mind raced with possibilities. Surely, he wasn't thinking of taking a shower. He needed to be gone, the sooner the better. The sound of a flush was followed by the sound of the tap running, and then, to my great relief, the door opened and he walked out. He came to me, still frozen in the middle of the living room, and bent to give me a kiss. I pulled away.

Hurt clouded the brown eyes behind the wire-rimmed glasses. 'I want you to know I really enjoyed being with you. I want to see you again,' he stated.

'What?' The word came out a gasp. Was he kidding? Here was a man responsible for me betraying my fiancé, albeit with a little cooperation on my part, and he was asking me for a date? Where was the one-nighter who couldn't get out the door fast enough? Who leaves saying, 'I'll call you,' but never does. Where was *that* guy? 'Are you crazy? You know I'm getting married.'

'You might want to rethink that, Maggie. All I know is I've never met anyone like you, and I want to see you again.'

'You don't know me, and you haven't met me. You met my drunken alter-ego last night and she's leaving town. I've made a big mistake. I love someone very much and I am going to marry him and what I did was wrong, very wrong.'

'You sure weren't acting like it was wrong last night. Or this morning. You were an animal in there,' he said, his eyes traveling down the hall to the bedroom door.

His words struck a nerve. Not because they were cruel, but because they rang true. So perhaps I had crossed the line into the animal kingdom. The problem was now that animal was back in its cage, and it needed to be in its cage alone. I had to get rid of the carpenter quickly, and as smoothly as possible. I decided to try rationalizing with him.

'Look, Steven. Last night, this morning, was fantastic. But that's beside the point. I've made a mistake. I've done something terribly wrong and now I'm scared, scared of what I did, scared of you. Scared that my actions of one night will blow something that I've invested a year of my life into. My fiancé is more important to me than anyone in the world. He is a wonderful, caring man, and I don't want to lose him. Because my libido clouded my brain, I've risked ruining everything. This can never, never happen again. You have to understand that.'

He shook his head. 'Maggie, you are making a big mistake if you go through with this wedding. The woman in that bed this morning sure wasn't madly in love with someone else.'

I wanted to scream, but I kept my cool. 'That's enough. I'd like you to leave now, please.'

He crossed the room to my desk where he picked up a pen and scribbled something on the pad sitting on the polished surface. He turned back toward me. 'This is the number for the job I'm working on. You can reach me there during the day.'

I walked up behind him and tore the sheet of paper from the pad, crumpling it in my fist. 'Don't you get it? I'll never call you.' For emphasis I stormed to the door and threw it open, taking a position on the threshold with my arms crossed.

'Then this is it?'

'This is it.'

Before leaving, he caught me by surprise, leaning down and brushing my lips gently with his. Then he stepped past me onto the landing. I shut the door behind him and turned the deadbolt, my ear pressed to the wood as his boots thumped down the flight of stairs. Relief flooded me upon hearing the entrance door squeak closed – as if that closure might shut out what had happened. Peeking from behind the white sheers in the living room, I watched him cross the street and climb into his truck. As he drove away, I hoped that he hadn't noted my address so that he could never find me again.

I went into the kitchen where a lonely bottle of Jameson sat on the counter beside two overturned shot glasses. More memory surfaced. His truck pulling up in front of my building. Inviting him in for one last drink seemed innocent enough. What could I have been thinking?

'To marriage,' I had toasted.

'To marriage,' he'd responded, drinking the whisky in one

gulp before placing the empty shot glass face down on the counter. And then he had buried his face in the soft skin of my neck. The sensation of him had been both disarming and familiar. Any resolve I may have had melted as he kissed along my collarbone and unbuttoned my blouse, slipping a rough hand under my bra. My last recollection was of him leading me to the bedroom, and the two of us pulling at each other's clothes. The rest was a blur.

Except for this morning. That was no blur.

I went back into the bedroom and stared at the scene of my transgression, wishing there was some cosmic way of turning back time, like hitting rewind on my VCR. The scrap of paper with his phone number was still clenched in my hand, and I hurled it into the wastebasket. I threw the windows open to clear the stale smell of lovemaking from the air and tore the sheets from the bed, shoving them into the washing machine. Then I showered in the hottest water I could stand, lathering myself over and over as if soap could wash him off me, thinking about Flynn the entire time and how hurt he would be if he ever found out about my unfaithfulness. But he could never find out. Never.

As I stepped from the shower, my tormented thoughts turned to Angie and the call I had yet to make. I wrapped myself back in my terrycloth bathrobe and went into the living room, picking up the phone to dial a number so familiar that I could dial it with my eyes closed. Carol Anne's chirpy hello rang out a minute later. Hers was the voice of yesterday, of ignorant bliss, the voice I trusted more than any other in the world. She was most likely sitting in her palatial kitchen making out her menus for the week and the grocery list to go along with it.

'It's me. I have some bad news.' My words sounded bland in light of the bomb to be delivered. In a trembling voice, I told her of Angie's death. There was an audible intake of breath, followed by utterances of disbelief.

'This just isn't possible,' she lamented. 'It can't be true.'

'I'm afraid it is.'

'Murdered?'

'That's what Kelly told Suzanne.'

'But I don't understand. If Suzanne dropped her off at home, how did she get to the park? It doesn't make any sense.'

'Nothing makes any sense,' I said, bursting into tears. 'Carol Anne, there's something else. Something else really bad has happened.'

'Worse than Angie being murdered?'

'Not worse, but bad.' My voice dropped to a level usually reserved for the confessional. Then I realized this was one confession that couldn't be delivered over the phone. It had to be delivered in person. 'Carol Anne, can I come over?'

'Of course,' she said, tossing me a much needed lifeline.

# THREE

## Kelly

Kelly Delaney climbed out of the squad car assigned to take her home and grunted an unconvincing thanks to the young cop behind the wheel. She let herself into the building's courtyard, the gate banging shut as she trudged the eight steps down to her garden apartment. She opened the door to an impatient meow. The cat was unaccustomed to being left alone this long in the morning.

'Hello, Tiz,' she said, stepping inside and kicking off her shoes.

The temperature in the small apartment was stifling, but after spending hours in the cold precinct in her damp running clothes, the heat was a welcome balm. For the cat's benefit she opened the windows, pushing them up as far as the nails pounded into the frames would allow. Though the neighborhood was a good one, it was the city after all. She was sticky with dried sweat and really needed a shower, but bathing seemed too much of an effort, so she plopped her grimy body onto the sofa. She was drained, both physically and emotionally. To call Angie's murder devastating would be gross understatement, but bearing witness to the lifeless body of her longtime friend made the tragedy even more cutting. Even now Angie's cold eyes glared from the front row of her memory, an image she knew she would carry the rest of her life. Another lousy burden in an already burdened life.

Didn't it figure, just when she was getting herself together and her life was headed in the right direction, things would turn on her. She shifted uneasily on the sofa and stared at the exposed pipes of the low ceiling. And to think the day had started out so well.

She had awakened early with a clear head and a clean conscience. No blinding headache. No sour stomach or boozy-tasting mouth. No trying to remember how she got home. No wondering what she said or did or whom she had fucked. No coming to consciousness fully dressed and realizing she was missing her underpants. Still, it was nights like last night that were always the hardest, being around old friends who could drink when she couldn't. That was when the temptation was the worst. But if last night served as a test, she had passed with flying colors. Not only did she not take a drink, she hadn't even wanted one. Well, hardly anyhow.

She kicked off the sheets and uncovered a ginger-colored ball of fur curled at her feet. A whiskered head unwound to give her a one-eyed stare. Discovered in a dumpster behind a Greek restaurant by a busboy taking out the trash, the cat had been near death when Kelly first saw her at the shelter, her coat matted with grease, her right eye blinded by bleach. A deliberate act or some unfortunate accident? One could never know. What Kelly did know was that when she saw the damaged creature quivering in the corner of its cage, she'd finally found something in more need of repair than herself.

When she first brought the cat home, in a kind of Holly Golightly way, she wasn't going to give the cat a name at all. But she had a change of heart after deciding she didn't want to resemble the lost soul Ms Golightly any more than she already did. The cat was officially christened Tizzy, the name that one of the workers at the shelter had tacked onto her cage, a name Kelly felt summed up both of their existences.

After taking a leisurely stretch, Tizzy jumped from the bed to the floor. Kelly swung her feet around and climbed out of the bed as well, stopping to fold it back into its day role as her sofa. She frowned as she fit the overstuffed rose-covered cushions into place. Flowered furniture wasn't her style, especially *pink*-flowered furniture, but she'd bought the sleeper-sofa second-hand, and the most important thing was that the mattress was comfortable since there was no space for any more furniture in the tiny apartment. Things were cramped enough as it was, with a kitchen table that doubled as a desk and a chest of drawers squeezed between the closet and the entrance. She would have preferred larger living quarters, certainly something above ground, but with money tight and school expensive, it was the best she could do on her limited budget. The upside of the cramped apartment was the location. It was situated on a quiet street only blocks from Lincoln Park, making it the perfect location for a runner.

The hardwood floor was cool beneath her feet as she padded past the corner kitchen into the bathroom. Brushing her teeth in front of the pedestal sink, she assessed the thirty-three-year-old face staring back from the mirror. Sure, it was prematurely wrinkled, but there was no getting around every one of those wrinkles was hard earned and then some. Luckily, her other features helped offset the damage and she remained pretty in a rough sort of way with the high angular cheekbones of a model, a mane of thick chestnut-colored hair remarkably free of gray, and deep-set welkin-blue eyes the color of the sky at dawn. And this morning, she noted gladly, those blue eyes were as clear as her head. No bloodshot roadmap. No glazed over glare.

She finished up in the bathroom and went back into the other room to prepare for her morning run. After getting dressed and feeding the cat, she did some stretches, laced up her shoes, and headed out the door. Being in no particular hurry, she stopped for a minute at the top of the stairs to take in the early morning tranquility. The courtyard was library quiet, the only sound breaking the silence a robin chirping in the overhead linden tree. A random breeze brought the heavy scent of magnolias to her nose, resurrecting ancient childhood memories. This was her favorite time, the early morning, that short-lived gap between impersonal night and intrusive day. It was the only time when being alone in the city wasn't such a bad thing.

In consideration of her neighbors, she shut the gate quietly behind her before starting down the tree-lined street. She ran slowly at first, picking up the pace as she turned onto Armitage Avenue. Her feet leaped nimbly from curb to street and back as she made her way past sleeping condominium buildings and darkened boutiques and overpriced dry cleaners. The intersection at Clark Street was deserted, so she crossed against the light and headed into the park. Her legs felt exceptionally strong and she glanced down to admire her thigh muscles at work, expanding and contracting like well-oiled pistons beneath her nylon shorts. Toned and sleek, it hardly seemed possible that only a year before those same muscles had hung from her bones like deflated balloons.

She skirted the shuttered zoo and arrived at the marked trail that ran the length of the park. She followed the course north, her legs carrying her effortlessly alongside the lagoon where the Lincoln Park Rowing Club was lowering its flat-bottomed boats into the water, beneath the crumbling Fullerton Avenue Bridge lined with hopeful Mexican fishermen, past Diversey Harbor, its slips newly swollen with boats back from dry dock. It was at the driving range she spotted the familiar hunched figure of Ralph ahead of her on the trail. Not quite firing on all cylinders, the old man walked the park end to end every single day, his pace only slightly affected by his age and a left leg a couple of inches shorter than the right. She called out as she neared him and he turned around, a gap-toothed smile crossing his dark face. He held out an arthritic claw, and she slowed enough to meet it with a friendly slap. He returned her slap with surprising strength.

'Wow, Ralph, with a right like that you should be in the ring.'

'Them days is gone, Missy,' rasped a voice sandpapered by age. 'Now you have a good one.'

'You too,' she tossed over her shoulder, resuming her previous pace. He shouted something behind her, but she had moved beyond earshot and his words died in the morning air. A minute later Belmont Harbor loomed into view, the luxury vessels mirrored in the still lake water like an Impressionist painting. Her untroubled mind veered off track upon spying the *Dermabrasion* floating placidly in its slip. One memory that remained painfully clear was the Sunday morning she single-handedly downed a pitcher of Bloody Marys and fell off the cruiser in the middle of the lake, nearly leaving Carol Anne Niebaum a widow when Michael had to jump in to rescue her. No wonder she hadn't been invited back since.

Pulling shutters across *that* memory, she rounded the marina and entered into the adjacent patch of woods where her run was brought to a screeching halt by a police car blocking the path, its lights flaring electric blue in the pale morning light. Yellow crime-scene tape was stretched behind the vehicle, anchored by trees on either side of the trail. A large-bottomed policewoman was turning the runners back, her hands directing them towards the sidewalk on the other side of the woods. Despite the policewoman's best efforts, a small group had gathered and was gaping at something on the other side of the yellow tape. Never one to pass up a car wreck, Kelly joined the crowd and sidled up to the barrier to see what was causing all the excitement. There was a tall thin policeman standing near the edge of the trees with his back to them, talking into his radio. A motionless figure covered in newspapers lay at his feet.

*Oh my God, is that a body?*

*Probably some poor homeless bastard.*

*Yeah, well, I've never seen shoes like that on a bag lady.*

Kelly pushed in for a better look, and what she saw turned her sweating body frigid. Jutting out from beneath the newspapers was a red stiletto attached to an immobile foot. She recalled commenting on a similar pair of shoes the night before.

*How in hell do you walk on those suckers, Angie?*

Without giving consequence any thought, she ducked the crime-scene tape and ran to the body. The crowd gasped collectively as she dropped to her knees and started tearing the newspapers away until her worst fear was realized. Angie's empty brown eyes stared at her from a whey-colored face, her raven-colored hair spread out like some cheap boudoir shot, her head at the angle of a doll with a broken neck. A grey tongue protruded from grey lips, frozen in some invective never to be heard.

'No!' she cried aloud, as a hand wrenched her to her feet with such force her shoulder was nearly dislocated.

'What in hell are you doing?' the thin cop snarled, holding her arm in a vise-like grip. His female counterpart had abandoned her post and was running toward them, her hand on her gun.

'Let me go,' said Kelly, twisting to break his grasp. 'I know her. She's my friend.'

After suffering an agonizing lecture on not compromising a crime scene, she was taken to wait in the police car. Sitting alone in the growing heat, she bit back tears and dabbed her eyes with her sweaty shirt. Before long the park was swarming with squad cars, so many she wondered if any were left on the street. Photographers hovered over Angie's body and forensics people scurried about the cordoned-off area, picking up God only knew what, and depositing it into plastic bags. She choked back an ironic laugh when an ambulance appeared – *as if anyone could do shit for Angie now*.

Eventually, a couple of detectives came to speak to her. They wore street clothes, short-sleeved button-down shirts with damp armpits and wrinkled dress slacks. One of them was a short fireplug of a man whose salt-and-pepper hair was overrun with cowlicks. The other was a lumbering giant with a shaved head round as a melon. They flashed silver stars at her from cheap wallets and introduced themselves.

The fireplug was Detective Ron O'Reilly, his voice a truck driving down a gravel road. Whiskey voice in the trade. Painfully bloodshot eyes the color of seaweed completed the picture. The giant was Joseph Kozlowski, his small black eyes like watermelon seeds in his massive face. His shoulders were set in a permanent slouch, his head bowed as if he had learned from banging into one too many doorframes.

Whiskey Voice did most of the talking, while the leviathan loomed aside taking notes on a crumpled notepad unearthed from a back pocket.

'Ms Delaney, we're from Homicide. We were told you knew the victim,' O'Reilly began.

*Homicide. Victim.* Two stinging bites that told a story. Kelly nodded, trying not to stare in the direction of the ambulance and the gurney being wheeled toward it. 'Yeah. We've been friends since high school.'

'We're sorry for your loss.' His attempt to sound sympathetic was beyond pathetic. 'The victim's name?'

'Angela Lupino Wozniak. Angie to her friends.' Kelly hesitated, and then added, 'But she may have been going by Lupino. She's going through a divorce.'

O'Reilly raised a brief eyebrow over a bloodshot eye.

'Uh-huh. And the last time you saw the victim was . . .?'

'Last night.'

This time the eyebrow remained raised. 'You were with her last night,' he echoed, his raspy voice barely disguising incredulity.

'That's what I just said.'

'Ms Delaney,' said O'Reilly, without bothering to look toward the giant for agreement. 'You wouldn't mind coming back to Area 3 with us so we can get some more information, would you?'

'Do I have a choice?' she replied, already knowing the answer to that question.

After a ride in an unmarked sand-colored Ford Crown Victoria with the air conditioning set to bring in the next ice age, they pulled up at Area 3 headquarters. It was housed in an ungainly brown building that sprawled half a city block. The parking lot was filled beyond capacity causing many vehicles to park on the sidewalks and the lawn. The irony of flouting the law in the very place it was administered was not lost on Kelly. After miraculously finding an empty space in the area reserved for detectives, the trio went directly into the building, bypassing the metal detectors everyone else was obliged to pass through. The lobby was a sea of desperate young faces.

'Stick close,' said Kozlowski. 'These ain't exactly model citizens. They do arraignments here.'

As if he was telling her something she didn't know.

Kelly was ushered up some stairs and into a large, fluorescent-lit room, its air conditioning set as cold as, if not colder than, the car had been. What was it with cops? she wondered. Did they have ice for blood? The room was filled with dozens of metal desks, all facing forward like some grand adult classroom, three-quarters of them empty. The desks that were in use were all occupied by men, most of them talking on the phone. While there were flimsy ashtrays on many of the desks, every desk held a Styrofoam cup, presumably containing coffee. All heads turned to follow Kelly in her running shorts and tank top as she crossed the room in the wake of the two detectives, her long brown ponytail streaming behind her.

They came to a stop at a paper cluttered desk with a plastic chair set beside it. 'Have a seat,' said O'Reilly. He passed behind her, leaving the faint scent of alcohol lingering in the air. Kozlowski grabbed a chair from the adjacent desk, turned it around, and straddled it. The chair was like a piece of children's furniture beneath his bulk. O'Reilly unlocked his top drawer and shoved the morass of papers inside. Kelly wondered what else he kept locked in that drawer. A little hair of the dog? Mouthwash to cover it up?

'Pardon the mess. I was catching up on paperwork when the call came in about your friend,' he said.

'You want some coffee?' Kozlowski asked.

'No, thanks,' said Kelly. She shivered and folded her arms across her chest. 'But a little heat wouldn't be bad.'

'Sorry about the temperature. We gotta choice between hot or cold and since it's summer we're going with cold. You wanna jacket or something?'

'No, thanks. I'll survive.'

O'Reilly flattened his hands on the desktop and spread his fingers apart as if to keep his balance. His thick hands bore the short nails of a nail-biter. He leaned in toward Kelly.

'You do what for a living, Ms Delaney?' he asked, the words more a command than a question.

'Me?' Kelly bristled, his brusque manner catching her off guard. She was none too fond of cops, with good reason, and this one wasn't doing anything to change her opinion. She told herself to chill out and be cooperative. This was about Angie. 'I'm a student at DePaul, working on my master's in Psych. I waitress on the side to make ends meet.'

'You knew the victim well.'

'We've been friends for over twenty years. Since Immaculata.' She filled in the blanks before he could ask. 'Catholic girls' high school in Winnetka.'

'I wonder if you could tell me what the victim did for a living.'

'I'd appreciate it if you'd stop calling her the victim. Her name is Angie.'

'Right, sorry.' A perfunctory apology. 'Angie did what for a living?'

'She's a department manager at Bloomingdale's.'

'Long time?'

'Thirteen, maybe fourteen years.'

'You said she was divorced?'

'In the process.'

'A nasty one?' The undisciplined right eyebrow raised slightly.

'I've never heard of a good one.'

'And the husband's name is . . .'

*Jesus, did this guy ever ask a proper question?* she wondered. His habit of framing questions as statements was annoying. 'Do you mean what is her husband's name?' she snapped.

He stared at her for a two-count before obliging her. 'Could you tell me her husband's name?'

'Harvey Wozniak,' she complied.

O'Reilly asked her what she knew about Harvey. Kelly gave a brief history of Angie's ex, a South Sider and commodities trader, fairly successful to her knowledge. He and Angie had been married ten years before separating. No, they didn't have children. Kelly felt no need to fill them in on the miscarriages.

'Let's go to last night. You said you were with the victim—' He corrected himself – 'With Angie last night.'

'Yes. At a friend's house in Kenilworth. We were having a bachelorette party for one of our friends who's getting married in a couple of weeks.'

'A big party?'

'More like a dinner, actually. There were only six of us. Unless you include the stripper.' If mention of a stripper derailed O'Reilly, he didn't show it, but Kozlowski coughed self-consciously into his hand.

'Names?'

She really wanted to punch him. 'Carol Anne Niebaum hosted the party. The bride-to-be is Maggie Trueheart. Suzanne Lundgren. Natasha Dietrich. Me.'

'You said six.'

The look she gave him would have stopped a pit bull in its tracks.

'Oh, right. The last time you saw the victim alive.'

'I take it that's a question,' said Kelly. 'About ten o'clock in Carol Anne's foyer. Natasha had left and Angie and Maggie and Suzanne were heading down to Rush Street. I took a pass.'

Before the conversation could go any further, a uniformed cop came up and whispered something in O'Reilly's ear. The right eyebrow went up again. 'That so?' He stood and gestured to Kozlowski who also rose, his chair squeaking in relief. 'You can wait right here,' O'Reilly instructed her, an order, not a request. The two detectives followed the uniform from the room, leaving Kelly alone to congeal in the cheap plastic chair.

A red second hand ticked off time on the white dial of the clock on the front wall. It was nearing eight, and she was supposed to be at Gitane's at nine to set up for brunch. At this point, there was no way she could make work on time, nor did she want to. It was abhorrent to think of dishing out egg-white omelets and endless cups of coffee on the heels of Angie's death. But the job paid her living expenses and tuition, and she couldn't afford to lose it. She eyeballed the phone on O'Reilly's desk. No one had told her it was off limits. She picked it up and dialed.

Her manager responded as expected, his underwear in a knot over having to handle the busy weekend crowd minus one server. *Like she wanted to be freezing her ass off in some police station. Like she planned for her friend to be dead. As if people found a friend murdered every day.*

'All right, you can take today,' he said in a huff. 'But you better be in tomorrow. I can't do a Sunday with only five servers.'

'I'll be there. I promise,' she said.

She placed the phone back in the cradle, relieved at having put a Band-Aid on her job. Then it dawned on her with a jolt that no one had checked the status of either Suzanne or Maggie. The two had gone to Rush Street with Angie. In all the chaos, they had slipped her mind. Wanting to be sure they were all right, she picked up the phone and dialed again. Suzanne answered on the second ring.

'Hey, it's Kelly. Are you sitting?'

'No, I was actually leaving to go into the office. You just caught me. What's wrong?'

'I'm at Area 3.'

'You're *where*?' Suzanne's voice was studded with judgment.

'Look, it's not what you think. I've got some bad news. You better sit down for this one. Are you sitting?'

'I am now,' said Suzanne.

'Something terrible has happened. Angie's dead.' Kelly went on to break the news as gingerly as she was capable.

'She was in Lincoln Park? But that's impossible. I dropped her off at home around three.'

'Well, she sure didn't end up there. She probably went out again.'

'But she was so drunk.'

'Yeah? That never stopped *me*.' Kelly looked up to see O'Reilly and Kozlowski coming back into the room. 'Look, I gotta go. Check Maggie, huh? I'll call you as soon as I get home.'

The two detectives reached the desk just as she hung up. Something about them had changed since they left her. They seemed more tense, especially O'Reilly. *They know*, she thought. O'Reilly took up his previous position behind the desk and Kozlowski straddled the defenseless chair again. O'Reilly tented his nail-bitten fingers and leaned in like Tizzy when she was ready to pounce.

'So . . . were you all doing coke at the party last night?'

'What?' she flung back, caught off guard by the question and the fact that he had finally posed one properly.

'Don't tell me you didn't know that Angie's nose was jammed with white,' he stated, staring at her in a way that made her feel like a germ under a microscope. 'What about the phone call you just made? Giving your dealer a heads up?'

The questions were so outlandish that Kelly's first response was nervous laughter. Then his inference set in and she leaned in toward him, resentful of the bleary-eyed cop reeking of alcohol. 'I do not do cocaine, Detective O'Reilly. And I don't *drink* either,' she added, stepping on the word drink for his benefit. 'I used the phone to call in to work. Then I called to check on Suzanne – who was with Angie last night and, for your information, who took her home. So why am I catching all this shit?'

'Why all the shit? Well, let's see. You were with the victim last night. Then you coincidentally stumble upon her body. Which you then tamper with, most likely destroying evidence. Added to that, you have a prior arrest for drug possession among other things. And you wonder why we're giving you shit? You tell me.'

So they knew. While she'd been sitting in this igloo playing penguin, they had been in some back room reviewing her history. Which, admittedly, wasn't real pretty. So she'd been to Area 3 a couple of times before. The first time was on a D and D before being sent over to County. Her cellmates that night were a prostitute in torn fishnet hose, a woman wearing a bathrobe and pink foam hair curlers, and a twenty-something in tight designer jeans – soliciting, domestic violence, credit-card fraud. The metal toilet bowl had overflowed uneaten baloney sandwiches. She had been released the next morning. Her second visit was for possession. The possession charge had supposedly been expunged by one of her lawyer customers. Guess that was a wasted blowjob.

'That was another life,' she said in defeat.

The seaweed eyes returned to her face, and he leaned back in his chair like a doctor finishing up a diagnosis. 'OK. You're done for now. Give Kozlowski contact info for the other girls, and we'll have a squad take you home.'

Tizzy mewed and jumped into her lap, jolting her gaze from the ceiling, startling her back to awareness. She petted the cat absentmindedly and thought about calling Suzanne. But even getting up to make a phone call seemed a Herculean effort. Her head weighed a thousand pounds, her eyelids a thousand more, and her body was covered in chainmail. Moving the cat aside, she stretched out with her long legs hanging over the edge of the sofa. She just needed to rest. She would nap for five minutes, no longer. As she lay there trying to erase the pale image of Angie's face from behind her closed eyes, she wondered what she had done in some past life to deserve the shit sandwich she got in this one. Was she captain of a slaver? Concentration camp commandant?

Whatever it was, it must have been heinous.

# FOUR

I merged into the traffic on the Edens, my thoughts seesawing between my indiscretion – a euphemism if there ever was one – and the horror of Angie's death. The combined weight of the two was overwhelming. I remembered learning in US History class that Teddy Roosevelt had lost both his mother and his wife on the same day and thinking that was more than a person could bear. While comparing my dilemma and Teddy's was a stretch, I was imploding under a double whammy that felt just about the same, the loss of a dear friend and the possible loss of a future husband.

My mind flashed back to sitting poolside at Carol Anne's last night, drinking wine with abandon while the girls showered me with the typical bachelorette gifts: edible underwear, a rubber tree made of condoms, a necklace strung with miniature penises, obscene books. I was thumbing through my personal copy of *The Kama Sutra* when the stripper arrived, a blond Adonis named Tony who was dressed like a policeman. His first move was to handcuff me to a lawn chair. His second was to crank up Joe Cocker's 'You Can Leave the Light On' on his boom box. Then he proceeded to liberate himself of his uniform piece by piece while we screamed like teenage girls with a peeping Tom in the window. Even Natasha, who usually had a stick up her ass, joined in the fun. After all, any woman would have had to be dead or mindless to not appreciate a body like Tony's, the contractile tissue perfection of his stomach, the smooth mounds of his biceps, his carved triceps, his broad shoulders.

Now Flynn has a nice build. He is tall and thin, ideally built for country-club sports, and I'm quite fond of his smooth, relatively hairless body. But this shaggy-haired blond creature gyrating in front of me came from an entirely different gene pool. He was primitive man at his best, and in my dreams he was swinging from tree to tree in the jungle, with me wrapped in his arms as willing victim.

The music ended just as Tony got down to his last article of clothing, a fuchsia G-string restraining a lump the size of a quarterback's fist. 'What do you say, girls? Should I take it all off?' he teased. With Natasha covering her eyes and Angie screaming for him to show us his gun, Tony shed that last bit of fabric, unveiling a package that would have made Sonny Corleone weep with envy. There was a moment of dumbstruck awe, after which the six of us let loose with howls so loud it was a miracle the real police weren't called in.

Later, after I had been freed from my bonds and an amply tipped Tony had taken his leave, I helped Carol Anne carry the glasses back into the kitchen. Her dark hair was damp from the humidity that managed to creep into the large, old house despite air-conditioning, and tight knots of it curled about her face. Her periwinkle-blue eyes sparkled at me, bright with impishness.

'What did you think of the entertainment, Maggie?' she said, suppressing a grin.

'I'll get you for this one, Carol Anne.' I took another sip of wine and checked my watch. It wasn't even ten o'clock. 'Wow, I guess we're getting old. This sure isn't like your party.'

'No, not quite,' my best friend concurred. 'But that was, like, a million years ago.'

Actually it was only slightly over ten years, but it did seem like an eternity. To celebrate Carol Anne's bachelorette party, we had commandeered a hotel suite downtown and most of us had never even gone to sleep. We had polished off cases of beer and filled the halls with the pungent scent of marijuana, much to the chagrin of the security guards, who were too intimidated to throw a group of good-looking twenty-somethings out on the street at four a.m. Now those times felt light years away, the freedom and spontaneity of post-college days traded in for careers or impatient husbands and children or both.

We went into the foyer where Kelly and Suzanne stood talking beneath the glimmering chandelier. Angela was absent, on one of her numerous trips to the bathroom. Natasha already had one foot on the threshold. Draped in designer clothes and expensive jewelry befitting the wife of a commodities trader, her dishwater hair highlighted into a golden shimmer, Natasha was the weak link in our group. She was the friend you tolerated, something like a bunion you put up with because you didn't want to suffer the pain of removal. Her mother and my mother had been Tri Delts together at Northwestern, which was how we came to be friends in the first place. History had cemented her position.

'Got to get home to relieve my hubby from childcare,' Natasha was saying, her excuse to bug out. *Did she really say 'hubby'?* I wondered. She put her head close to my ear and raised a hugely diamonded left hand to her mouth to insure secrecy. 'See you next Saturday,' she whispered, referring to the lingerie shower she was holding for me at her Lake Forest home, something I had tried to beg out of to no avail, something in all honesty I was not looking forward to. She said goodnight to the others and walked down the driveway to her Mercedes.

I turned around and the reason for her secrecy presented itself. Angie was back from the bathroom and was standing beside me with a freshly lit cigarette in her hand. It was a given that Angie wouldn't be invited to the shower. The two were oil and vinegar ever since Angie had appropriated Natasha's boyfriend in the ancient days of senior year. They had come to an uneasy truce over the years and only tolerated each other because neither wanted to leave the group.

'Rushing home to Mr Dietrich, no doubt,' said Angie caustically. 'Though why anyone would rush home to an ignor-anus like Arthur Dietrich is beyond me. I don't care how much money he has.'

'You mean ignoramus,' I corrected.

'No, I mean ignor-anus. He's one of the biggest assholes I've ever met.' She smiled a nasty but engaging smile, her white teeth gleaming against her Mediterranean features. I watched jealously as she took a drag from the cigarette and released a steady stream of smoke. Angie had been smoking almost compulsively since she had arrived, despite, and in spite of, raising the ire of the reformed smokers. She had also been consuming alcohol at a healthy pace. I suppressed a sudden urge to grab her cigarette and take a drag off it, to savor the unhealthy acrid smoke, to feel the lift as the nicotine violated my lungs. The longing had never completely gone away since quitting smoking after college. I also had been tempted to follow her on one of her many forays into the bathroom where I suspected one would find the source of her fidgety behavior. My hunch was she was doing cocaine, an occasional indulgence of my college years, and yet another vice that was but a dim memory.

A damp breeze blew in the open doorway, and a wave of melancholy swept me, partly inspired by days gone by, partly by the enormity of the step I was taking. The bachelorette party was my final goodbye to my youth and wilder times, and I didn't want the rite of passage to end. There was no reason for me to go home early. Flynn was in New York with his Dartmouth buddies for his own bachelor party, and I really wanted to let loose one last time. As if we were on the same wavelength, Angie verbalized my thoughts.

'Hey, I don't know about you guys, but I'm not ready to call it a night. Let's head down to Rush Street and leave our mark.'

'C'mon! My last night out,' I sang in a voice amplified by wine.

'Not for me,' said Kelly forcing a weak smile, her narrow freckled face fixed in a mild but firm expression. There was a restrained sadness lurking behind her transparent blue eyes. 'Tables to wait in the morning. Need a steady hand.' Then she added the answer we'd really expected. 'Besides, it's still too hard for me to be in bars. You all have a good time. I'm outta here.'

We watched her go down the walk in her tired jeans and T-shirt and climb into a battered red Honda with grey duct tape holding one of the headlights in place. The car died on the first start, then caught on her second try. A minute later her taillights receded into the night.

'God, I hope she makes it home in one piece,' Carol Anne worried. 'That thing barely looks roadworthy.'

'No kidding. I hope she's been to confession recently,' Angie quipped. Then she turned on Carol Anne like an attorney with closing arguments. 'What about you, Mom? Can we drag your sorry ass out of the burbs for the night? You can stay at my place.'

Carol Anne shook her head emphatically, sending the dark tendrils quivering. 'Sorry, girls. Michael promised to quit his card game early, and we're going to take advantage of the kids being at his mother's. It's been a long time since we've been alone in the house.'

'Wow! After all these years you still have the jones for each other? That's almost enough to renew my faith in the institution of marriage,' Angie spewed. Her voice softened as she added, 'Almost.' Then she pounced on her last victim, Suzanne. 'So I guess it's just you, Maggie and me.'

'Well, I don't know. I've got to go into the office tomorrow,' Suzanne hemmed. Angie wasn't having any of it. She was on Suzanne like a frat rat on a case of Heineken.

'Eat shit and die. We've barely seen you since you started your job. You're coming with. You can count your money with a hangover.'

Suzanne's eyes traveled from Angie to me, weighing the options. We were her oldest, dearest friends. Friends who held her head over the toilet when she'd had too much to drink. Friends who sat with her as she cried out the loss of a boyfriend. Friends who held her together after her brother's death.

As if she could read Suzanne's mind, Angie added, 'Friendship comes with obligations.'

'All right, I'm in,' Suzanne acquiesced, less than enthusiastically. 'But I need to make a call.'

'Use the phone in Michael's office,' said Carol Anne.

'It's gotta be business, cuz all her friends are here,' Angie said wryly, stepping onto the front porch to grind out her cigarette. Suzanne disappeared down the paneled hall, blond and tall and slim in her tailored black suit. She was back a few minutes later.

'All set,' she said.

'What was that all about?' Angie asked.

'Had to change some business.'

'Told ya,' Angie directed at me.

After one last attempt to get Carol Anne to join us, Suzanne, Angie and I took leave of her beautiful old mansion with its shutters and trellises and climbing vines. Carol Anne appeared to be watching us from the doorway, but I had a sense she was really looking beyond us. She gave us a final wave and closed herself behind the thick wooden doors.

Standing in the driveway, the night sky was overwhelming, millions of pinpricks of light stretching in all directions, each star clear and distinct. I'd forgotten how much closer the stars were in the suburbs, and I was overcome with a sense of tininess, of being insignificant amid their vastness. Their beauty was nearly eclipsed by a low-hanging moon, full and fat, a golden orb hanging just beyond reach. The three of us stood as if in a trance, listening to the rustling of small animals in the woods and enjoying the fragrance of newly growing things, sounds and smells rare in the concrete city. The sensory overload transported me back to the sultry summer nights of my teenage years living in the sheltering cocoon of suburbia, to a time with no ties and a whole future ahead.

'Well, let's get going,' said Angie, bringing us abruptly back to this world. The spell was broken. 'Maggie, you ride into the city with me. Suzanne already got to catch up with you on the way here.'

I looked to Suzanne for approval. Being the sort to dance with them that brung you, I didn't want to jilt Suzanne after she had gone out of her way to pick me up after work. But Suzanne didn't seem to mind making the drive alone. 'Fine with me. I need to drop my car off at home anyway.'

'OK,' I yelled louder than I needed to, as if volume would insure Suzanne was going to join us. 'We'll see you at The Overhang, right? You're not going to wimp out on us?'

'I will see you at The Overhang,' she replied with conviction. She climbed into her BMW and a minute later the smooth hum of the German engine faded into silence. Angie retrieved her keys from her unwieldy purse, and we screeched out of the driveway and fishtailed onto the road. All right, so back then we weren't quite as vigilant about drinking and driving as current day, but that night, even I questioned the wisdom of allowing Angie behind the wheel.

'Are you sure you're fine to drive?'

'Of course I'm fine to drive. Most drunken driving accidents are by people falling asleep and I'm wide awake,' she said, and then as if trying to reassure me, she reached into the pocket of her slacks and pulled out a little glass vial. 'Feel like a bump?'

My suspicions were confirmed. She was doing coke. I was going to decline the offer when that renegade ember flared within me again. For one last time, I wanted to act outside of the day-to-day conformity that ruled my life. I took the vial from her, filled a tiny spoon with white powder and sniffed. 'Whoa. It's been a long time since I've done any of this,' I said, already infinitely alert and capable of great things. 'Flynn's not big on drugs.'

'I only do it on special occasions,' said Angie, her eyes fixed on the road as she merged onto the expressway. I had a feeling much of Angie's life was a special occasion these days. 'So how'd you like the party?'

'Great to see everyone, of course. But I wish Natasha would talk about something besides kids and babies. You know. Breast pumps. Potty training. Enough already.'

'Yep. I had to laugh though when she told how that cretin Arthur fainted in the delivery room. Harvey always swore he would never set foot in one.'

'Was he squeamish?'

'Hell, no. But he always said the last thing on earth he wanted to see was a little bald head popping out of his favorite place.'

'That sounds like Harvey,' I said. 'How are things with him anyhow? Any communication between you two?'

'Not since he found another favorite place,' she said morosely, stepping on the gas.

The Overhang was as tightly packed as a womb. Friday nights on Rush Street were always a madhouse. But after finishing off the last of Angie's coke in the self-park a few blocks away, we were both up for the challenge. We worked our way inside the club and secured seats at the bar just as a couple was vacating them. We moved up the potency level from wine to vodka and savored the icy-cold alcohol as it saturated our already frozen throats.

The clientele was predominately young, recent entries to the post-twenty-one demographic. The women were carefully dressed to look as though they hadn't thought about it, wearing multi-layered T-shirts or Madonna-style tops that at one time would have been considered underwear. The men wore jeans or baggy pants cinched tightly at the waist and loose fitting shirts buttoned to the neck. Standing out were the nine-to-fivers, those left standing from Happy Hour that is, the men in traditional suits, the women in the work suit of the era with matching skirts and jackets and grosgrain ribbons tied into bows at the necks of their blouses. Never much one for fashion, I felt unexceptional in plain beige slacks and a silk blouse and wished I'd thought to wear something more exciting for a change. Angie was a standout in her spiked red heels and tight-fitting slacks, a Gucci scarf draped across her low-cut blouse.

'She Drives Me Crazy' by the Fine Young Cannibals was playing, and the mating dance was in full swing, males and females checking each other out with a critical eye, any thought of safe sex a subject to be broached later on. For now, life was carefree and the only imminent danger was not coming up with a viable partner for the night.

Angie nudged me and nodded at a couple of men across the room. The far side of the median age, they had dark, slicked-back hair with sideburns creeping down their faces and wore twin black Members Only jackets. The top buttons of their shirts were opened, revealing heavy chest hair and even heavier gold chains.

'Look. A couple of extras from *Saturday Night Fever*,' Angie quipped. They caught us staring at them and, taking it as an invitation, started working their way in our direction. 'Oh, shit,' said Angie, looking down into her drink. 'Don't acknowledge them and maybe they'll go away.'

'I don't think so,' I giggled, watching them swagger towards us. 'What's wrong? You don't want to meet a couple of your soul brothers?'

'Maggie, I'm serious. Don't encourage them. Once they come over here, we'll never get rid of them. I know the animal. Macho West Suburban Italians who think you'll be impressed because they know Jimmy the Juice or Louis the Hooch. These kinds make my skin crawl.'

'Too late now,' I said, as the two men made contact.

'Excuse me, ladies, do you mind if we reach over youse here

to order a drink?' asked the taller of the two in a voice thick with the nasal twang of urban Chicago. Angie ignored him and I shrugged as if to say, 'It's a free country.' He leaned in and extended a gold Rolexed wrist toward the bartender. His accomplice turned his attention to me.

'We couldn't help but notice youse ladies sitting here. Nice too see someone in this joint whoose been out of diapers for more than a couple a years.' Angie groaned audibly at his lame compliment. He talked with his hands in stereo, pointing first at himself, then his amigo, and then back at himself, his gold bracelet dangling over his own Rolex, his pinky ring facing the floor. 'I'm Sal, and this here is Joey. What are youse girls names?'

Regrettably, my mother raised me never to be rude, leaving me no choice other than to oblige him. 'I'm Maggie,' I said, trying to avoid Angie's evil eye.

'Jesus H. Christ,' she spouted under her breath. 'Now we'll never get rid of them.' Clearly oblivious to Angie's hostility, Sal asked her name again.

'Isabel Sanchez,' she punted.

'Isabel. Now that's an unusual name.'

'Unusual for her too,' I said, unable to resist. Angie shot me another nasty glance.

Joey procured a couple of drinks and handed one to Sal who cupped it in his gold-laden hand. 'Would either of youse ladies like to dance? Isabel?'

'No thanks,' Angie replied. 'I make it a policy to never dance with someone wearing more jewelry than me.'

The mouthful of vodka that spiked up my nasal passages would have been painful had I been able to feel my nose. Both the men chose to ignore Angie's sarcasm. They were probably used to passive aggressive rejections. They continued trying to make small talk until I, too, wearied of their presence and was relieved when Angie said, 'Look, guys, my friend here is getting married in a couple of weeks, and we really want to talk, so do us a favor and get the fuck lost.' That was all Angie. She was never one to mince words. Or worry over their appropriateness.

Sal's face turned so red, I feared what might come out of his mouth. But before he could say anything a young blonde bursting out of a black leather dress appeared from nowhere and worked her way in beside us. 'Well, look whose here,' Sal said to his buddy, his eyes glued to the cleavage pushing out from her low-cut neckline. Her broad hips hiked the dress up above the knee, exposing her fleshy thigh. Her long hair was cut in layers, frozen into place by what must have been at least a can of hair spray. 'How about a dance, baby?' he asked.

'I'm not interrupting anything?' she asked, tilting her lacquered head in our direction.

'Nah,' Sal answered for us. 'These two old gals want to be alone. They're celebrating an upcoming wedding.'

The girl sized Angie and me up like we were a couple of relics from the Middle Ages before smiling a broad wide-toothed smile at Sal. 'Let's dance,' she said, and the two of them merged onto the crowded dance floor.

'Now that's a babe,' said Joey, as if we had any interest in his opinion of the girl or anything else he had to say for that matter.

'Yeah,' said Angie. 'Snappy dresser.'

'What d'jou say?'

'I said nice dress. The only problem is it needs to be a couple sizes bigger.'

'You know, honey. I don't think I like your sense of humor. And I don't think I like you. There's a word for you that starts with a C, but I'm too much a gentleman to use it. And let me tell you something else. That little girl's father could buy and sell a piece of trash like you, so she sure don't need your approval.' He drained his drink and slammed it down on the bar. Then he turned and walked away, nearly smacking into Suzanne who was standing behind us. The bemused look on her face told me she had been taking in the scenario for some time.

'See why I don't like bars,' she said, edging in closer to us. 'Who were those horrible men, anyhow?'

'A couple of guys looking to buy on the Gold Coast,' Angie replied. 'I recommended your building.'

It was a rare occasion to be in a bar with Suzanne. Her attitude towards financial success left little space for wasted time, a trait she had displayed as far back as high school. She had set very high goals for herself early on, and her tunnel vision left her little time for leisure activity. But if possessions were the measure of success, she was right on the mark. Draped in designer clothes, wearing diamond earrings and a Cartier watch, I figured there was about $20,000 worth of her perched on the barstool next to me. She drove a BMW and owned a penthouse condominium. Lord knows how many fur coats she laid claim to. But the impressive thing about Suzanne wasn't what she had, but that she had done it on her own. Most of us who had careers weren't making anywhere near enough to budget for what she owned. The only women we knew with that sort of booty got it through marriage.

With all distraction gone, we turned towards our drinks and for the time being we were three old friends out on the town. Suzanne wasn't a workaholic, Angie wasn't going through a messy divorce, and I wasn't under the stress of planning my mother's idea of a perfect wedding. We ordered one round of drinks and then another and the talk flowed like the booze. I complained about my job at the *Chicagoan* while Angie complained about hers at Bloomingdale's. Suzanne remained silent on the job front. Then Angie complained about her lack of sex life, and I weighed in on mine.

'Flynn and I have a pact. His idea. No sex for the month before the wedding. He wants the honeymoon night to be special.' I took a sip of my drink and heard myself confess, 'To tell the truth I don't really miss it, our sex life isn't all that exciting anyway.'

'What the . . .' Angie's eyes went wide. 'And you're not even married yet? The one thing I could say about Harvey is our sex life was the best. He was, like, the horniest guy on the planet. It got so if I wasn't in the mood I had to change in the bathroom, cuz the second I got naked he was all over me. Until . . .' Her voice drifted off before she added, 'It may have been hell in the end, but it sure was great for a while.'

Three young professionals wearing their ties wrapped around their heads like urban Indians, sent over a round of shots. Something called a woo-woo, a concoction of vodka, peach schnapps and cranberry juice. They were sweet and went down far too easily. I flagged the bartender. 'Three more woo-woos here. And three for the guys who bought them for us.'

'Those guys just left,' he said, as he poured us three more shots. I looked down the bar and the three tie-clad men were indeed gone. Two of their stools had been commandeered by a couple, the third by a guy looking very out of place in a blue work shirt, his dark curly hair brushing the frames of his wire-rimmed glasses as he peered down into his beer.

'Then send the hippie a woo-woo. He looks like he could use it.'

The bartender came back and told me Work Shirt had said thanks but no thanks. Having achieved the amusing stage of drunk, I peeled off three dollars and handed them to the bartender. 'OK. Then give him this and tell him his next beer is on me.'

We toasted ourselves and threw back our woo-woos. When I glanced back in Work Shirt's direction, his seat was empty. 'Looks like he took the money and ran,' I laughed. A moment later, my three singles appeared on the bar next to my empty shot glass. I swiveled around to see the recipient of my generosity standing behind me. He did not look amused.

'I believe those belong to you,' he said, nodding at the money.

'Hey, get a sense of humor,' I said. 'It was a joke. You didn't want a drink, so I sent the money instead. Get it? It's no affront to your masculinity if that's what you're worried about.'

The firm set of his jaw relaxed and the trace of a smile appeared on his lips, carving dimples into his cheeks. 'Sorry. I'm not from around here. I guess your city humor is lost on me.'

I should have stopped there, taken my three bucks and waved him off. I know I should have. I should have. I should have. But instead I pulled out the charm, asking lamely, 'Oh? Where are you from?'

'New Hampshire.'

'New Hampshire. I don't think I've ever met anyone from New Hampshire. What brings you to Chicago?'

'I'm a carpenter here on a job.'

'Oh, a carpenter.' That explained the work shirt. 'I don't know many carpenters either. What's your name?'

'Steven Kaufman.'

'Maggie Trueheart.' I held out my hand and he met it with his own, a strong workingman's hand. 'Kaufman? Isn't that Jewish?'

'Yes,' he replied defensively. 'Something wrong with that?'

'Not at all. I just don't think I've ever met a Jewish carpenter. I thought all Jewish men were doctors, lawyers and bankers.'

'Are you Christian?' he asked.

'Catholic,' I admitted.

'If I'm not mistaken, a Jewish carpenter started your religion.'

'Touché, Steven Kaufman!' And with booze-inspired boldness, I added, 'Do Jewish carpenters from New Hampshire dance?'

He shrugged and I grabbed his hand and tugged him towards the dance floor, leaving Angie and Suzanne at the bar. The B-52s' 'Love Shack' was playing as I fell into my best imitation of someone who could dance. The carpenter danced awkwardly, his arms swaying to and fro from his squared shoulders as if he wasn't sure what else to do with them. 'Love Shack' segued into Tina Turner's 'Private Dancer', and my mind turned to Tony, the stripper, and his provocative moves. *I'm your private dancer, dancer for money.* The vodka and the woo-woos had really taken hold, not to mention whatever residual cocaine was still floating in my system. I closed my eyes and began mimicking Tony, rotating my hips and torso in a circular motion. My arms were stretched over my head, my body slinking to the hot pulsating beat of the music, and I was the sexiest woman alive. *I'm your private dancer, dancer for money, do what you want me to do.*

The song ended, and I opened my eyes, surprised to see the carpenter standing there instead of Tony. That's how far gone I was. He was staring at me with a dumb look on his face. 'That's some kind of dancing,' he said.

The next song had just started when I felt someone tugging at my arm. I turned into the melee to see Suzanne standing in the middle of the dance floor, fighting to keep her balance amid the jostling dancers. 'I think it's time to get Angie home,' she shouted over the din, pointing behind her. Angie was slumped on a barstool, her face on the bar. 'Are you ready?'

What did she mean was I ready? Did she really expect me to go now? When I was having so much fun? This was my last night out as a single woman and I wanted to relish it. I looked at the carpenter doing his best to keep a beat. He was an innocent tradesman from New England. Certainly no harm could come from another dance or two.

'I thought it was girls' night out,' I yelled back.

'C'mon, Maggie, let's go.'

'You guys go. I'm staying.'

'You're kidding.'

'No. It's all right. He knows I'm spoken for,' I said obstinately, waving my engagement ring in his face. 'I'll be all right.'

She stared at me sternly and shook her head. 'It's your party,' she shouted. 'I can't babysit everybody.' I mouthed goodbye over the noise and turned my attention back to the dance floor. The next time I looked at the bar, Angie and Suzanne had gone.

# FIVE

## Suzanne

Suzanne stood in the window of her high rise looking out over Lake Michigan, watching the white triangles of the sailboats dance gracefully against the cobalt blue while she replayed Kelly's call over and over in her brain. *Something terrible has happened. Angie's dead.* Her eyes drifted up the shoreline and came to rest on Lincoln Park, lush and green against the grey buildings that banked it. She shuddered at the thought of Angie's body laying somewhere within, cold as concrete itself. Her heart ached with a sadness that only one who has suffered permanent loss can understand. Her brother dead at twenty-one. Now her best friend at thirty-three.

Her mind flashed back to sitting in the cab, watching Angie weave an unsteady line up the walk. Her wobbly wave at the door. What had happened after that? Had someone been waiting for her inside? She thought of Kelly saying that being drunk never stopped her from going back out. Is that what happened? Had Angie ventured back into the early hours alone? Would things be different today if Suzanne had gone inside with Angie and put her to bed? But it had been nearly three o'clock, and Suzanne had been so bone tired her only thoughts had been of her own bed.

Too late, she regretted going to Rush Street with the girls last night. She didn't even like bars. They were noisy and crowded and people were always spilling on her expensive clothes. And that was before taking into account how infantile the men turned after a few drinks. But Angie had been insistent. Refused to take no for an answer. Going up against Angie when her mind was set on something was like going up against a force of nature. If only she had refused to go. If only. Then today she would only be suffering Angie's death as an aggrieved third party instead of feeling somehow responsible. Or worse, maybe the death wouldn't have occurred at all.

With her plans to spend the morning at the office scuttled, she picked up a dust rag to busy herself while waiting for Kelly to call back with more details. Moving about the large apartment dusting furniture rendered spotless by the housekeeper the day before, her insides felt as empty as a hollowed out gourd. Sunlight streamed into the room from the east and struck a Venetian vase gracing the cocktail table, setting it aglow in a kaleidoscope of red, blue and orange. Despite her sadness, she stood back to admire the phenomenon, filled with the pride of ownership. The vase was truly a thing of beauty. Bought on a short-lived trip to Venice, it represented a whole lot more than the thousands of lire it cost. It brought back clear harsh memories of the day the financial bottom had almost fallen out of her world. It served as a constant reminder of how fragile a lifestyle could be.

A ring of the phone sent her rushing into the kitchen. Fully expecting to hear Kelly's voice, she was surprised when the daytime concierge announced there were two detectives from the Chicago Police Department in the lobby who wanted to speak with her. She told the concierge to send them up and waited in the foyer with one eye pressed to the peephole. A minute later the elevator doors opened and two distorted figures emerged, one stubby and one gargantuan. Suzanne had the door open before they could knock.

When O'Reilly and Kozlowski saw Suzanne framed in the entry, tall and slim and blonde, dressed in fitted jeans and a crisp white blouse, they reacted the same way most men did upon seeing her for the first time. They stood up straighter and sucked in their stomachs. 'Ms Lundgren, sorry to drop in unannounced. We got your name from Kelly Delaney,' said O'Reilly, barely able to breathe with the effort of holding in his paunch. Both detectives reached into their pockets to pull out their wallets.

'That won't be necessary,' said Suzanne, waving off the proffered badges. 'I know who you are and why you're here.'

'You know who we are *supposed* to be. Don't ever let a stranger into your apartment without verifying who it is. A couple of slobs like us could be axe murderers.'

'I'll take that under consideration the next time a friend turns up dead,' she said dourly. She ushered them through the foyer and into the living room. O'Reilly let out a low whistle as he took in his surroundings. He figured the space could easily fit three pool tables without any crowding. The polished hardwood floors were scattered with oriental rugs and the walls were adorned with modern art that didn't do much for him, but he knew had to be expensive. While he didn't know much about this sort of stuff, no one needed to tell him everything he was looking at was beyond a cop's pay.

'Nice place you got here.'

'Thank you. I'm very proud of it.'

Suzanne directed them to a pair of beige slipper chairs and seated herself on a peach couch across from them, resting her hands in her lap.

'That sure is beautiful,' said Kozlowski, his small eyes fixed on the Venetian vase.

'It's Murano glass. I bought it in Venice.'

'Venice. Now that's a place I'd like to see before I go.'

'You should go. It's very special,' she said.

'We're sorry about your friend,' said O'Reilly, shooting his partner the evil eye to cut the small talk. 'You know her long?'

'Over twenty years.' Suzanne's eyes started to well and she banked the tears with a linen handkerchief. The way O'Reilly was studying her made her uneasy, though she had no way of knowing he was mentally comparing her to Kelly, who he found about as rough around the edges as Suzanne was polished.

'We understand that you were at a party with Angela last night, and that she left with you and . . .' *Damn*. The goddess in front of him had him so flustered he'd forgotten the bride's name.

Kozlowski came to his aid. 'Maggie Trueheart.'

'That is correct.'

'And you did what after that?'

'We went down to Rush Street to a club called The Overhang. It was Angie's idea. I went along under duress.'

'Under duress? Why do you say that?'

'I'm not really one for bars. I only went because Angie insisted.'

He tented his fingers under his chin and leaned in towards her. 'Tell me a little bit about what happened in that bar.'

'Well, Maggie and Angie had been there a while before I arrived, because I had to go home to drop my car off. Let's see. In short order, a lot of alcohol was consumed, including some shots. I have to confess to drinking a lot more than I usually do, but not a ridiculous amount since I intended on working this morning. When Angie was barely able to stand, I took her home.'

'And you got home how?'

'Taxi. I literally had to pour her into it. We went straight to her building in Old Town, and I made the taxi wait until she was inside.' Suzanne's facade started to crumble, making it a fight to keep her lips from quivering. She held the handkerchief to her mouth. 'I watched her go inside.'

O'Reilly asked about the party and Harvey, and she pretty much told them the same things Kelly had told them earlier. They appeared to be wrapping it up when Kozlowski asked out of the blue, 'Didn't the bride leave with you?'

'No. She was dancing and wanted to stay, so Angie and I left alone.' Suzanne thought of taking a last look at the dance floor before herding Angie out of the bar. Hoping she hadn't made a mistake leaving Maggie behind. Like she'd said, she couldn't be everyone's babysitter. It was hard enough just being Angie's.

Suzanne walked them to the door and waited as they summoned the elevator, standing halfway in her apartment and halfway in the hall. Then, no longer able to contain her apprehension, the question spilled from her lips: 'Do you think there was someone waiting for her in her home?'

'Want the truth?' O'Reilly asked.

Suzanne nodded.

'Nah. We've already checked her house. No signs of break-in or violence. She probably decided to go back out on her own. Seen it a million times.'

'As soon as you are certain, will you let me know? I need to know if I delivered her to her death.'

'We will,' Kozlowski said in a comforting manner.

The elevator doors closed on them, and she went back into

the apartment and stood without purpose in the middle of the living room. She wished she would hear from Vince, so she could tell him what had happened. She recalled the disappointment in his voice when she called from Carol Anne's last night to tell him she was going out with Maggie and Angie. She didn't know why he should be the one to be so upset. He was the one who was married.

She picked up the rag and went back to dusting.

# SIX
## Kelly

Kelly's fitful sleep was filled with dreams of Angie. They were in biology class dissecting a frog, but the frog's neck was broken and its head was tipped sideways. Angie was laughing and Kelly couldn't understand what was so funny. But the lab was at Carol Anne's house and Angie was dancing in the red stilettos. The dream shifted to Kelly's apartment, and a living Angie was hovering over her, spewing obscenities. Kelly tried crawling behind the flowered couch to hide, but Angie followed her, swearing at her from the horrible whey-colored face.

'Why are you so angry, Angie?' Kelly implored.

'Why? Why?' the ghost screamed, its glassy eyes widening with ire. 'Because it should have been you instead of me. That's why. It should have been you.'

Kelly awoke from her nap soaked in sweat. She had overslept for work again. She was going to be fired. She had been warned. She ran to the closet and pulled out her uniform before realizing that her job wasn't in jeopardy. That she had called Gitane's to explain why she wouldn't be in today. That these days, she was about the most reliable person on the planet.

She went into the kitchen nook and poured herself a glass of water, drinking it down in noisy gulps. Her smelly running gear was stuck to her. Not wanting to put off a shower any longer, she went into the bathroom and turned on the water, abandoning her clothes on the floor. She stepped into the shower and stood beneath the unrelenting stream, wanting for all the world to swirl down the drain along with the sweat and the soap and the water. Her dream came back with a vividness that made her shudder. Angie's face looming before her, pale and accusatory. *It should have been you instead of me. It should have been you.*

Angie was right. It should have been her.

\*    \*    \*

Perhaps the color of Kelly's life would have been different had her mother not gotten sick. She was a change-of-life baby, her two brothers well into high school by the time she was born. They had finished college and were starting their own families when her mother was diagnosed with stage four colon cancer. Kelly was ten. Her father, a successful patent attorney, travelled frequently for his job which meant leaving young Kelly alone to take care of her mother for days at a time. Her adolescence was spent watching her mother suffer the pain of radiation and chemotherapy, listening to her woeful tears at night after the indignity of a colostomy. Despite the doctor's dire prognoses, her mother hung on for years longer than anyone would have guessed, wanting more than anything to see her daughter grow into a woman.

Kelly was in her junior year of high school when the cancer metastasized to the vital organs, and it became clear her mother's fight was nearing the end. Kelly took charge and for the last months of her mother's life, rushed home from school to be with her, to spoon-feed her when she no longer wanted to eat, change her colostomy bag when she was no longer able to do it for herself. Her father offered to hire nurses, but Kelly refused. The intimacy the mother and daughter shared in life would reach all the way to the end.

Her mother died on Christmas Eve. Kelly felt an initial relief that her mother's suffering was over, but that did little to soften her grief. The person she loved most in the world was gone forever. Standing at the funeral beside her father and her two brothers with their wives and children, she felt like she was among strangers. No one but Kelly really knew what her mother had suffered. A part of her had been scooped out that could never be refilled.

Much to Kelly's chagrin, her father married his secretary barely a year later, a Chinese American woman named Clara. Kelly was traumatized, not only by the presence of this stranger in the house, but that her father could forget her mother so easily. To make things worse, Clara was only ten years older than Kelly and resented her stepdaughter's presence in her life as much as Kelly resented Clara's. Though they remained in the beautiful Georgian-style house where Kelly had been brought up, her stepmother lost no time in marking her new territory, changing out her mother's antiques for modern pieces, replacing her heirloom dishes with Crate and Barrel. Kelly hated her new stepmother so much she avoided home as much as possible, dividing her after school hours between her friend's houses. Her favorite refuge was Angie's house where the noisy and spirited fighting that went on during meals was the polar opposite of the feigned politeness of her own home. Kelly could see her father was ecstatic with his healthy young wife, a woman who was doing her best to wipe out any traces of Kelly's mother, and then Clara went one better by getting pregnant.

Graduation couldn't come fast enough. She didn't even mind that her father missed the ceremony because Clara was in the hospital giving birth to Kelly's half-sister. Graduation meant college, and college was her ticket out of a house with dark memories and an infant who cried all night long. She signed up for summer school at the University of Illinois in Champaign and left home two weeks after graduation. She threw herself into her studies, never addressing the lingering pain of her mother's death, an open wound that wouldn't scab over. She seldom spoke to anyone about her mother's death, not even her best friends, as if it wasn't any big deal. But it was a big deal, and it was crushing her from within.

She finished college a semester early, graduating with a teaching degree, and came back to Chicago. Since her teaching job wasn't to start until the following September, and not wanting to return to her father's home – where Clara made her feel as welcome as an ex-wife – she rented an apartment in Old Town and took a temporary job tending bar at a Rush Street club called Oliver's.

At least the job was supposed to be temporary. She loved tending bar from her very first night. Her head had been so buried in her studies during college that she hadn't had a social life. Now her time was spent in a place that was crowded and noisy and exciting, not to mention filled with attractive men who seemed attracted to her. The added benefit was that the money was terrific. In her first week, she made as much in tips as her monthly teaching salary was going to be in September.

She also found something else at Oliver's, a place she

belonged. Alienated from her father by his wife and young baby daughter, and the two brothers she barely knew busy with their own wives and children, her co-workers became the family she didn't have. Oliver's employees were a close-knit group, bouncers and waitresses and bartenders who worked the vampire hours, the nine-to-fivers on the flip side of the clock.

Since their day was winding down when the rest of the world was just starting theirs, there were often after-hours parties that lasted until long after the sun had come up. It was at one of those parties that a fellow bartender handed her a rolled-up hundred-dollar bill and a mirror with a white line of powder. Kelly knew what cocaine was, had seen it around college, but had never tried it. It was supposed to be the rich man's drug, a drug with no side effects, so she figured what the hell. She sniffed up the line, and the instant the drug hit her nervous system, Kelly felt a well-being she hadn't known since before her mother got sick. She had found something to blunt the rawness inside her. She had found a new best friend.

Occasional parties turned into regular parties and she fell into a cycle of drinking and snorting coke after work, getting home after noon and crashing until it was time to get up for work again. By the time September rolled around, she had lost all interest in teaching. She started her new job, but continued drinking heavily and doing coke, and was fired after three weeks for coming in late or calling in sick. Which didn't bother her at all. She went back to bartending at Oliver's and the decadent lifestyle that accompanied it.

She kept up that pace for ten years. Being young and resilient, her body somehow survived the abuses being heaped on it. During that time, she had a few fleeting relationships, but the drugs and booze always trumped any possibility of commitment. That didn't rule out sexual activity; there were more one-nighters than she could count. Or remember. Blackouts were a common occurrence. She even got pregnant once, but nature took care of things and she miscarried before having to decide what to do about it.

Her job at Oliver's came to an end when the bar was bought by a national chain with strict rules, and she was fired for drinking on the job. That wasn't really a huge problem, because after all her years working on Rush Street she had made enough connections that she had no trouble finding work. Her new job was at a dive-bar named Finnegan's just around the corner from Oliver's. The owner was an Irishman with consumption issues of his own who didn't mind if she drank while she worked. In fact, he would sit at the bar while she was working and drink with her. Her drinking escalated to the point that sometimes she was barely able to stand by the end of her shift. The coke kept her going, but it was eating up so much of her income, there were times she barely made rent.

Kelly rarely saw her father or brothers, and hardly knew her half-sister. As for her old friends, whenever they made a lunch or dinner date with her, she invariably cancelled at the last minute or didn't show up. Then one time when Kelly failed to show for a third rescheduled lunch with Angie and Carol Anne, they decided to go in search of her. After repeatedly ringing her entry buzzer to no response, they slipped into her building on the heels of a departing occupant. They took the stairs to the third floor and banged on her door until it finally cracked open. What they saw nearly put them into shock. Kelly's hair was an unwashed tangle, her face so puffy and bloated her cheekbones had all but disappeared, her pale blue eyes sunken into her head. She was a train wreck.

She tried to keep them out in the hall, but Angie pushed right past her into the apartment. Turned out her living conditions were worse than her face. The kitchen sink was stacked with paper plates and carryout cartons, a banquet for the roaches that skittered in the mess. The floor tile was caked with dirt and spilled drinks. A plastic trashcan erupted vodka bottles. Dirty laundry was piled everywhere and an unmade bed with gray sheets was visible through the open bedroom door. The carpet hadn't seen a vacuum in months, if not years. A mirror on the coffee table was dusted with white.

Carol Anne was so shocked she couldn't find words, but Angie found them just fine. 'Jesus, Kelly, what is this shit?' she yelled in disgust. 'This is beyond gross. I can't even imagine what must be growing in your bathroom. What is wrong with you? You're living like an animal. Actually, my apologies to animals everywhere. You're worse.'

Kelly blinked several times, trying to pull herself to full consciousness. God only knew what time she had gone to bed. 'I know it's a little messy. I've been working a lot. I was going to clean up this afternoon,' she slurred.

'Clean up? With what? A fire hose? A blow torch?' Angie wasn't letting up. 'It's a good thing you didn't show for lunch. We would have been thrown out of the restaurant for breaking the health code. C'mon you're fucking thirty-one years old and you look like crap. Do you want to die? What is wrong with you?'

Far more the diplomat than Angie, Carol Anne tried rationalizing with her. 'Kelly, we're your friends and we care about you. This isn't right. You need help. We want to help you.'

Through the veil of drugs and alcohol, Kelly heard what was being said and she didn't like it one little bit. She started to rant. They didn't understand, couldn't understand. They hadn't grown up with a sick mother in a dark house that smelled of illness and radiated pain. Their mothers had been healthy and whole. They didn't have a father who forgot them for a woman nearly her age and a baby that never stopped screaming. How could anyone who had parents that supported and loved them understand her pain? She had carved out her own niche and did what worked for her. She hadn't asked anyone for anything, and no one was going to tell her what to do. Her resentment fomented as if they were interlopers in white coats, there to haul her off to a padded future.

'Leave,' she hissed, her eyes narrowing in the jaundiced face. 'Get the hell out of my apartment.'

Carol Anne tried pleading with her. 'Kelly, don't you see we care about you. We want—'

Angie cut her short. 'Forget about it. Don't even waste your time. She's too far gone. We won't win this argument.' She grabbed Carol Anne by the arm and pulled her out the open door.

Kelly was standing bizarrely defiant amid the detritus, a queen in her garbage castle. 'Eat shit and die,' she howled and she slammed the door in their faces.

Six months later Kelly was finally shocked to her senses. She had finished work early and was trying to score some coke.

Police pressure had dried up her regular Rush Street sources, so she hopped a taxi to Boystown and a gay bar named The Zone where the bartender usually had eight-balls for sale. The shit was really stepped on and a huge rip-off, but hey, she was desperate.

The Zone was packed to the rafters with good-looking men, none of whom bothered to give her a second look when she walked in. She took a seat at the bar. Lyle, an anorexically thin man with a wispy moustache and weepy eyes, acknowledged her with a nod.

'What'll it be, sweetie?' he asked, floating over with a coaster in his hand.

'Hey, Lyle, I was wondering if you had a ticket for the movie?'

He put the coaster down and shook his head. 'Sorry, no can do. The pipeline is dry. The heat's on here same as Rush Street.'

'Crap,' said Kelly, pondering where to try next. She really needed a bump. There was a guy in Wrigleyville she'd scored from before who might be worth a go. She slammed a shot of Jagermeister and headed out the door. She was on Lincoln Avenue trying to hail a cab when a heavily muscled black man came up the stairs from The Zone and approached her.

'Couldn't help but notice you was looking for something in there, and my first guess is it wasn't a date. Maybe I could help you out?' He unearthed a small glass vial from the inner pocket of his leather jacket and waved it in Kelly's face. 'Some of the finest blow around.'

'Only blow around,' she said warily, eyeing him and then the vial. 'Any samples?'

'Sure, but not here. Follow me.'

He led her around the corner to the alley where a black Cadillac was parked in front of a sign that read *WE TOW*. 'My name's Lemont,' he said, holding the passenger door open for her. 'C'mon inside and I'll give you a taste.'

Kelly knew it wasn't exactly wise to get into a stranger's car, but her desire for the drug overruled any sense of self-preservation. She climbed into the car and pressed herself against the passenger's door, keeping as much distance between them as possible. Lemont inserted a tiny spoon into the vial and brought a mound of white powder up to her right nostril. She inhaled it faster than an anteater. Another mound disappeared up her other nostril as quickly. The welcome jolt rushed through her system.

'Wow, that's some good stuff,' she said. 'How much?'

Without answering, Lemont reached under the seat and pulled out a flask of Jack Daniels. He twisted the cap off and held it out. She took a swig directly from the bottle. He gave her another snort and she took another swig of Jack. She was feeling pretty good, totally cool and in control. Another snort and another go at the bottle. 'Yeah, I'll definitely take a couple of grams,' she said, reaching into her purse for money. That was the last thing she remembered.

When she pried her eyes open, it was broad daylight. She was naked on a bare mattress in a room with the paint peeling so badly portions of the wall studs were visible. Lemont slept beside her, his dark muscles shining in his nakedness. A cockroach skittered up the wall.

She sat up slowly, grimacing at the soreness between her legs. She knew the source of the soreness, but in the grand scheme of things, that was no big deal. Getting out of there was. Her clothes were piled in a corner of the room, her purse nowhere to be seen. Great, it had her keys and her money. She had no idea where she was or how she was going to get home.

Careful not to disturb the sleeping man beside her, she crawled off the mattress to her clothes and dressed quietly. Just as she was getting ready to make her exit, the door burst open. A woman in a Chicago Bulls T-shirt and black stretch pants fell into the room, a gun quivering in her right hand. Her glassy eyes told Kelly she was higher than a kite. When she saw Kelly, she swung the gun directly at her.

'How dare you fuck my man, bitch,' she shouted.

Her man, who by now was wide awake, sat frozen on the mattress.

'Fenicia, calm down,' he commanded.

'Calm down? Calm down?' She swung the gun in his direction, pointing it between his legs. He covered himself with a broad hand.

'That won't help you none,' she screamed, moving further

into the room. 'I'll blow that hand away along with your cheatin' dick.'

Seeing that Fenicia's attention was concentrated on her man, Kelly bolted out the open door and down the hall. A couple of men snored on the two sofas in the living room as she let herself out of the apartment. Screens lining the open hallways told her she was in one of Chicago's housing projects. Worse still, she was on a high floor. Knowing better than to take an elevator, she hurried along the graffiti-covered walls to the stairwell. She started running down the stairs as quickly as her shaking legs would take her, the smell of urine overwhelming her the entire way.

She was nearing the second floor when she encountered two gangbangers standing in the center of the stairwell blocking her way. They wore sagging jeans and T-shirts, and their cheeks were smooth with the dewiness of youth, but their dark eyes were old. She tried to go around them, but one of them grabbed her arm.

'Whoa, Mama. You can't just go down for free. They's a toll.' She tried to free herself from his grasp, but his grip was tight. 'You deaf? They's a toll. If you don't got no money, we gotta collect some other way.'

Before she could even try to escape, he had pinned her to the wall. She struggled to slide away, but he was entirely too strong. He put his mouth to hers and tried to force it open with his tongue. His breath made her want to retch, a combined scent of tobacco and alcohol and unbrushed teeth. The other teen moved in beside him and the next thing she knew they had her by the arms and legs, holding her stretched out between them. She struggled to free herself, wriggling her captive limbs, but between their youth and strength her efforts were wasted. Two more gangbangers appeared from nowhere, eyeing her like a rarely seen commodity. 'We gonna have a nice piece of pale booty,' she heard one of them say as a hand went under her shirt and tore off her bra. 'You up for a little partying, ain't you, Sunshine,' said the other. And then the four of them laughed, their laughs so nasty that both her bladder and her bowels threatened to loosen. She wondered if letting go of her fluids might prevent them from raping her. Her mouth was so dry she couldn't scream if she tried though she knew screaming probably wouldn't help anyhow.

*Oh no, God. Please, God. Don't let this happen*, she prayed as they started carrying her struggling body up the stairs. *Please. Please.* If she could only get out of this in one piece she would change. She would stop drinking. She would stop doing drugs. She would call her father. *Anything. Please, God.*

Kelly felt a blast of air beside her ear, and a split second later the sound of a gunshot reverberated in the stairwell. Her head whipped upwards to see the stoned woman from the apartment standing above them. She was holding her gun and the weapon was aimed at Kelly's face.

'You boys let her go. She mine.'

'Motherfucker, she crazy!' The gangbangers dropped Kelly and scattered. The next thing Kelly knew she was somersaulting down the concrete stairs, banging her head repeatedly along the way. Another bullet ricocheted past her, the whistling sound from the first still fresh in her ears. She slammed to a stop at the ground floor, splitting her lip open. Without wasting a second, she crawled out the open doorway and found herself in a grassless common area strewn with shredded paper and fast-food wrappers. She stood up and took off running as fast as her battered body and wobbly feet would allow. She didn't stop running until she saw a police car on a side street.

The cops were kind enough to pretend they believed her story about getting off at the wrong subway stop and somehow ending up in the middle of Robert Taylor Homes. They drove her to a safer neighborhood, and one of them even gave her the fare to get home.

That day she quit her job and went to her first AA meeting. Afterwards, she stopped at the animal shelter and adopted the cat. When she got home, her first call was to Angie to apologize.

Kelly turned off the shower and watched the last of the water spin down the drain. She put on her tattered bathrobe and went back into the other room. She picked up the phone and stood holding it with her hair dripping onto the floor, her finger hovering over the dial. This call would not be to Angie, but about her. She was most certainly at the morgue by now, a number with a tag on her toe, her parents awaiting the nasty task of identifying her. Angie's father would tell his wife to wait in the hall, but Angie's mother would insist on seeing the body of her only daughter. Mrs Lupino would nearly faint while Mr Lupino held her in his quivering arms.

She thought of how close she had come to putting her own father through the same scenario and felt a bittersweet sting as she envisioned him standing over her cold flesh, a tear splashing the lens of his tortoiseshell glasses. An image of her stepmother patting him on the shoulder came next and the sweetness to the sting dissolved.

*Stop perseverating on your own misery*, she told herself. *There is more misery to be shared.* Two hours after leaving the police station, she finally called Suzanne.

# SEVEN
## Suzanne

Suzanne didn't hide her displeasure that it had taken Kelly so long to get back to her. 'You're a little late. Your friends just left.'

'My friends? What friends?'

'The detectives assigned to Angie's case. O'Reilly and Kozlowski.'

'You mean Mutt and Jeff? Don't call those two morons my friends,' said Kelly, shivering anew at the thought of the icebox where she'd spent the better part of the morning. 'What did they want?'

'They wanted to know about Angie,' Suzanne replied, her ire softening at the gravity of the discussion. 'About us and what we did last night. About me taking Angie home. They told me she was doing coke,' she added.

There was silence before Kelly spoke again. 'I should have known by the way she was acting last night.'

'Kelly, we all should have known.'

They talked about Angie and the circumstances and how horrible it was before the conversation hit a wall of futility. With nothing else to add, nothing else to be done, they hung up, each left to deal with Angie's death in her own universe. Suzanne put the phone down on the kitchen table and stared out her window at the canvas of sailors and power boaters on the lake. The vacuum of loss returned in all its intensity.

Suzanne met Angela their freshman year of high school when alphabetical coincidence placed them next to each other in homeroom that morning and every other morning for the next four years. Lundgren. Lupino. How do you sit next to someone for that long and not become friends? Despite having completely different personalities and dispositions, their friend-ship had been rock solid from high school through college and beyond. Suzanne had even served as Angie's maid of honor. But in the years that followed Angie's wedding they drifted apart, so that they didn't speak daily anymore, and they stopped sharing secrets. One might have thought it was because Angie got married, but in actuality it was Suzanne's own commitment that proved the greater impediment to their friendship. Suzanne was married to her job.

Suzanne couldn't remember a time when she hadn't wanted to be rich. Finding that path to riches had been her driving force in life. When she was growing up, she resented that her family was of modest means compared to everyone else in Winnetka, where poverty was not belonging to the right country club. Second to that was not belonging to any country club, which was Suzanne's situation. Her parents were immigrants from Sweden who owned a toy shop on Green Bay Road next to couture dress shops and linen stores where sheets cost about as much as a used car. She had secretly envied her peers, who got their allowances from attorneys and CEOs and third generation industrialists. Suzanne had to work for her money, spending long hours behind the counter at Skanda, the family store, so she could buy herself the kind of clothes her friends got to buy with their father's credit cards.

Suzanne's ambitions made her far more serious about school than any of her friends. She was taking college-level classes as a sophomore, always working that bit harder to insure an A. Her grades and test scores won her a scholarship to Purdue where she majored in finance. After graduation, she went on to get her masters at the University of Chicago. When she was hired by one of the best brokerage firms in Chicago, no easy task for a woman at the time, she was certain her payday had arrived.

She quickly learned otherwise. While her gold-embossed business cards read *Financial Advisor*, her job was basically as a salesperson working the phones to drum up customers to financially advise. The firm provided her a modest draw and a list of prospective clients, doctors, lawyers and other professional people. Unfortunately, everyone in the business worked from the same list of candidates. Hammered to death by solicitors, the prospects seldom took her calls. The times she did manage to finesse her way past a secretary, more often than not the beleaguered prospect banged the phone down in her ear. A successful call was when the prospect stayed on the line long enough for her to practice her pitch.

After six months of dialing her fingers raw, she had yet to open a single account. She was lost in despair, questioning her choice to become a broker, her dreams of riches tumbling before her. Then one night while she was riding home on the bus in a pounding rain, trying to figure out how she was going to pay her rent on her miserly draw, the bus pulled to a stop in front of a huge construction site. Suzanne turned her head toward the window and saw dozens of construction workers in yellow ponchos, working in the rain. A building boom was underway and the city was one big construction site. Inspiration struck. What about construction workers? They had to be making decent money and since they wouldn't have college loans to pay off, most of it would be discretionary income. After all, how much could a person spend on beer?

She did some investigating and learned construction workers were averaging well over $40,000 a year, the pay scale climbing higher for men who worked the higher floors. That was more than some people at her firm were making, including herself. And when it came to construction workers, Suzanne realized she had that something extra going for her. Her looks. Nearly six feet tall, blessed with the Scandinavian combination of blonde hair, blue eyes, and perfect skin stretched over amazing bone structure, she was beautiful. She wasn't in the least bit vain about her beauty, but she wasn't beyond using it to her advantage. Being face-to-face with potential male customers would give her an advantage she didn't have on the telephone.

The next day was bright and sunny. She put on extra makeup and started visiting construction sites, asking the site manager's permission to speak to their employees about financial counseling. Had she tried this pitch at a law firm or corporate headquarters she most certainly would have been shown the door, but with all the testosterone bouncing around a building site, well, suffice to say, they not only welcomed her, she had carte blanche.

Within a year, she had opened hundreds of small accounts. And since they were operating in one of the greatest bull markets of all time, her clients were making a lot more money than the lousy five percent the credit union was paying. Word about Suzanne spread, and soon she was doing business with the general contractors themselves, who then started referring her to their suppliers. It wasn't long before she was handling the portfolios of so many presidents and chairmen of the board that she found herself in the top tax bracket. Right where she wanted to be.

Suzanne had an unfulfilled taste for extravagance dating back as far as she could remember. Her parsimonious parents looked down on any kind of waste, and thrift was always revered in their household. Now that she was making so much money, it was time to fill those desires. She went shopping with a fervor.

First on the list was a penthouse condominium on the lakefront with south, east and north views which she proceeded to decorate in a manner straight out of *Architectural Digest*. She drove a BMW convertible. Her clothes were the finest couture, and she was a recognized regular at Chanel. Monthly facials at Elizabeth Arden and haircuts from the top stylist at Sassoon were de rigueur. A black willow mink and a sheared beaver armed her against those brutal Chicago winds while diamond earrings, Mikimoto pearls, and a Cartier watch fed her self-esteem.

A good percentage of her purchases were financed, and the payments gobbled up much of her paycheck, but it was 1986, and the markets kept going up along with her income. Suzanne turned her head from the vortex of debt that sucked her money out as fast as it flowed in. She was confident her client list and her own investments would continue to grow. In the meantime, her cash flow covered her payments with lots of wiggle room.

Until October 19, 1987, a day later named Black Monday, when the bubble burst. The DOW dropped 22.6 percent in one day, and more than $500 billion dollars of wealth evaporated, gone to parts unknown. Along with the vaporized money went the portfolios of most of Suzanne's customers – as well as her own.

To make matters worse, the crash occurred while Suzanne was on her first vacation in three years. She was sipping an espresso in a Venice café when grumblings about some disastrous problem in the markets caught her ear. Since this was well before the now ubiquitous cell phone, she ran for her hotel and the television. When the extent of the implosion became clear, she tried calling her office. The lines were tied up for hours before she was able to get through. Her assistant confirmed things were as bad as, if not worse than, she had heard. She arranged for a flight the next morning and after a sleepless night caught a six a.m. flight from Venice to Frankfort and on to Chicago. If she could have flown out sooner, she would have, but it seemed most of Venice wanted to get out.

By the time she landed at O'Hare, clutching her precious Venetian vase to her breast, the damage was beyond repair. In truth, there was little she could have done to save her customer's portfolios even if she had been at her desk that fated day. The system had been so overwhelmed that getting out of positions had proved nearly impossible. But try telling that to someone who has just lost twenty-five to fifty percent of his or her net worth. Many clients lost confidence in Suzanne for being out of town when the crisis hit. She hadn't been there to take their calls, and the broker covering for her had been in his own swamp. Scores of them showed their displeasure by closing their decimated accounts.

She tried explaining to her clients that their losses were only on paper and that the market would come back again, but they still wanted out. She tried convincing them to buy now while prices were low, but nobody was listening. Her small customers, the construction workers, went back to the credit union where they knew their money would be safe. The only thing she was able to sell to her remaining clients were certificates of deposit, which paid a miserable commission. The realization set in that, with any luck, her income would be one-quarter of what she had made the previous year.

There was no way to service her debt on so little income. The mortgage. The car payment. Her credit card accounts. She pared back on shopping. No more dining out, no facials, no new purchases. She even decided to sell some pieces back to the jewelers who had so happily sold them to her. When she learned the offer was twenty cents on the dollar for a necklace she was still paying off, she nearly died. But desperate for cash, she sold it at the discounted price anyhow.

With her cash reserves drained, she found herself forced to liquidate her own holdings, taking losses on stocks and mutual funds she was certain would come back in time. But there was no time. And though it was the last thing in the world Suzanne wanted to do, it soon became apparent that she was going to have to sell the lakefront condominium. Her fortieth-floor residence with its herringbone floors and crown molding and elegant wainscoting was the pinnacle of everything she had worked for. After sacrificing social life, love life, and family to own something so grand, the thought of losing it was devastating. For the first time, she envied married women like Natasha and Carol Anne who didn't have money woes because their husbands were big earners. Maybe putting up with a husband was worth it if it freed a person from worry.

The beast was hungry. It needed money now. Even if she listed her condo right away at a fire-sale price, it would still take a while to sell, even longer until the closing. There was no sense in asking her parents for a loan. They made it no secret they considered her spending reckless. Asking them for money would only get her a lecture, and a long lecture at that. The situation looked hopeless.

Then the real-estate developer, Vince Columbo, came into her mind. One of her few big clients whose account remained active, he was the most prominent developer in the city and his bottom line remained huge, even with the downturn. Suzanne had long suspected that he was attracted to her, but she had ignored his subtle advances. He was married, and she had no interest in ever being someone's second choice. But ever the astute businesswoman, she had used her physical assets to maneuver him into a business relationship, while deftly keeping that relationship professional. Suzanne surmised that the reason Vince's accounts remained active was because his interest in her remained active. Maybe she could leverage his infatuation with her into a loan. Under normal circumstances, such a drastic move would have been abhorrent. But these were trying times.

Her call to his office was put straight through, and he readily accepted her lunch invitation for the following Friday. To discuss some investing options, of course. She dressed with special care that morning, choosing a royal-blue suit that flattered her creamy complexion and enhanced her blue eyes. She arrived at The Pump Room early and settled into the cushy leather of the corner booth, beneath vintage photos of Chicago celebrities and Hollywood icons. Her eyes were cemented to the door. At exactly noon, Vince Columbo walked into the room wearing a fitted grey suit and red tie, his silver hair swept back from his widow's peak. The way he stood out among the tony crowd told her he had taken the same care in dressing as she had.

He greeted her with a businesslike handshake, and they made small talk, Suzanne hoping the tension in her voice wouldn't give away her apprehension. The waiter interrupted and they ordered quickly, shrimp cocktails followed by Dover sole. Suzanne chose a bottle of Chablis Premier Cru from the extensive wine list and nodded her approval when the sommelier poured her a taste. Knowing Vince to be a baseball fan, she steered the conversation to the Cubs' upcoming season opener. Suzanne made it a point to be well-versed about the sports world. The knowledge came in handy when dealing in the world of men.

'What's your opinion about lights in Wrigley Field?' she asked, taking a sip of the wine.

'Long overdue. Cubs need to come into the real world. I know a lot of people are fighting it, because they hate change, but my philosophy is accept change or die. People who are unwilling to make or accept change end up swimming in the same pond their whole life. And that water gets so murky they don't see the opportunities out there.'

Suzanne nodded as she bit into a Parmesan crisp. Normally, the crisp would have melted on her tongue, but she was so nervous that it stuck to the roof of her dry mouth. She took another sip of wine, larger this time, to loosen up both the Parmesan crisp and her tongue.

'Vince, this is very embarrassing, but I have a confession to make,' she managed eke out. 'I brought you here under false pretenses. I didn't really ask you to lunch on business. Not normal business, anyway.'

He put down his glass and stared at her with unblinking dark eyes.

'We've known each other five years or so now, and – well, I consider you a friend,' she continued, wondering if this whole thing was a colossal error in judgement. 'I just don't have anyone I can go to, and I thought of you, and I think you are aware of my integrity and my work habits.' She stopped talking. This wasn't going right. Despite all her practice, both in her mind and in front of the mirror, she realized she couldn't make the 'ask' after all. 'This is a mistake,' she said, switching from wine to water.

'What is it, Suzanne?' His eyes were compassionate, as he tried to draw her out.

Back to the wine. Take a deep breath. It was like diving into a cold lake. She thought of the one-week vacation her family took each summer when she was a child, to northern Minnesota where her mother's relatives lived. She and Johnny would dip their toes into the icy lake and scream as the cold cramped their feet. After repeated tries to wade in failed, they learned the least painful way was to just dive in and get it over with. After the initial shock, the water wasn't bad at all. The anticipation was worse than the actuality.

She dived.

'I need a loan,' she blurted.

His face gave no indication of his thoughts as she explained her situation. She told him about all her lost clients, and her own losses, that she would sell her condominium as soon as the real-estate market recovered, and when it did sell she would pay him back with interest. She didn't see the stock market recovering any time soon, but she was doing her best to find good value out there and she was certain it was only a matter of time before she would be in the black again. He cut her short when she said that, of course, she would provide a promissory note and—

'How much?' he asked.

'What?'

'I asked how much.'

Could it be possible he was actually considering lending her the money? 'Right now I need forty thousand,' she said, and then she held her breath.

Without a word, he reached into his jacket and pulled out a checkbook. He wrote a check for forty thousand dollars and made a notation in the memo line that read 'loan'. He handed her the check and she stared at it with incredulity. It had been so easy. She'd thought at the very least she would have to do some more explaining, pleading her case. But in her hand was a check for forty thousand dollars, totally above board by virtue of that one little word in the corner, loan.

'Thank you,' she said, looking him firmly in the eye. 'Let's discuss the terms of the payback.'

'Suzanne, I'm not worried about the payback. I know you'll pay me back as soon as you can and at fair market interest.' He was smiling as he spoke, and she found herself noticing how attractive he was. 'I feel more secure lending you this money than I would some members of my family. But there is one string attached.'

*Uh-oh*, she thought. *It had been too easy.*

'I want you to have lunch with me once a week. To discuss the market, of course. And maybe a little baseball.'

Suzanne didn't have a naïve bone in her body, and she knew where he hoped their lunches would lead. But that didn't worry her; she could handle herself. The most important thing was Vince's loan would keep the debt collector from the door for the next couple of months. She would deal with the other issue if and when it ever came up.

'Deal?' he asked.

'Deal,' she answered, and they shook on it.

When the check came, she grabbed for it. He tried to wrest it from her, but she held firm. 'Please, I invited you to lunch,' she said. 'This one is on me.'

He didn't argue, and she pulled out her American Express card and laid it on the table. It was the last check she would pick up.

# EIGHT
## Angie

Angie stood inside her entry watching out the front window until Suzanne and the cab were entirely out of sight. She had caught a second wind in the taxi, and home wasn't where she wanted to be. Home was just too lonely a place these days. Finding a cab on her quiet street was an unlikely proposition, so she started walking towards Halsted Street where they would be numerous. A car came from behind, and she turned to see if it was a cab, but it was a passenger car, which drove past, turning at the next street. She was spooked a little, walking alone down the deserted street, the click of her heels echoing in the darkness. Once she thought she heard someone behind her, but it was only the trees swaying in the breeze. Nevertheless, she picked up her pace, the clicks of the stilettos coming at closer intervals until her walk turned into a high-heeled run.

She was sweating when she reached Halsted, but the active street relieved her anxiety. Patrons were emerging from the local pubs wearing khakis and cardigans and topsiders or running shoes – far less style-conscious than the Rush Street regulars. She toyed with popping into one of the neighborhood bars for a quick one, but time was running out and the vial in her purse was empty. The stuff in that vial was the only thing that eased the pain, and her mission was to see it filled.

She hailed a cab and gave the driver a Newtown address. The cab stank of body odor, so she rolled down the window and rested her head against the doorframe, her eyes taking in the scene with lazy indifference. The cab stopped for a red light, arm's length away from a couple so completely engaged in each other they didn't see her. The man she knew well, the petite blonde woman she didn't. They were laughing about something, the man's arm wrapped possessively about the woman. Angie stuck her head out the open window.

'Harvey!' Angie screamed. 'Over here, asshole!'

Her estranged husband turned his head, his eyes wide with the shock of seeing Angie hanging out of a taxi. The blonde stared in ignorance. The light changed and the taxi started moving. Angie pushed her torso out the window and continued screaming as nearly everyone on the sidewalk turned to watch. 'That's right, you no good son of a bitch. Go ahead, flaunt it in public. You can't even wait until the divorce is final. I'm going to get you for every cent you have, you bastard. I'll see you in court, you lousy Polack!' The couple disappeared from sight, and she settled back into her seat, feeling sorry for herself.

*What went wrong, Harvey*, she was thinking, *that you treat me like this? Didn't I always look good for you, keep your house clean, make your favorite foods? Wasn't the sex great – at first anyhow? Why couldn't you have been more under-standing of me? Couldn't you wait until I was feeling better? Didn't you know how hard it was losing those babies?* Angie pictured the *For Sale* sign in front of their home, the profits of the sale to become the spoils of divorce, and her eyes filled with tears.

She was searching her purse for a tissue when the cab came to a lurching stop in front of her destination, a dive named The Zone. Her purse tumbled from her lap, landing upside down on the litter-covered floor. 'Goddammit, look what you did! You should be more careful,' she snapped.

'Four dollars, lady,' said the cabbie.

She wanted to curse him out for even charging her. She retrieved her wallet from the floor and took out a ten. She placed the wallet on the seat beside her and continued collecting her things from the rubbish-strewn floor, stuffing lipsticks and lotions and the empty vial back into the oversized bag. She was so pissed there was no way in hell this guy was getting a tip. When he finally held six singles over the seat back, she grabbed the money and shoved it into her purse. Then she jumped out of the cab and slammed the door behind her.

Her wallet still sitting on the seat as the taxi pulled away.

The pavement was undulating as she walked down the dark

steps to the bar's entrance, clutching her purse tightly to her side. She stumbled once or twice before she made her way to the concrete landing. She yanked the door open with a vengeance and went inside.

# NINE

I pulled into Carol Anne's driveway and parked behind
Michael's silver Porsche with MD2020 plates. I was beyond
relieved to arrive at my destination in one piece, especially
after having had to pull over to the shoulder of the Edens to
throw up . . . twice. Even now the dry heaves teased the back
of my throat. But in the scheme of things, no matter how sick
I felt, anything was better than being in my apartment with its
suffocating atmosphere of guilt. I opened the car door and sat
immobile, listening to the sound of lawnmowers running in the
distance and birds chirping in the trees, the consoling sounds
of suburbia. Sounds anchored in happy childhood.

I was still sitting in the car when Carol Anne came running
down the driveway, her face laced with tears. I pulled myself
out of my red VW bug and took her in my arms. We crushed
one another close in grief.

'I just can't believe it,' she repeated over and over, her
tears wet against my cheek.

'I know. I know.' It was the only response I could muster.

We stepped apart and stared into each other's faces. Carol
Anne's eyes were puffy and red from crying as to be expected.
But they were also ringed in black as if she hadn't slept. I
knew that face from adolescence. Something else lurked behind
those eyes besides the death of a friend.

'Are you all right? You look almost as bad as me.'

'As I,' Carol Anne corrected me, sniffling.

'Jeez, I was the English major. As I.'

Carol Anne took her turn to give me the once over, noting
my scarlet eyes and whisker raw face. 'What happened to you?
You look like you've been through a blender.'

'Tell me.' My stomach had settled, but my head was still
pounding relentlessly. 'I really need a cup of coffee.'

We went into the house and through the foyer where six of us said our good-byes the night before. Reduced to five forever more. As we walked arm in arm through the living room, I glanced out the window at the kidney-shaped pool in the back. In my mind's eye, Angie was out there, egging the stripper on with her foghorn lungs, her bottom shaking in her tight slacks, her breasts jiggling in her low-cut shirt. Her taunt echoed in my brain. *Let's see the gun, Officer Tony.*

'It's like I can hear her,' said Carol Anne, putting words to my thoughts.

'Yeah, me too.'

We took the service hall, past a dining room with a Wedgewood ceiling installed during the Jazz Age, and ended up in the kitchen. Carol Anne poured two cups of coffee from the carafe and we sat down at the granite island beneath a ring of copper pots. The house was eerily quiet, the absence of pounding feet, blaring TVs, and baby's cries almost louder than their presence.

'Where's Michael?' I asked, taking a cautionary look around.

'He's still sleeping.'

'So late? I thought he was an early riser.'

'We were up late,' said Carol Anne.

So maybe that explained the black rings under her eyes. Married people taking advantage of the kids being gone for the night. Good for them. The stability of her marriage only served to remind me of how I'd jeopardized my upcoming one. We talked about Angie being dead and speculated about what might have happened, my mind only half on the subject matter as my actions pounded on my conscience like an irregular heartbeat. The guilt continued to build until it was a pot ready to blow its lid, and I couldn't hold it back any longer. 'Carol Anne, this is going to sound demented that I need to talk about myself at a time like this, but there's something I need to unload. Something really, really bad.'

Her dark blue eyes grew wide in her tired face. 'You killed Angie?'

'Don't even joke.' Keeping my eyes riveted to the door in case Michael made an appearance, I whispered ever so quietly, 'I cheated on Flynn.'

'You what?' Her response was both reflexive and loud.

'Shhh,' I pleaded, searching her face for understanding. She was my best friend in the world, and I needed her on my side.

Our friendship dated back to kindergarten and we understood each other in ways no one else could. We shared common backgrounds, both coming from families of all girls, Carol Anne the third of four, me the middle born of three. Growing up, we found in each other someone who knew what it was like to have a know-it-all older sister and a spoiled-brat younger one, someone who wasn't competing for Daddy's attention or trying to steal your favorite shirt. We knew everything about each other – or so I thought at the time. There was an unspoken pact between us that not only would each other's secrets always remain secret, but we would never sit in judgment of one another.

So my hopes for absolution were pretty much dashed to smithereens when Carol Anne's next words were, 'Oh . . . My . . . God. Have you lost your mind?'

'Thanks for the vote of confidence.'

'I'm sorry, you just took me by surprise. With Angie and all, this is just too much.' She saw the shattered look on my face and relented. 'Tell me what happened.'

Piece by piece, I recounted my story of meeting the carpenter in the bar and buying him a drink, of dancing with him, of letting him drive me home and inviting him into my apartment where one thing led to . . . well, another. When my story was finished, I lowered my aching head into my hands as if hiding from my mistake could make it go away. 'Last night was just one big fucking nightmare. Now Angie's dead and I've done this horrible thing. It's all so surreal. Here I am marrying this great guy and I go and screw up like this. I'm going to hell. I know I am. Oh, God. What if I'm pregnant?'

Her eyes widened more than I'd ever seen them widen. 'Don't even think it. You used something, didn't you?'

'This morning. But not last night.'

The silence screamed. The way Carol Anne stared at me reminded me frighteningly of my mother. When she finally did speak, her tone was the sort reserved for the worst of offenders. 'You have lost your mind! I can almost understand about last night. You were really drunk. But this morning? There was a "this morning" too?'

My shame and humiliation were complete. 'God as my witness, I don't know what possessed me. It was like some kind of temporary insanity. After Suzanne called and told me about Angie, he was so comforting and suddenly I wanted it – wanted him – so much that I didn't give a hoot. I know I should have stopped myself, but I didn't want to. *Then*. Now I'm so ashamed I don't know what to do.'

'All right. All right, stop punishing yourself. That's not going to solve anything.' I felt a modicum of relief, as Carol Anne turned sympathetic. 'This sort of thing probably happens more often than people care to admit. Like some last fling. You made a huge mistake, but you'd never do that to Flynn again, right?'

Flynn's name opened fresh floodgates of guilt. For reasons beyond my comprehension, the guy was so totally in love with me that sometimes my feelings for him seemed lukewarm in comparison. But fanned by the flames of impending loss, my love for him surged to a newfound intensity. I loved him more than anything on this planet. 'Cheat on him again? Not in a million years. Now I realize how really important he is to me.'

'See,' she comforted me. 'So maybe this happened for a reason. And as far as being pregnant, the odds are against it. I'd worry more about disease.' She pursed her lips and rethought her statement. 'When is your period due anyway?'

'Ten days.'

My words fell with a thud as both of us counted backwards in our heads. There couldn't have been a worse possible time.

'Oh, it'll be OK,' said Carol Anne with false assurance.

'And if it isn't?'

'You're still doing the celibacy before marriage thing?' I nodded feebly.

'Abortion?' The look I gave her ended all discussion on that topic. 'Then I guess you'd have to tell him it's his.'

'Tell him what is his?' The male voice nearly sent me to the floor. Having slackened my vigil on the door, Michael Niebaum had snuck in behind us and was standing in the middle of the room, a Grateful Dead T-shirt hanging over the top his jeans, his thick black curls still shiny wet from a shower. Lucky for me, he hadn't heard the first part of the conversation.

'Choice of the rehearsal dinner entrée,' Carol Anne rebounded.

'Back so soon?' Michael said to me, obviously not interested in anything to do with my rehearsal dinner. He kissed the top of Carol Anne's head from behind. The tenderness of the gesture nearly made me cry. 'Why didn't you just stay overnight?'

'Believe me, I wish I had.'

'I'm afraid there's some terrible news, Michael,' said Carol Anne, spinning around on the stool to face her husband. 'Angie's been found dead.'

In my entire life, I have never seen anything like the look that passed over Michael Niebaum's face. His great dark eyes glazed over like they were gazing into the depths of some unspeakable horror and he drained of all color. He turned abruptly away and went to the coffee pot where he poured himself a cup with trembling hands.

'What happened?' he asked, staring out the window with his back to us.

'We're still not quite sure, but it looks like she was murdered. Kelly was out running this morning and saw some kind of commotion in Lincoln Park and there was a body and . . . it was Angie. Isn't it just beyond belief? I mean, we were just with her last night . . .' Carol Anne's voice trailed off and then came back afresh. 'Michael, they found her near Belmont Harbor of all places.'

'What?' When he turned he had recovered some of his color, though he was still chalky for a person whose complexion was a natural tan. He stood contemplating what Carol Anne had said. Then he grimaced and his hands went to his abdomen. 'Excuse me, I'll be right back,' he said and he darted from the room.

'Are you all right?' Carol Anne called behind him. 'He has an irritable colon,' she explained. 'I guess the news about Angie is as shocking to him as it is to us.'

The phone rang, and Carol Anne looked at me warily as she picked it up. 'Hello. Yes. Yes, this is she,' she said. *Police*, she mouthed. I listened silently to her side of the conversation.

'Yes, I do know about the murder. Uh-huh. When? This afternoon? Yes, I'll be here.' There was a pause followed by, 'Maggie Trueheart? Well, actually . . .'

Terror overcame me. I couldn't talk to the police. Not yet. I had no idea what they would ask me about last night and an even worse idea of how I might answer without sealing my own coffin. I waved my hand back and forth in front of my throat as if I was cutting it. Which I pretty much wished I were. My ever-perceptive best friend came to my aid.

'Actually, she was here, but she just left. Yes, officer. I mean, Detective. Yes, I'll see you then.'

Carol Anne hung up and her eyes darted at me. 'The police are coming out here to talk to me about Angie. Why were you hushing me?'

'Because they'll want to talk to me and I can't talk to them right now.' Panic gripped me as I jumped to my feet. Guilt and sorrow were now in the back seat, having given way to the deeper-rooted instinct of survival. Something told me I was going to have to tell some lies and I didn't want to have to do it in front of Carol Anne. Or Michael. I grabbed my purse and headed for the door. 'I've gotta go.'

Carol Anne walked me down the driveway and stood beside me as I started the car.

'Are you sure you're OK?'

'I'm not sure of anything, Carol Anne. Except that the way I'm feeling right now, things would be better if I was the one in the morgue.'

'Don't say that, Maggie,' said Carol Anne, reaching into the car and touching my shoulder. 'They're coming here to talk about Angie. They don't know about you and they don't care about you. Don't worry. I'm on your side.'

'Thanks, C. A. I needed that.' I started the car and pulled down the long driveway.

# TEN

My thoughts were on Flynn the entire drive back into the city, the man I was to marry in two weeks, the fiancé I had betrayed. We'd met at Natasha and Arthur's Memorial Day party last year, a set-up on their part I was to later learn. Having finally taken off the extra thirty pounds I'd been carrying since high school, I was acting both clever and flirtatious. After years of being chubby and funny, you know, the girl with the great personality, my trimmed-down version was the cute girl with the great personality. No more chubby in the equation.

Flynn and I hit it off right away. We had a shared love of sushi, music and movies. He had driven me home and we sat in his car in front of my apartment until two in the morning, comparing favorite movies. We both had the atrocious taste to like Doris Day movies and *Airplane* but to also appreciate the classics like *The Third Man* and *Casablanca*. He found it intriguing that I had chosen to attend a state school like the University of Iowa and major in literature when he'd gone Ivy League at Dartmouth with a major in Finance. He walked me to the door that night and gave me a warm, but not too warm, kiss good night, and I sensed my vanilla life was about to change. When he called to ask me out the next day, I was certain.

And my life did change. For the first time since high school, I was part of a 'we.' It wasn't just me anymore, or me and the girls. There was a man in my life. And according to every woman around, Flynn was quite a man. He was good-looking, a dedicated son and brother, and loved by all his friends. He came from a wealthy family, but he was successful in his own right, having started a swiftly growing software company – whatever software was. He told me that first night that he was going to be worth at least nine figures, and at thirty-six, he had a good leg up on those riches. He had already put a down payment on a house for us in the Gold Coast that we would close on after the honeymoon. The house was more of every woman's dream – every person's dream for that matter. Four stories of hardwood floors, granite baths, and hand-carved balustrades. But as the wedding drew nearer, I found myself having trouble getting excited about the dream home. It felt so excessive. My mother castigated me for being blasé about my good fortune, herself ecstatic that after her long years of worry, her thirty-three-year-old daughter would no longer be living in a one-bedroom rental apartment in a building without proper security.

The truth is, I'd been blasé about a lot lately, including Flynn. I wasn't sure if I fully understood what being with one person forever really meant. Except for my first love in high school, my experience with the opposite sex was limited. Before Flynn came along, my relationships had consisted of brief affairs and even briefer one-nighters. As a fat girl, it's easy to get them to sleep with you – once. Getting them to come back was the tricky part.

If I didn't know how lucky I was to have Flynn, there were plenty of people to remind me. I attributed my lack of enthusiasm to the pressures building up before the wedding. It was all so tedious, the engagement parties and showers, the requisite thank-you notes that followed. The decisions that my mother treated like life-changing events: invitations, registering for china and silver and crystal, pre-cana with the priest, picking out the three thousand-dollar wedding gown and bridesmaids' dresses, choosing a band, flowers, menu, cake, weekly measurements for the wedding dress, finding hotels for out-of-town guests, rehearsal dinner arrangements, and more. The list went on and on. I was drowning.

I asked myself what was wrong with me. Here I was nearing my mid-thirties, an age where most single women were already planning cruises together, and I had connected beyond most women's wildest expectations. Most women would have loved to be in my shoes. I should have been crazed with happiness. Carol Anne had made a good point. Right now, in the fallout of my indiscretion – what else could I call it – Flynn had become the most important thing in my world. I loved him so much at that moment that maybe, in a backhanded sort of way, my cheesy behavior might have a positive result.

I decided then and there I would spend the rest of my life making it up to Flynn by being a perfect wife and companion. Of course, he could never know the hurtful thing I had done. It was my duty to protect him from it forever.

Which brought me back to Angie's murder. Not to diminish it at all, Angie had been very important to me, but the police would undoubtedly want to see me this afternoon. I was disgusted with myself for being so worried about what they might ask. But I couldn't block my fear. What if they asked if I left the bar with Angie and Suzanne? What would I say? My intention was to do everything possible to help find who had murdered my good friend, but the police could never find out what I was doing while it happened. Never. Find. Out. Things were on a need-to-know basis, and they had no need to know.

When I let myself into my apartment, the red light on my answering machine was blinking. I played back three messages from Flynn telling me to call him in New York, and a message from a Detective O'Reilly, telling me he needed to meet with me as soon as possible. I called Flynn at his hotel first, taking a deep breath before speaking to him, wondering if he would sense my betrayal over the line.

'Hi,' I mumbled.

'Maggie, where have you been? I was beginning to get worried.'

'I was at Carol Anne's.'

'Weren't you just there last night?'

'I had to go back for something.'

'You sound strange. Is everything all right?'

Before he could ask any more questions, I told him about Angie, hoping that he would assume the odd tone in my voice was due to my friend's murder. Which in part it was. Of course he had a slew of questions about the murder, but I cut him short before he could ask too much.

'I'm really too upset to talk about this right now,' I said.

'Of course, I understand that you can't talk, honey. What a shocker,' he said. 'I hope they get the bastard.'

'Me too,' I said, one of my few honest statements in the conversation.

'See you tomorrow then. I love you,' he ended.

'Me too,' I echoed.

The phone was barely back on the hook when there was a knock at my door. I opened it to two men, one quite large, the other short, holding out badges. It didn't take a genius to figure out who they were. Evidently, they had decided to take a detour down Guilt Alley before heading to Carol Anne's. I cursed myself for opening the door.

Of course, they wanted to know all about last night. Sitting with them at my dining table, fighting off a headache that made me want to peel my skull back, I did my best to reconstruct the previous night's activities without sharing any incriminating information. While O'Reilly did most of the talking, his partner's small eyes swept my apartment like he was taking an inventory, the matching ecru sofa and loveseat bought at a discount furniture warehouse, the small nook that housed my office, the bookshelves that bowed under the weight of my favorite hardcovers and Shakespeare's collected works, the boxes I had been filling piecemeal for the move after my wedding. Kozlowski's silence made me more nervous than the ruddy-faced Irishman's questions, especially when his probing eyes travelled to the open kitchen door. The bottle of Jameson had been put away, but two shot glasses remained tipped upside down on the drain board. My blood pressure rose as I wondered if he noticed them.

O'Reilly was asking me something, but I was so distracted it sailed over my head. 'I'm sorry, could you repeat that?'

'You have any problems with anyone during the night, like in the bar?'

'Maybe one slight problem.' I told them about the West Siders Angie told to eff off. 'Telling people where to go was nothing out of the ordinary for her.'

'Any more contact with them after that?'

'No. They left a while later with some young girl – she was obviously more interesting than we were.'

'So you girls left the bar at what time?'

'Suzanne and Angie left around three.'

'And you?'

'I left a little later.'

Things became problematic when Kozlowski dropped the shoe I had been dreading.

'Why didn't you leave with them?'

My heart was pounding so uncontrollably it was a wonder it wasn't pulsing through my shirt, like on cartoon characters. The way he asked the question suggested I had something to hide. Which I did. But, though what I'd done with the carpenter was wrong, it wasn't illegal, and bringing it to their attention served no purpose. 'Because I was dancing and I didn't feel like going home yet,' I said with a paper towel tongue.

'Were you dancing with someone you knew?' Kozlowski pressed.

*I'm sorry, but what in hell does that have to do with the price of eggs?* 'No, I was just dancing with a bunch of different people.' Now I'd lied to the police. Which probably was illegal.

'So what time did *you* leave The Overhang?'

Was it my imagination or had the big detective's eyes darted back into my kitchen? Was he noting the two shot glasses? I wanted to run into the bathroom and heave out my insides for the third time that day. *The bar lights had come on. Blindingly bright lights.* 'After last call. About three thirty.'

'And how did you get home?'

'I took a cab.' I told myself I better get used to that lie. It slid off my tongue like an oyster. It was mind-boggling what one could do when survival was at stake.

O'Reilly had started speaking again, but my mind was racing so badly I only caught the tail end of his question. 'He's what kind of guy?'

'He? Who?' The blood was pooling in my ears, my head spinning so hard I feared I might faint. Was he asking me about Steven Kaufman?

'Her ex. Harvey. He's what kind of guy?'

'Harvey?' Relief. The pounding slowed. This is what guilt does to a person. O'Reilly didn't want to know about the carpenter. He wanted to know about Harvey. Praise God. 'He's a good person overall. He came from nothing and made a lot of money and is real happy about it.'

'Why the divorce?'

'He cheated.'

'It's a nasty divorce?'

'There's some animosity, of course. Especially over their real estate. Angie swore she was going to get their building and everything in it if it killed her.' I paused upon realizing what I had just said.

'You think Harvey Wozniak is capable of harming his ex?'

I thought back to how deliriously happy Angie and Harvey had been in their first years together. He was like a puppy with its tongue hanging out around her, all flustered and animated and happy. He had begged for Angie's forgiveness after he cheated on her, but she would hear none of it. Was it possible his love had spun so far in the other direction that he could take her life? I couldn't see it. 'There's no way Harvey killed Angie. He really loved her.'

'Were you aware that Angie was doing coke last night?' O'Reilly asked.

I shook my head no. *Another lie, but once again this was on a need to know basis, and they had no need to know.*

'So you wouldn't have any idea who her source could be?'

Another shake of the head, and that was the truth.

No one has ever been as relieved as I to see the backs of those two cops' heads receding down my stairs. I gave myself an A for getting through my interview without them tripping over my secret, but my guilt still hung on me like a sack of gravel. Though I had brought the burden upon myself, it was a burden nonetheless. Guilt mixed with fear made a potent mix. My mind explored different scenarios. What if they questioned the bartender from The Overhang, and he remembered seeing me leave with the carpenter? Would that send O'Reilly and Kozlowski back to me with more questions? I prayed that the cops would find Angie's killer soon, before there was any more digging into my actions of the night.

Then I told myself to stop being paranoid. The police weren't interested in my private business. It was Angie's life they were concerned with. Or her former life.

My headache had evolved into a lead ping-pong ball banging

the sides of my skull. Vowing to never drink again, I took two Tylenol and went into the bedroom. The bare mattress served as yet another reminder of my sin. I lay down on the bed and cradled my head in my arms, wondering how was I ever going to be able to face my fiancé tomorrow and thinking about how much I was going to miss Angie.

# ELEVEN
## Angie

Angie met Harvey on a crazy Saturday during the Christmas season when the store was so understaffed that Angie found herself working the floor in the lingerie department. Elbowing her way down a crowded aisle, she couldn't help but notice the husky, dark-haired man in a Blackhawks jacket rummaging through a rack of lacy nighties, his eyes turned sheepishly downwards.

'Can I help you?' she asked, deciding to have some fun with him. He looked up with droopy eyes reminiscent of a bloodhound, and his face turned crimson. Angie was quite certain that if he could have disappeared at the moment, he would have.

'Uh, yeah, I'm looking for a gift.' His nasal accent placed him from the Southside. Working class.

'For your wife?'

'Uh, no. A special friend.' He cleared his throat twice.

'Lucky girl.' Angie sorted through the rack until she came to a black wisp of a baby-doll nightie with feather trim. She held it out. 'Would this be her size?'

'I'm not sure,' said Harvey, who by now was the color of a boiled beet. Apparently, size was a consideration that hadn't occurred to him.

'Well, how does she compare to me?' Angie teased, meeting his droopy eyes directly with her own. 'Would you say she's about my size? Or is she larger? Smaller?'

Harvey took a closer look at Angie. With her full-lipped smile, high chest and wide hips, sensuality oozed from her pores. Suddenly, his flat, thin girlfriend was looking at a rather meager Christmas.

He took the nightie from Angie and held it in front of her. 'This looks about right. I'll take it. And can you wrap it?'

She rang up his purchase and wrapped it for him in colored

tissue. She placed the box into a Bloomingdale's bag and handed it over to him. 'I'm sure she'll enjoy it.'

'I don't think so.' He handed the bag back to her. 'It's for you.'

It was Angie's turn to flush, standing frozen behind the counter while dozens of Christmas shoppers vied for her attention. Emboldened, Harvey smiled at her and asked, 'So, where are we having dinner tonight?'

Angie had regained her equilibrium. 'How about Morton's? I like red meat.'

Angie didn't wear that nightgown until her wedding night. To both the delight and frustration of her future husband, she was a virgin and intended to remain in that rarefied state until she was married. Her flirtatious and often lewd behavior was a put-on. Her father was a notorious philanderer, his escapades so blatant that practically everyone knew about them. Raised in the shadow of her father's behavior, Angie had strong opinions about sex and the hurtful detritus it left behind. She was never going to take sex casually.

When Angie put on that nightie the first night of their honeymoon suite at Las Brisas, it turned out the wait had been worth it – for both of them. Harvey proved to be the kind of considerate lover Angie read about in books, and her timidity melted under his guidance. She found that sex was something she really enjoyed. Which worked out quite well, since her only aspiration in life was to have children and raise a family.

She and Harvey were both thrilled when not long after the honeymoon, they learned she was pregnant. They bought a three-flat in Old Town and rehabbed it into a single-family home with three bedrooms and a nursery. Then came the first miscarriage. Angie's doctor assured her that it wasn't unusual for a woman to miscarry her first pregnancy, so she and Harvey enthusiastically tried again. A second pregnancy ended in miscarriage too. Then a third.

After the fourth, Angie was inconsolable. She couldn't understand why her body, so obviously built for bearing children, was betraying her. When she suffered the fifth miscarriage, instead of turning to Harvey for support, she shut him out. She wouldn't let him touch her, because she couldn't bear to fail again. The bedroom that had been such a source of joy for them became an embittered battleground, her husband seeking to fill his needs, Angie refusing him.

This went on for nearly a year until the afternoon Angie came home early from work and found Harvey in their bed with a blonde from the trading desk.

If Angie had been inconsolable over her inability to bear children, Harvey's infidelity was even worse. He swore it was the first time he had strayed, the only time. That the woman had given him a ride home and he had succumbed in a moment of weakness. He vowed it would never happen again. Angie would hear none of it. After watching her mother silently endure her father's extra-marital affairs, she had no intention of suffering through what her mother had suffered. Harvey pleaded with her – reminded her they hadn't had sex for months – asked that they go for counseling. But there was no changing her mind. Infidelity ranked as the highest betrayal in her book. She threw him out of the house and started divorce proceedings. And refused to look back.

# TWELVE
## Carol Anne

With the kids back home, the noise level in the kitchen had returned to its usual ear-splitting normal. Cara and Eva were fighting over the television remote while Michael, Jr. squealed for attention from his high chair. Barely a sound registered with Carol Anne, who was parked in front of the sink peeling potatoes. There were far too many other unsettling things occupying her mind. The loss of Angie, by murder no less. And what Angie's parents had to be suffering. She couldn't even begin to imagine how devastating it must be to lose a child. Next was her best friend's idiot move, sleeping with a stranger at the risk of losing everything. But trumping all her concerns was her marriage to Michael. Something was terribly wrong between them.

He had been at the hospital dealing with a liposuction complication when the police appeared at the door. With the children still at their grandmother's, it had been haunted house quiet as she sat with them in the living room answering their questions. They asked her about the night before, about Angie and the other girls, about Angie and Harvey, about the condition Angie had been in when she left. If she had known Angie was doing coke – which of course she hadn't. Detective O'Reilly did most of the speaking while his silent partner took notes. They had been very businesslike, and it had been easy to be direct and honest with them. Not that Carol Anne had anything to hide. At least she didn't think so until the very end of the interview.

'And your guests left about what time, Mrs Niebaum?' O'Reilly had asked. She appreciated being referred to as Mrs Niebaum. She loved the sound of her married name.

'I'd say they were all gone by ten.'

'And as I understand it, Mrs Lupino drove downtown with Ms Trueheart.'

'That's correct.'

The short detective nodded, his thick-fingered hands folded in his lap. 'You were here alone after that.'

'Yes. The children were at my mother-in-law's, still are actually, and my husband was out playing cards.'

'I hope he won,' Kozlowski joked, the first thing he'd said since introducing himself at the front door.

'Actually, he did. He better have. He played late enough.' The moment the words escaped her mouth she wanted to rein them back in. Was that a glimmer of enlightenment in O'Reilly's eye? His right eyebrow twitched, and he touched a hand to it to calm it.

'And your husband got home at what time, Mrs Niebaum?' he asked.

It was probably a routine question, she told herself. Nevertheless, she didn't want them to know that the birds were chirping when Michael climbed into their bed. Not only would that be beyond humiliating, it was none of their business. She hoped neither detective noticed her hesitation before answering. 'Michael got home just after midnight.'

They had gone after that, leaving her alone in a house that suddenly felt bigger and emptier.

The girls' shrieks reached an intolerable level, piercing her private thoughts, grinding her sensitized nerves like one of those infernal leaf blowers the gardeners used. Her hand slipped and she sliced her knuckle with the potato peeler. Turning from the sink, she snapped at them in a tone they seldom heard.

'Cara. Eva. Stop it. Now, dammit!'

Stunned to learn their mother had a breaking point, they ran from the kitchen and disappeared down the hall. The baby's cries grew louder, so she lifted him from his high chair and held him against her. When he quieted, she returned the pacified infant to his high chair and started feeding him pureed carrots. Her mind circled back to Michael.

He hadn't touched her in months, the bed they shared used only for sleeping. For the first time in their fifteen years together, Carol Anne suspected another woman. Enough women passed through his office on a daily basis that having an affair would be as easy for him as plucking a petal off a daisy. But the confounding thing was, he didn't show any of the cheating signs she read about in magazines. He hadn't bought sexy new under-wear or started spending an inordinate amount of time in front of the mirror. There was no scent of another woman's perfume on his clothes. There were no mysterious calls to the house, followed by a hang-up. So she decided her imagination was working overtime – that he was just tired from working too hard – the excuse he always gave when she questioned the lack of intimacy in their marriage.

But the day's events brought back her suspicions on a completely different level. Michael had skulked in at five a.m. and awakened her from sleep – if you could call her restless tossing sleep. He apologized for being so late, explained that he had been winning big at the poker table, that it was in bad taste for a winner to walk away. Then he made love to her for the first time in months, nullifying her anger about his late arrival. All that mattered was that he had made love to her for the first time in ages.

Her newfound happiness came crashing down when she witnessed his reaction to Angie's death this morning. He had turned as white as the blinds on her kitchen windows, his hands shaking so visibly she feared he would miss his coffee cup. Hardly the hands of the surgeon who could take twenty years off a woman's eyes. While there was no denying Angie's death was an unexpected tragedy, Michael seemed inordinately disturbed by it. After all, Angie was her friend, not his. That's when the unthinkable occurred to her. Could Angie have been coming between them? Had the breakup of Angie's marriage pushed her to dabble in someone else's?

She was still pushing carrots into the baby's mouth when she sensed him standing behind her. Michael had a most annoying habit of entering a room without announcing himself, and then saying or doing something that made her jump from her skin. Sure enough, a light touch on her shoulder caused her to jerk the spoon from the baby's mouth. 'I hate it when you sneak up on me like that,' she said, turning to glare at him before returning her attention to the baby. 'How's the patient doing?'

'She'll be all right. Had to put in a couple of drains. Of

course, lipo on Mrs Cavanaugh was a complete waste. She's gonna eat herself back to fat in no time. Only this time the fat's going to end up around her waist instead of her ass. Thank God they pay in advance.' He wrapped his arms around her from behind, and she put down the jar of baby food and rotated toward him, burying her face in his chest.

'Michael, why did you act so weird today when you heard about Angie's death?' she asked without looking up.

His body tensed and he broke the hug. He grasped her by the upper arms more firmly than she was accustomed to and looked at her in a manner that frightened her. 'What are you talking about? A friend of yours is murdered and you think I'm acting weird? As compared to what? It's not like we get this kind of news every day.'

'Oh God, Michael. You're right,' she apologized, not wanting to anger him. 'I just get so afraid sometimes. You and the kids are everything to me and if anything ever happened . . .'

He folded her back into the hug and held her tighter this time, rocking her gently back and forth. 'Honey, a horrible, barbaric thing has happened. It's understandable that you're upset. But don't read things into a situation that aren't there.'

Secure in her husband's embrace, Carol Anne began to think maybe she was overreacting. But there was an unfamiliar timbre in his voice, an almost forced normalcy. A sense that something wasn't right came over her, lingering after he went upstairs to get ready for dinner. She worked to suppress the feeling. This curly-haired character was the focal point of her existence, the only man she had ever loved, and nothing would ever change that. Her troubled thoughts overshadowed the grief she should have been feeling for her deceased friend.

# THIRTEEN
## 13 Days Until

The biggest hurdle after eating of the forbidden apple was facing Flynn when he arrived home from New York on Sunday afternoon. I'd begged off from picking him up at the airport, but couldn't reasonably get out of going out to dinner with him that night. Since he left the choice of restaurant to me, I intentionally chose our favorite sushi restaurant so I wouldn't have to sit across from him and look him in the eyes for an entire meal. I was afraid what his trusting blues might read in my cheating greens. Not yet ready for him to set foot in my apartment, I told him I would meet him outside the restaurant. The moment he turned the corner, casually dressed in his stonewashed jeans and cranberry Polo shirt, my eyes filled with tears. He hugged me, and I buried my head in his chest, unloading rivers of salt on Ralph Lauren's pony, not truly sure which was prompting the tears more, my own behavior or Angie's death. The entire time, he rubbed the back of my head with his smooth hand and kept repeating, 'It's OK, Mags. It's OK.'

When I regained control, I wiped my tears away and glanced at him briefly. Then my eyes went straight back to the sidewalk. 'Welcome home,' I said.

Sitting side-by-side at the sushi bar, we talked about Angie's death. I told him everything I knew about her murder, that Angie had most likely left her apartment after being dropped off by Suzanne and been killed some time after that. Luckily, he didn't press me for any real details about the evening. The less said about that night the better. I had fibbed – if you could call it that – and told him Angie, Suzanne and I left The Overhang at the same time, but that we had taken separate cabs because Suzanne was taking Angie home. That statement left a gaping hole in my story since Angie lived closer to my Old Town apartment than Suzanne's Lake Shore Drive penthouse, in which case it would have only made sense for me to escort Angie home instead of Suzanne. Flynn didn't notice.

But then Flynn wasn't looking for holes in my story. There was no reason for him to distrust me. In an effort to lighten the mood and move the subject off Angie, he recapped his weekend in New York with his fraternity brothers, a weekend he said would take his liver at least a month to recover from. They had started out Friday night with drinks at Fanelli's followed by steaks at Gallagher's and ended the night in a roast at P.J. Clarkes. On Saturday night they'd dined in Hell's Kitchen before the guys took him to a gentlemen's club in a seedy Westside neighborhood.

'You want to know what I was thinking while I was watching those girls at The Incubator,' said Flynn, taking my hand. 'I was thinking that they had nothing on you. I was wishing I was back here with you or that you were with me in New York.'

'I wish I'd been in New York too,' I echoed in all honesty. If I'd been in New York, none of this would have ever happened.

I swiveled my chair sideways and studied his sweet face, the slope of his nose and his strong chin. I reminded myself how lucky I was, something my mother was always quick to remind me of as well. 'There aren't many men around like Flynn, especially for women in their thirties,' she repeated, ad nauseam. 'I told you you'd find someone if you lost that weight.'

*As if you had nothing to do with the weight, Mother*, I wanted to say. A picture of sandy-haired, sleepy-eyed, rebellious Barry Metter found space in my brain and my stomach sank with a last bit of pain for my young self.

I had fallen for Barry just as hard as Carol Anne had fallen for Michael, my uninitiated heart as vulnerable to first love as a native to colonial disease. He was older and smarter, saw the world through a different lens. He had radical beliefs and lofty ideals for solving world hunger and getting out of Vietnam before he made draft age. We met during winter of my Junior year and were inseparable all that spring and through the summer. And as young love in its rawest form would have it, he began pushing me to go all the way, telling me that if I really loved him, I would prove it. Being a good Catholic girl, I refused him that proof, but did permit him do things that would have appalled my parents.

But then September drew near, and I was confronted with Barry leaving for Berkeley. I decided that proving my love might be the only way to keep him tied to me across the two thousand or so miles between Winnetka and California. Then, the perfect night presented itself. My parents were going to see *La traviata* downtown and not expected home until late. With my older sister already away at college and my younger sister spending the night with a friend, the house was mine.

Barry climbed up the elm outside my bedroom so that none of the neighbors would see him come into the house. I waited at the window wearing the yellow negligee my parents had given me for Christmas. When he took me into his arms, we were Romeo and Juliet, two young lovers so taken with each other the rest of the world failed to exist. Barry was gentle with me and I only felt the mildest discomfort as he pushed his way into the uncharted territory. He was atop me with the sheets pushed to the foot of my bed, when my bedroom door opened. Just my luck, the electricity had gone out at The Lyric and the opera had been cancelled.

To this day, my mother's shrieks still ring in my ears. She wanted to see him in prison for statutory. With Barry already eighteen and me only sixteen, there was a good chance she could have made it happen. Instead, Barry was banished from my life, and I was grounded for last weeks of the summer. Barry left for Berkeley without me even having a chance to say goodbye. I lay in my room crying for days afterwards, refusing to eat.

Two weeks later, I donned my grey plaid uniform and went back to Immaculata for my senior year. In the weeks that followed I still wasn't eating, had no taste for food, yet the waistband of my uniform started getting tighter. My mother confronted me with the truth before I had permitted myself to become fully aware of it. With my older sister away and my younger sister premenstrual, my mother and I were the only tampon consumers in the house. And when she noticed the seal on the box of Tampax under my bathroom sink remained unbroken, it didn't take long for her to draw her conclusion.

Before I knew it, the Catholic of all Catholics whisked me to her Jewish gynecologist for a D and C. What were my options? I was sixteen with an ex-boyfriend two thousand miles away. And when my mother's mind was made up, like natural events such as a tornado, she was not a force to be challenged. I was a slave following orders. I did as I was told, studying the ceiling with my legs spread as my uterus was scraped clean. That night, still numb over the loss of Barry, and even more numb over the loss of his potential child, I started to eat again.

Boy, did I ever start to eat. I buried myself in food to ease the pain. I ate like a glutton, hamburgers and chips and ice cream. I couldn't get enough food. I kept eating until I'd put thirty pounds on my five-foot-three frame.

I never saw Barry again. His father was transferred to California later that autumn, so there wasn't even a chance of seeing him when he came home at semester break. Not that I would have wanted him to see him the way I looked then, blown up like the Hindenburg. In time the pain lessened, but that did nothing to lessen the thirty pounds. The weight stuck with a vengeance through the rest of high school, college, and afterwards. In part, I attributed my success at the *Chicagoan* on being overweight. My fat shielded me from any distracting interests, like a boyfriend, leaving me plenty of time to dedicate to a job I didn't even like.

Then, one day while waiting to make a sales call on an insurance agency that advertised in the *Chicagoan*, I started leafing through a trade magazine in the waiting room and came across a picture of Barry. He had won some award for being the top insurance producer in his county. His face was soft and flabby, his hairline had receded, and the smirk I had so loved had evolved into a white capped-tooth smile. The article mentioned how proud his wife and two children were of him. His rebellious streak had matured into bland conformity. At that moment, I realized that somewhere deep inside my consciousness had been a vision that we would be together again. That vision now evaporated.

In the weeks that followed, I stopped overeating. Just like that. I stopped gorging on hamburgers and French fries and cookies and ice cream, and started eating wholesome foods like fruits and vegetables and fish. I started walking to work instead of driving or taking a taxi. I started doing sit-ups and push-ups. And pound by pound the weight melted off until one day I got on the scale and it read one hundred and ten pounds. My exact weight the summer I loved Barry.

My exact weight the day I met Flynn.

Every word I spoke the rest of the evening to Flynn was forced and contrived, like he was a stranger I couldn't wait to get rid of. The irony was he was the same person I'd dropped at the airport on Thursday evening. I was the one who had changed, who had violated a trust, who was now the stranger. And as hard as I tried to act normal, normal was hard to find. An immense sense of relief passed over me when Flynn pulled up in front of my building to drop me off. But before I could get out of the car, he pointedly asked me if everything was all right. I blamed my odd behavior on Angie's death, which was partially true. Then I bolted from his car and went up to my apartment, grateful that we weren't living together yet, so I could be alone with my guilt.

# FOURTEEN

## Suzanne

Vince sat on the edge of the bed watching her dress, the sheets draped across his spent penis. His stare was so intent that even as she pulled her black jersey dress over her head, she could feel his eyes on her. When she bent her arm to reach the zipper in the back, he jumped from the bed and pulled the zipper the length of the sheath in an almost religious manner. His eyes stayed riveted to her while she sat at her vanity, knotting her blonde hair into a perfect bun and applying a light coat of lipstick. When she slipped the heavy gold bracelet he had given her onto her wrist, he nodded with approval.

Then her façade fell apart. She dropped her head to the back of her chair and let out a sigh. She pressed her eyes closed and held them tight, searching for peace in the dark behind her lids. There were no words to describe how much she dreaded this funeral. The wake had been painful enough: the morbidity of the funeral home, Angie's weeping mother and broken father, her three brothers trying to stand tough, the grieving faces of family and friends, the pain exacerbated by the unanswered questions of who and why. The past days had been exceptionally hard on Suzanne, bringing back seething memories of Johnny's death. She thought time had scarred over that wound, but Angie's death had torn it wide open and the pain was fresh as ever.

When she reopened her eyes, Vince was staring at her with concern. She forced a weak smile. 'I better get going.'

'Are you sure you're all right? You look pale,' he said, his voice fringed with new worry.

She started to nod yes and then stopped, shaking her head from side to side in a very emphatic no. Fighting for control of her emotions, she sat down next to him on the bed that had been the source of sweet ecstasy only minutes earlier. 'Oh, Vince. I just can't stop feeling this is somehow my fault. I mean, I know it's not, but I can't help it. Every time I see Angie's parents, this sense of culpability gets worse. I feel so responsible.'

'But how could you be responsible?' he soothed her. 'You didn't make Angie go back out.'

'But I made her go home. You can't understand.'

'Help me to understand.'

'It's too difficult,' she said.

Vince wrapped a comforting arm around her. She squirmed out from under his arm and gave him a quick peck on the lips. The kiss was a far cry from her earlier needy kisses.

'I don't want to be late. Be sure to lock up when you leave,' she reminded him.

She let herself out of the apartment and took the elevator to the garage. As she inched into the morning traffic, she adjusted her grip on the steering wheel and the gold bracelet reflected the morning sun. She couldn't help but smile at its simple beauty. Vince had presented the bracelet to her at one of their earlier lunches. She had turned it down at the time. Now she stared at it with the satisfaction of a cat on a warm car hood. Despite everything sad going on, the prize of possession could always elevate her mood.

The lunches with Vince had started out innocently enough. For a solid month of Fridays, she joined him at a fine restaurant where they shared a fabulous meal washed down with expensive wine. His behavior was always that of perfect gentleman, rising when she approached the table, keeping himself at an appropriate distance at all times while they dined, a polite peck on the cheek when they parted ways at the end of the meal. Their conversations were seldom about business, but more about arts and sports and history. Sometimes they discussed politics, but since they were both conservative and were both fans of the current president, George Bush, each was preaching to the choir.

He only spoke about himself once. Emboldened by a third glass of wine, she had asked him how he had achieved his success. He told her of being born in Pittsburgh forty-two years before to elderly parents who died within months of each other, leaving him an orphan at age eight. For the eight years that followed, he had been handed off from relative to relative, months here, a year there, never having a room he could count on much less a place he called home.

'But don't feel sorry for me,' he said upon seeing her pitying look. 'My childhood made me who I am. It created a will in me to succeed, a will I might not have had if my life had been normal.'

Wanting to be self-sufficient, he dropped out of high school at sixteen and took a job in construction where the pay was good and jobs were plentiful. He loved every aspect of the business, of creating something where there had previously been nothing. He enjoyed the danger and skill involved working high up in the sky. He appreciated the mathematical symmetry of the structures he worked on, how tons of steel and concrete could be integrated with miles of wire and plumbing to form magnificent structures. He loved battling the elements and solving problems.

'I decided that what I wanted to do was own a company that would design and erect buildings. So I went to night school, got my GED, and started taking classes in architecture and engineering. My whole life was study and work, study and work.'

He paused momentarily as if deciding whether to go farther, and then without Suzanne prompting him, he continued. 'I was so solitary, all alone. Then a guy I was working a project with introduced me to his sister, Anna, and I found myself with my first girlfriend. And my first lover. Which was great until she got pregnant. I got married when I was nineteen. I was twenty when I became a father.'

There was no hesitation before his next words.

'But you want to know something? Even though I got trapped into marriage at an early age, my daughter is worth it. I love her like nothing else on this planet.'

Having passed that hurdle, he continued his story. The family ended up relocating to Chicago where construction was really booming. He got a job with a small company where the owner took him under his wing, teaching him the business end of construction. When his boss decided to retire, Vince bought the company and started not only building, but developing his own buildings.

'And now, in case you didn't notice, Columbo is probably the most visible sign in the city. It's my passion and I'm very good at it. I thrive on the competition in the bidding process, dealing with the unions, working out design problems. I have no idea what else I would be doing if I wasn't developing properties.'

Suzanne stared at him over the rim of her wine glass. 'That's quite a story. You have a lot to be proud of,' she said, not quite sure why he had enlightened her about his family life. His history made no difference to her. She had no intention of ever getting involved with him, and so she let it drop.

He never spoke about his family after that, and she never asked about them. Their lunch conversation returned to the previous topics of art and sports and history. Then one Friday, he presented her with an expensive bottle of French perfume. She tried to decline the gift, but he insisted she take it, explaining it was really just a small token, a lagniappe. Suzanne accepted it warily. The following Friday there was another gift, this one far more pricey, a gold Bulgari bracelet. This time she firmly refused to accept his offering. Their arrangement was strictly business and gifts suggested something more. He shrugged and put the bracelet back into his suit pocket.

When they finished lunch and were waiting for the waiter to bring the check, he surprised her by saying, 'Suzanne, a beautiful woman should have beautiful things. I'm going to continue buying you gifts and you are free to refuse them. But I'm going to save them hoping the day will come when you will accept them.'

Her blue eyes glassed over. 'Suit yourself, Vince, but I'm not for sale.'

The following Friday, he presented her with a strand of black pearls which she glimpsed at admiringly before turning down. The next week, he brought a Cartier tank watch. And so it continued for several more weeks until, against her better instincts, she found herself growing attracted to this self-made man in more than a platonic way. It was nearly impossible to not be charmed by him. He was successful, intelligent, and handsome. He had come to her rescue when she had so desperately needed it. They shared many traits. Both were driven to succeed; both realized success came at a cost; both appreciated the material things that accompanied success. They loved the fine arts, music, and literature, but had little interest in social trappings like parties and galas. They were both solitary souls, their greatest satisfactions coming from their work.

He was her friend. He was her confidant. He was her financier.

And then he was her lover.

It happened at their twelfth lunch. Vince must have sensed her resolve was wavering, because when she arrived at the Ritz Carlton that day, instead of being shown to a table in the hotel's restaurant, she was ushered into a private dining room. Vince waited beside a bottle of Taittinger Comtes de Champagne chilling in a copper bucket. He lifted the bottle from the bucket and showed it to her.

'My favorite,' he said.

'Not bad,' she agreed, knowing full and well that the bottle price was stratospheric. Her practiced eyes surveyed the room. A large oriental rug covered most of the rose-colored marble floor. A pair of Louis XIV chairs upholstered in rich cream-colored brocade sat before a mirrored wall. The strains of a Brandenburg concerto filtered in from invisible speakers. A table for two draped in Irish linen sat beneath a glittering crystal chandelier, set with fine china, heavy silver, and sparkling crystal. Suzanne had never imagined such scenes existed anywhere outside the movies or one's fantasies.

'I hope you don't mind by-passing the restaurant,' Vince apologized. 'I just couldn't tolerate listening to other people today.'

'Well, I can't complain about the amenities,' she said. Her eyes registered the open door at the far end of the room and the huge four-poster bed inside. Weeks before she would have been insulted by what it suggested. That day the sight made her knees tremble.

There was a discreet knock at the door and a white-jacketed waiter entered wheeling a cart with a mound of caviar nestled in ice, accompanied by toast points and crème fraîche. Vince pulled out her chair, and she sat quickly, grateful to feel the solid seat beneath her. He took the seat opposite her and smiled.

So much blood had rushed to her cheeks, she was certain she had turned the same color as her red suit. The waiter poured the Taittinger, served the caviar and disappeared. Without exchanging a word, they clinked their glasses and drank. Though the champagne was excellent, the taste barely registered. Unfamiliar sensations coursed through her, her breath registering in shallow puffs. She had been pursued by plenty of men in her life, but school and then work had always come first, and her sexual experiences were limited. She felt an unfamiliar giddiness. Was it the Taittinger or the man?

Their usual small talk drifted into silence as the electricity between them continued to grow until the only sound in the room was the concerto. When the waiter reentered to pour more champagne, it was Suzanne who broke the silence, surprising herself with her own words. Looking boldly into Vince's eyes, she said, 'Have him hold the next course.'

The waiter retreated, leaving them alone. Vince remained rooted to his chair, his eyes transporting him across the space between them. He longed to go to her, but his body was responding in a manner that would most certainly give itself away were he to stand. Her skin was glowing and rosy, her pupils enlarged in the sapphire blue circles of her irises. His nerves were more primed than the day his daughter was born.

When he found words, he delivered them in an unwavering voice. 'Suzanne, I want to make love to you more than I've ever wanted anything in this world.'

His words pleased her greatly because her feelings mirrored his. Every fiber of her wanted him to touch her, to consume her. A side of her she never knew existed took hold and she took the initiative, rising from her chair and walking around the table, lowering herself onto his lap and wrapping her arms around his neck. His hardness beneath her confirmed his words, and she relished her newly discovered power.

Their first kiss lasted minutes, neither one wanting or willing to break it off. Suzanne had never experienced anything quite like that kiss. It took her to another dimension, as if he was an extension of her. The kiss was warm and deep and the most carnal thing that had happened in her life. She wanted it to never end.

No longer ashamed of his physical state, Vince stood with her in his arms and carried her into the bedroom, kissing her passionately as he laid her on the bed. His lips were caresses, moving from her neck to her cheeks to her eyelids. He unbuttoned her suit jacket and lowered his mouth to the mounds of her breasts. He unzipped her skirt and slid it over her hips, his excitement enhanced by the lacy garter belt and hose she wore, a prescient change on her part from her usual pantyhose. It was her turn to undress him and she took her time, pressing her lips to the flesh as she opened each button of his shirt. When she ran out of buttons she reached for his zipper.

Then it was his turn again, and he lowered her onto her back, continuing to kiss her as he removed her bra, the garter belt and hose, the wisp of panty beneath. He was frenzied and wanted to lick every inch of her, and nearly did so, his excitement growing stronger as she lay beside him moaning. And when he could stand it no longer, he climbed atop her, pressing himself at the sweet spot between her legs.

'Are you ready for me?' he panted.

'I'm not using any birth control,' she managed between gasps. This turned him on all the more. The knowledge that she wasn't on the pill or carrying her own condoms told him this scenario was alien to her, that she didn't sleep around.

He, however, was prepared. He retrieved a condom from his pants and rejoined her in the bed for what turned out to be the best lovemaking either had ever experienced in their lives.

They finished lunch in bed, taking breaks between courses for another round of lovemaking. As day drifted languidly into evening Suzanne lay in his arms fully satisfied, finding it hard to believe there was something more exhilarating than opening a new account or receiving a huge bonus check.

'I brought something for you,' said Vince, kissing her forehead. He reached into the nightstand and produced a cache of small boxes. Her heart leapt as she realized he had brought all the gifts she had turned back: the gold bracelet, the black pearls, the Cartier tank watch. But there was an additional box this time, the signature blue box with the white ribbon from Tiffany's.

Her breath caught in her throat as she opened it. She wasn't quite sure if she was relieved or disappointed at the exquisite pair of diamond-and-emerald earrings flashing iridescently in the lamplight.

'Oh, Vince, these are stunning,' she said.

'So will you take my gifts now?'

'My mercenary side will always out in the end,' she said, climbing out of bed and going to the mirror. Completely naked, she put on the earrings, the pearls and the bracelet and turned for his approval. 'What do you think?'

The sight of her with the strand of dark pearls hanging to the middle of her long slender waist stirred him again, and he put out a hand to pull her back to him.

It was after midnight when her newfound happiness hit the first speed bump. She was dozing in his arms when he awakened her. When she met his eyes and saw an apology in them, the smile that had begun to crease her lips turned downward.

'I have to leave you now.' He pulled her close and put his lips to her ear. 'I have never, ever, felt like this about a woman. You have been under my skin since the first time I saw you. Being with you is better than I ever imagined it could be.'

Suzanne put on a mask of indifference. He was telling her she was the most special thing in his life, but he had to go home to his wife. It wasn't a surprise, but it stung nonetheless. For him to leave her after the magnitude of the step they had taken today was disappointing. Why hadn't he arranged some lie so they could spend this first night together? Hell, she hadn't even called the office to tell them she wouldn't be back after lunch. She had put herself on the line, and now he was deserting her.

'Please don't look at me like that,' he said, reading her mind. 'Don't judge me. Not after something so important has happened between us.'

*Welcome to the real world*, she thought. What did she expect? 'I'm sorry you're leaving,' she said without any argument.

She met his goodbye kiss with cool lips, his caress of her cheeks with cool eyes, not wanting him to find any neediness in her. Once he had gone, she ran a bath in the marble tub and poured in some deluxe bath salts. The scent of lavender tickled her nose as she eased into the steamy water and gave some more consideration to her situation. This did not have to be a bad thing, she realized. In fact, having a lover and a life of her own could actually be having the best of both worlds. She had never looked for commitment in the first place, never wanted a family, so why not roll with it?

She crawled back into the bed and sniffed the pillows. His scent was there in the linen, masculine and musky. She put a pillow between her legs and another beneath her head. Feeling very sexy and content, she drifted off into a trouble-free sleep.

A florist's box was waiting outside her apartment door the next morning. Inside were two dozen long-stemmed yellow roses. The accompanying card read, *To the most special woman in the world. Love, Vince.*

She never gave his marital status a second thought again. She was going to enjoy their relationship for what it was. While she questioned the wisdom – not to mention the moral aspects – of carrying on an affair with a married man, Vince added an element to life that she'd never known was missing. Their time together was filled with excitement and passion. Vince gave her something to look forward to, an intense physical outlet. Every minute with him brought pleasure. Accepting that the affair couldn't go anywhere made it all the more enjoyable. No need to ruin things by overanalyzing. They were two people sharing each other's minds and bodies. That was enough for her.

The sound of multiple horns pulled Suzanne from her reverie. The light had changed and she was holding up traffic. She was on her way to a funeral. As she touched the accelerator and the BMW surged ahead, she could feel Angie's disapproval coming from above.

# FIFTEEN
## 10 Days Until

I sat in the window picking flint from my black Gap skirt and watching the street for Flynn's silver Audi. This would be our first time together since the awkward dinner on Sunday night. My nerves were frazzled and my stomach churning so loudly, I could only pray it wouldn't announce itself during the funeral. The last few days had proved beyond the pale, trying to find normal when I wasn't quite sure what normal was. My life had spun so dramatically out of control that I didn't even feel like myself, but rather like someone suspended above me looking down on my hapless other self.

I had avoided Flynn altogether on Monday, using the excuse that there was so much to be wrapped up at the *Chicagoan* before the wedding that I needed to work late. That was actually true. A sales director's responsibilities didn't stop even if one of your best friends was murdered and you cheated on your fiancé and you were the bridal half of the world's most excessive wedding. My paperwork was backlogged as a result of having taken off so much time for wedding preparations, and the calendar told me ten days remained to pull everything together.

In a bit of dumb luck, Flynn was called out of town on Tuesday and didn't get back until late, sparing me the ordeal of attending Angie's wake with him. The heart-wrenching event had been difficult enough as it was, filled with moaning and wailing and tears. I had gone with Suzanne, who had been so overwrought that we only stayed an hour.

But now here I was again, in a state of apoplexy at the prospect of facing my fiancé. Not wanting to take the chance that he might come up to sinful Eden, the moment I saw his car pull into the street I was down the stairs and out the door. He hadn't been in my apartment since *that* day, and I feared if he visited the scene of the crime he might sense something different.

Since we hadn't been together the last couple of days, I'd been able to drop the guilt shield, but today it would have to be raised again.

I walked towards his car feeling vulnerable. The air smelled of damp pavement from an earlier rainstorm, and the sun was just peeking out from the last of the black clouds, promising a Chicago humid day. A near perfect day for a funeral. I stopped beside the car to compose myself, taking a deep breath before opening the passenger's door. The smell of cleaning solution usurped the smell of damp pavement. Of course. It was Wednesday. Flynn's day for his regular hand-wash. Funeral or no. He greeted me with a white-toothed smile. I sat down and buckled myself in, the seat belt preventing me from giving him anything more than a kiss on the cheek.

'That was romantic,' he said, his smile morphing into a disappointed pout.

'Flynn, I'm burying one of my best friends today.'

'Sorry. I'm being disrespectful.' He put the car in gear and drove off without another word, no doubt nursing wounded feelings while I sat wrapped in a cocoon of deceit. The radio was playing a Whitney Houston song, 'I Want to Dance With Somebody Who Loves Me'. An uninvited image of the carpenter on the packed dance floor of The Overhang popped into my brain, an image I immediately suppressed.

After suffering through twenty minutes on the snail-paced surface streets, we merged onto the Dan Ryan. Flynn started driving fast, as if he was in a race against time, weaving swiftly through cars without leaving much margin, sometimes crossing four lanes at a time. He loved to drive aggressively, and I usually said something about his risky behavior, but at the moment a fatal crash seemed the perfect solution to my problems. When we reached the Edens spur, he started driving even faster. As the off-ramps sped by, the curves arcing round to neighborhoods of identical, split-level houses, I realized it was time to break the silence, if not for me then for the safety of others.

'Thank you for coming to the funeral,' I said, hoping my voice rang true. 'I know you had a big day at work today.'

'I wouldn't even think of letting you go through this alone.' He seemed pacified and brought the car's speed closer to the posted limit. 'Maggie, what's the matter?'

'Why do you keep asking that?' I sighed, lobbing the ball back at him in a best-defense-is-a-good-offense tactic.

'Well, I know this death has been hard on you, but you just aren't yourself. Ever since I got back from New York, it's like you're a different person.' When I didn't say anything, he added, 'See, that's what I mean. What is wrong with you?'

'I'm sorry.' I racked my brain for some reasonable excuse. It was unfair to torture him like this. 'I'm just exhausted and a little depressed, I guess. Don't take it personally.'

He took his hand off the wheel and patted mine. 'Well, think of something nice. Like our wedding. Hard to believe it's less than two weeks to lift-off, isn't it?'

'It sure is,' I replied. That was the honest truth. The last months had flown past. I thought about all the wedding gifts piled in my childhood bedroom. The place looked like a bazaar.

'You know, Mags, one of the best days of my life was the day I met you,' Flynn said as we pulled off at Tower Road and headed east through the forest preserve, the overhead trees in full bloom. 'I've never told you this, but from the beginning the thing I liked best about you, aside from your stellar person-ality, of course, was you weren't one of those predatory women out there for money. You have real substance.

'And you made me laugh. You really made me laugh. Promise to keep making me laugh after we're married?'

'I'll do my best,' I answered, wondering if he'd heard the joke about the bachelorette party where the bride . . . Another unwanted image popped into my mind, the carpenter smiling at me on the dance floor like he'd known me forever. I admonished myself, wondering where these thoughts were coming from.

And even worse, how could I be thinking them on the way to a friend's funeral?

# SIXTEEN
## Vince

All alone in Suzanne's apartment, Vince thought about the spell she cast on him. How everything she did left an impression. He pictured her squaring her shoulders as she walked out the door on her way to the funeral, standing tall like a soldier readying for combat. The image tugged his heart in a way he had never experienced. He remembered how confidently tall she stood the first time he saw her on one of his construction sites. But this time it was a different tall. Her rigid posture was braced against the pull of sadness. He wished more than anything that he could have gone to the service with her – been there to fold her in his arms, to lend her a shoulder to cry on.

Less than a week had passed since he'd last seen her, but it felt like a lunar year. He was glad he decided to stop in this morning unannounced, and gladder still when she welcomed him with open arms. They had made quick, torrid love. He thought with satisfaction of watching her slip the bracelet he had given her onto her slim wrist. God, he had missed her so wildly these past days.

Rolling back onto the bed, he pushed his face into the sheets and breathed deeply of her scent, etching it into his olfactory sense for later enjoyment. Then he showered and dressed for the second time that day. He stood in front of the bathroom mirror knotting his tie with the image of her bedroom reflected through the open door. As to be expected, the room had real style, from the Frette linens to the Biedermeier sleigh bed to the Japanese prints adorning the walls. Suzanne had class, something his wife could never have, something all the money in the world couldn't buy. In Vince's mind, Suzanne was pure perfection. His obsession with her made him crazy with fear that she didn't feel as strongly about him as he did about her.

When he asked her about her past relationships, she told him the few boyfriends she'd had were so inconsequential they'd left no imprint. But certainly it wasn't possible that someone as beautiful, as perfect as Suzanne, had never had a love affair. There had to have been some great passion in her life.

Vince had noticed that there were very few personal photos displayed in Suzanne's apartment. Surely she had mementos somewhere, pictures of her earlier life, life before him. Suddenly, he was struck with an idea that so violated her privacy he hated himself for even thinking it. But at the same time he knew he would act on it. He zeroed in on her walk-in closet, hesitating only briefly before stepping inside. Like the rest of the apartment, it was orderly beyond imagination, the clothes organized by color like paint chips from lightest to darkest. He started randomly opening drawers, lingerie, hosiery, T-shirts, silk scarves, finding a glimpse of her in each one. Moreover, every drawer held a lilac-scented sachet, the smell he associated with her in those exquisite moments between dress and undress.

After exhausting all the drawers without finding anything of a personal nature, his search turned to the overhead shelves. They were lined with handbag filled sacks and boxes of shoes labeled in black marker. Black Ferragamo pumps. Gold Gucci sandals. His eyes travelled past the shoes to the corner of the closet, and it was there he claimed his victory. Wedged between the last shoebox and the wall were three tired-looking photo albums. He reached up and took one down.

The photos inside appeared to be from Suzanne's teen-aged years. There were shots at the beach, in a school auditorium, lounging in a park. He assumed the girls often posing in the pictures with her were the friends she talked about all the time; the plump redhead was the one getting married, the dark haired one with the large bust the dead girl. He put the first album back and took down the second. These were clearly college photos. Scenes of a leafy campus. Crowded parties with men and women drinking beer and smoking. He was relieved to find there was no photo of Suzanne arm in arm with a special someone, no one on the receiving end of that personal smile that so knocked his socks off.

The third album was a cracked leather-bound folio, much older than the others. The first page held an aged Polaroid of a little girl staring at a newborn in a crib. A second photo on the same page was a family photo of a little blond boy and a slightly older blond girl and two blond adults, sitting next to a stream on a blanket with a picnic basket in the center. Their smiling faces radiated happiness. The family matured over the next pages, Suzanne evolving into a stunningly beautiful young woman, the boy into a handsome young man. There were pictures of her father setting up a Christmas tree. Her mother taking a turkey from the oven. There were First Communions and graduations and birthdays. The entire album was inhabited by the small family: Suzanne, the boy and the two adults.

The last page held a yellowed news clipping.

> *Local Man Killed in Hit and Run*
> *John Anders Lundgren, 22, of Winnetka, was killed in an early morning crash on Green Bay Road when the vehicle he was driving was forced off the road by another vehicle that apparently swerved into his lane. A witness to the crash said that the driver of the other car, a black Cadillac, had been driving erratically and appeared to be drunk. The witness was unable to get the license plates of the vehicle because he stopped to assist at the accident. Lundgren was taken to Evanston Hospital where he was declared dead on arrival.*
>
> *Lundgren was returning from Chicago after taking his sister home following a family birthday party.*
>
> *He is survived by his parents, Lars and Inga, and sister, Suzanne.*

Vince slid the album back into place feeling he had just peeked into Pandora's box. Though Suzanne spoke about her parents occasionally, she had never mentioned a brother, much less a dead one. Now he understood why she was taking Angie's death so especially hard.

He knew he should be ashamed of himself for invading her privacy, intruding into her private world. But he was so obsessed with her that he couldn't help himself. And this intrusion was small compared to his previous one. The previous intrusion was something far more invasive than rummaging through a closet. If she ever learned about it, she would most certainly hate him. But she would never learn about it, because he couldn't bear to live if she hated him.

# SEVENTEEN

lynn's hand was an alien claw escorting me into Donovan Brothers Funeral Home. We walked into the mortuary to a service so large that several salons had been combined and the room was still packed to the gills. The front half was filled with family alone. Angie was, after all, Italian. So many floral arrangements lined the walls, the place could have passed for a nursery. To either side of the closed casket stood easels with collages following the arc of Angie's life: childhood, high school and college. The glaring void was the absence of wedding pictures, almost as if the marriage had never occurred.

Ida Lupino stood in front of her daughter's sealed remains sobbing loudly, her huge bosom heaving. Beside her stood Angie's father, stoically patting her shoulder, his bronzed face somber beneath his thick head of silver hair, his face wearing the grief of a parent when the natural order is reversed. He bore little resemblance to the sartorial man who had walked his beaming daughter down the aisle behind her eight bridesmaids not so many years ago. Angie's three older brothers completed the picture, wearing grim black suits, their handsome faces pulled downwards, their wives alongside them looking helpless.

I spotted Kelly sitting next to Arthur and Natasha in the center of the room, her thick hair laced into a tight braid. Like nearly everyone else in attendance, she was dressed in black. Natasha looked elegant in an expensive black suit. Arthur's pinched face looked peeved, as if he would rather be anyplace else. Carol Anne and Michael were seated behind them holding three places. I gave Flynn the nod and we worked our way over to them and took two of the open chairs. Flynn fell into conversation with Arthur in front of him while I talked to Carol Anne.

'Suzanne's not here?' I asked.

'Not yet.'

'I hope she's all right. She was really having a tough time at the wake last night. You know, déjà vu all over again. How's the family holding up?'

'I think that scene speaks for itself.' My gaze turned toward the front of the room where Mrs Lupino's sons were practically carrying her to her front row seat in preparation for the services. Angie's sisters-in-law circled around their mother-in-law trying to console her. My heart clutched in agony.

'And you?' Carol Anne whispered. 'How are you holding up?'

'Not too well.' I turned toward the back of the room to search for Suzanne and spotted Albert Evans standing among the latecomers congregated in the rear. Albert had been Angie's assistant manager and one of her boon companions, a total pillar during her separation. I had spent many a pre-Flynn cocktail hour sipping wine with Angie and Albert, suffering through the finer points of retail. Impeccably dressed in a slim Italian suit, Albert looked more like he belonged at a fashion shoot than a funeral. But he wore the expression of a child who had just been told his dog was hit by a car. We locked eyes and I gave him an ironic smile. He acknowledged it by raising his handkerchief to his eyes, soaking up a sincere tear with pressed Irish linen. His partner, Julian, stood beside him giving support while looking somewhere between appropriately mournful and bored.

It was then Suzanne walked in, looking far too beautiful for the occasion. I waved her over and we shared hushed hellos, as the tall balding priest stepped up to the podium. Father Carroll was a longtime friend of the Lupino family and had presided at Angie's wedding. Now he would bury her.

'All rise,' he said, and we assembled as told. He recited the Catholic prayers for the dead, prayers I first heard at my grand-mother's funeral when I was eight, his monotone chant punctu-ated by an occasional sob from Mrs Lupino. After finishing the ritual prayers, the priest sprinkled the casket with holy water and invited the mourners to pay their last respects before leaving for the funeral Mass.

The chairs emptied and a line formed as people shuffled to the front of the room to pass before Angie's remains. Carol Anne stopped to touch brush the casket with her hand. Michael nodded respectfully. Kelly touched the casket too, as did Suzanne, whose shoulders heaved with a choked-back sob. Arthur steered a dry-eyed Natasha past and then it was my turn.

Angie's high school graduation picture was perched on the casket lid, her face angelic beneath the black cap. I recalled the drunken pact the six of us had signed that graduation night, a solemn agreement that if any one of us died prematurely, there was to be no mourning. Instead, we were to throw a party and prop the corpse up in a corner with a beer in one hand and a joint in the other. I thought of the rosary beads Ida Lupino had most likely laced through her daughter's stiff fingers and thought about how much better they would serve Angie than a beer and a joint.

'Goodbye, my friend,' I whispered, touching the casket, tears clinging to my eyelashes. Flynn gently prodded me, and I stepped away from the casket, wiping my eyes with my fingertips. This time Flynn's reassuring hand felt like it belonged.

When we stepped into the lobby I was surprised to see Harvey hunkered down in the far corner like a pariah, his curly head bent in apology. I hadn't seen him since he and Angie had separated and he looked terrible. His face was mottled in pain and dark rings encircled his eyes as if he hadn't slept for some time. Certainly he must be thinking if only he and Angie had stayed together, this travesty wouldn't have happened. *Too late now, Harvey.* No rewrite of history could change this outcome. He looked up just then and saw me. I gave him a sympathetic nod as Flynn and I walked past him and out the door. I wanted to reach out and touch his hand and say how sorry I was, but I didn't.

Moving out of the dim lights in the funeral home into the sunlight was blinding. But even with my eyes frozen in a sun-blocking squint, they couldn't miss Detectives O'Reilly and Kozlowski stationed in the parking lot. Wearing suits instead of shirtsleeves, they were trying to look unobtrusive as their eyes addressed each person who walked from the funeral home. A chord of fear passed through me. They were two people I never wanted to see again. I cozied up to Flynn, more for their benefit than my own, hoping seeing me with my fiancé would deflect any future unwelcome questions.

'See those two men over there? They're the cops on Angie's case,' I said in a low voice.

'You mean the two bad suits? I thought they were relatives from Cicero,' said Flynn.

I hushed him and checked to make sure none of Angie's family was in earshot. 'What do you suppose they're doing at the funeral?'

Flynn gave me a look usually reserved for someone he considered stupid beyond belief. 'They're checking out the crowd. Standard for this sort of thing, I'm sure. You know. Criminals returning to the scene of the crime.' He donned his Ray-Bans and accepted an orange *FUNERAL* sticker from one of the Donovan brothers. We got in the car and Flynn put the sticker in the lower left windshield, careful not to press so hard it would leave adhesive on the glass.

While we sat in the car with the air conditioning running, waiting for the procession to the church to start, I thought about what Flynn had said about criminals returning to the scene of the crime. I couldn't see how anyone here could have had anything to do with Angie's death.

# EIGHTEEN

The mourners were invited back to the family home after the services. By the time Flynn and I arrived, the streets were so filled we had to park five blocks away. Walking alongside a ravine beneath oak trees dense with summer foliage, I was reminded of the hundreds of times I had walked this street in my youth. Whether it was crunching on autumn leaves or watching snow fall between the denuded branches, this street always held a particular sweetness. That sweetness was gone now.

The sting deepened when we reached the house. The modest four-bedroom Colonial of my first visit had grown over the years to a sprawling giant, numerous additions taking it to the boundaries of the heavily wooded lot. Angie's father seemed to add a new wing with each major business deal. Or maybe it was with each new girlfriend, as a way to keep his wife occupied. It was no secret that Mr Lupino was a philanderer. Angie had known from sophomore year that her dad was a cheater. She had cried when she told us. But if Mrs Lupino knew about his dalliances, she never let on. They were Italian after all, and no matter how late her husband got home, he was lord and master of the manor and dinner was always waiting for him. Ironically, he was a true family man and a devout Catholic who gave generously to the church. Every Sunday found him in the front pew with his wife and children, the best-dressed man in the place.

Dozens of children were playing in the front yard, Angie's nieces and nephews and young cousins finally set free after a grueling morning of good behavior. Children were revered by the Lupinos, making it all the more tragic that Angie hadn't been able to have any of her own. It seemed there was always a small army of children on the premises, especially on the weekends when the Cicero relatives came to visit. When I was growing up, the chaos of Angie's house was so inviting and vibrant compared to the quiet reserve of my own that I loved spending time my free time there. My few cousins lived out of state and were practically strangers, so large family gatherings were totally foreign to me, making the Lupino gatherings seem even more enjoyable than they probably were.

Flynn and I squeezed into the house and worked our way down a crowded hall into the kitchen. With all the equipment and activity in the room, it looked more like a restaurant than a residence. Several large-breasted women labored over gas ranges with boiling vats of pasta and open grills of sizzling sausages. Long stretches of countertop were heaped with bowls of penne and meatballs, platters of fried chicken, trays of antipasto, baskets of crusty bread. A round table in the bay window was covered with sweets, cookies, cakes, and ricotta-stuffed cannolis, sabotage to every diet I had ever started. It was no mystery that I maintained much of my former weight by gorging myself at the Lupino table, world's away from my mother's table where one protein, one starch and one vegetable were the rule.

A woman with arms the size of my thighs and a mound of gray hair pinned atop her head stood in front of the range stirring a pot. Upon seeing me, she put down her spoon and came rushing over, her ample body moving with surprising grace. She wrapped her huge arms around me, and hugged me so close I could barely breathe.

'Oh, sweetheart, who could ever believe a day like this could happen?' she said, shaking her head in answer to her own question. She released me and turned her attention on Flynn who looked frightened she might hug him too. 'Does he belong to you?'

'This is Flynn Hamilton, my fiancé. Flynn, this is Rose, Angie's aunt.'

'Handsome, but too skinny,' Rose said, managing a feeble smile. 'You too,' she said, eyeing me up and down. 'You're wasting away to nothing.' Relieved to have a crusade, she piled two plates high with food and thrust them at us. 'Here now, go outside and eat. *Mangia, mangia.*' Her mission accomplished, she turned her energy back to the pots bubbling on the six-burner range.

'That scene was straight out of *The Godfather*,' said Flynn, as we walked out the back door. The yard was filled with people sitting at café tables around the pool or on the lawn. We found a place in the shade and put down our plates. I made myself comfortable on the grass while Flynn went back inside for drinks. I was picking at my food when I spied Albert Evans standing by himself, looking overwhelmed at his equally overloaded plate. He saw me and came over.

'May I join you?' he asked.

'Of course. Where's Julian?'

'He had to go back to work.' Albert removed the Irish linen handkerchief from his pocket and unfolded it, placing it on the grass before sitting down. He studied his plate as if the food was going to eat him instead of the other way around. 'Isn't this ridiculous? Some gargantuan woman corralled me in the kitchen and wouldn't let me escape until she'd given me enough to feed the better part of Outer Mongolia – wherever that is.'

'Angie's aunt. That's the Italians for you. No matter the disaster, it's always important to eat. They talk lunch at breakfast and dinner at lunch.' I put my fork down on my plate. My stomach was queasy, so I had no appetite. 'How are you holding up without your old boss?'

He turned teary and reached into his pocket for his handkerchief before realizing he was sitting on it. He touched his thumbs to his eyes. 'It hasn't been easy. Angie wasn't only my boss, you know, she was one of my best friends. I loved her very much. It's so beyond the beyond that she met such a violent death. I just hope she was messed up enough to not suffer.'

'What's that supposed to mean?' I asked.

Albert looked around surreptitiously and leaned in close to me. 'Oh God, I've been practically dying keeping this to myself. Swear yourself to secrecy?'

I crossed my heart.

'I saw Angie right before she was murdered.'

'What? How could you have seen Angie?'

'I was in The Zone and she came in just before closing.'

'The Zone? What would Angie be doing in The Zone?' I knew of the Boystown bar because it advertised in the *Chicagoan*. With its almost exclusively gay clientele, it didn't seem the sort of place Angie would patronize. Especially on her own.

His face changed from sad to guilty. 'I think she came in to score.'

'So you think she got her coke there?'

The guilty look thickened. 'I turned her on to a bartender acquaintance who deals a little on the side. She was so depressed after her breakup with Harvey that I thought a bump from time to time would make her feel better. So I introduced her to Lyle. I was only trying to be helpful.'

'Nice move, Albert.'

'How could I know she'd end up so out of control? I mean, really.'

He seemed to be trying to convince himself rather than me. 'Did you talk to her that night?' I asked.

'No. I was with friends and she didn't see me. I didn't go up to her because . . . well, you know how abrasive Angie can get. Especially when she's fucked up. I didn't feel like dealing with her.'

'Oh, Albert,' I admonished him. 'Maybe if you'd talked to her things would be different.'

'Fuck me. Tell me I haven't had that thought about a million times. But there's more to the story. After she scored, on her way out, she stopped to talk this good-looking dark-haired dude sitting by himself. You could tell they knew each other and you could tell he wasn't happy to see her there. She said something to him that made him look like he was going to punch her. Then she left.'

'Oh my God, have you told the police about this?'

'That's the problem. I can't. If I tell the cops she was in The Zone, they'll go after Lyle. You may think it's a brave new world, but lots of cops are real homophobes and have a hard-on for gays. No pun intended. Lyle called me the minute he saw Angie's face on the news and begged me to keep my mouth shut.'

'But, Albert, what if the guy she talked to killed her?'

He hung his pomaded head. 'I've been eating a guilt sandwich over this all week. I haven't slept in days.'

*You're not the only one eating a guilt sandwich. Or not sleeping.* But I was finding a saving grace in Albert's confession. If the dark-haired guy Albert saw turned out to be Angie's killer, then her murder would be solved and I wouldn't have to deal with the police asking me more questions and possibly stumbling over my secret. 'Albert, you have to call Area 3 headquarters and ask for Detective O'Reilly. He won't care about Lyle. He just wants to find out who killed Angie.'

He paused and rolled his eyes. 'I'll think about it, Maggie. Seriously. But in the meantime remember you promised not to say anything.'

'But, Albert, this is different.'

'Let me handle this my own way. Otherwise, I'll deny the whole thing.'

'Albert, you've got to do what's right.'

Our conversation skidded to a halt as Flynn arrived armed with two glasses of wine. Carol Anne and Kelly were trailing behind him. Albert stood and picked up his handkerchief, folding it primly before placing it back in his pocket. He nodded at the girls and walked away, leaving a mound of untouched food on the grass.

'What's with him?' asked Carol Anne, settling in on the lawn. Her navy suit made her blue eyes look bluer, but there was something unreadable in them I couldn't pin down.

'I guess he lost his appetite,' I replied, taking my glass of wine from Flynn. 'Where's Michael?'

'His pager went off during Mass. There was some emergency and he had to go to the hospital.'

'A plastic-surgery emergency?' quipped Kelly, forking an immense meatball into her mouth.

'They happen,' Carol Anne replied defensively.

'What about Suzanne?' I asked.

'She went back to work. If you ask me, seeing Angie's family was just too emotional for her. Hitting too close to home,' Carol Anne added.

I envisioned Suzanne so folded up in grief the day of her brother's funeral, she had to be escorted to the car with one of us holding her up on each side. I thought of my own siblings, the two sisters I was sandwiched in between. We may have had our differences, but I couldn't imagine the world without them. The same way none of us could imagine the world without Angie.

Flynn and I stopped to say goodbye to Angie's parents on our way out. This turned out to be the most difficult task yet. There was finality to this goodbye that colored the air like a bad haze. Angie's mother hugged me and cried, while her father stood beside her owning the same pained silence he had at the wake and the funeral.

'If we only knew who did this horrible thing . . .' Ida Lupino sobbed.

My thoughts zoomed straight to Albert Evans. Under circumstances like this did I really have to keep his secret? Would he do the right thing and come forward? If he did, would it unlock the mystery of Angie's death and provide the Lupinos some modicum of relief?

The problem was there were too many secrets to keep. Including my own. After begging off with the honest – for once – excuse that my next day was going to be hellish, I had Flynn drop me at the office where I lost myself in work until well after midnight.

# NINETEEN
## Kelly

The black cloud descended while Kelly was lacing up her running shoes. It was like the moon passing between the earth and the sun, eclipsing all light and leaving her in inky shadow. When it came it was without warning like a train barreling through a crossing. But unlike a train, it did not recede within minutes. It lingered ominously, sometimes for hours, sometimes for days.

The phenomenon had started taunting her after her mother's death. Over the years she'd employed different strategies of dealing with it. In high school, she'd lock herself in her room with a good book. In college, she buried herself in her studies. The booze and drugs and one-night stands came later. Though the cloud had been in remission since her sobriety, it had been simmering just beyond the horizon. Now it had reappeared with a vengeance, a squall of depression crushing her towards a rocky shore.

She felt a sense of worthlessness, of insignificance, of help-lessness, the sentiment that her life was one big pile of shit. Here she was in her thirties trying to jumpstart a life she never started, and the challenge seemed hopeless. She wasn't like the other students in her college classes, their eager young brains effortlessly sponging up knowledge while she had to labor for it, their trajectories already programmed for success. She envied their enthusiasm and wished she had felt the same way at their age.

Catching up was a bitch. It seemed all her friends were coasting in early middle age instead of reaching like she was. They were set with families or careers, homes and nice cars, no financial worries like how to pay tuition and next month's rent. They had people in their lives. Husbands, boyfriends, children. So Suzanne was flying solo, but her job was the only lover she'd ever wanted. Kelly had never had a relationship with someone she could lean on, someone to come home to. She told herself being alone didn't necessarily mean being lonely. But Kelly was both. Alone and lonely. She wished that life were something to be enjoyed instead of endured.

It was almost humorous that she was studying to be a psychologist. She hated shrinks. She'd spent enough time on their couches after her mother's death and found most of them to be sanctimonious people with their own problems. She imagined she could do a better job of helping people than they did. That's why she wanted to be one of them. At least there would be one shrink out there who understood people's pain.

The cat sidled up to Kelly and regarded her with one-eyed concern. *Enough self-pity*, Kelly reprimanded herself. *You have no one other than yourself to blame for your laggard existence. Don't let that black cloud put you back where you were. Get out there and run it off.* She finished lacing up her shoes and headed out the door.

The early morning sky was a lapis blue dotted with white cotton, the air still cool as she cut through the courtyard and started down the street at her warm-up pace. Before long her body fell into its regular rhythm, her muscles growing more fluid with every stride. But while her body was co-operating, her head still wasn't right. The dark cloud hovered over her, blocking out the blue sky. It followed her into the park, and she ran faster in an attempt to outrun it. But it refused to be outrun, sinking lower and lower until it was upon her, enfolding her, Angie's contorted face looming within. *It should have been you.*

Finding it hard to breathe, she stopped and bent over in search of oxygen, her hands resting on her knees. Anyone watching would have thought she was going to be ill. Her heart was racing in incomplete beats and the world spinning in a way that confused up with down. It was a full-fledged panic attack. Pushing past the feeling she was going to faint, she turned back on unsteady legs and headed for home. Crossing Clark Street was a herculean effort, and the rest of the walk was pure misery. The cat greeted her with a questioning meow when she opened the door. Kelly threw her shaking body onto the pink-flowered sofa.

The panic subsided slowly, taking its hand off her one excruciating finger at a time. If she ever felt like she needed a stiff drink, now was the time. She could handle depression, but the panic was entirely unmanageable.

She couldn't do this on her own any longer. She needed to talk to someone.

# TWENTY
## 8 Days Until

Friday morning found me wondering why I hadn't just slept at the office since it had been well after midnight when I left the night before. I glared at the monumental pile of work to be attended to. Sales figures. Reports. Projections. The pile seemed to be growing instead of diminishing, and losing the day of Angie's funeral had just put me that much farther behind. My period was due, but had yet to present itself. Flynn was getting testy with me for all my avoidance of him. In fact, the backward relief of my workload was being able to use it to avoid my fiancé. My guilt had not diminished one iota in recent days, but rather, had grown stronger, a weed threatening to choke me off. Even more disturbing, uninvited flashes of Steven Kaufman, on the dance floor, in my bedroom, kept popping into my brain. As much as I tried to repress the images, they refused to stay down. During my few restless hours of sleep last night, he had appeared in a dream and asked me not to marry Flynn. Freud said you are everyone in your dreams. Could I be this stranger I never wanted to see again?

I checked my calendar. There was a note to call the bridal shop about the bridesmaids' dresses. Another to call the florist. Yet another to call Flynn's mother with a count for the rehearsal dinner. I was so entirely overwhelmed I longed to disappear, to go home and curl up in a corner with a good book. It seemed like years since I'd had time to read for pleasure. My apartment was filled with boxes of unread books, but the recent demands on my life left no time for reading. Much less time to write. I'd always thought there was a book inside me trying to get out and it was just a matter of time. But real life didn't leave much time. Besides, in order to write, you had to have something to write about.

The phone rang and Sandi, the receptionist, informed me that there was a Kelly Delaney on the line. Did I want to take the call? Not really, I thought, but I took it anyhow.

'Aren't you usually out running right now?' I asked.

Kelly's voice sounded garbled as if she was talking through water. 'I didn't run today. More important things to do like cut my toenails. Do you have a few minutes?'

A few minutes was exactly what I didn't have. 'For you, I have plenty of time. What's up?'

'I'm in a kind of bad way. I really need to talk. I mean, I could go to an AA meeting, but it wouldn't be the same as talking to a friend. I was wondering if we could get together some time today. I wouldn't bug you, but I don't know who else to call.'

*Of all times, Kelly.* I checked my schedule. Staff meeting. Luncheon meeting. Sales calls to key customers. I was so slammed, I barely had time to hit the john. The first crack in the day came around three o'clock, time I had counted on to weed through more paperwork. But the desperation in Kelly's voice couldn't be ignored. What good is a friend if she can't throw her own life in the crapper to help out? 'I can't get away until this afternoon. How's three? You OK till then?'

'Three's fine.' She already sounded better. 'Meet me at the Mayfair Regent. I'll buy you tea. Or a drink if you want.'

'The Mayfair? I guess you're not looking to get lucky.' The expensive hotel was an outpost for blue-haired ladies and the gay men who accompanied them.

'I want peace and quiet.'

'All right. I'll see you at three.'

'Thanks, Maggie. Thanks a lot. I know you're really busy. You don't know how much I appreciate this,' said Kelly.

'That's what friends are for.'

I hung up and gave work another try, but my mind wouldn't sit still. A sharp jab in my pelvic area drew my attention. A sign of my period coming? Or a sign of something else? I closed my eyes and prayed for debilitating, painful cramps. Then, I questioned the wisdom of counseling Kelly when my own state of mind was so radically scrambled.

*    *    *

I slipped from the office at 2:45, ignoring the 'you've got to be kidding me' look Sandi gave me on my way out the door. It was no secret how much work I had to do. I arrived at the Mayfair just before three and hurried past the uniformed doorman into the staid lobby. It was an oasis in the craziness of the city with rich paneled walls, a frescoed ceiling and a young Asian woman playing a calming harp. The room was populated with well-dressed elderly women and much younger men whose ivory silk jackets sported colorful pocket squares. Kelly was watching for me from a sofa in the far corner. Her eyes reminded me of an animal in hiding.

'You OK?' I asked as I joined her on the sofa.

She shrugged. 'When I was a little girl, after Mom got sick, my Aunt Betty used to take me Christmas shopping on Michigan Avenue and we would come here afterwards. We'd sit in this room with all our packages, and have tea. I always looked forward to that day. It was so special to me. I suppose that's why I wanted to meet here. Everything bad disappeared for a while when I was here.

'Aunt Betty died not long after my mom. Heart attack,' she added. Though her pale blue eyes remained dry, they projected the depth of a thousand tears. 'I still miss her.'

A white-jacketed waiter rolled over with a cart and laid out plates of finger sandwiches and scones with strawberry jam and clotted cream. We selected a tea and he spooned it into china pots that he covered with quilted cozies before wheeling the cart away. The ritual was so civilized that for the first time in nearly a week I felt almost human. Kelly poured herself a cup of tea and stared at it.

'Maggie, I don't know what's wrong with me. Ever since Angie's murder I feel like I'm falling apart again. I need to talk about it before something bad happens.' She didn't need to elaborate what something bad might be. I had a good idea. 'You know I hate asking for help, so I doubly appreciate you being here for me.'

'Get a life. I already told you that's what friends are for.'

'I mean, it's been really hard this past year. And all things considered I think I've been doing pretty well. But since Angie's death, well, I feel like I'm walking backwards toward that pit. I just can't keep her out of my mind. I feel like I was so locked up in my own problems, I wasn't a good enough friend to her. She used to call me after her breakup with Harvey, but I was so busy with school and work and all that I just never found the time for her. I could tell she was hopped up at Carol Anne's. I should have said something to her, but I didn't.'

'Kelly, you couldn't have saved Angie. No one could.'

'Maybe not, but I could have tried. She tried with me. I saw myself in her the other night, the anxiousness, the pacing. Deep down, I knew there was more going on with her than drinking. But I've been so dominated by my own recovery, all I was thinking about was myself. Now I wake up every morning seeing her looking at me with blame in her eyes. And sometimes it happens at other times. It's giving me anxiety attacks. Today was so bad I couldn't even run.'

'You've got to stop beating yourself up,' I said, raising a cup of soothing tea to my lips. My hand trembled ever so slightly as I put the cup back in the saucer. 'How about me? I was with her in the bar that night.'

Kelly followed my nervous hand, and then looked me in the face. She studied me in a way that made me feel as transparent as her welkin-blue eyes. Were they seeing through me? Could they read my own distress?

'What's wrong?' she demanded, shifting the thrust of the meeting. Suddenly she was the take-no-prisoners girl I knew in high school. The one who would take charge of a problem and solve it. A math equation. A sick mother.

'Me? Nothing. What are you talking about? I thought we were here to talk about your problems.' I picked up a cucumber sandwich. Though my appetite was non-existent, I took a large bite to avoid having to speak.

'There is something wrong, I can tell. C'mon, Trueheart, I've only known you for, like, a hundred years. What is it?' My silence only made her probe deeper. 'Are you having second thoughts about your wedding?'

I swallowed the bit of sandwich. I wanted to say *absolutely not*, that Flynn was the center of my universe, and I couldn't wait to become his wife in exactly one week and one day.

That's what I wanted to say. Instead, I found myself back in the confessional. 'I cheated on Flynn.'

'You what?'

'It's true.' Pushing through my humiliation, I told the story of meeting the carpenter in The Overhang. Of bringing him into my house and into my bed. Of my fears of being pregnant. Kelly let out a low whistle.

'Whoa. Maybe you're the one who should be in a program.'

'I don't need to hear that right now,' I said defensively.

'OK, sorry. But you know something. When we were at Carol Anne's the other night, aside from my suspicions about Angie, I got the feeling you weren't really all that excited about getting married.'

'Of course I'm excited about getting married. Flynn's the greatest guy on earth. I'm sure everyone has some second thoughts.' I wondered if my argument was to convince myself as well as Kelly. 'It was a stupid drunken fling. That's all.'

'And if you're pregnant?'

'God forbid. I'll know soon enough. I'm blocking it until then.'

'And what if you are pregnant?' she repeated.

'I don't know. Maybe I'll go to New Hampshire and look the guy up,' I joked half-heartedly. 'I could get one of those really ugly red-and-black lumberjack coats and we could raise sheep.'

The pale eyes widened. 'Did you say New Hampshire?'

'Yah. The guy was from New Hampshire.'

Kelly put her teacup down so forcefully, she nearly broke the saucer. She leaned her narrow body close to me. 'Please don't tell me he was driving a truck. A white GMC pickup truck.'

I spun through blurred images of him squeezing his enormous white truck in between two cars in front of my building. A hugely unsettling feeling swept over me. 'How did you know that?'

'Holy shit,' said Kelly. 'That same truck was parked on Carol Anne's street last Friday night when I was leaving. I noticed it because the New Hampshire plates caught my attention, the slogan, *Live Free or Die*. What the hell was he doing there?'

This newfound information wasn't sitting well with me, but I had to nip Kelly in the bud before her enthusiasm led to my disaster. 'Stop it. That's crazy. There's no way he was outside

Carol Anne's. It's got to be a coincidence. There are probably thousands of white trucks in this world?'

'With New Hampshire plates? In the state of Illinois right now? There can't be that many. In fact, I'll bet you there's only one. My creep detector is telling me there's something weird about this. Maggie, what if he was stalking Angie and had something to do with her death?'

'Stop again. You know he couldn't have killed Angie. He was with me when she was killed.'

Kelly had the audacity to roll her eyes. 'Are you sure about that? You admit you passed out.' Undeterred, she continued her tormenting train of thought. 'There's no good reason for this guy to be in Kenilworth and then end up in The Overhang. We've got to tell Mutt and Jeff about this.'

'You mean the cops? Kelly, don't even go there. We don't know that was his truck in Kenilworth. And you know what telling this to the cops could mean for me.' I recalled my conversation with Albert Evans after the funeral, insisting he tell the police about seeing Angie in The Zone. Great. Now, I was a hypocrite as well as a liar and a cheat. But the stakes were too high for me to be anything other. 'And if you're my friend you won't even think about talking to them.'

'But what if this guy left while you were passed out and killed Angie?' she whined.

'And then came back to my apartment and got back into bed without waking me. I don't think so.'

Kelly was not to be put off. 'What if he's some kind of kinky serial killer? What if he comes back for you? If anything happened to you and I knew all about this weirdo, then I'd never ever friggin' forgive myself. Think about that.'

'And how about if you ruin my life? Please, Kelly, promise me you won't say a word to the police,' I begged.

'Shit,' said Kelly, catching the pain in my tortured face. 'OK, I promise. But I sure don't like it one bit. And you gotta swear to me, if you see that guy anywhere again, on the street, in a store, in church, you'll friggin' go to the police.'

What do they say about no good deed going unpunished? My effort to help Kelly had turned on me, and now I had to worry about her on top of everything else. Not to mention the other worry that had just been added to my laundry list. That being, if it was Steven Kaufman on Carol Anne's street, what in hell was he doing there? There was no logical answer to that question.

'I promise,' I said.

# TWENTY-ONE

F lynn and I were at the Acorn on Oak listening to a fiftyish
patron sing an off-key rendition of 'Loverly', while the
accommodating piano player did his best to earn a good
tip. The Acorn was right out of the fifties, a dimly lit room with
upholstered chairs on heavy wheels, camp without trying to be.
Flynn called it the perfect sneak joint.

'So what did you think of the movie?' he asked. We had just
seen *Big* at Water Tower Place.

'I liked it OK,' I answered, 'though I thought it would be
funnier.' After leaving the Mayfair, I had been so agitated I
toyed with cancelling our standing Friday night date, but then
decided it was unfair to Flynn. Besides it was time for me to
start inhabiting my regular world again. *Big* had been my choice.
I figured it would be safe, nothing controversial, no sex, some
laughs. And it had filled the bill, a mindless respite from
everything that was haunting me, work, wedding, infidelity and
pregnancy, in ascending order. For a blessed couple of hours
the antics of Tom Hanks as a 13-year-old boy who steps into the
shoes of a grown man dominated my universe. It was the perfect
escape. Clever. Funny. Brainless.

I actually walked out of the theatre in a good mood.

Until I saw the promotional poster in the lobby where a
guilty-looking Tom Hanks ponders the words: *HAVE YOU
EVER HAD A REALLY BIG SECRET*. It was hard not to
shudder.

'Yeah, I thought it would be funnier too,' Flynn was saying.
'Maybe we should have seen *Crocodile Dundee II*.'

'Spare me sequels. So how was your week?' I was working
to produce innocuous conversation in an attempt to stop being
the horrible company I'd been of late.

'It was actually pretty productive despite . . .' His voice

tapered off. I knew he meant to say despite missing a day, but he let it go. 'How about you?'

'I'm chugging along. If I don't hang myself this week, I guess I never will.'

He took a sip of beer. 'Anything new on Angie?'

'*Nada*,' I said, my thoughts circling round the white truck on Carol Anne's street. After all, what *were* the odds of two white trucks with New Hampshire plates being anywhere in Chicago on the same night? Had to be less than one in a million, and there were what, like three million people in Chicago. Not counting the suburbs.

I realized he was talking again. 'I just can't believe the police aren't doing anything more about it. What a bunch of Keystone Cops.'

To my immense relief, Flynn spotted a couple he knew and they stopped at the table to say hello. He asked them if they wanted to join us, and they did, thankfully, sparing me any more awkward conversation.

In the taxi on the way home, Flynn asked me if he should come up.

'Probably not, Flynn. You know Natasha's having that stupid shower for me tomorrow, and I'll have to get an early start. Thank God this is the last one.'

'That's all right,' he said. 'It would probably be too tempting. I don't want to break our vow.' With that he wrapped a possessive arm around me and pulled me close. He kissed me deeply, and I felt myself give way in his arms. It felt almost right again. Maybe things were going to be OK, I thought. Just maybe they would be OK.

# TWENTY-TWO
## Vince

Vince was silhouetted in Suzanne's dining room window watching the city unfold below him, hundreds of individual dramas playing out behind hundreds of yellow squares of light. A mother rocked her baby, an elderly woman warmed milk in a pan, a couple entertained at a dinner party, a young man took something from the refrigerator, probably a beer, and returned to his living room to watch an enormous television. If the beer drinker were to look up, what would he think of the man in near darkness, holding a wineglass and peering down on him? Vince's gaze pivoted to Lake Shore Drive. The line of cars crawled in the Friday night traffic, their white headlights a stark contrast to the yellow streetlamps, the dark void of Lake Michigan stretching lonely and black to the other side of the slow-moving parade.

He took a sip of wine and noted the finish, how the taste lingered in his mouth. Just like Suzanne. The taste of her lingered long after they were apart.

He turned from the window and looked at her sitting at the table, her blonde hair glowing gold in the candlelight. She'd hardly spoken a word at dinner and only eaten a few bites of the filet he'd picked up at Gibson's. Her moodiness since her friend's death had gotten worse. Admittedly, she had suffered a loss, but he was having trouble understanding her behavior. He walked over and emptied the last of the '61 Latour into her glass. The wine was ridiculously expensive, but when it came to satisfying Suzanne, no price was too high. He held the empty bottle out and looked at the label.

'Sixty-one was a good year,' he said.

'It was. My brother was born that year.'

Vince wanted to throw the bottle through the window, wishing he'd bought the '82 instead. He wanted to say something, but he was fairly certain he wasn't supposed to know she'd had a brother. Instead, he placed the empty bottle on the sideboard and walked behind her to rub her shoulders. The feel of her flesh beneath his fingertips awed him. She was feminine and soft and muscular and firm at the same time. She was contradiction and harmony. Cool and hot. Reserved and passionate.

'Your brother?'

She stood abruptly, breaking away from him, and went to the window. Her reflection in the glass was haunted and severe. 'Yes, my brother. I never told you this, but I had a younger brother. He was killed in a car accident. It was a long time ago, right after I got my job.'

She stopped to take a sip of wine, her eyes peering out across the lake.

'He was run off Sheridan Road by a drunk and hit a tree. There was this man who saw the whole thing and pulled over to help. Johnny wasn't wearing a seat belt and had been thrown from the car. His neck was broken. The man waited with my brother until the ambulance came. Johnny died on the way to the hospital.

'And as much as I appreciate that man for stopping to help, there's a part of me that wishes he hadn't stopped at all, that he'd followed that driver and gotten his license plates instead. Then maybe we would have found out who killed my brother. Maybe there could have been justice. Or at least some closure for my parents and me.'

Vince started to speak, but Suzanne held up a hand.

'No,' she said, waving him to silence. 'There's something else about that night. Johnny was killed because he gave me a ride back into the city. It was my mother's birthday, and my car was in the shop, so I'd taken the train out to Winnetka. My parents wanted me to spend the night, but I insisted on going home because I wanted to be at my desk early in the morning. They didn't want me to take the train that late so Johnny drove me home. And got killed on his way back. Can you imagine the guilt I carry for that? I've felt responsible for his death every day since.'

She stopped to compose herself and this time Vince knew better than to interrupt. 'Now, I've lost one of my dearest friends and it's the same thing. The bastard who took her life is out walking around. They'll never find him – I know it. No one will ever pay for Angie's death. Just like no one has ever paid for Johnny's.' Tears started to flow, trailing dark streaks of mascara down her cheeks. 'Except me. I'll pay for the rest of my life. Don't you see? Johnny died because he took me home. And Angie died because I took her home.'

He had never seen her cry and her unhappiness tore at his heart in a way he never thought possible. He went to her and held her close, cupping her heaving shoulders as she buried her face against his chest. Her eyes were ringed in wet mascara, her cheeks smeared black. Her nose was running. And the more she cried the more he loved her. The ice maiden had melted, and it only made her all the more alluring. It unhinged him to know his feelings for her could grow any more intense.

'Suzanne, honey, listen to me.' He tipped her chin up with his fingers so that he was looking directly into her eyes. 'I'm going to fix this. I'm going to find out who killed Angie.'

She stopped crying and, oddly enough, started laughing through her tears. 'Oh, Vince, please . . . you can't find Angie's murderer.'

'Yes. I can,' he said, his face tight, his black eyes filled with determination. 'In this world, there's very little that can't be done if the price is right. Money can open doors the police can't. I know someone who does this sort of thing. He will find out who killed Angie.'

She blinked back another round of tears. 'You're serious, aren't you?'

'Dead serious. Seeing you like this is torture to me.'

'You really think you can find who killed Angie.'

'I know I can.'

'God, you're wonderful.' She sniffed and wiped her nose with the back of her hand. 'I must look delightful.'

'You've never looked more beautiful.' He meant it. Taking her face in both hands and pressing his mouth to hers, he tasted the salt of her tears on his lips. He drew her gently to the floor.

Any voyeur would have enjoyed quite a show.

It was nearing midnight when Vince got home. He went directly downstairs and headed to his home office, walking past the custom-made bar still under construction, careful not to step on any abandoned tools in the dark. His office was his haven, an entirely masculine room with heavy leather furniture and a large oak desk. He took a seat behind the desk and pulled his personal address book from the top drawer. Turning to the letter B, he ran his finger down the page until it found the name he was looking for. Belchek, Charley. Belchek was a Chicago cop who'd been thrown off the force for using unethical means to extract confessions. He'd turned private investigator shortly afterwards, and a highly effective one at that. He'd helped Vince win a bid on a crucial job years ago by digging up some unpleasant information about the competing developer and his young protégé, and leaking it to the newspapers. Vince hadn't needed Belchek's particular skills since then, but he sure needed them now. Despite the late hour, he suspected the ex-cop would still be awake. He punched out the number on his private line.

The voice on the other end was straight out of a noir film.

'Belchek.'

'Charley. It's Vince Columbo.'

If Charley Belchek cared about the time, he gave no indication. 'Vince, been too long. I see you done good by yourself since we done our business. See your signs everyplace.'

'I can't say I have any complaints,' said Vince, ignoring Belchek's implication he might not have done as well otherwise. He got straight to the point. 'I'm looking for some information. There was a woman killed in Lincoln Park last week named Angela Lupino Wozniak. I need to find out who did it.'

'That's a strange request, but hey, it ain't my business to know why you want to know what you want to know. This kind of information could be possible, but it'll take a lot of coin and I'm making no guarantees. How much you willing to invest?'

Vince didn't hesitate. 'As much as it takes.'

'There'll be a lot of palms to grease depending on the caliber of who did her. You know, gang, organized, oddball, whatever. It'll cost ya at least forty K.'

'And I need to know fast,' Vince added.

There was silence on the line as the ex-cop did some calculating. And then, 'Make it sixty.'

'Done,' said Vince.

# TWENTY-THREE
## Ron

Ron O'Reilly was riding that rail between true slumber and drunken stupor, dreaming in fitful patches. The dismissal bell was ringing, and he was waiting for his sisters and brothers outside St Mary of the Brook. He had promised his mother he would always take care of them. The bell grew louder and louder. Ringing, ringing. His eyes flicked open. It wasn't a school bell ringing. It was his telephone. He turned on the light and squinted at the bedside clock. 5:15. A half-filled glass of whiskey rested on the nightstand beside him.

He picked up. 'O'Reilly.'

It was the watch commander at Area 3. 'Ron, we just got a call that Angela Wozniak's wallet turned up over at the Yellow Cab depot.'

Ron rubbed his eyes and willed himself to consciousness.

'You shittin' me. It's been a week.'

'No shit. Know it's early, but thought you'd want to know.'

'I'm there,' said O'Reilly. He called Koz, rousting him from sleep as well, and told him to be ready in fifteen minutes. Then he rolled out of the bed and hit the bathroom, filling the sink with icy water and plunging his face into it. The cold water took his breath away, but it woke him up. Finally, he brushed his teeth twice and gargled with Listerine Mint. *That should do it*, he thought.

The morning sky had turned robin's egg blue by the time they drove through the chain-link entry of the Yellow Cab depot, a Flanders Field of mustard coffins bearing the headstone TAXI. A sign at the gate read *Patrolled by guard dogs* accompanied by the picture of a German Shepherd with its teeth bared. O'Reilly popped his fourth Altoid of the morning and offered one to Koz who declined. He pulled up next to a gray cinder-block fortress situated in the middle of the lot. The sound of barking dogs filled the air.

'Where're they?' asked Kozlowski, hesitating to open the door. 'I'm not big on Shepherds. Somehow they see a big guy like me as a challenge.'

O'Reilly pointed to a chain-link pen where two German Shepherds paced like tigers in a cage, their open jaws warning visitors back. 'Over there, big guy. You're safe.' They went to the cinder-block building where a security guard let them in and directed them to the office. Inside the square windowless cubicle, a couple of uniformed cops waited alongside a black man whose long spiderlike legs and arms were little more than skin and bones. A tired-looking white woman with bad skin, and an even worse brown wig, was seated behind a Formica-topped desk. A checkbook-sized Gucci wallet sat on top of the desk.

O'Reilly nodded to the cops, the man, the woman. His head hurt badly and he hoped the breath mint was enough cover the previous night's sins. The woman, Rosie Harding, was the night office manager. The human skeleton, Mashal Anouye, was introduced as the taxi driver connected to the wallet. O'Reilly picked up the wallet and flicked it open. A photo of a living Angela Lupino Wozniak smiled at him from between dozens of credit cards. The billfold compartment held several crisp hundred-dollar bills.

O'Reilly dismissed the cops and took the only other open chair in the room, opposite Anouye. Kozlowski leaned against the wall as unobtrusively as his size would allow.

'Somebody want to explain to me about the wallet?' O'Reilly asked.

Rosie Harding spoke before the driver had an opportunity. 'Mashal turned this wallet in last Saturday morning at the end of his shift, around five a.m. I locked it up in the safe. It's our policy to keep valuable items under lock and key until someone calls to claim them. When Mashal stopped in this morning to see if anyone had claimed the wallet, I checked the safe. I looked inside for identification this time and realized it was that woman they found in Lincoln Park. So I called the police.'

'That right, Mashal?' O'Reilly demanded.

The black man shifted his legs nervously, his knees moving like a spider in a tight spot. 'Yes, it is, sir,' he said in British-accented English.

'Where are you from, Mashal?'

'I come from Kenya, sir, but I've been in Chicago over ten years now.'

'Not quite as warm here, is it?' Kozlowski piped in.

The black man's head turned momentarily toward the giant leaning against the wall. 'No, sir.'

'So tell me about this wallet?' O'Reilly continued.

'Well, it was one week ago, Friday night, sir, or actually Saturday morning, as you prefer. I was on my way down Halsted when a woman hailed my taxi. I almost didn't take her because my shift was finished, but I thought, well, one last fare couldn't hurt. The moment she got in the taxi I was sorry I picked her up because I realized she was very, very drunk.'

'What happened then?'

'She asked me to take her to a bar, sir, up on Lincoln Avenue. The Zone. But I must advise, sir, of something very strange that happened along the way. At the corner of Halsted and Armitage, she leaned out the window and started screaming at someone. While I don't remember what she said exactly, it was something unfriendly about seeing him in court. When we arrived at the bar, she seemed in a hurry. When I gave her her change, she jumped out of the cab. Without giving me a tip, I might add. I turned off my light and came directly back here, sir, to the depot.

'As it is my habit to check the back of the cab before turning it in, I did so, and that's when I noticed this wallet lying on the back seat. She must have forgotten it.' He pointed at the wallet. 'In keeping with company regulations, I turned it in here, sir, to the lost and found.'

'And it's been locked up ever since?' O'Reilly asked Rosie Harding. When she nodded, he added, 'I don't suppose you ever think about trying to contact the owner of a lost item?'

She gave him a disingenuous look. 'You can't believe how much crap people leave in taxis. We'd be on the phone all day.'

O'Reilly turned back to Mashal who was shifting in the chair like the seat was made of broken glass instead of wood. 'So the reason you checked to see if the wallet was claimed is . . .?'

'Because, sir, often a grateful person leaves a reward for the driver when they retrieve a lost item. I would have checked on it sooner, but I've been out sick.'

After pressing Mashal for more information, O'Reilly learned the man was undergoing chemotherapy for a lung tumor, the reason he had been absent the past week, most likely the reason he didn't seem to be able to sit still. After dismissing the driver with an admonition not to leave town, O'Reilly dropped the wallet into a plastic bag and handed it over to Kozlowski. Rosie Harding sat silently behind the desk.

'You should really consider trying to reach out to your customers,' were O'Reilly's last words. 'It would be a great public service.'

The sun was fully risen when they walked back outside, and the day heating up. The sound of the barking dogs echoed in their ears as they climbed back into the Ford. O'Reilly turned the ignition key and waited for the air conditioning to come on. His face was throbbing. 'Can't believe they didn't look in the wallet for ID. Bunch of fuckin' idiots.'

'I wouldn't exactly call it the best policy,' Kozlowski agreed.

'Think there's a chance the cab driver did her?'

Kozlowski shook his head. 'Don't think so. Guy looked like a wind off the lake could blow him over. Besides, why would he turn in the wallet without taking the money?'

'Yah. Right. She sure seemed to keep enough on hand to feed her habit,' O'Reilly agreed, as he put the car into drive. 'But at least now we know where she went before getting whacked.'

# TWENTY-FOUR

## Kelly

The morning dew was still in the air and the sun rapidly on the rise as Kelly ran along the lakefront. Her head was on a lot straighter than it had been the day before, but her body was fatigued from lack of sleep. She had tossed and turned all night, making the cat's night as miserable as hers, unable to stop thinking about the truck from New Hampshire on Carol Anne's street. The cops needed to know about that truck and the carpenter, and she was trying to work out how to do it without breaking the promise she'd made to Maggie at the Mayfair.

Five miles into her run, she turned around and headed south, bypassing the woods where Angie's body had been discovered. She doubted she would ever run through those woods again. She was on the sidewalk near the totem pole at Addison, when she spotted Ralph, and it dawned on her she hadn't seen him in days. She slowed for his outstretched hand. His grizzled smile stretched his stubbly cheeks.

'Hello, Missy!' he said, reaching out for their traditional slap.

'Yo, Ralph! What are you doing over here? Aren't you off course?'

'Won't go through them woods no more. Nothin' good in there.'

She gave his hand a slap and kept going. She had run a quarter mile past him when his words caught traction like spinning wheels hitting solid dirt beneath mud. 'Holy shit,' she cried aloud. She turned around and started to sprint.

'Ralph, wait,' she called when his lopsided body came back into sight. By the time she caught up to him, her breath was coming in short bursts. 'Why d'you say that about the woods, Ralph?' she panted.

His answer almost knocked her backwards. 'I seen somethin' bad happen there.'

'Bad like what, Ralph?' she asked, still panting from her all out run.

The old man's lips grew taut over his gummy smile. He nodded as if he was trying to make a big decision. Toeing the dirt with one of his tired shoes, he looked at Kelly nervously. 'I don't want no trouble.'

'Of course not, Ralph. I'm your friend. There won't be any trouble. Now tell me why you won't go into those woods.'

'I seen a man carrying a daid girl.'

Kelly's heart felt it might stop. 'Ralph, can you tell me exactly what you saw?'

'Well, Missy, it was 'bout a week ago. I was walkin' like usual down the path – sun was gettin' ready to come up but hadn't come up yet. I gets up early, about three thirty, four. Used to clean them downtown bars, so's I had to be up 'bout that time of the morning for nigh thirty-five years. Since retiring, I just cain't break the habit. Anyhow, I's walking and I seed someone near the trees carrying somethin' big over his shoulder. I thought I best make my presence known, so as not to startle him or nothin', so I said, 'Howdy.' Well, the very second he heard my voice, he dropped his load and took off runnin'. So's I went up to investigate, and I sees it was a girl he was carrying. Poor thing. Neck's all broke – that's clear as day. I didn't want no trouble, but I felt bad for her laying there like that, so I got some newspaper out of the trash and covered her up till someone could come and bury her proper. Then I didn't know what else to do, so I kept on walkin'.'

Kelly didn't know whether to laugh or cry. She'd always known Ralph to be a few cards short of a deck, but not this short. Covering up a dead woman with newspaper instead of notifying the police. But despite his limitations, maybe Ralph saw enough to describe the murderer. Probably not the world's most credible witness, but at least it was a start.

'Ralph, did you get a look at the person who was carrying that girl?'

'Not much a one. Like I said, it was dark and he was near gone the very second he heared my voice.'

'Can you explain him at all?'

'He was kind of big, reached nearly to those low branches, and he was dark.'

'Dark, like a black man?'

Ralph shook his head no. 'No'em. He was white-skinned as you. I mean he had dark hair. And he was wearing dark clothes. That was about all I could tell he was gone so quick.

'Now, Missy, don't go tellin' no one about this. I don't want no trouble with the police. I had trouble with them once in my life, back when I was a drinkin' man, and believe you me, you don't want to go there twice.'

*Don't I know*, Kelly thought.

'But, Ralph,' she pressed on, 'this wouldn't cause you any trouble with the police. They'd love you for telling them about it.' She touched the old man's arm softly. 'They might even give you a reward.'

His eyes lit up. 'I never thought about that. Getting a reward. I never got no rewards in my life. Tell 'em they can look for me here in the park.'


O'Reilly was slouched in a booth at Ann Sather's watching his partner demolish a five-egg bacon, cheese and onion omelet. His own stomach was so dicey coffee and toast was about all he could manage, and the toast was a stretch at that. Koz scraped the omelet plate clean and moved on to a stack of pancakes. O'Reilly blew on his steaming brew. His partner was big, but still, how could anyone eat all that food?

'Haven't they fed you recently?'

'Missed my breakfast,' the giant replied between bites. 'Melissa and I usually have breakfast in bed on Saturdays.'

The image of a shirtless Kozlowski in bed with a plate resting on his stomach sent his own stomach roiling. Happily, his pager buzzed in time to interrupt the image. He looked at the pager and swore aloud at the number on the display. It was Kelly Delaney. That broad was one gigantic pain in his balls. She'd called three times in the last twenty-four hours to ask about the investigation. To O'Reilly's mind there was nothing worse than a meddling citizen. What did she think they did with their time anyhow? Play pinochle?

He left Koz alone to finish off his breakfast and found the pay phone. Kelly picked up on the first ring. 'Detective O'Reilly, I have to talk to you,' she demanded.

'And this is about what?'

'What the hell do you think it's about? I've got some important information for you. It's too hard to explain on the phone. I need you to come to my apartment.'

'Just so happens we're in the neighborhood,' he said reluctantly. 'Be there in ten minutes.'

Kozlowski was still working on his pancakes when Ron returned to the table. 'Better finish up,' he said. 'Kelly Delaney says she's got something for us.'

'Like what,' said the big cop, drawing a napkin across his mouth.

'I don't know. She says it's important. Maybe she's found the Tylenol killer.'

Kelly was still wearing her damp running gear when O'Reilly and Kozlowski appeared on her doorstep. She invited them to sit at her tiny kitchen table. They hadn't been seated for more than thirty seconds when a wail penetrated the room, an ungodly sound like a person being tortured. Both cops jumped from their seats, looking to the corners of the small space, ready to draw their service revolvers.

'What in the hell is that?' O'Reilly asked, his head pin wheeling around the room.

There was an even louder second howl. Kelly looked at them sheepishly. 'That's my cat. I have to lock her in the bathroom when I have visitors. She's not terribly fond of strangers.' She thought of the medical bills she was still paying off from the time Tizzy lanced into the calf of a plumber, who she'd called in to unclog the toilet.

They sat back down and Kelly couldn't help but notice the tremor shaking O'Reilly's hand even though it rested on the table. She wondered about his drinking and if it impacted his job performance. Not that his life was any of her business, but her friend's lives' were. She already had one dead friend. She wanted to make certain that number didn't rise to two due to his incompetence.

'So if you could be so kind as to bring us up to date . . .' he said.

Kelly went on to describe her encounter with Ralph and how the old man had surprised a large dark man carrying Angie's body the night of her murder. O'Reilly was starting to think this might be a significant break until Kelly added that Ralph was the one who put the newspapers over Angie's dead body.

'He covered up the body,' O'Reilly said in complete disbelief.

'Yes. Like I said, Ralph is a little eccentric. He did it as a sign of respect.'

'And he didn't tell anybody about it. If this Ralph is for real, he could be in some trouble.'

'Please don't go there,' Kelly said. 'Ralph's afraid of the police, which is why he never said anything. But that doesn't change what he saw. You've gotta find him and talk to him.'

'I don't suppose you have an address for Ralph?' O'Reilly's tone told Kelly he hardly took her or Ralph seriously.

'Not exactly. But you can find him in Lincoln Park near the totem pole. He promised to be there this afternoon.'

'Got that, Koz? The totem pole.'

'Don't make fun of me,' said Kelly defensively. 'You guys haven't come up with anything.'

'Actually, we have come up with something,' O'Reilly countered. 'Angie's wallet turned up this morning. She left it in a taxi the night she was killed. We would've had it sooner, if the village idiot hadn't kept it under lock and key. We also learned she took that taxi to a bar called The Zone. You familiar with it?'

'Familiar with it? That place was my pharmacy for years.'

'Probably Angie's pharmacy too. Got a name for me?'

Kelly balked. Even in her new life, she didn't want to cause trouble for anyone from her old one. Apparently O'Reilly read her mind, because he said, 'Don't worry about your friend from The Zone. We're homicide, not vice. If we turned in every drug dealer who tipped us off, we'd have to commandeer the Hilton for holding space.'

'All right. His name is Lyle. I was going to tell you anyway. Finding out who killed Angie is the most important thing.'

'Got it. Lyle,' O'Reilly said. Tizzy let out another howl. 'Holy Jesus, it sounds like there's an exorcism going on in there.'

'We have a cat,' said Kozlowski. 'They just need a little understanding.'

Though Kelly didn't want them to leave yet, the cops were pushing back from the table. She was wrestling with how make them aware of the man from New Hampshire. They were nearly through the courtyard when a loophole presented itself. She had sworn to Maggie she wouldn't say anything about the man from New Hampshire, but she hadn't sworn a thing about the truck.

'Wait,' she called out. 'There's something else.' O'Reilly's irritation was clear as he turned around to face her.

'You might want to know about a suspicious truck parked on Carol Anne's street the night of the party.'

# TWENTY-FIVE
## 7 Days Until

I t was a half-hour past the given time on the invitation when I pulled into Natasha's Lake Forest driveway, my Volkswagen a pebble in a sea of Sevilles, Mercedes and BMWs. Arthur Dietrich's manor resembled a satellite of Oxford more than a home. It even had a name, Ferrydale, but don't ask me what that stood for. The current house stood on the bones of a mansion that had already been considered ostentatious when it was built during the Gatsby-esque 20s. If Arthur Dietrich wanted to do ostentatious one better, he had succeeded. He was all about appearances, from his good-looking wife and kids to his house to his Bentley with the GREED E 1 plates. The son of a mail carrier, he had obtained his initial wealth through savvy trading and taken it off the charts by shorting the market just before the '87 crash. Typical of Arthur, he actually bragged about the move. I had never been too fond of him. He was a blowhard and a braggart, but my emotions toward him were mixed since it was through Arthur that I had met Flynn.

Standing in front of massive entry doors more befitting a medieval church than a residence, I smoothed my hair and took a deep breath. Natasha might be irritated at me for being late for my own shower, but my mother would be furious. And when my mother was furious, it made everyone's life miserable.

Natasha's butler answered the door. Yes, butler. Imported from England, he was one of the growing trends among the new wealthy. Hobbs ushered me into the foyer where Natasha was talking with two of my mother's bridge partners.

'Our guest of honor, finally,' she announced, floating over to kiss me on both cheeks in her best imitation of Mrs Astor. 'We were getting worried about you.'

'I'm sorry. Traffic was insane.'

I made my excuses to my mother's friends, and we walked

together down a wide hall, thick with oriental rugs and recently acquired collectible paintings. The rest of the guests were seated in the arboretum, drinking white wine and chatting politely amid potted orange and fig trees. Most of the women were my mother's age, in their mid-fifties and beyond, wearing designer clothes and carrying purses straight from the pages of *Vogue*. Dressed in a simple beige shift I'd picked up on sale at J.Crew, and clutching a battered Coach bag, I was without doubt the least fashionable person in the room. My mother was seated on a rattan settee, wearing a canary yellow suit, a Hermes scarf draped across her shoulders and clusters of pearls at her ears. My younger sister, Laurel, sat next to her looking pissed that she had to be in attendance. I could hardly blame her. She was as battle-weary of the shower circuit as I was. Our older sister, Ellen, lived in New York City with her husband and kids, and had been lucky enough geographically to miss all seven of the previous showers.

My mother shot me a withering glare when she saw me. Then she pasted a smile over the glare and sailed her perfectly made-up face across the room to cull me aside like a sheepdog would an errant lamb. 'Margaret Mary,' she said tersely, her use of my legal name putting me on notice. 'Do you have any idea how utterly déclassé it is to be late for an event held in your honor?'

'Please, Mother, save it. I'm really not feeling too well.' Unlike the excuse I'd given Natasha about traffic being horrible, this was the truth. I'd spent the entire morning in the bathroom heaving my guts into the toilet, hopefully from a parasite in last night's hamburger and not that other possibility.

My mother regarded me seriously, motherly concern trumping her anger. She put a palm to my forehead. 'You do look a little pale. Oh Lord, don't tell me you're getting sick. Not now.'

'Mother, stop! It's probably just a touch of food poisoning. Now c'mon, let get this show over with.'

'Maggie!'

In no mood to share another word with her, I stepped back into the arboretum. Being a seasoned shower veteran at this point, I issued warm greetings to everyone and made my apologies for being late. I fussed over Flynn's mother and her friends, many of whom I was meeting for the first time. Natasha's mother was there, of course. As one of my mother's best friends, she was the principal reason I had no choice about this eleventh-hour shower at her daughter's house.

Of course, I was well aware of Natasha's motive for sponsoring this superfluous event. Though Arthur's wealth was substantial, his new money didn't necessarily gain them entree into the circles that Natasha wanted to travel in. With Flynn's mother and her friends in her home, Natasha had assembled a cross section of the women who belonged to the best clubs and served on the most important boards of Chicago and the North Shore. These were women who could finance a new wing to the Art Institute or deliver a gorilla to the Lincoln Park Zoo with a few phone calls. Natasha was a social climber with no summit in sight. Having this group in her house was a step towards the top.

The butler announced that lunch was served and we filed into the formal dining room. An extravagant buffet of pastas, salads, shellfish and smoked fish was set on a long table around exotic flower arrangements in crystal vases. We filled our plates and retreated to the terrace where tables with open umbrellas were arranged around a scaled-down version of the Trevi Fountain. I maneuvered myself next to Carol Anne, who was the only one of our group who had accepted the invitation. Both Suzanne and Kelly had begged off, and rightfully so. Hoping to speak to my best friend confidentially, I tried not to explode when Natasha plopped down on the other side of me, quashing my intended conversation. I waved off a glass of wine and asked for an iced tea. My stomach was churning in a manner that made any thought of eating reprehensible, so I used my fork to rearrange the crab salad on my plate to give the appearance of having consumed some of it. My behavior did not escape my mother's watchful eye.

'Honey, you are so like your mother!' she called from the adjacent table.

The terrace quieted and all eyes turned to her. I put down my fork and waited in dread to learn what made us so alike.

'I was such a nervous wreck before I married your father, I couldn't eat either. My dressmaker got so tired of taking in my wedding gown, she told me not to come back until two days before the wedding.'

Everyone laughed, leaving me to squirm uncomfortably under the magnifying glass of being the central figure. Sometimes, I just couldn't believe the triviality that fell from my mother's lips. I stuffed some crab into my mouth in direct defiance of her words and fought back the impulse to deliver it directly back to the plate.

The spotlight turned from me as the guests resumed their previous conversations. Natasha, looking incredibly chic in a cream-colored dress that was most likely from some Oak Street boutique, gave me a wry smile, a piece of spinach stuck on her front tooth. Usually, I would have pointed out the green flag, but the mood failed me. Let one of the other women deliver the news, or, better yet, her husband after everyone had gone. 'So what's the latest news on Angie?' she probed in a tone that sounded far too satisfied.

'Last I heard, she was still dead.' Then, feeling I had been too strident, even if it was directed at Natasha, I added, 'From what I've heard, the police don't have anything.'

'Well, I've heard there were drugs involved. Personally, I think she was looking for someone to sleep with and it turned on her.'

'Natasha, that's a horrible thing to say. You know Angie was the last person in the world to look for a one-nighter.'

'I don't think so. In fact, I know otherwise. She tried to seduce Arthur once.'

Carol Anne nearly choked on her food, while it was a challenge for me to suppress an ear to ear grin. Angie had been vociferous in her dislike for Arthur Dietrich, calling him *the walking price tag*, as he was always eager to share just how much his acquisitions cost. Including Natasha. He talked about his wife and her jewels and clothes as if they were part of his portfolio. Angie's other nickname for him was *the space invader* because when he was around her, he was exactly that.

Natasha was not put off in the least by our responses. 'Go ahead and laugh, but Arthur told me that Angie came on to him at your engagement party here last winter, Maggie. As he was coming out of the bathroom. He said he practically had to fight her off.'

I knew of the incident Natasha was referring to, but it hadn't played out quite the way she described. In fact, it was a drunken Arthur who had cornered Angie leaving the restroom, shoving her against the wall as he tried to shimmy one of his paws up her blouse. Instead of being insulted or angry, Angie had laughed him off and walked away. His bruised ego must have driven him to turn the story around and carry it back to his wife.

'Natasha, I'm sorry, but there's no way Angie came on to Arthur.'

'She did too. And that's exactly what I told the police. You know the problem with you two,' Natasha said, including Carol Anne. 'You're too trusting. Truth is, there's always someone out there waiting to screw you. If I've learned one thing in life, it's to keep one eye and one hand on what's yours, because as soon as you relax someone's going to try and take it from you.' There was blessed relief when the butler came up and whispered something in Natasha's ear. 'I have to see about the coffee,' she said, putting her wine glass down and following him into the house.

'Wow, she's strung tight,' said Carol Anne.

'Nothing new there.'

'So how are you feeling anyhow, my friend?'

'I'm surviving, but barely.'

'Any sign of you-know-what?'

'No, but I've still got two more days before I enter the panic phase.'

We stopped talking when my younger sister came and sat down in Natasha's vacated seat. 'I just wanted you to know that after watching this circus, if I ever get married, I'm eloping,' she said.

'Don't I know,' was all I could say.

A bell rang and all heads turned toward the open patio doors. The butler announced that coffee was served and the procession of women filed back into the dining room where the table had been transformed into a French patisserie laden with fruit tarts, crème brûlée and dozens of chocolate selections. There was even an espresso machine set up at the end of the table. I skipped dessert and had a decaf cappuccino with skim milk. I thought how the coffee could be a metaphor for my life. Coffee without the kick. Milk without the fat. An unsatisfying version of the real thing.

Following dessert, I played the good bride and opened the beautifully wrapped boxes awaiting me on a linen-draped table near the fountain. Despite being billed as a lingerie shower, I was relieved that most of my gifts were tasteful items like satin robes or elegant nightgowns, each held by me up to a chorus of oohs and aahs. That all changed when I got to the gift from Flynn's mother. I opened the carefully wrapped box and folded back the tissue. It held a cherry-red lace teddy with a cutaway crotch and nipples. My face turned as crimson as the teddy. I looked at my future mother-in-law questioningly, and she nodded. I held up the flimsy piece for all to behold.

'Can you tell I want to see Maggie pregnant right away?' said Marguerite Hamilton. The entire terrace burst into laughter with the exception of the bride-to-be who wanted to crawl into a wormhole and die. I placed the teddy back in the box hoping her wish about me being pregnant hadn't already been fulfilled.

# TWENTY-SIX
## Ron

They sat on a quiet side street in the shade with the windows rolled down. O'Reilly watched his partner tuck into two Big Macs and a large fries, while he drank some more black coffee. 'Where do you put all that food, anyway?' he asked his partner.

'Man's gotta eat.'

'Yeah, I know, but you ever think about leaving some for the rest of the world?'

He took another jolt of brew. It was late afternoon, and to say he was exhausted from the legwork he and Kozlowski had put in since the predawn wakeup would be understatement. After parting company with Ms Delaney that morning, they had hunted down Lyle from The Zone who was none too happy to be rousted from bed in his Boystown apartment. He played box of rocks dumb as they threw questions at him about Angie, rubbing his sleep-encrusted eyes and swearing he didn't know who she was. Hadn't seen her in his life. Finally, O'Reilly explained quite succinctly that he and Koz were homicide, not vice, and if Lyle was helpful, vice might never get wind of his extracurricular occupation. Otherwise, well . . . to put it in football terms, they'd put narco on him like pass rushers on a quarterback.

So Lyle had cooperated. Yes, Angie had come into The Zone around three a.m. to buy a gram. She'd also ordered a drink, but when it came time to pay for the drink and her collateral purchase, she couldn't find her wallet. Knowing her to be trustworthy, Lyle comped her the drink and fronted her the gram based on her promise to come back the next night.

'So then she left right away?' O'Reilly asked.

The rail-thin bartender ran a hand through his thinning hair. 'Actually, she stopped to talk to someone on her way out.

Dark-haired guy. Good-looking. I'd never seen him before. He seemed a little agitated after talking to her.'

'But they didn't leave together?'

'Nah. She left alone. He stayed a while longer.'

'You're sure he stayed.'

'Yah, I'm sure. I said he was good-looking, didn't I?' he said, a wistful look creeping behind the sleepy eyes.

After they finished with Lyle, they visited Harvey Wozniak at his rental apartment. He was no stranger to them. They had interviewed him right after the murder. Though he had no alibi for the time period when Angie was killed, the shock on his face when they'd told him about her death had seemed so real O'Reilly hadn't considered him a person of interest. Until now. After talking with the taxi driver this morning, he'd put Harvey back into the possibility pool. It didn't take an Einstein to figure out who Angie had been yelling at from the cab.

When they showed up at his apartment unannounced, Harvey had been a bundle of nerves. His hair-covered hands twitched the entire time the two homicide detectives sat on his shabby sofa and interviewed him, their faces impenetrable walls of copness that made him sweat.

'Why didn't you tell us you saw Angie the night she was killed?' O'Reilly asked, his gaze a cocked revolver.

The scene came back to Harvey all too vividly, walking down Halsted Street in the early morning hours with his hand on Jennifer's arm and his thoughts in her pants. Hearing his name called. Seeing his estranged wife hanging out the window of a taxi, screaming profanities at him like a woman possessed. *You lousy cheating Polack! I'll see you in court. I'll get every penny.*

'Why didn't I tell you I saw Angie? How could I? I mean, here she's cursing me out one minute and then turning up dead the next. And me with no alibi. Hey, I watch TV. I know how that looks. Mistakes are made in this world all the time, and sometimes people pay for crimes they didn't commit.'

'So you're telling me you dropped your date off and went straight home?'

'Like I told you before. Yeah.'

'I'm going to assume you've been intimate with her.'

'Jennifer? Yeah. Not that it's any of your business.'

'So why didn't you sleep with her that night?'

'How can I explain it? My mood changed after seeing Angie. I just felt like being alone. Look, the day I met Angie, it was like the thunderbolt in *Godfather II*. I never hoped to have a woman like her for a wife. Our first years together were beyond fantastic until she shut me out of the bedroom.

'Doesn't it just figure, the first time I cheated – and it was the first time – with this hot gal from arbitrage who gave me a ride home, Angie comes home from work unexpectedly? My entire life went into the crapper after that day. I lost my wife and my house. My luck has gone to shit. I have margin calls more often than not these days. Look at this piece of shit I'm living in. Rental furniture.

'So you ask me why I didn't sleep with Jennifer that night. Let me give it to you straight. Sex with Jennifer is OK, but compared to sex with Angie it's skim milk to cream. I lost interest.'

Harvey smacked his leg in frustration. At his life, at his situation, at his loss of Angie. O'Reilly couldn't know which. 'I didn't kill Angie,' the big man said, his eyes filling with tears. 'You've got to believe me. I loved my wife.'

After leaving Harvey, they went in search of Ralph, the mysterious walking man. They found him easily enough. Having taken Kelly at her word, he had not strayed from the totem pole since morning. He retold his story of seeing a tall dark-haired man drop Angie's body in the park and run off. And of covering the dead body in newspapers so she wouldn't get cold.

'You'd know this man if you saw him again?' O'Reilly queried.

The old man had nodded. 'Yessir, I believe I would.'

O'Reilly questioned his own sanity for even considering the eccentric Ralph as a witness. He watched his partner finish off his second Big Mac, wondering how the man would ever be able to eat dinner.

'So what are you thinking?' Kozlowski asked, draining his cola with a loud slurp followed by a belch.

'I'm thinking about putting Wozniak in a lineup. Bring in the fruit from The Zone and the crazy guy in the park.'

'Do you really think Wozniak did her?'

'No. But might as well rule it out.'

'What about the white truck in Kenilworth?'

'What about it?'

'Think it's anything?'

'You shittin' me? When Ms Delaney told us about that truck I wanted to ask her what the hell she was smoking? Forget about that fucking white truck. It's nothing.' O'Reilly started the car. He was dying for a drink, could already taste the beer slipping down his throat at his neighborhood tavern. But before allowing himself the pleasure, he figured they might as well make one more stop. 'All right, Koz. Since we're in the neighborhood, let's pay a quick visit to the bride. Then let's call it a day.'

# TWENTY-SEVEN

I t took me three trips to ferry the shower gifts from my Volkswagen to my apartment. Sadly, the only meaning all those glossy boxes held for me was the obligation to write thank-you notes. I sat down on the sofa and pulled my legs up beneath me, feeling relieved to be back in my cocoon and away from prying eyes. I had barely eaten a thing at the shower and was having stomach pangs that I recognized as hunger. I went into the kitchen to make a peanut butter sandwich and was three bites in when there was a knock at the door.

'What the flock,' I cried aloud, trying not to swear at my solitude being violated. I put the sandwich down on the counter and went to the door. My appetite disappeared the moment I looked through the peephole and saw the two homicide detectives standing on the landing. *Now* what did they want? Given the option between talking to them and throwing myself out the window, I would have opted for the window, except that my apartment was only on the second floor, so it probably wouldn't have done the job. I opened the door.

'Good evening detectives,' I said in a highly controlled attempt at cordiality. 'What can I do for you?'

'Hope we're not disturbing you,' said O'Reilly. 'But we learned some new information today that we want to run past you.'

'Of course, come in.' I held the door open, nearly deafened by the sound of my pulse in my ears, terrified that the new information might have something to do with the carpenter. 'Shower gifts,' I explained, moving a pile of boxes from the couch to make room for them to sit. My arms filled with boxes, I tripped over the area rug and Flynn's mother's gift flew from the pile, spilling the crotchless teddy onto the floor. O'Reilly barely seemed to notice, but Kozlowski's ears glowed scarlet and he turned his head toward the kitchen. This time there were no shot glasses on the counter. Only a peanut butter sandwich missing three bites.

'Like I said, shower gifts.' I stuffed the wisp of lingerie back in the box and tossed it on top of some other boxes in the corner of the room. My space-clearing efforts turned out to be for naught as the detectives remained standing.

'This should only take a minute,' said O'Reilly. 'We just have a quick question for you. You ever hear of an establishment called The Zone?'

His question was balm on a pulled muscle as I realized they hadn't come to ask me about Steven Kaufman. They were asking about The Zone. The vise of fear loosened.

'So you've spoken to Albert?' I asked, assuming that Angie's assistant manager had finally contacted them about seeing Angie before her murder.

'Albert? Albert who?' O'Reilly's perplexed look told me my assumption was incorrect. Oh well, you know what they say about assuming. Now I was stuck.

'Albert Evans. He worked with Angie.'

'We don't know anything about an Albert Evans.' The right eyebrow shot up over the bloodshot eye. 'Maybe you can enlighten us.'

Figuring Albert would have to accept my honest mistake, I told them of our conversation at the Lupino residence after the funeral, adding, 'He was supposed to get in touch with you.' O'Reilly was clearly pissed off, his face ruddier than usual. I hated being caught in a lie, even if it was only a lie of omission. Of course, there was a bigger lie of omission casting its ominous shadow across the room, my dalliance with the carpenter, but luckily it was only visible to me.

'Well, he didn't get in touch with us.' O'Reilly suddenly looked inspired, the redness diminishing. 'This Albert a big guy? Dark-haired?'

'He's the complete opposite,' I replied, thinking of Albert's narrow shoulders and pale coloring. 'He's got a slight build and light hair.'

'Angie was seen talking to a big, dark-haired guy in The Zone. Harvey Wozniak ever frequent The Zone that you know of?'

I actually stifled a laugh. 'Harvey in The Zone? No way. He's a homophobe. You wouldn't find him within ten miles of a gay bar. He used to dread Bloomingdale's Christmas party because of all Angie's gay co-workers. He spent the entire night with his back against the wall. I swear, if he dropped his wallet at that party, he would have kicked it home. Besides,' I added, 'it couldn't have been Harvey. Albert knew Harvey. He would have recognized him.'

'Hmmph,' O'Reilly grunted. 'Next time someone gives you some information, don't assume they contacted us. You contact us. Got it.'

'I will. I promise,' I said, one eager hand on the knob. Having dodged yet another bullet, I was giddy for them to be gone. But before they could start down the stairs, Kozlowski stopped and uttered his first words of the evening.

'Wait, Ron. I want to ask about the truck.'

The ball hit me from behind, and I fought not to stagger under the blow. There was no doubt in my mind which truck he was talking about. I cursed Kelly for betraying me. Clutching the doorknob tightly to steady my shaking hand, I stood there wondering if this was the end of life as I knew it.

'Right.' O'Reilly gave his partner a sideways glance that I was meant not to see. 'You happen to know anyone from New Hampshire?'

*Shit.* I was caught. I was getting ready to come clean when I looked into O'Reilly's face and saw a blank slate. Kozlowski wore a dumb look too. Were they playing me, or were they in the dark about my connection to Steven Kaufman? With my future hanging in the balance, I kept my face as opaque as theirs. 'Why do you ask?'

'Oh, somebody reported a suspicious white truck with New Hampshire plates near the Niebaum house last Friday,' O'Reilly answered. His tone of voice told me he hated wasting his time.

'No, I don't recall ever meeting someone from New Hampshire,' I volunteered. It was amazing how the lies just kept piling up.

The moment they left I ran into the bathroom and gave back the three bites of peanut butter sandwich. My torment was complete. What would happen if the police did connect

Steven Kaufman to me that night? Could I be brought up on charges? Would it make the papers? I thought of Flynn and my parents and my total shame if that were to happen.

When my stomach had nothing left to give, I went into the bedroom. Clammy with sweat, I pulled the damp J.Crew dress over my head. As I wriggled out, I caught sight of my silhouette in the full-length mirror. After so many years of seeing the fat girl with mounds of swollen flesh, it was still hard to believe the slim figure with the concave stomach and lean legs belonged to me. An inexplicable impulse came over me, and I went back into the living room to retrieve the teddy Flynn's mother had given me. I put it on and struck a slutty pose in front of the mirror. Seeing my nipples poking through the transparent material and the patch of curly auburn hair peeking from the cutaway bottom, made me feel incredibly sexy. I fantasized about being thrown onto the bed and being taken in wild, passionate love.

The problem was that in my fantasy, Flynn wasn't doing the throwing. Or the love making.

My eyes travelled to the wicker wastebasket under my desk. It hadn't been emptied for a week. I turned it over and started sorting through tissues and bits of paper until I found what I was looking for. A crumpled scrap with a number written on it. The number Steven Kaufman had written on my pad that morning. 708-925-1014. I picked up the phone and started to dial, stopping as I thought better of it. I waited a minute and dialed again, this time the entire number. The moment the phone started ringing I hung up. I had no idea why I placed the call and no idea what I would have said if we had connected.

I changed into some baggy sweats and called Flynn to cancel our dinner date, telling him that Natasha's shower had left me exhausted. He sounded disappointed, but said he understood. I crawled into bed and fell fast asleep, sleeping soundly until a tremendous orgasm wakened me. I lay in the dark with my heart pounding wildly. I'd been dreaming and in my dream the carpenter had broken into my apartment and was standing over my bed.

'Are you dangerous or are you here to make love to me?' my dream-self demanded.

'I'm dangerous,' he said, tearing the covers from the bed and climbing on top of me.

It occurred to me that I was disappointed it had only been a dream. *What in the hell is wrong with me*, I asked my deeply conflicted self. I was split into three realities. One longed to see the carpenter again. One knew that to do so was not only wrong, it was rank stupidity. And then there was a disturbing third voice that told me I should be downright afraid of him.

# TWENTY-EIGHT

## Suzanne

The Sunday bells of Holy Name Cathedral carried forty floors to Suzanne's apartment where she sat in her kitchen reading the Sunday *New York Times*. In a perfect world she would have already gone to the office, but an early morning call from Detective O'Reilly, asking if he and Detective Kozlowski could stop over, had temporarily derailed her plans. She'd phoned down to the weekend doorman to tell him that she was expecting visitors and returned to her newspaper. She was halfway through the *Week in Review* when the doorbell rang. She opened the door and was surprised to see Vince standing there instead of the cops. He was holding a hefty bouquet of tropical flowers in his right hand.

'Vince, what are you doing here?' she asked.

'I came downtown to check a job. You know, you should have the doorman call you before sending up your visitors, sweetheart. I could be some depraved maniac.'

'He usually does. It's just that I told him—' Before she could say anything more, Vince silenced her by covering her mouth with his. He stepped into the apartment, kicking the door shut behind him. The flowers fell to the floor as he slipped a practiced hand beneath her cotton skirt and up her thigh, grabbing her by the right buttock.

She gasped aloud. 'You are a depraved maniac.'

'You turn me into one,' he replied. He led her hand to the front of his trousers where his rigidness pushed madly against confinement, his excitement only serving to intensify hers. One minute earlier sex had been the furthest thing from her mind. Now it occupied it entirely.

Vince pulled sharply at her lacy bikini until it tore away. Moving slightly away from her to gain access to his zipper, he almost stumbled over the flowers. Kicking them aside, he freed himself from his pants and lifted her onto his erection with a groan, barely able to contain himself as he rocked her back and forth. 'Oh, God,' she uttered, holding onto him desperately, her feet stepping into empty air. He pulled up her blouse and then her bra, lowering his lips to her right nipple and circling it with his tongue. She moaned in contentment and pushed her body closer to his, trying to bring him in more deeply.

The world was only Vince and her and then it was just her and it was happening, that exquisite pleasure bordering pain, and she shrieked in ecstasy. He had reached that point too, and grunting like a rutting animal, he plunged even more deeply into her and emptied himself.

They remained motionless for seconds, both savoring the lingering pleasure, both gasping for air. Then he lowered her so her feet were once again touching the floor. His hands were resting on her butt, the two of them still trying to catch their breath, when her doorbell rang. Vince stared at her in astonishment.

'You're expecting someone?'

'Oh, shit,' she said, using language she seldom employed. 'It's the police. They want to talk about Angie.' She quickly pulled her blouse down and straightened her skirt.

'I'll wait in the bedroom,' Vince whispered, an impish smile on his face.

'Here, take this with you.' Suzanne picked up her torn bikini and tossed it at him. Vince held the delicate piece of material to his nose for a delicious moment and disappeared down the hall. The doorbell rang again, more insistently this time. Suzanne checked the peephole and saw O'Reilly and Kozlowski waiting in the hall. She smoothed her hair and opened the door.

'Please forgive me. I was in the restroom,' she said, hoping her clothes were all back in the right place.

'Hope we're not disturbing you,' said O'Reilly.

'I've said I'd do anything to be of help.'

She stepped aside to let them in. Kozlowski bent over and picked up the discarded bouquet from the floor. In her haste to make herself presentable, Suzanne had overlooked it. He handed it to her and she laid it on a table, offering no explanation of why it had been there. Was it her imagination, or did a knowing glance pass between the two men? She led them into the living room and they assumed the same seats as their previous visit, the men on the silk slipper chairs, Suzanne poised on the peach couch. The early morning light radiated through the Venetian glass vase, casting its colors onto the tabletop.

'So you said on the phone, you've learned something new,' said Suzanne.

'That's right,' said O'Reilly. 'For starters, we now know that after you dropped Angie off she went to a bar called The Zone and scored some coke.'

Suzanne pressed her eyes shut, plagued by the same doubts that had been tormenting her since the murder. If she'd gone into Angie's house that night and put her in bed would she have stayed home? If she'd left Angie in The Overhang, would there have been a different outcome? There could never be a way of knowing. When she opened her eyes, both detectives were staring at her, O'Reilly with seeming impatience, Kozlowski in a more compassionate manner.

'Angie was observed having a heated discussion with a man in The Zone, a tall man with dark curly hair,' O'Reilly continued. 'Do you have any idea who that might be?'

'That could describe Harvey.'

'We know it wasn't Harvey. Could that description possibly fit Michael Niebaum?'

'Michael Niebaum?' Suzanne was stunned by the question. The notion that Carol Anne's husband could be involved in Angie's death was past impossible. 'Michael is tall with dark hair, but there is no way he had anything to do with Angie's death.'

'It's been suggested by one of your friends that Angie had a thing for other people's husbands. Dr Niebaum was out that evening.'

'That's the most ridiculous thing I've ever heard,' said Suzanne, wondering who could ever make such a suggestion. Then the image of Natasha flashed in her brain. She crossed her arms indignantly. 'Angie never had an affair with anyone's husband except her own. If anything, she was frigid. Furthermore, let me assure you, Michael Niebaum is a wonderful husband and father. There is no way he was having an affair with Angie. Not by a stretch.'

'Hey, we're just homicide cops, not the morality police. We've got to ask the tough questions.'

To Suzanne's surprise, Kozlowski chimed in. The big man was so quiet, she sometimes doubted he had a voice. 'Maybe you want to ask Ms Lundgren about the truck?'

O'Reilly was bugged by Kozlowski's obsession with the white truck, but what the hell, Koz was his partner after all, and he realized it was in his best interest to humor the big guy. 'You didn't happen to notice any unusual vehicles parked on Mrs Niebaum's street that night? Specifically a white truck with New Hampshire plates?'

'No. I don't recall a white truck. But why does New Hampshire ring a bell?' She tweaked her memory, trying to remember where she had heard something about New Hampshire recently. It wasn't like the state came up outside an election cycle. Then it dawned on her. 'Oh, I know why New Hampshire rings a bell. There was a guy from New Hampshire in the Overhang that night.'

Ron O'Reilly sat back so hard he nearly tipped the chair over. Kozlowski moved in forward. 'Could you describe him?'

Suzanne took an audible breath. 'Now that you mention it, he was tall and he had dark curly hair. But as I recall he wore glasses.'

O'Reilly picked up the baton. 'Gotta a name for him?'

'I couldn't tell you anything more about him. Maggie's the one you should ask. She was the one talking to him. In fact, she was dancing with him when Angie and I left.'

O'Reilly's face grew redder than ever as he digested this new information. He thought about the bride-to-be denying knowing anyone from New Hampshire just yesterday. He thought of how odd the blonde sitting across from him had been acting when they came in. He thought of the evasive manner in which Mrs Niebaum had answered some of their questions. Why did he feel like all these women were hiding something?

Suzanne saw them to the door, hoping they wouldn't notice the wet spot on the back of her skirt or the cloudy white rivulet running down her leg. Then she went to join Vince in her room where he lay on the bed reading an article in *Town and Country* about the most romantic restaurants in Paris. He'd already made up his mind he was going to take Suzanne to the city of light. First class. They would get a suite at the Ritz. He would order up some champagne and from there . . . well, he only hoped they got out to see the city a little bit.

'Did they put your feet to the fire?' he asked mockingly.

'No, but I hope I haven't made a lasting impression,' she replied, taking off the damp skirt and tossing it onto the bathroom floor. She crawled onto the bed beside him, touching his cheek with her nose. 'They asked a lot of odd questions though. About Carol Anne's husband, for one. I think Natasha put it in their ear that Angie might have been having an affair with someone's husband. But, aside from that being out of the question, I don't know where they came up with Michael. Carol Anne and Michael have been joined at the hip since day one.'

Vince was barely listening to a word she was saying. The mere presence of a skirtless Suzanne next to him was enough to get him worked up again, the touch of her hand on his stomach electric. His appetite for her was relentless, like a bug bite that only stopped itching while it was being scratched. And when it wasn't being scratched, it itched all the worse. More maddening was that he wanted more than her body. His feelings went deeper than mere animal desire. He wanted her in her entirety, body and soul, wanted to know that she would always be his.

'And there was one other odd thing they asked about,' she continued, her head resting on his chest in a way that she could hear the steady beating of his heart. 'Supposedly there was a truck from New Hampshire parked on Carol Anne's street the night of Maggie's party. Crazy enough, Maggie was dancing with some guy from New Hampshire in the Overhang that night. Isn't that a weird coincidence? I mean, how often do you meet someone from New Hampshire?'

Vince's heart skipped a beat any a doctor would have noticed. Suzanne noticed it too, and she lifted her head and looked him in the face. He wore a pained expression, his lips drawn tightly together, his dark eyes fixed on her bedroom wall. 'Vince, are you all right?'

'A muscle spasm,' he replied. He laid next to her trying to wish his heart rate back to normal; he was as close to panic as a man of his nature could be. So the police were looking for a man from New Hampshire in connection to the murder. Well, that was just great. It was now critical that Angie's murderer be found soon, before they could find the man from New Hampshire, before certain facts came to light that could ruin him in Suzanne's eyes forever.

He needed to put in a call to Charley Belchek and light a fire under his ass.

# TWENTY-NINE
## Carol Anne

Michael eased the *Dermabrasion* out of its slip while Cara and Eva ran giddily about the deck, both of the girls wrapped in life vests. Pacified by the churn of the boat's engines and the warm sun on his face, Michael, Jr. kicked contentedly in his car seat. It was their first time out this season, and seeing the happiness on her children's faces, away from the poison of television, Carol Anne wondered why she had fought Michael so hard over getting the boat in the first place.

Purchased with the spoils of vanity, the *Dermabrasion* was a thirty-eight-foot cruiser with two staterooms, a galley to rival most land-locked kitchens, and the best navigational equipment that silicone could buy. Carol Anne gave silent thanks to the women who had underwritten this extravagance with their tummy tucks and eye lifts and unreasonably enormous breast implants. She looked down at her small chest, smaller still after the last baby, and smiled. There would be none of that for her. Though her husband's trade was making people what they weren't and holding the ravages of age at bay, she accepted what nature had given her and was willing to take what time would bring.

The boat chugged through the glassy water of the marina at a no-wake speed, past docks of equally fine vessels. As they pulled from the calm harbor into the chop of the lake, the boat started to rock. Carol Anne looked back at the skyline, the high-rises like grey teeth against the blue sky. Against her will her eyes brushed the woods where Angie's body had been found, and she felt hugely unsettled. It was unnerving how close her body had been to the harbor. Michael opened the throttle, the prop bit into the water and the boat lurched forward. As the girls screamed in glee, Carol Anne allowed herself suppress all unpleasant thought. Nothing was going to spoil this idyllic day.

Michael drove the boat for some time without stopping. When they were far enough offshore to be alone, he put the engine in neutral and called down to the girls, 'Anyone want to drive?' Piercing squeals followed as Cara and Eva clamored up to the bridge on their long skinny legs, each one fighting to be the first, the sounds of *let me let me* carrying over the water.

Carol Anne picked up the baby and sat in her deck chair nursing him. She watched his perfect little hands clutch her and his dark inquisitive eyes take in everything around him, rendering her so overwhelmed with love she feared she might burst. Her miracle baby, he was so long in coming, he may have never come.

When was it that the physical aspects of their marriage began to wane? Was it after the second baby or had it started before that? For the last years, their sex life had been practically non-existent, months passing without any physical contact between them other than a hug or a kiss. Whenever she broached the subject, it would turn into an argument and Michael would grow defensive, blaming their lack of intimacy on the pressures of work. The arguments would always end in the same way, rote, unsatisfying sex followed by more barren months.

While things were certainly different after Eva's birth, in retrospect, their lovemaking had already tapered off long before that. Maybe not too long after they were married. With Michael in medical school and then interning, there hadn't been a lot of spare time for sex, and after the girls came along there was even less. Each pregnancy and birth brought more prolonged barren spells. Carol Anne told herself this was how mature love was, and contented herself in raising the girls and taking care of her family. She had tried everything imaginable to make him more interested in her: sexy lingerie, scented body lotions, dirty movies, everything short of hanging from a trapeze and she would have had one mounted in the ceiling if she thought it would help. She couldn't understand his lack of interest in her. She kept her figure, did the best she could with her unruly hair, and knew the face that stared back at her from the mirror was still attractive. She asked herself daily what was wrong with her that he was no longer interested in her.

But when they went six months without any relations, Carol Anne had gone to Michael and cried. Their son was conceived that night after he had made dutiful love to her. Afterwards, Michael had given her physical attention on a weekly basis until her belly was swollen with the baby, and once again the bed they shared was only used for sleep. It had stayed that way since Michael, Jr.'s birth.

But suddenly in the last week, Michael had done a complete turnabout. Since Angie's death, he had made love to her nearly every night, which added up to more times than they had made love in the preceding year. Carol Anne didn't know what to make of it, but she wasn't complaining. She hadn't forgotten the look on his face when he learned about Angie's death. Maybe her death had shocked him into realizing that it was possible to lose someone dear to you. Or was there some darker reason? The one she had ever so briefly suspected. That he had been involved with Angie, and with Angie out of the picture, his love for her had returned.

Carol Anne refused to believe such a betrayal was possible. Michael had been her best friend since they met, and they had weathered the storms of young love together. The bedrock of their marriage was strong. She put away her doubts. Right now her biggest care in life was that they thrive as a family.

While Carol Anne nursed the baby, the girls took turns driving the boat until Michael cut the engine and let them drift. She went below deck with the baby and put him in his car seat while she prepared a lunch of turkey sandwiches, carrot and celery sticks, and, as a special treat, potato chips. She never served chips at home, didn't want the kids to get too fond of junk food, but this was a special day. And it would appease Eva, who missed peanut butter sandwiches. Ever since Cara developed a peanut allergy, peanut butter was a forbidden commodity in their house. Even so, Michael kept an ample supply of EpiPens in the boat's first-aid kit – just in case.

Carol Anne put out juice boxes for the girls and a cold beer for Michael. A Tab for herself. Leaving Michael, Jr. secure in his car seat, she carried the tray of food and drink upstairs and had just placed it on the table when the sound of an approaching boat drew her attention. There was a speedboat coming toward them with two men on the bow and a third one piloting. All three men were thin and bronzed and nearly naked in nylon thongs. They were waving at the *Dermabrasion* with an odd familiarity. As she stood there watching, the engines started up and Michael called out, 'Hold on!'

Carol Anne was thrown against the railing as the boat jolted forward. The tray slid from the table, spilling lunch onto the deck.

'Michael! What are you doing?' she screamed. Even over the roar of the engine she could hear wails coming from below. She rushed down into the cabin to check Michael, Jr. He was crying, but otherwise all right. When the boat finally slowed, she marched back on deck with the baby in her arms. 'What the hell was that all about?' she shouted up to the bridge.

'Mommy swore,' yelled Eva.

'Mommy swore,' her sister echoed.

'Those people in that boat – I didn't want to deal with them,' he replied, his voice barely audible over the churning engine and the wind whistling in her ears.

'You knew them?'

'They're part of a group of moochers who're always hanging around the marina. Ever since they found out I'm a plastic surgeon, they don't want to leave me alone. If we'd let them tie up, we'd never get rid of them. This is our family day.'

'Don't you think that was rude, gunning away like that?'

He brought the boat to an idle without answering her. They were alone in the water, the phantom boat nowhere to be seen. 'How about we have lunch here?'

Carol Anne looked at the tray lying on the deck and shook her head in frustration. The sandwiches had survived intact, but there were potato chips and carrot and celery sticks strewn all over. She cleaned up the mess and carried the bowls back below deck to refill them. Michael and the girls came down from the bridge and the family sat in the sun, eating in peaceful contentment with the waves lapping the sides of the boat. Michael took a long drink from the beer, his eyes veiled but his smile broad. He put the can down and wrapped an arm around each of his daughters.

'It doesn't get any better than this, does it?' he asked.

As perplexing as her husband's behavior was, Carol Anne decided to let it go. No matter what, she was determined nothing was going to ruin this day.

The June sun was still high as they chugged back into Belmont Harbor, the water flat in the breathlessly still evening air. Michael docked the boat, only slamming into the pilings a couple of times, much to the amusement of the girls. Leaving the children on the boat while their father fiddled with the engine, Carol Anne started the first of many trips to load up the car. She had just put the cooler down on the ground next to the Volvo when she became aware of the two men watching her from a sand-colored car parked two spaces over. The doors opened and they got out. Warning bells sounded when she recognized them as the detectives who had come to her house after Angie's murder. *What are they doing here?*

'Pardon us for disturbing you, Mrs Niebaum,' said the bulldog she remembered as Detective O'Reilly. 'Do you mind if we speak with you for a minute?'

'Of course not,' said Carol Anne, not really meaning it.

The larger one picked up the cooler and put it in the back of the car for her. 'That's some beautiful boat you have,' he said.

'Yes, we're very lucky to have it,' she concurred. 'We've only had it a couple of years and didn't get a lot of opportunity to use it last year – me being pregnant and all. We're really going to make the attempt this summer.'

'You ever get the chance take it out at night?' O'Reilly asked.

Carol Anne hesitated. The question seemed odd, and the unpleasant vibe coming from the detectives even odder. She planted her feet firmly and put her hands on her hips. Like a lioness facing off a predator outside the den, she sharpened her mental claws. Her sole purpose was to protect the pride. 'What's this all about?'

'Mrs Niebaum, I want to ask you again what time your husband came home last Friday night – or Saturday morning – as you prefer.'

She tried to remember her lie, to keep it consistent. 'I told you before. He came home shortly after midnight.'

'Is your husband here? We'd like to speak with him.'

'He's on board with the children. I'll get him for you,' Carol Anne said, doing her best to sound cavalier with a tongue turned to cotton. The good feelings of the day had just gone up in smoke, leaving a tar pit smoldering in their place. She walked back to the boat on ankles made of wood, her head spinning like batter in the blender.

'Michael,' she called out breathlessly, as she climbed down the steps into the cabin. He poked his head from the engine room and she went to speak with him away from the girls who were entertaining their baby brother with a set of plastic dinosaurs. 'The police are here. They want to talk to you,' she whispered.

'What the hell?' His face blanched and his eyes went to the open hatch.

'Not here, they're in the parking lot,' Carol Anne said. 'Michael, I told them you got home around midnight the night Angie was killed. I know it's a lie but I didn't want them to know how late you'd been out. I didn't think they'd understand.'

The color returned gradually to his cheeks. 'That's all right, honey. You did the right thing. I'll talk with them and be right back.'

Carol Anne remained with the children, trying not to explode with anxiety as she finished cleaning up. The children were getting fidgety and it was all she could do to keep them below deck. There was no reason for them to be up top while their father was talking to the police – especially if something terrible happened. She wasn't sure what terrible was, but somewhere in her imagination handcuffs were involved. *Not that there was any reason for handcuffs*.

'Where's Daddy?' asked Cara. 'Are we going home now?'

'Daddy'll be right back. Now be a good girl and get the rest of your things together.'

While the girls gathered up their clothes and books, Carol Anne finished wiping down the galley, alternating between wanting to cry and wanting to scream. She had never felt so confused and frightened in her life. Ten minutes passed, and then another ten, before Michael finally appeared in the doorway.

When she saw him wearing his usual, easy smile, she finally let herself relax. All that worry for naught.

'Well, gang, are we ready to go?'

'Daddy, Daddy,' the girls clamored noisily, scrambling up the steps behind him. Carol Anne picked up the baby and followed.

In the car on the way home, with the girls in the back seat absorbed in their coloring books, Carol Anne quietly asked Michael what the detectives had wanted.

'Nothing really. Someone had put it in their heads that Angie and I might have had an affair.'

'You call that nothing?' Revisiting her unvoiced fear, Carol Anne grabbed the opportunity to clear the air. 'Well, did you?'

'Honey, don't be ridiculous!' He gave her a quick, sincere look before turning his eyes back to the road. 'I can't believe you even asked me that. I swear to you I never had an affair with Angela. Or any other woman.'

She watched him drive with his eyes fixed on the road. Though she believed he was telling the truth, the feeling something wasn't right nagged her nonetheless. But despite everything coming at her, her world was currently back in place, so she held her tongue and rode the rest of the way home in silence.

# THIRTY

## Vince

Vince's foul mood was further exacerbated when he pulled into the driveway and saw his wife's Mercedes parked at the front door. No matter how many times he told her to put the car in the garage – they had three spaces – she regularly left it in the circular drive, making the house look like a shoot for a car ad. As if their stately abode wasn't enough of a declaration of wealth, she had to prove to the world what she had. *Once a peasant, always a peasant*, he thought.

He pulled his Seville into the closest bay and closed the door. Giovanna had insisted on the Mercedes. He wasn't a believer in imported cars, preferring to buy American. This country had been good to him, and he wanted to be good back to it. He was a standup citizen. He voted and paid his taxes. Well, most of them anyway.

He entered through the garage and stormed into the kitchen.

'Giovanna!' he called out, his voice filled with none-too-subtle anger.

Maria, the El Salvadoran housekeeper, poked her head from the pantry and pulled it back like a turtle retreating into its shell. She knew when it was best to stay out of her employer's way. Vince's trajectory took him through the kitchen to the entry hall where he stopped at the foot of a winding staircase and shouted again. 'Giovanna!'

A moment later his wife's head popped over the railing, her long brown hair flowing loosely over her shoulders. 'Vince, what's the matter with you, howling like a mad man? You'll scare hell out of Maria and I'll end up looking for a new maid.'

'Goddammit, Giovanna. How many times have I asked you to park the goddamn car in the garage? How many times?'

'Calm down, Vince, or you'll burst an artery. I had some packages to bring in. I'll move it in little while.'

Packages, packages. All the woman ever did was shop. 'I've got some work to do, I'll be down in my office,' he yelled, bringing an end to the conversation if there was one. He took the winding stairs to the lower-level game room where a picture window looked out onto a landscaped yard and pool. With a bar under construction, the room resembled a battle zone with tools and half-sawn pieces of wood scattered about. Vince ran an appreciative hand along the seamless cherry wood of the unfinished bar. The workmanship was as close to perfection as he had ever seen. Then, as if he were punishing the bar for something it had done, he banged it so hard his hand stung.

He went into his office and closed the door. Sitting behind the massive oak desk, he spun the Rolodex until he found the name he was looking for. He was already speaking before the receptionist spit out the name of the hotel.

'I want room thirty-four. And if he's not in I want to leave a message.'

But the resident was in. 'What's up?' he said upon hearing Vince's voice.

'What's up is I want you here immediately.'

'Hey, man, it's Sunday.'

'If you want to keep your job, get your ass out here right away.' Vince slammed the phone down even harder than he had slammed the bar. So what if the asshole was the greatest craftsman on earth, he sure was lousy at following instructions. Vince's anger was so out of control he felt like his head might fly off. Giovanna was right. He got far too angry for his own good. His doctor had warned him it was unhealthy to get so mad, that it wreaked havoc on his blood pressure, but this was one of those situations where he couldn't help himself.

There was a light knock at the door. It cracked open and Anna stuck her head into the room. 'Am I disturbing you?' she asked, flashing her dark eyes at him.

His mood softened immensely. He was glad to see his daughter was wearing her hair in its natural raven color again; she dyed it so often he was never quite sure what to expect. One day it was blonde, another day carrot orange. Giovanna had assured him hair was just hair and easily changed, not like tattoos which seemed to be the coming trend. Those would be tougher to get rid of.

'Come in, baby. You know you never disturb me.' She opened the door the rest of the way and walked into the room. Her tight jeans and a skimpy top bordered on trashy, and Vince reminded himself to have Giovanna talk to her about the way she dressed. Then he reminded himself that her mother didn't dress much better herself, always opting for flashy as opposed to subtle. He wished Anna had a better role model; someone with class, someone like Suzanne.

Clothes aside, Anna was very much her father's daughter, and he adored her. She had inherited his intelligence and his single-mindedness. From the earliest days of childhood, she had tackled everything head-on the way he did, whether it was learning to ride a bike or getting good grades. She was relentless when she wanted something and never wavered. She'd just finished her junior year at the University of Illinois, pulling straight As in architecture. The plan was next year when she graduated, Vince would bring her into the company as a partner. She'd already started learning the business from the ground up, working for him during all her school vacations.

'Where have you been all day, Daddy?' she asked. 'We were supposed to go to brunch, remember?'

He slapped his forehead. He'd been so focused on seeing Suzanne this morning that he'd completely forgotten brunch at the club with his wife and daughter. 'I'm sorry, baby. Something came up on the Delaware site. I hope you understand. We'll do it next Sunday for sure.' He hated lying to his daughter, and fear momentarily gripped him as he realized how out of control his emotions had become. He was a man holding onto two ropes, his family pulling one way and Suzanne pulling the other. Lately, the pull of Suzanne's rope had become so strong, he wasn't sure how long he could hang on to both. After a childhood of being handed off from family to family, never sure whose table he would be sitting at next, he had sworn to himself his daughter would always have a stable home environment and nothing, much less a mistress, would ever break up his family. He'd used women and disposed of them as he wished, usually providing a healthy stipend to ease their pain. But that was before Suzanne. She was far too important to be dismissed. There was no good solution to his problem.

'OK, Daddy. Next Sunday. No forgetting this time.'

'I won't forget, sweetheart. I promise.' Regrettably, that meant no lazy Sunday morning in bed with Suzanne.

His daughter perched herself on the arm of his chair and wrapped her arms around his neck. 'You and Mom are more important to me than anything in the world. Nothing can ever change that, right?'

For a moment Vince thought he read something knowing in her eyes, but that was impossible. There was no way she could know about Suzanne. He had been beyond careful. 'And nothing will ever change how important you are to us. But some day you'll find some man even more important than us, and you'll raise a family of your own. Of course, he'll have to get my approval, and I will accept nothing short of perfection for my daughter. So I guess you're not going anywhere for a while,' he joked. Then his tone turned serious, and he added, 'Just be sure to be selective.'

'Thanks, Daddy,' she said, easing off the chair. 'I love you.'

'I love you too, sweetie.' He watched her walk out the door, the swing of her soft bottom making his father's heart skip a concerned beat. God, he hoped she listened when he warned her about being selective. Lately, she'd been seeing some grease-ball she met in a bar, a guy way too old for her. Giovanna told him that it was just a passing phase, like the different hair colors, and if he made a big thing out of it that would force her even closer to him. He hoped his wife was right. He couldn't think of anything worse than having a goombah like that for a son-in-law.

A half-hour later there was another knock on the door. 'Come in,' he called gruffly. The door opened and Steven Kaufman sauntered in wearing a blue T-shirt and torn jeans, his curls pulled into a ponytail.

'So what's so important you make me drive all the way out here on a Sunday?'

'What's so important?' Vince seriously tried to control his temper, keeping his blood pressure in mind. But it was a losing

battle. 'What's so important is that we got a serious problem.
Remember that extra job you did for me last weekend?'

Steven shrugged. 'You mean spying on your girlfriend? Like
I told you, you don't have to worry about her. There sure weren't
any other guys on her radar.'

'Yeah. Well, you did something I asked you not to.'

'I don't get you.'

'You made contact with the girls. You danced with the bride.
I told you to keep your distance.'

A disingenuous smirk crossed Steven's lips. 'So? What's the
big deal about that?'

'Don't you read the fucking papers? The big deal is that one
of her friends went and got herself murdered that night. And
someone reported a truck with New Hampshire plates on the
street in Kenilworth. And then, how do you think it looks when
some guy from New Hampshire turns up in the same bar with
them? It looks like you were stalking them. That's the big deal.'

The smirk withered and Steven lowered himself into the chair
opposite Vince. 'Which girl?' he asked.

'What?'

'Which girl was murdered?'

'Well, it wasn't Suzanne and it wasn't the bride, so it was
the other one. Angie. I'll never forget that name, I've heard
Suzanne cry over it enough.'

Steven put a hand behind his head and tugged at the ponytail.
'I didn't kill her.'

'Jesus. I sure as fuck hope not. But that doesn't change the
fact that the police are asking about you. And if they find you,
you damn better have an alibi for later that night.'

'Well, in fact, I do have an alibi.'

Vince's black eyes were ice picks into Steven's skull as he
ran the logistics in his head. 'Don't tell me. Please don't tell
me. Not the bride?' When the carpenter didn't respond, Vince
felt his blood pressure ascend to the hazard level. Forgetting
his sore hand, he slammed the desk again. 'I asked you to follow
Suzanne, not fuck her girlfriend.'

'She started it. She bought me a drink.'

'Fuck,' said Vince, leaning back in his chair. 'What a fucking
mess. The police are looking for a white truck with New

Hampshire plates and since New Hampshire plates ain't exactly in abundance here in the Land of Lincoln, they're going to find you. And when they do, they're going to ask you why you were in Kenilworth and later on in that fuckin' bar. And what's your answer? That you were following your married boss's girlfriend at his request. And what were you doing when Angie Wozniak was killed? You were banging the bride. This is not a good situation for you or me, not to mention the bride.'

Steven bristled at Vince's last words. 'Hey, I'm sorry. Like I'm supposed to know somebody was going to get killed that night? I'm no happier about this than you are. Believe me, I have reasons of my own for not wanting trouble with the police.'

By this time, Vince was so deaf with anger, he could barely hear. He didn't give a squat about Steven's personal reasons for not wanting to talk to the police. And he didn't care squat about the cheating bride either. What he cared about was Suzanne. He didn't want to even entertain the notion of what might happen if she found out he had her tailed. Would she hate him? Never talk to him again? That would kill him.

There was only one solution for this mess, and that was for Steven Kaufman to disappear until Charley Belchek found Angie's murderer. After that no one would give a rat's ass about some guy from New Hampshire. He had no doubt the former cop could do the job, but he didn't know how long it might take. In the meantime, Vince didn't want Kaufman driving that truck around and being pulled over and brought in for questioning. No, the carpenter was going to have to go into hiding, and what better place to hide him than under Vince's nose.

'So this is what we're going to do. You're going to put your truck in my garage and leave it there until this blows over. You can stay here and finish up your work on the bar. Maria will fix up a room in the help's quarters. I'm sure it will beat the flea trap you've been staying at in the city.' He unlocked his bottom desk drawer where he kept his strongbox. Inside were cash, several sets of keys, and a spare garage door opener. He used to keep his .45 in there, but since the market crash he was more comfortable keeping the gun taped beneath his top desk drawer. He counted off five hundred-dollar bills and placed the money and the garage door opener in front of Steven. 'Here's something for your trouble. Now hide that truck right away, before someone notices the plates.'

Steven stood wordlessly in front of him, thinking over his position. He didn't like answering to Vince, but he was in a tough spot, and right now he didn't have a better solution. He meant it when he said he couldn't talk to the police. And Vince was right about another thing. Any place was more comfortable than the transient hotel where he'd been staying. He put the money in his wallet and picked up the garage door opener.

'Where should I park?'

'Take my wife's spot. The middle bay. And Kaufman, by the way, stay away from my daughter.'

'I didn't even know you had a daughter,' said Steven walking out the door.

'Good, keep it that way,' Vince called to his back thinking Steven Kaufman was just the kind of loser that Anna was always drawn to.

Giovanna Columbo shook her head with frustration. There was no understanding her husband. Here she was pulling her car into the garage like he asked – no, demanded – and she opens the door to find the carpenter's truck parked in her space. What was the man's problem? Oh well, never mind. She liked leaving the car out front anyway. She pulled back around the circular drive, and parked it back in front of the entrance, just like in the glossy magazine ads.

# THIRTY-ONE
## Ron

Monday morning was grey and rainy, and the barometric pressure was wreaking havoc with Ron O'Reilly's head. Four aspirin and two cups of coffee hadn't brought any relief. Sitting at his desk in agony, wishing he could stop all blood flow from the neck up, he tried to block out the noise of the other detectives working the phones. The desk next to his sat empty. Koz was at the dentist after spending a sleepless night with a toothache.

Working on the Angela Lupino Wozniak case only made his headache worse. He pretty much thought that Niebaum did her, not only because Natasha Dietrich planted the seed, but because the good doctor had a boat moored in Belmont Harbor, not far from where Angie's body was found. Even if Dr Niebaum wasn't banging Angie, one thing was for sure: Michael Niebaum was not home at midnight Friday. He may have been a good liar, but his wife wasn't.

But complicating things was the mystery man from New Hampshire. His presence in Kenilworth and later on in The Overhang was troubling. After talking to Suzanne Lundgren, they'd put out an all points for a white GMC pickup with New Hampshire plates, and if the guy were still in the state, he'd turn up. In the meanwhile, it was time for O'Reilly to have another little talk with the bride-to-be.

But that could wait. The first order of business today was to hunt down Albert Evans, Angie's elusive assistant manager. They'd gotten his contact information from Human Resources at Bloomingdale's, but a call to his apartment yielded a recorded message saying he was in New Buffalo for the weekend and wouldn't be back until Monday. O'Reilly left had an ominous message alluding to the serious nature of withholding evidence, betting that would elicit a phone call from Evans sooner than later.

The bet paid off a second later when his phone rang.

'O'Reilly.'

'This is Albert Evans,' came a voice clearly constricted with fear. 'I believe you are looking for me.'

'That would be an understatement, Mr Evans. I need to speak with you regarding the death of Angela Wozniak. You available to come and see right now?'

'Oh, that wouldn't be possible. I'm just leaving for work.'

'I could meet you there.' When O'Reilly's words were met with silence, he added, 'Or we could meet for a cup of coffee. This shouldn't take too long.'

There was still a prominent quiver in Evans' voice. 'I guess we could meet for coffee. Do you know Peaches on Rush Street? If I catch the next bus I could be there in thirty minutes.'

'Good enough,' said O'Reilly. 'What are you wearing, so I'll know who you are?'

'With all this rain, I'll be in my olive drab trench, but actually, I know who you are. You were outside the funeral. Salt-and-pepper gray and, well, no offense here, but you dress like a cop.'

'A half-hour then.' O'Reilly hung up, thinking it was a good thing Albert Evans was such an observant bugger.

O'Reilly picked out Angie's assistant manager the moment he walked into Peaches. He was wearing the aforementioned olive drab trench coat and carrying a black umbrella with a duck's head grip, his hair amazingly in place despite the downpour. His eyes jumped around the room until they found O'Reilly in the corner booth. He hung up the raincoat and deposited the umbrella in a brass holder at the door before making his way across the busy room.

'I'm Albert Evans.'

'Have a seat,' O'Reilly half offered, half commanded. Evans slid obediently into the booth and sat there looking trapped. 'I understand you saw Angie Wozniak right before she was murdered.'

Albert's eyes came to rest on his manicured hands. 'I'm

so sorry,' he said, not daring to look up. 'I know I should have contacted you. Especially since I cared so much about Angie. She was more than my boss, she was a true friend and an angel. And she had such wonderful taste. We miss her so much at the store.' He picked up a spoon and started fidgeting with it. 'I suppose that's not what you want to hear about.'

O'Reilly raised a crooked eyebrow and stared wordlessly.

Albert put the spoon down and looked up uneasily. 'The night she was killed, Angie came into The Zone late, about an hour before closing. It was obvious she was really messed up. I was with a group of friends, so I ignored her. I mean, I loved her like a sister, but she could be a nasty little bitch when she was drunk. I didn't feel like dealing with her.

'She had a drink at the bar. Then on her way out, she stopped to talk to someone, a big good-looking guy who was sitting alone. I remember him because I noticed him when he came in. He looked pretty agitated after she talked to him. He left a while later.'

'Why didn't you report this before?'

Albert shrugged stupidly and picked up the spoon again. 'Look,' said O'Reilly in no uncertain terms, 'if you're worried about getting your buddy Lyle in trouble, get over it. I've already talked with him and if he lands in the shit it won't be because of me.'

'You know about Lyle?' Evans was visibly shocked.

'You think we sit around doing nothing? Damn straight we know about Lyle. Now tell me everything about the man you saw Angie talking to.'

Relieved to have the onus of betrayal lifted, Albert opened up. 'Well, I'd say he was late thirties, big, dark and really hunky. He had curly hair.'

'Was he wearing glasses?'

'Definitely not. My taste doesn't run to men in glasses.'

'Could you identify him if you saw a picture?'

'Oh, yes,' Albert gushed, eager to be helpful now that he had been exonerated.

O'Reilly laid a picture of Harvey Wozniak on the table. 'Is this the man you saw in The Zone?'

Albert shook his head. 'No way. That's Harvey, Angie's ex. Besides, I said he was hunky.'

O'Reilly laid another photo beside Harvey's. Albert's pale eyes grew wide and his guilt grew deeper. 'My God, this is incredible. That's him. That's the guy Angie was talking to. The picture doesn't do him justice, though. Who is it?'

'Never mind,' said O'Reilly, picking up the photo of Michael Niebaum he had gotten from the DMV. 'You would be willing to identify this man in a lineup, yes?' he asked.

'If it helps find who killed Angie, I sure would,' said Albert.

Kozlowski was sitting at his desk, trying to negotiate coffee from a Styrofoam cup into his mouth after five shots of Novocain. His toothache had kept him up all night, and he had no one to blame for it but himself. His wife had been nagging him forever to go the dentist and he'd ignored her. Luckily, she wasn't the sort of wife to give him *I told you sos*, although after all the pain he'd suffered, he was going to listen to her from now on. He never thought he'd be so glad to see a big needle. After his dentist numbed him up, he had drilled for so long, Kozlowski was surprised he hadn't struck oil.

He took another stab at the coffee, but with his mouth so numb, the coffee spilled straight down the front of his shirt. He threw the cup into the trash and looked up to see O'Reilly entering the room, his face glowing the usual red. Koz wondered if he'd already stopped for a drink. Sometimes he reeked so badly of the previous night's booze, the smell oozed from his pores. On those days, Kozlowski rode with the window down. He couldn't understand how anyone could poison himself the way his partner did. Himself, he wasn't much for the stuff; maybe an occasional beer, but that was about it.

Thank God, the man didn't smoke. That would have been intolerable.

'We got a positive ID on Michael Niebaum talking to Angie in The Zone,' O'Reilly said triumphantly, tossing the DMV photo onto his desk.

'Thaths great, thoud we move on him?'

'What the hell's wrong with you?'

'Novocain.'

O'Reilly nodded in momentary sympathy. 'No. I don't see Michael Niebaum as a flight risk. Not yet anyway. And we still need to run out that New Hampshire ground ball.'

'So what now?'

'Let's go visit the bride,' said O'Reilly.

# THIRTY-TWO

## 5 Days Until

I was blissfully absorbed in last month's sales figures and next month's quotas, happy to be doing anything other than face my wretched life, when the buzz of the intercom jolted me back to reality. Sandi Lane's voice did little to disguise her morbid curiosity. 'There are two gentlemen in the lobby who would like to see you. A Detective O'Reilly and a Detective Kozlowski.'

I grabbed my forehead to keep my head from flying off my shoulders, wondering what in hell had prompted the two cops to show up at my office. Despite my abject terror, I managed to calmly ask her to send them to my office. Meeting them in the lobby was out of the question. Not with a receptionist who made *Bewitched*'s Mrs Kravitz look like an ostrich with its head in the sand. Besides, it was doubtful my rubber legs would have made it down the hall. Not to mention my bladder.

A minute later the two detectives were in my office. Their presence was suffocating, causing me to question if there was enough oxygen in the office for the three of us. I shuffled the papers on my desk in an effort to show *I really don't have time for this*.

'Sorry we didn't call first. We were in the area,' O'Reilly lied.

'You sure seem to be *in the area* a lot,' I countered.

They helped themselves to the two chairs in front of me and got right down to business. 'There's something we need to run past you,' O'Reilly continued without acknowledging my statement. 'You recall the other day when I asked you if you knew anyone from New Hampshire?'

Boom. That shoe sure hit the ground hard. I worked my best poker face, my mouth closed as I waited for his next words to fall.

'We spoke with Suzanne Lundgren yesterday, and she told us you girls met someone from New Hampshire in The Overhang the night of Angie's murder. That you were talking to him.'

I stalled, staring at O'Reilly for seconds that felt like years. So Suzanne had turned Judas on me. Coughing to buy myself a few more seconds of life as I knew it, I agonized over just how much to reveal to these cops. That's when O'Reilly made a strategic error that gave me an easy out.

'Do you remember him now?' he pushed.

*Remember. Thank you for that, detective.* With so much of that night a fog, how could he know what was lost to alcohol? Surely he was familiar with that scenario.

'Detective,' I said sheepishly. 'I'm not proud of it, but I was pretty drunk that night. I vaguely remember dancing with some guy in The Overhang, but whether he came from New Hampshire or the moon, I couldn't tell you.'

'I never said you were dancing.'

I flinched, but managed to recover. 'Oh. Well, I do remember dancing, but that's about all.'

O'Reilly's bloodshot eyes continued evaluating me, searching for the crack in my story. But my face was blank; those late nights of five-card draw in college were paying off. His next words held a sharp edge. 'You're saying you don't remember anything about this guy?'

I shook my head and shrugged. 'Sorry.'

O'Reilly tried some more probing, but was unable to derail my claim of drunken ignorance. Finally, he gave up and they left. I felt like I'd just survived a congressional drilling. As much as I abhorred lying, I had gotten damn good at it. In all truth, if I thought for one moment there was a remote possibility Steven had something to do with Angie's death, I would have come forward. I truly would have. But what I knew about him and what he was doing when Angie was murdered was no one's business but mine.

The rest of the day was a write-off. The dual pressures of work and the wedding were killing me, and worst of all, my period had yet to show, a half-dozen hopeful trips to the bathroom yielding nothing more than pristine white toilet paper. I arrived home that night feeling beyond overwhelmed. With so many deadlines to be met, I really should have worked late, but Flynn was coming over for dinner and I couldn't put him off yet another time. I'd been treating him poorly enough as it was.

I was chopping vegetables, enjoying the brainless repetitiveness of it, when the phone rang. I was sorry I answered the moment I heard the voice on the other end. It was my mother. Having endured dinner with her the night before to go over last-minute details, I thought I was off the hook for a while.

'I'm calling to remind you about the final fitting for your dress on Thursday.'

'Mom, didn't we talk about that last night? It's on my calendar. Look, I'm trying to get dinner ready. Is there anything else?'

'How are you coming with the thank-you notes from the shower?'

Getting rid of my mother when she had her mind set on something was more difficult than killing a poinsettia. 'They're still in the thought process.'

'I suggest you get them out of the way now. Then you won't have to worry about them on your honeymoon. And don't forget to specifically mention the gift.'

As if I had any intention of writing thank-you notes on my honeymoon. I envisioned the beaches of St Bart's and listening to the surf without a care in the world. 'OK. I'll start them tonight. I gotta go. Flynn's here.'

I had become such a facile liar, I barely recognized myself any more. Then again, when I thought about it, I hadn't recognized myself for a long time. Going back even before Angie's death and my night with Steven Kaufman.

I put down the knife and took a seat at the table. It was time for a heart to heart with myself. What had happened to that free-spirited youth who was going to travel and write? Where had the teenager who never wanted to live a conventional life gone? I had hidden behind that thirty extra pounds for so long that when I came out from beneath them, I was in my thirties and had given up on my dreams. Now it seemed I was willing to settle for someone else's.

Time was flying too quickly. Graduation felt like yesterday.

My original plan after college had been to take a year off to backpack around Europe, to collect experiences for a someday book. My mother had quashed that dream from the get-go. 'Europe will be there for the rest of your life, but if you don't start your career now, you'll fall behind everyone else.' So instead of spending a year discovering new places and people, I did a whistle stop tour of London for a week and Paris for a week and came home to sell advertising space. What allowed me to let my mother control me like that? Why hadn't I stood up to her and done what I wanted?

I'll never forget the way my mother's eyes lit up the first time I brought Flynn to the house. She couldn't have been happier had I brought home the Golden Calf. Not long afterwards he offered me the diamond, and I took it. Having grown used to passion being out of my grasp, I assumed that applied to marriage too. Life with Flynn would be comfortable and secure. I needed to accept my good fortune at finding someone like him.

Then I was seized with the vision of a door that could never open again.

Steven had awakened in me someone long buried, the person who had been missing since high school and Barry Metter. I'd taken enough psychology in college to know there was a reason I hadn't emptied the trash basket with Steven's number in it. In fact, that same scrap of paper with his number had been relocated to my vanity drawer. Though we'd only spent those few drunken hours together, I couldn't put him out of my mind. I ached to reach out to him, to ask him if he was thinking of me too. Then reality pounded me with a resounding *Hello?* There is no such thing as true love. That's all a fairy tale. Like the dreams parents pass on to their children and then take away.

I read once middle age snuffs out more creativity than war or disease combined. Is that what had happened? Had middle age snuffed me out? Was I marrying Flynn because I loved him or because it seemed like the smartest thing to do?

*Let the unopened doors remain unopened.* I capitulated. My future was with Flynn, who would be arriving at any moment. I picked up the knife and went back to chopping vegetables.

\*     \*     \*

'I hope this isn't a preview of our married life,' he said of my lackluster kiss at the door. He pulled me close and kissed me fully on the lips. He wasn't a particularly passionate person, so it took me by surprise when his kiss grew deeper, his tongue probing my mouth as he slipped a smooth hand under my blouse to my breast.

'They feel bigger,' he said sexily.

'My period's due,' I answered, breaking his grasp and turning away.

'No wonder you're acting so weird.' He looped his arm around my waist and drew me close again. 'You know, I've been thinking about our little abstinence pact and maybe it's not such a good idea after all. I mean, it's not like Saturday's going to be our first time.' He kissed my neck and his hand went back to my breast. To my chagrin, I found myself annoyed by his overtures.

'C'mon, Flynn. The abstinence pact was your idea and we've gone nearly a month. We should see it through.' Tossing him a crumb, I gave him a lingering kiss on the lips and went back into the kitchen to see about dinner. Flynn sulked for a while in front of PBS *Newshour*, but by the time we sat down to eat he had moved beyond his frustration. He talked about work and how the new software would revolutionize things. He talked about the wedding and how flattering it was that nearly all of his Dartmouth buddies were coming in for the occasion.

'Why wouldn't they come, Flynn? You're a great guy.'

'That's what I tell myself every morning,' he said, only half ironically. 'But I'm beginning to wonder if you think so.'

'Why would you say that?'

'You have to ask? You've been weird ever since I got back from New York. We've barely talked in the last week.'

'So we have to have this conversation again,' I said, falling back on my list of excuses. 'Angie's death. Work. The wedding plans. My mother. When it's all over, I'll be better. I swear.'

I forced myself to be talkative through the rest of the meal, clowning about the women at the lingerie shower and telling him about the sexy teddy his mother had given me. We ate pasta and salad and Flynn drank most of the bottle of Chianti. When we finished dinner, instead of hanging around to watch a movie on the VCR, like he normally would, Flynn opted to leave.

'You better get some rest, Mags. You're really not yourself.' He hesitated and added, 'You're not getting cold feet, are you?' I wanted to hug him and say, *Yes I am and thanks for under-standing*. But the question was meant to be rhetorical. The thought would never occur to him that I would be anything other than thrilled to be his wife. And rightfully so. He *was* a great guy. He wrapped a warm arm around me, and I found comfort in the embrace, but it was the sort of comfort found in a good friend or the brother I'd never had. 'Don't worry so much. In five days, you'll be Mrs Flynn Rogers Hamilton III. In seven days, we'll be sipping mojitos on the beach. And when we come back we've got the new house, and then we can get on with starting a family.'

He winked at me and headed down the steps. I stood on the landing, watching his blond head recede until the entry door closed behind him, thinking that he was the greatest thing that had ever happened to me, that I was a Jekyll and Hyde. How stupid I was to risk loss of him with someone like Steven Kaufman. My mind fixated briefly on the carpenter's hands and their strong touch, but I pushed the thought back.

As I did the dishes, my mind seesawed back and forth, wondering why I hadn't just let Flynn make love to me. It would have covered for me if I were indeed pregnant. But thank god I still had some integrity left. That was one lie I could never live through.

I prayed. *Please God, just let me get my period, and I promise I will never deceive him again.*

# THIRTY-THREE

## Carol Anne

The girls were at day camp and the baby taking a mid-morning nap, leaving Carol Anne alone in her kitchen. While her cookbook was opened to 'Chicken Piccata', her focus was on a robin building a nest in the crabapple tree outside the window. As she watched the bird's busy beak fix twigs into place, creating a secure nest to lay her eggs and hatch her chicks, she was reminded of herself. Her sole purpose in life was keeping the nest safe for her family.

She worried that her nest was threatened. She worried about it from her first conscious moment until she gave way to sleep. Not that worrying was something new for Carol Anne. She had always been a chronic worrier, the type who assumed the worst when someone didn't show up on time or answer the phone. That there had been a car accident or a heart attack or a plane crash. She stayed one step ahead of disaster with transistor radios and flashlights stashed strategically throughout the house, a month's supply of bottled water in the basement, rope ladders beneath all the upstairs beds in the event of a fire. But her latest worry had grown so overwhelming it squeezed out all the others.

Michael was acting stranger than ever. The night before, he kept hovering behind her and clearing his throat as if preparing to say something. When he finally opened his mouth to speak, something innocuous would come out like, 'What's for dinner?' or 'How was your day?' Carol Anne knew him well enough to know he was waiting for the right moment to spring something on her; he'd done a similar dance a few years ago when he was pushing to buy the *Dermabrasion*. But her sixth sense told her this time it was something far more serious than a boat.

There was only one thing to resort to when she was this unstrung. She needed a smoke. After rooting around in the towel drawer, her fist closed like a crane around a rock on the cellophane-wrapped pack she kept hidden beneath the terry-cloth dishtowels. She brought it to her nose and sniffed the tobacco right through the seal. Smoking was reserved for emergencies and no time qualified like the present. She lit a cigarette off the gas burner and took a deep puff. The nicotine hit her nervous system immediately, delivering a much appreciated calm. She looked upward and thanked God for small favors.

When the cigarette burned down to the filter, she lit a fresh one and pondered the ironies of life. People sure weren't what they appeared to be, especially when it came to happiness. She thought of her best friend, on the cusp of a dream marriage, threatening to destroy it all because of a one-nighter. And Kelly still trying to fill the void left by her mother's death. Suzanne all alone in her sky palace. Natasha living with her control freak husband Arthur. Was anyone truly happy?

Her mother had appeared to be happy when she was raising Carol Anne and her two sisters. So it was a complete shock when her parents divorced after her youngest sister graduated high school. How long had they endured each other for the benefit of their kids? Carol Anne didn't know the answer to that question, but she knew her own happiness hinged entirely on her family, on Michael and their children. As long as they were together, there was no problem that couldn't be worked out.

She ground out the second cigarette and was contemplating a third when she caught a movement in her peripheral vision. In his usual stealthy way, Michael had crept in unannounced. He would be angry with her for smoking – like any doctor he was vehemently opposed to it. But when she turned to face him he didn't even mention the cigarettes, didn't appear to have even noticed them. He wore the face of a stranger.

'What's wrong? What are you doing home? Are you all right?' Her questions were rapid fire, her voice peppered with wifely concern.

'Carol Anne, we have to talk.'

The taste of the nicotine on her tongue turned nauseating. His tone forewarned of something ominous. She had anticipated this moment, fretted over it. Now that it was upon her, she was so frightened she wanted to turn and run. But she held her ground.

'Is this about Angie?' she whispered.

'In a way, yes.'

'Did you kill her?'

'God, no. Don't be ridiculous,' he said, his face breaking into his easy grin, and for that moment he was her Michael again. Then the opaque veil reappeared, heavy and unfamiliar. 'This is not easy for me.'

*Oh my God, he wants a divorce*, she thought. She barely drew breath as she studied his pain-twisted face. An extended silence was broken by the sound of the icemaker dropping ice. She waited with wretched patience, straining not to scream *tell me*.

'Do you remember the first time we made love?' he asked casually, working to tease the smile back onto his face.

Could she ever forget? It was at Tower Beach on a blanket she'd smuggled from her bedroom and couldn't return afterwards because of all the sand in it. Her mother looked for that blanket for years. Carol Anne had been afraid the police would come along and catch them in the act, but Michael had calmed her fears, telling her that people in love deserved to share it. Afterwards, she knew they were locked together forever. She was sixteen.

'Of course, I remember. And I've never made love to anyone else.'

He turned his back to her, unable to face her with what he had to say. 'I have.'

The verbal slap left her cheeks numb. So her suspicions were true. He was having an affair. No longer caring about his disapproval, she reached for another cigarette and lit it, waiting for him to continue.

'This is going to hurt,' he admitted, 'but I've got to tell you the whole truth. It's the least you deserve. For a long time, there's been something different about me. Actually, it's been for my whole life.

'But it came to a head a year or so after I finished medical school. I started having these intense sexual dreams, wet dreams that woke me in the night. I hid them from you. Then Cara was born. And Eva, and they went away for a while. But I kept having troubling thoughts, and I missed the dreams. Then one day a person entered my life who forced me to face my fears, someone who understood my internal discord.

'This person said, "I know what's bothering you." And we talked, and when the truth came out, and I felt light, like the weight of the world had been lifted from my shoulders, like suddenly life was something to be celebrated. We ended up having an affair.'

Tears swelled Carol Anne's eyes as the entire bottom fell out of her world. 'Was it Angie?'

'No, it wasn't Angie. It was an intern at the hospital.'

'Are you still having an affair with her?'

'No.' Michael bent his head back and stared at the ceiling. His next words were barely audible. 'My affair with him ended a long time ago.'

The words slammed her like a hurricane. She wanted to correct him, to say, 'You mean *her*,' but in her heart she knew there had been no mistake. He was telling her something she may have suspected, but had seemed so reprehensible she had buried it away with things she didn't want to think about. Now there was no denying it. Now the world made sense. It explained why they lived as best friends, practically brother and sister. And suddenly, the young men in the boat on Sunday made sense too.

'You had an affair with a man,' she said, surprising herself with her calm delivery of the statement.

'Yes.'

'Have there been others?'

'Yes.'

That's when Carol Anne lost it. She threw herself at him, striking his chest with her fists. He took the blows without even trying to stop her. 'You're telling me our marriage is a lie,' she screamed. 'You bastard. You bastard.' When she realized the violence of what she was doing, she dropped her hands to her sides and stared at him through teary eyes. 'What about AIDS, Michael? What about me? Did you ever think about infecting me? Did you think of that?'

'I always practiced safe sex,' he said matter-of-factly.

'Is that supposed to console me?' She went to the table and sat down, resting her forehead in her hands. 'You said this was about Angie in a way. What way?'

'I saw Angie the night she was murdered. In a gay bar.'

'What? I don't understand.' Carol Anne's head came out of her hands and she stared at him in confusion. 'Why are you telling me this now?'

He stretched his hands toward her, opening and closing them as if reaching for something unattainable, his eyes rimmed red as he fought back tears of his own. 'I had a visit from Detective O'Reilly this morning. Someone saw me talking to her in the bar.' His shoulders hunched and he continued. 'The night of your party for Maggie, after the card game broke up, I was feeling needy, so I went into the city to look for . . .' He took a deep breath to fuel his next words. 'Well, I went to a few places. Finally, I stopped in this place called The Zone, and who do I see there but Angie. She was totally messed up, but not too messed up to figure out why I was there.

'She made some comment about the uselessness of marriage and left. I finished my drink and got out of there. Then at Angie's funeral service, I saw this guy who had been eyeing me in The Zone that night. I was pretty sure he hadn't seen me, so I decided I'd better not go to Angie's parents after the service – just in case he showed up there.'

'So there was no medical emergency that day?'

'No,' he admitted, looking her directly in the eyes. 'But it gets worse. They want me to come in for a lineup. Supposedly, there's some witness who can put me in the park carrying Angie's body. Which is impossible, because I wasn't there.'

'A lineup? You can't go in for a lineup. What if someone saw you? Think of what that could mean to your reputation.'

'I know,' he said, sounding defeated.

'But Michael, when you came home that morning, you made love to me. It felt like you really meant it. Were you faking it?'

'No. You have to understand how conflicted I am. I love you with all my heart. After seeing Angie in the bar, I got in the car and started driving just to think things through. I drove all the way to Wisconsin border. All I could think about was how horrible it would be to lose you and our family, and it scared the living shit out of me. You and the kids are the most important things in my life. So I made a decision to tell you everything and go into therapy to fight this problem. As soon as I made the decision, all I could think of was getting back home and making love to you. I want us to stay together. That's the truth.'

Carol Anne barely drew breath as she analyzed the situation. Her husband had just confessed to sleeping with men. That was devastating enough, but on top of that he was suspected of murdering Angie. Which was worse, she wondered, her husband being gay or being a murder suspect? She decided being a murder suspect presented the greater threat to their family at the moment. She could picture the headlines. Married north suburban doctor, renowned plastic surgeon, frequenter of gay bars, suspect in murder. It wouldn't matter if he was guilty or innocent, he would lose his clientele. The damage would be done in the eyes of the public. And what about Cara and Eva? How would the other children treat them knowing their father was under suspicion for such a crime?

If Michael's therapy succeeded, which she wanted to think it would, what good would that do them if his career was ruined?

The most critical thing was protecting her children from any harm. Angie's case was high profile, and she couldn't risk Michael being associated with it. She went to her husband and massaged the back of his neck the way she used to when he came home after long days of interning. She would take care of this if it took all her wiles and then some.

He could not be part of a lineup. That was all there was to it.

'Don't worry, Michael. Everything is going to be OK,' she reassured him. And it was going to be OK. She would see to it. Things were so much easier once you knew what you were battling.

# THIRTY-FOUR
## Ron

With Kozlowski out after yet another sleepless night with the bad tooth, Ron had gone on his own to visit to the Evanston medical offices of Dr Michael Niebaum. Medical offices. Talk about a euphemism. The waiting room was more like a hotel lobby, right down to the coffee bar and the marble finishes. Or maybe a bordello, considering all the good-looking babes passing through.

The good doctor had agreed to see him right away. He'd come clean when O'Reilly told him he was seen speaking to Angie in The Zone. But then he actually had the cojones to give O'Reilly some song and dance about driving to Wisconsin afterwards to do some thinking. More likely he'd driven east to Belmont Harbor and not north to the land of milk and cheese. The good news was Niebaum had agreed to a lineup. The bad news was O'Reilly needed to locate the peripatetic Ralph to make that lineup happen.

Now he was back at Area 3, waiting for his regular breakfast of aspirin and coffee to kick in. His phone rang, and when he picked up he was surprised to hear the voice of Niebaum's wife. He pictured the pretty, soft-spoken woman trying to cover her worry when they spoke in the parking lot on Sunday. Even if she was a liar, his heart went out to her for her being married to such a total asshole.

'What can I do for you, Mrs Niebaum?'

'Detective O'Reilly, it's imperative that I speak with you as soon as possible. Could you come out to the house?'

*Imperative*. Strong word. Maybe she was ready to confess that her husband hadn't arrived home any time near midnight that night. She was a little late for that. Or was there something else she wanted to share with him? Though he had just gotten back from the northern suburbs, his head was throbbing and any excuse to get out of the 'office' worked for him. It had been a late night at the neighborhood tap.

'I'm on my way,' he said.

The cigarette burned to the quick between her fingers. *Quitting again is going to be really hard*, she thought as she stubbed out the last embers in a saucer. After listening to Michael's soulful confession, she had convinced him to go back to work. What were they going to do? Stare at each other? The moment he left she had called Detective O'Reilly. Now she had some magic to perform.

The sound of Michael, Jr, crying upstairs caused a curse to slip from her mouth. She'd been optimistic to think he'd sleep much longer. She went up to the baby's room and found him standing in his crib, his small fingers grasping the rails firmly, his face red with the anger of abandonment. Upon seeing his mother, his tears stopped like a faucet being shut off and a beaming smile lit his countenance. It was his first time standing. An unstaunched wave of love flowed through her at the sight. 'My little miracle boy,' she said, lifting him from the crib. 'You will never know what a true miracle you are.'

She was changing his diaper when the doorbell chimed. She hurriedly finished and rushed down the stairs with the baby clenched in her arms. The door opened to a tired-looking Detective O'Reilly replete with bloodshot eyes and rumpled clothes. His graying hair stood up at its cowlicks, giving him the appearance of having just rolled out of bed.

She looked over his shoulder expecting to see his large partner shadowing him. 'Are you alone?' she asked.

'Detective Kozlowski is indisposed this morning.' He forced a smile meant to put Carol Anne at ease. An awkward silence followed, punctuated by the sound of the infant's gurgling.

'Do you mind if we go into the kitchen,' she said finally. 'I can put the baby down in there.'

'Don't mind at all. I'm most comfortable in kitchens.' As she led the way through the expensively decorated house, he couldn't help but think of Suzanne Lundgren's elegant apartment in the clouds. And of Natasha Dietrich's Lake Forest mansion. Angie Wozniak's friends sure did live high. Then he thought of Kelly Delaney's cramped studio apartment. Well, some of her friends anyway.

When they got to the kitchen, she put the baby in his walker and offered him a cup of coffee. 'How do you like it?'

'Black. And strong.' His hand trembled as he raised the cup to his lips. The rich blend was far better than what they drank at the station. 'So you wanted to talk to me about something, Mrs Niebaum?'

Carol Anne had been rehearsing the lines in her head ever since hanging up with him. About what a good man Michael was, a good father, a talented and dedicated professional. About how damaging it could be if certain information got out. About how much she depended upon him. Now that it was time to speak, the words dried up before they could reach her tongue. She lit a cigarette to boost her courage.

'Sorry, these are only temporary, but entirely necessary, I'm afraid.' She took a deep drag and waited for the nicotine to deliver. Exhaling the smoke away from the baby, she stubbed the cigarette out and stared at it. 'I understand my husband is a suspect in Angie's death.'

'We like to call it a person of interest,' said O'Reilly.

'Why? Because he was seen in the same bar as Angie?' Her eyes were hooded as she looked to the floor in her personal shame. 'Yes, he told me about being in The Zone. In fact, he's told me a lot lately. More than I ever cared to hear. But his being in that bar has nothing to do with Angie's death. It's just a coincidence they were there at the same time. Nothing more.'

*And is it a coincidence that you have a boat moored practically yards from where her body was found?* O'Reilly wanted to say. But he reined in the urge. Her vulnerability appealed to his sympathetic side. She was not only pretty, she seemed so decent, and her pale skin and dark frizzy curls reminded him very much of his deceased mother. While O'Reilly didn't know for certain why Michael Niebaum was in The Zone at three a.m., he did know it couldn't bode well for his marriage. His distaste for Michael Niebaum grew stronger. Whether or not Niebaum had anything to do with Angie Wozniak's death, his lifestyle left another victim, his pretty wife.

'Michael told me you want him to come in for a lineup,' she said, her soft voice turning chill. She reached for another cigarette, but thought better of it. She turned to him, begging him with her eyes. 'Detective O'Reilly, you just can't put Michael in a lineup. You have to understand what it could do to his career. He has a reputation to keep up. If anyone were to see him in the police station, or wherever you do those things, it would ruin our entire family . . . our lives.'

'Mrs Niebaum,' said O'Reilly. 'Why did you lie to us before? Why did you say your husband got home at midnight when he didn't?'

She knew she was strong, but a person could only handle so much. So many things were coming at her from so many directions, she felt she might implode. Though she worked to keep up her bravado, she was near the edge, her hands shaking from nerves and her vision blurred by banked tears. O'Reilly saw her dilemma and tried not to let his sympathy for this woman override his obligation as a homicide cop. He would not let himself be dissuaded by a woman's tears. No matter how much she reminded him of his mother.

'I don't know why I lied. I'm not a liar,' she confessed, gritting her teeth in an effort to maintain control. 'Maybe I was embarrassed by the hours he was keeping. Maybe I sensed there was some kind of trouble. But you've got to believe me, Michael Niebaum never had any relations with Angie, and he certainly didn't kill her.'

O'Reilly wasn't so sure about that, but a bulb lit in his skull when Carol Anne used the word relations. Niebaum was obviously queer or bisexual. What if he was having relations with multiple people? Like maybe he and Angie and the guy from New Hampshire were some kind of threesome. That could explain a lot. He needed to subpoena Niebaum's phone records. Who a person talks to can answer a lot of questions. But getting a subpoena could take a lot of time, and O'Reilly was in a hurry. He looked at the desperate woman in front of him.

'I'll tell you what, Mrs Niebaum. If you're so certain your husband had nothing to do with Angie's death, there's something you can do to help prove it. I'll make you a deal. I'll hold off on the lineup in exchange for all your husband's phone records.

Home and office. If I have to go through regular channels it can take days, but with your permission—'

'We'll provide the records,' Carol Anne said, her face a picture of relief. For a minute, he thought she was going to throw her arms around him. 'We'll do anything to prove Michael's innocence. Anything.'

On his way back to the city, O'Reilly passed one of those chain restaurants that offered mediocre food served at a big square bar. He made a U-turn and pulled into the lot. After all, it was lunchtime and a cold one might help him back into equilibrium. His first beer disappeared in one uninterrupted gulp, and he ordered a second, sipping at it slowly as he rolled possible scenarios around in his head. Extramarital affair. Jealous homo lover. Homo love triangle. Too bad Koz wasn't there to bounce things off of. Then again, if Koz were there, they wouldn't be here. He ordered a third beer and paid the check.

As he walked back to the car, his thoughts turned back to Carol Anne Niebaum's situation. Even the rich get to be miserable, he decided.

# THIRTY-FIVE

## Kelly

Gitane's had been its normal crazy, with people in suits rushing through lunch, ladies in designer wear doing exactly the opposite. Kelly arrived at work on the heels of a Biopsych exam she hadn't done well on, leaving her distracted her entire shift. Twice she had forgotten to drop food orders until she noticed the customers craning their necks in search of her, and once she had even given a table the wrong check. Luckily they had noticed before she ran their credit card. Otherwise the error would have come out of her pay.

But the exam wasn't the entire reason for her lackluster performance. Her mind was still preoccupied with her belief that the man from New Hampshire was somehow connected to Angie's murder. Telling the cops about the white truck hadn't seemed to move them along at all as far as finding the guy. She had come to the conclusion there was no other option than to tell them the whole story.

'Sorry, Maggie,' she said aloud, as she dug in her apron for a quarter and headed to the pay phone outside the ladies' room. She was happy to find O'Reilly at his desk. 'I hate to be a nuisance, but I really need to talk to you about something important in Angie's case.'

'I don't believe that for a minute, Ms Delaney,' he replied. His hangover had improved after having a hair of the dog, but talking to her brought it back with a vengeance.

'What? That I don't have something important to tell you?'

'No. That you hate to be a nuisance.'

'Ha. Ha,' she said without humor. 'I really need to meet you.'

'We're pretty busy over here,' he said, in hopes of putting her off. The last thing he wanted was to waste more time with this meddling pest. 'Can't you just tell me over the phone?'

'I said it was important.'

'All right,' he conceded. 'Where do you want to meet?'

'I'm just finishing up my lunch shift. How about O'Dwyer's on Dearborn in about fifteen minutes?'

O'Reilly glanced up at the white dial on the front wall clock. It read two forty-five. 'All right. Three o'clock,' he said. *And it better be good.*

Koz called in a minute later. 'So good to hear you're alive,' O'Reilly chided him. 'Where the hell you been?'

'In and out of dentith's chairs. They finally pulled the thucker. Now Melissa's all pithed off, because she hath a thing about people with mithing teeth. Says she can't be around a hillbilly. Looks like I hath to get a bridge. Which ain't cheap. There goeth the new fishing pole,' Kozlowski lamented. 'I mithing anything?'

'Head over to O'Dwyer's. We'll be meeting with Kelly Delaney, so it's probably a good thing you're still anaesthetized.'

'Ms Delaney. What's up with her thith time?'

'I don't know, she wouldn't tell me. Maybe she wants to join the force.'

The first thing to hit Kelly's nose as she walked in the door were the familiar smells of stale beer and rotting wood. A few of the old regulars sat at the bar, chasing their afternoon shots down with beer. She liked to stop in her former place of employment from time to time just to remember how bad it was, kind of like the Fitzgerald character who took one drink a day so he wouldn't start to imagine liquor was better than it was. Except unlike Fitzgerald's character, there was no way she could even have one drink a day. That much she knew.

She sat down on a wobbly stool at a wobbly table in the window and nodded to Eddy, the bartender who had worked the day shift for as long as she could remember. He returned her nod with a lame smile, his stained yellow teeth as big as a horse's in his bony face. He was drinking what looked like a glass of ice water, but Kelly knew better. The only water in that glass was the ice.

The waitress came over and Kelly ordered a diet cola. It was déjà vu watching Eddy go through the mechanics. Glass, ice, soda gun, straw, give glass to waitress, sip his own drink. She wondered how much longer before Eddy succumbed to liver disease or stepped out drunkenly in front of a moving car.

Kelly felt guilty about what she was about to do, but she'd rather be hated by a living Maggie than crying over a dead one. When she was a little girl and her mother punished her for something, she always said, *This is hurting me more than it's hurting you*. That's how she felt about breaking her word to Maggie. But it had to be done.

Kelly picked up an abandoned *Chicago Tribune* from the table next to her and started working the crossword puzzle. After years of idle time standing behind bars, she had become a whiz at them. Nearly all the boxes were filled when she looked up to see Detective Kozlowski coming toward her, his swollen right cheek giving him the appearance of one very large bald chipmunk.

'Ms Delaney, mind if I join you?' His voice was slurred, and for a moment she wondered if he was taking lessons from O'Reilly. Then he touched his cheek with one of his mitt-like paws. 'A hundred-dollar filling just turned into a five-hundred-dollar bridge.'

'Don't you hate spending money on teeth? I sure do. Take a load off. And for God's sake, would you call me Kelly? It makes me feel old having somebody my age calling me Ms Delaney. Makes me feel like a teacher or something.'

'Call me Joe, then.'

'Joe,' she said, looking down at the unfinished crossword. 'You wouldn't know a six-letter word for a medicinal plant, would you?'

'I should. I used to kill a lot of time doing crosswords during stakeouts.'

'Damn. One empty square is stopping me from solving the whole thing.' She thought about what she'd just said. 'Is it anything like that in homicide? One empty square effs up everything?'

Kozlowski moved a finger under his slightly tight collar and wished his partner would show up. He was uneasy around women except for his wife, and was always afraid of saying something that might sound stupid.

'It's more like a whole lot of squares. And it's being able to prove it. Lots of times we know who the perp is, but if we don't have enough for the DA to convict, then it's a waste even making an arrest.'

'Does that happen often?'

'More than you would ever care to know.'

Kelly thought about her close encounter in the projects. She knew those teenagers wouldn't have given her a second thought if they'd killed her, and she wondered if they ever would have been caught. The waitress reappeared, having noticed another warm body at the table. Kozlowski ordered a club soda.

'I'm not much of a drinker,' he said. 'Never have cared much for the stuff or the effect it has on me.'

'Guess your partner makes up for you.' Kelly watched for the giant's reaction.

'Ron may like his pops, but that doesn't make him a bad guy,' he said in O'Reilly's defense. 'And I've never seen a harder working cop. He should have made lieutenant a long time ago.'

'Maybe his drinking is holding him back.'

Kozlowski shrugged. 'He's Irish, what can I say? His life hasn't been exactly easy. His mother passed when he was just a kid and he had to practically raise his siblings by himself. His father was drunk all the time. Just to show what kind of a guy he is, he took care of the old man until he died a couple of years ago.'

'What about a wife?'

'He was married once, but it didn't work out.'

*No wonder*, thought Kelly. But for the first time, she saw O'Reilly as something more than a drunk. She wondered how his mother had died, if she had been eaten away by cancer until she was little more than bones inhabiting a tired robe. Had a young Ron O'Reilly cried himself to sleep every night too? Did the loss of his mother inhabit his psyche the way it did hers? Was alcohol filling the vacuum left by her death?

'That's a shame about his mother,' Kelly said sadly. The door to the dingy bar opened and O'Reilly stepped in. He did a quick inventory of the room, his eyes hovering over the bar, before joining them in the window. The waitress was back before the barstool had a chance to squeak.

'Somethin' to drink?'

'A cup of coffee.'

'Are you sure you don't want anything stronger?' Kelly teased. The look he gave her told her she was pushing it. The waitress went away shaking her head, hoping the three teeto-talers taking up her best table would leave before the cocktail hour started.

'I have something important to share here,' said Kelly. 'This is so sensitive it could ruin someone's life. I'm betraying the confidence of a friend. But I'm so worried about her safety that I feel I don't have a choice.'

O'Reilly shot Kozlowski a look that said *Spare me from amateur sleuths*. He couldn't wait to hear what the reformed-alcoholic-drug-addict-turned-jogging-psychology-student-waitress was going to spring on them now. He didn't have to wait long for his answer. Kelly leaned in close and spoke in a voice barely above a whisper. 'If you want to know more about the guy from New Hampshire, you've got to talk to Maggie Trueheart.'

O'Reilly suppressed a groan. She had dragged them down to the seedy bar for nothing. 'We've already spoken to Maggie,' he said. 'She vaguely remembers dancing with him at The Overhang, but that's about it.'

O'Reilly slapped a ten-dollar bill down on the table and stood to leave.

'No wait,' Kelly pleaded, raising her voice. 'That's not the whole story. She lied to you. She did more than dance with him. She slept with him.'

A few of the patron's heads turned. O'Reilly sat back down. This time she had his attention. 'With all due respect, if that's the truth, how could this guy have killed Angie if he was other-wise occupied?'

'Here's what I think happened. He slipped Maggie a rolfie, either in the bar or at her home. Believe me, I know how easy that is to do. After she was out cold, he went and killed Angie, then came back to Maggie's bed. If he's caught, what better alibi?'

'But what's his motive?' Kozlowski puzzled aloud.

'That's the part I don't know. But you gotta admit it's just too weird he was outside Carol Anne's house and then at The Overhang. And then hosed my friend.'

O'Reilly nodded, more to himself than anyone else. His instincts about Maggie Trueheart hiding something had been right all along. Now he knew what it was. He thought about Carol Anne Niebaum's lie and his doubts about Suzanne Lundgren's honesty. He wasn't the morals police, but what was with these women anyhow? he wondered. Did any one of them tell the truth?

'Now this is what we have to do,' Kelly continued, the plan mapped out in her mind. 'Maggie can't know I narced on her. You've got to make up something like one of her neighbors saw her getting out of the New Hampshire truck. Or that the bartender saw her leave with him. Tell her anything, just as long as it keeps me out of it. I wouldn't be doing this if I wasn't scared shitless that he might come back for her. I couldn't live with myself if that happened.'

'Oh, don't worry, we'll talk to her,' said O'Reilly, getting up from the table for a second time with Kozlowski following suit. They were halfway to the door when the big cop froze and swung around to face Kelly. 'Yarrow,' he said.

Kelly looked down at the crossword and smiled. 'Yep. Yarrow. Thanks, Joe.'

When they were out on the street, O'Reilly raised a crooked eyebrow at his partner. 'Yarrow? What the hell is that code for?'

'Six letter word for a medicinal plant.'

'Oh,' said O'Reilly. Evidently something had transpired between the two before he arrived. He didn't know why he found their familiarity irksome. There was no denying the Delaney woman was a bona fide pest. Aside from the obvious reasons for wanting to find out who killed Angie Wozniak, another huge incentive to solve the murder was to get her ass off of his.

# THIRTY-SIX
## 3 Days Until

I worked late on Tuesday and was back in the office first thing Wednesday morning. My sleep had been fitful; one chaotic dream rolling into another. Dreams of Flynn, of my wedding, of Steven Kaufman. There were still several deadlines to meet before the end of the week, and the pink slips in my inbox were multiplying. I wanted to cover my ears and open my mouth like the character in *Silent Scream*. If only life had a pause button. Or better yet a rewind. I wished for a black hole to come and swallow me. It would be a merciful end.

My period still hadn't come. My breasts were swollen and tender, my abdomen bloated like I'd pigged out on the buffet at India House. I couldn't recall ever feeling this uncomfortable before my time of month. Ever. I tried convincing myself that it was premenstrual tension, that stress was causing my period to be late, that there was no way I could be pregnant from one slip-up. But if that was the case, then why were my breasts falling out of my bra?

My desk phone rang. It was my boss, Marian Roche, the publisher of the *Chicagoan*.

'I wonder if you could come up and see me.' Her voice was all business. I felt the catgut tighten. Marian was not one to take time out for praise. She only called upon someone when there was a problem.

'Of course. I'll be there right away.'

I took to the elevator to tenth floor and walked the long glass hallway of executive offices, stopping in front of the nameplate: *M. Roche*. She was elegantly dressed, her head of prematurely silver hair bowed over a broad glass desk as transparent as the walls. She waved me in, her gray eyes probing my face like a doctor trying to make a diagnosis.

'How are you coming along?' she asked without offering me a seat.

'I'm fine,' I lied, another lie among lies. My gaze drifted out the window to Grant Park where softball players tossed a sixteen-incher in the morning sun. 'Some prenuptial jitters, but otherwise I'm OK.'

The look on her face told me that her question had nothing to do with my personal well-being. Marian had little time for such frivolity in her universe. At forty-five, she had survived three marriages, the first two to divorce, the last to the widowhood which left her owner and publisher of the *Chicagoan*. The magazine was her spouse now, and she was competitive. Her entire raison d'être was to put out a superior product that kept her readers' loyalty as well as her advertisers.

'I know you've got a lot on your plate, but I need to take the temperature on the August deadlines.' She stared me down with laser-like precision. 'Are you going to make it across the finish line by Friday?'

I squirmed. 'I'm a little behind schedule.'

'What's a "little behind"? If you need some extra bodies to help you get it in under the wire, just say so. I've got them.'

How I wished extra bodies were the solution. Extra bodies couldn't get inside my head to help me focus. Extra bodies couldn't make me sleep at night or wash away my guilt. But I had to do this on my own – pull it out of somewhere. In the long game, this job I hated might be the only thing I had left to support myself and maybe another. 'Thanks, Marian, but it's the kind of stuff that would be impossible to delegate out. I plan on working late the next couple of nights. Don't worry – I'll get it done.'

'All right, Maggie. I have faith in you. But remember, if you need help checking off some of those boxes, I'm here.'

Marian was nicely telling me that if I didn't get the job done there was no one to blame but myself. I left the publisher's office resolved to block out all collateral worries and concentrate on my work. That resolve crumpled the moment the elevator doors opened at my floor and I saw Detective O'Reilly seated in one of the Mies chairs, thumbing through the latest copy of the *Chicagoan*. This was getting to be far too regular. Sandi was doing her best to pretend his presence was nothing out of the ordinary. When he saw me, he closed the magazine and stood up.

'Ms Trueheart, you have a couple of minutes?'

'To be honest, detective, no I don't. I don't even have a few seconds.' My voice was shrill, my vocal cords constricted with stress. I was tempted to march down the hall and leave him and his rumpled clothing standing in the lobby. In reality, I didn't have the nerve. 'Come with me,' I acquiesced.

Sandi's eyes followed us down the hall. Thank God my office didn't have a glass wall like Marian's. We went into my office and I closed the door behind us. 'Detective, I'm sure you can appreciate I have a lot to do before this weekend, so can we make this lightning quick?'

'That depends on whether you are going to tell me everything you know this time.'

'Everything I know about what?'

'About the New Hampshire man.'

My stomach issued an obscene grumble that felt mild compared to the activity around my sphincter muscles. But, never one to fold, I continued my bluff. 'Look, I've already told you everything,' I said more coolly than I'd ever thought possible.

'Ms Trueheart,' he said unequivocally, 'one of your neighbors placed a white GMC pickup truck with New Hampshire plates on your street the night Angie Wozniak was murdered. We are looking for the owner of that truck. Now, if you have information that you're not sharing with us, I can bring you up on criminal charges ranging from aiding and abetting a criminal to obstruction of justice.'

Busted. I was so busted. I'd bluffed my way out twice, but this time the only choice was to throw in my cards. There was no mistaking the implicit threat behind O'Reilly's words. He seemed the type who would happily escort me from my wedding in handcuffs if that's what it took. I slumped into one of the office chairs.

'Detective, the guy you're looking for couldn't have had anything to do with Angie's death. He was with me all night,' I admitted. 'And as you probably know, I'm getting married on

Saturday. If this gets out, I don't have to tell you what kind of a problem it will cause me. I don't understand why the entire Chicago Police Department is so interested in my behavior.'

'Your behavior isn't anyone's concern. But his is. I just want to ask him a few questions, that's all. I promise to treat your situation delicately. The reason I came alone is to assure you that this will be handled as discreetly as possible.'

My humiliation was complete. 'But don't you understand? He left the bar with me and was with me until the next morning. Do I have to paint a picture of why he couldn't have had anything to do with Angie's death?'

'You yourself admit you'd been drinking heavily. Were you awake the entire time he was there? Can you be certain he never left your apartment?'

I searched the blurred memory for the umpteenth time. Shots in the kitchen, his lips on my neck, the two of us making our way tempestuously to my bedroom. My next recollection was Suzanne's call. No, in all honesty I couldn't be certain he was in my apartment the entire time, but c'mon, it was probably only a few hours between . . . it and the next . . . it. 'You can't possibly think he ran out and murdered Angie and then came back? That doesn't make any sense.'

'Nothing makes sense until it makes sense. Now, a name please.'

'Steven Kaufman,' I uttered in quiet defeat.

'And do you have any contact information for him?'

The inevitable final surrender. 'His phone number is at my apartment.'

'Let's go get it.'

'What? Now?' My eyes leapt to the flotilla of work on my desk. Then again, getting everything finished before my wedding was beginning to look less critical. At this rate, I might just have the weekend free to finish up. And lots of weekends to come. 'Yeah, why not?' I said.

The shower gifts were still piled in the corner, sharing space with boxed up books and knickknacks to be moved to the new house upon our return from St Bart's. An open suitcase for the honeymoon lay on the sofa. It was still empty.

Leaving O'Reilly alone in the disaster area, I went into my bedroom. The number was in my top vanity drawer beside memorabilia from my past life: cocktail napkins with scribbled notes, postcards from London and Paris, matchbooks from favorite restaurants. I picked up the crumpled piece of paper and stared at it. Then I grabbed one of the postcards and copied his number onto it. When I went back into the living room, O'Reilly was standing in the window staring at my door. I handed him the slip of paper and he stuffed it in his pocket.

'You mind if forensics came over to see if they can lift a fingerprint?' he said.

And I thought things couldn't get any worse. I envisioned a van full of overall clad men piling into my apartment and leaving a trail of black powder in their wake. Try explaining that one to the neighbors. Or Flynn. Or my mother.

'That won't be necessary.' I replayed Steven in my kitchen pouring Irish whiskey into two shot glasses. I went and got the bottle and gave it to O'Reilly. 'His prints will be on this.'

I wondered if he would be tempted to drink it.

When I got back to the office things were quiet, the receptionist who filled in for Sandi during lunch hour barely looking up from her *People* magazine. I went into my office and shut the door. An inexplicable calm came over me, like a person who has come to accept her own death. The mountain of work suddenly seemed surmountable. I sat down at my desk and attacked it with fervor.

# THIRTY-SEVEN
## Ron

It was late afternoon and AT&T had just faxed over a list of all outgoing calls from the Niebaum residence in the days prior to Angie's murder. Hundreds of numbers had been dialed, but one stood out. Glaringly. The night of the murder an Oakbrook number had been dialed that matched the number the bride had given him for Steven Kaufman. The phone number was assigned to a Vincent Columbo. He stared at the two numbers and couldn't believe his luck.

'Koz, you find this as interesting as I do?' O'Reilly asked, handing the printout and Maggie's scrap of paper over to his partner.

Kozlowski took a quick look. 'Beyond interesting.'

'Columbo. Columbo. Wonder if it's the developer?'

'One way to find out,' Koz echoed.

Traffic was bumper to bumper on the Eisenhower, the setting sun blinding drivers in a way that brought traffic to a near halt. Even with the air conditioning running full blast, O'Reilly was sweating out the evils of the night before. Kozlowski opened the window for some relief. They drove west until they reached the exit for the Oakbrook Mall and got off the expressway, driving further west. Speeding along through swaths of pastoral green, they finally reached Chewton Glen. Two grandiose stone towers marked the entrance, but there was no gate.

'Guess they're not much on security,' O'Reilly observed.

'Not yet anyhow,' Kozlowski agreed.

They turned into the subdivision and followed a road lined with oversized houses around a man-made lake. They came to a stop in front of a huge Greek revival with a three-car garage. There was a Mercedes-Benz parked in the circular drive. A sign posted on the front lawn notified visitors that the house was protected by Safeway Systems.

'Let's cool our heels for a while,' O'Reilly suggested. They drove to the end of the block and turned around, parking in front of a vacant wooded lot where they could see the front of the house. After a few minutes a dark-haired woman wearing a tank top and tight white slacks came out the front door and drove off in the Mercedes. Not long afterwards, a Cadillac Seville pulled in and parked in the far garage.

'The master of the house?' Kozlowski queried.

'Good guess. What say we go and have a little talk with Mr Columbo?'

They pulled into the driveway, parking in the space vacated by the Mercedes.

'We're definitely dragging this place down,' said O'Reilly, as they got out of the unmarked car. They rang the doorbell and a Hispanic woman answered. Visibly rattled when the detectives flashed their stars, she left them standing on the front porch and hurried off in search of her employer. She returned shortly thereafter, asking them to *follow me please* in heavily accented English. She took them through an opulent entry and down to the lower level, past some scattered tools and pieces of wood to an office at the far end of the room. Vince Columbo was sitting at his desk watching a muted Cubs game. The window behind him framed a pool with landscaped grounds sloping down to the lake.

They fished their stars out again and Vince took a disinterested look before turning off the game. 'What can I do for you, gentlemen?' he asked, his dark eyes piercing and intent as he leaned forward over his desk.

O'Reilly addressed him in his best deferential manner. 'Mr Columbo, we're from Area 3 Homicide, and we wonder if we might ask you some questions?'

The housekeeper was hovering nervously in the doorway. 'It's OK, Maria. You may go. These gentlemen are not from immigration.' She crossed herself and walked away, a whispered prayer trailing behind her.

Vince got up and closed the door. He gestured toward a couple of leather chairs in front of the TV and took a seat on a leather sofa opposite them. 'You said you have some questions?'

'Mr Columbo,' O'Reilly began, his sweat finally starting to dry in the cool of the air-conditioned office. 'A little over a week ago a woman named Angela Lupino Wozniak was murdered and her body found in Lincoln Park. Did you know this woman?'

'No, I did not know her,' said Vince, the mention of the name putting him on alert.

'You've never met her?'

'No. Absolutely.'

'Not even for a drink or something innocent like that?'

'I told you I don't know the woman.' He didn't try to cover the irritation in his voice. 'Listen, gentlemen, while I have nothing to hide, I'm more than a little leery of two Chicago police detectives showing up at my door unannounced and grilling me about a dead woman I've never met without giving me any clue as to why. Perhaps you would like to enlighten me here.'

'Simply put, Mr Columbo, your phone number has been linked to a person of interest in the case. This is an informal inquiry, but it's been my experience that people with nothing to hide are generally very cooperative. Now, are you willing to answer a few more questions?'

No sooner had O'Reilly voiced his request than the office door opened and a striking young dark haired woman wearing painted on jeans slipped into the room. Her face took on a look of total surprise when she saw the two detectives. 'Oh, excuse me, Daddy. I didn't realize you had company.' Without waiting to be asked, she pulled the door closed behind her, gone as quickly as she had come. Vince found himself wishing she didn't wear such tight clothes.

'Beautiful girl,' said Kozlowski.

'My daughter. Tell me I don't die a little every time she walks out the door with some knucklehead.' Vince resumed the conversation. 'I want to make it clear I am not comfortable with this situation and I won't be railroaded. However, I will answer any questions I find to be reasonable. Any other questions you can ask in the presence of my attorney. Fair enough?'

'Fair enough,' O'Reilly replied, unfazed. It wasn't like having an attitude was anything new to him. 'First off, who lives here?'

'Myself and my wife and my daughter, when she's not away at college, and the housekeeper part-time,' said Vince.

'No one else.'

'That is correct.'

'You know anyone who lives in Kenilworth?'

'I know several people from Kenilworth. I've done some projects there.'

'Specifically, do you know Michael and Carol Anne Niebaum?'

'No.'

'Do you know of any reason why someone from their house would have called here on the evening of June 6?'

'I told you, I don't know those people or why anyone would—' He stopped mid-sentence. Suzanne had called him that night to tell him she was going out with the girls and couldn't keep their date. He got up and went to the door and opened it, sticking his head out to make sure that his daughter had gone. He resumed his seat opposite the detectives. 'I did receive a call from Kenilworth that night. It was from my girlfriend. She was attending a party and she called me down here on my private line.' His gaze shifted from one detective to the other. 'Man to man, I hope this can remain between us.'

'This girlfriend have a name?' O'Reilly asked.

'Suzanne Lundgren.'

O'Reilly was stunned. Suddenly he had a better idea of where those flowers on the floor had come from on their last visit to her. He tried to remain cool.

'But you never met her friend Angie?'

'No. I've only heard of her through Suzanne. Who is extremely distraught over her murder, I might add. Because of my fondness for Suzanne, there is nothing I would like better than to see the culprit brought to justice.'

O'Reilly nodded appreciatively before going for the jugular. 'Do you know anyone named Steven Kaufman?'

Vince had to work hard to keep his face placid, trying to figure out how the cops had come up with the carpenter's name. 'Why do you ask?'

'He was seen around the girls that night.'

'Steven Kaufman was doing some work for me here at the house. He was working on the bar you just walked past out there.'

'Any idea why he might have given out your phone number as his own?'

'He's staying in some transient hotel downtown, so I gave him this number to use for suppliers and deliveries. But, unfortunately, he's turned out to be as transient as his hotel. He hasn't shown up to work this week.'

'Any idea why Mr Kaufman was in Kenilworth last Friday evening?'

'None at all.' Vince was prepared for the question. He couldn't tell them the reason Kaufman had been in Kenilworth, nor could he tell them that the man they were looking for was upstairs in the servant's quarters, probably watching TV.

On his way out, Kozlowski ran a hand over the smooth surface of the unfinished bar. His father had been an artisan from the old country and he knew great craftsmanship when he saw it.

'This is some beautiful work. It's a shame Kaufman didn't finish it before he disappeared.'

'Isn't it though?' said Vince.

The Mercedes pulled into the driveway as they were pulling out. O'Reilly checked his watch, one of those plastic jobs that runners used. It kept excellent time. The digital display read six o'clock. Past cocktail hour. He watched in the rear-view mirror as the same dark-haired woman they'd seen before got out of the car and began unloading groceries. 'If I had a wife who looked like that, I sure wouldn't be out screwing somebody else,' said O'Reilly.

Kozlowski made no comment on his partner's observation, saying instead, 'Don't you find it a little odd that Columbo's wife is hauling groceries in the front door of that house.'

'What do you mean?'

'Well, there's a three-car garage, and you know there's gotta be a garage entrance to the kitchen. Don't you think Mrs Columbo would want to go in that way instead of dragging the groceries through that whole big house?'

'Maybe the garage is full.'

'Well, his daughter's home, so that's one space. We saw Columbo park in another. But what about the third space? Who's parked there?'

'The housekeeper?' O'Reilly offered.

'Maybe so, but seems kind of odd to give a garage spot to the help. But here's something that's bothering me more. You see all those tools lying around the floor in the game room. They're expensive. Seems weird to me that a tradesman would run off and leave his tools.'

O'Reilly didn't have to think long before saying, 'You know Joseph, you are a friggin' genius. You're going to make lieutenant before me, I swear. I guess what we need to know now is who is parked behind door #3?'

# THIRTY-EIGHT

## Suzanne

S uzanne walked in the door and went directly to the den to play her messages. An electronic voice told her she had received six calls. The first caller was Vince. His tone of voice told her something was bothering him.

'It's me, baby. Just checking to see if you're back from your parent's house yet. I'll try you later. Don't call me.'

*That's curious*, Suzanne thought. *He's never said that before.*

The next message was from Kelly. 'Wanna go to the wedding together on Saturday?'

Vince again. 'You're not home yet? I hope you're all right?' Actually, she wasn't all right. It was the anniversary of Johnny's death, a night she always spent at the family home. It was a solemn, depressing evening that opened up old wounds.

The fourth call was from Detective O'Reilly. 'Please call me when you get this.'

A fifth message was from her father, probably placed the second she'd walked out the door. 'Hello, honey. It's Mom and Dad. Call us as soon as you get in so we know you got home safely.'

The last call was a hang-up, but she had no doubt it was Vince again.

She called her father first. He sounded both anxious and tired. 'Hello, Suzanne?'

'Yes, Poppy, it's me. You can go to sleep now. I'm home.' She could hear her mother in the background asking if everything was all right. She pictured her father in his cotton pajamas, bathrobe tied tightly about his thin waist, nodding his head to let her mother know their little girl had gotten home in one piece.

'Good night, sweetheart. Your mother and I will sleep better knowing you're at home. We love you.'

'I love you too,' she echoed.

It saddened her that her parents would forever live in the shadow of Johnny's death, two aging people stuck in a groove, moving back and forth from store to home like robots, spending far too much time over yellowing picture albums. Sometimes Suzanne wanted to scream, *You've got to let him go. You have to move forward with your lives instead of sinking into oblivion.* Tears welled in her eyes, tears for her parents, for Johnny, for herself. *You've got to let him go too, Suzanne.*

The telephone pulled her from her web of resurrected pain.

'Hello,' she answered flatly.

'Baby, you're finally home. It's after eleven. I've been trying to reach you all night.'

'Well, I'm here now.' The disconnect in her voice troubled Vince, and he had the frightful thought that the police had spoken to her about Kaufman. Luckily, she put that fear to rest right away. 'I've just spent one of the most depressing nights in my life. Sometimes I think if not for me, my parents would just cease to exist. And now Dad's talking about selling his business since there's no one to take it over. I know they want me to run it, but I can't seem to explain to them my aspirations run higher than Skanda.'

'Poor baby,' he said, so intertwined with her that her unhappiness became his own. 'Can I do anything?'

'No, Vince. There's nothing you can do.' Then as if a magician had waved his wand, her tone changed and became more upbeat. 'Three calls tonight. To what do I owe this momentous honor?'

Vince steeled himself. He had a most unpleasant task to take care of – and it needed to be handled right away. 'I've got to see you. Now.'

'Tonight? It's so late already. Can't it wait until tomorrow?'

He wanted to say, yes it can wait until tomorrow and a thousand tomorrows after that. It can wait for eternity and a day. But he didn't have the luxury of time. He had to get to her and explain his actions before it was too late. He needed to make her understand and hope that she wouldn't hate him.

'I wish it could wait, but it can't. There's no traffic this time of night. I'll be there in forty-five minutes.'

Though she was exhausted, the urgency in his voice made her agree to let him come. She wondered what he told his wife when he left the house at odd hours like this. Did he create some kind of construction emergency? The thought of him lying to his wife was unattractive, so she pushed it out of her mind. Then a more unsettling notion occurred to her. What if he was coming to break off their affair? The possibility had never occurred to her before. The time they had spent together had been so blissful, so exciting, that she couldn't remember what life was like before him. The fantastic things he gave her, the places they went to eat, the sex. Above all the sex. A shiver passed through her at the mere thought of it. She couldn't believe she had gone so many years without any intimacy. For the longest time she thought sex wasn't important. Now she couldn't think of living without it.

Ironically, his marital status mattered to her less than ever. After that first night together, when Suzanne realized the rules of the game, she had come to terms with the wife's existence and felt very unthreatened by it. Vince clearly adored her, and how many wives could make that claim. He was there for her physically, psychologically, and even financially if necessary. She didn't need anything more.

Then another thought nearly as disturbing crept into her mind. What if he was coming to tell her that he was leaving his wife? That could be as bad as losing him. Their relationship was perfect just the way it was – he was there for her, but she still had her own space. Suzanne enjoyed her independence and felt absolutely no need to marry. She had no desire for children, believing the odds of children bringing pain were as high as the odds of them bringing happiness. She would never put herself in a position to suffer like her parents.

Suzanne lived on her own terms, content with her life as it was. So as she sat in the window, watching the city lights below her, she hoped whatever Vince was coming to tell her was something she could handle.

The phone woke her. She had dozed off. The doorman was calling from the lobby. Yes, please send Mr Columbo up. She met him at the door, and he walked past her without so much as an embrace, the intensity in his face frightening, his eyes dilated like a wounded animal. He looked older, less handsome, perhaps because his mouth was drawn down at the corners. His right cheek was twitching uncontrollably. Her heart beat with unhappy fear. *Help me, God. He's leaving me.*

'What is it, Vince,' she asked quietly.

'Can we sit down and talk?'

'Of course.'

Acting more like an unexpected guest than a lover, he followed her into the living room and sat beside her on the sofa, leaving an intentional gap between them. He drank her in with his eyes. For the first time since they met, her body held no physical desire for him. His entire being was on edge like a soldier who knows the enemy is waiting to spring from somewhere in the dark. In this case, the enemy was the truth.

'Suzanne, I care for you deeply,' he began, almost meekly. 'More so than I ever have for any woman.'

Suzanne opened her mouth to speak, but Vince hushed her with a raised hand.

'Wait until I'm finished. I think you know me pretty well, and you know the sort of guy I am, the kind who when he wants something he goes after it one hundred percent. Nothing stands in my way. I feel even stronger about you. I want you one hundred ten percent.

'I wake up thinking about you. I think about you all day. You are the last thing on my mind before I go to sleep. I need to hear your voice at least once a day or I go crazy. My feelings for you make my wife so secondary she practically doesn't exist.'

He rose from the sofa and began pacing the room, his hands clenched into tight fists. In a matter of seconds, Suzanne's thoughts seesawed from *Help me, God, he is leaving me* to *Oh my God, he's leaving his wife.*

'Please, don't hate me for this,' he said, placing one foot deliberately in front of the other. 'I don't know any other way to tell you, so I'm just going to spell it out. The night of the bachelorette party, when you were out with the girls, I . . .' His voice trailed off as the words stuck in his throat.

'You what, Vince? What?' she demanded.

He stopped and bowed his head. 'I had you followed.'

'You *what*?' The very idea was so ludicrous, she laughed aloud.

'It's true, I had you followed. I had a man who works for me follow you to Kenilworth and later downtown. He was with you and the other girls in The Overhang.'

A numbness spread over her as the reality of what he was saying began to gell . . .

'I don't understand this, Vince. I've always been up front with you, told you where I'm going and what I'm doing. I've volunteered all that information because I wanted to. I have no idea what would make you mistrust me like this.' Her face glowed red with anger. Her life was not her own. She was as kept a woman as had ever been kept. 'Didn't I call you that night to tell you what I was doing? Didn't I? Maybe it would have been better if I just shouted my plans out Carol Anne's front door. Hell, you'd think I was the one who was married and cheating.'

He stared into her eyes without blinking. 'That's the problem, Suzanne, don't you see? I'm married and you don't seem to care. You don't complain or ask about my wife or if we have a sex life or even what she looks like. That's not normal. If you loved me, you'd be bugging the shit out of me about my wife. But you've never said a word. That makes me question your seriousness in this relationship.

'So when you told me you were having a girls night out that Friday, I went a little crazy. You *never* go out with the girls. I had to know if that was really what you were doing. If I found out you were with someone else, I'd die from jealousy. I'm insane over you, Suzanne. You've turned me into a crazy man.' He got down on his knees in the middle of the room and put his hands together in prayer. 'I plead insanity. Forgive me.'

Though she wanted to be angry, the sight of him on his knees made her burst out laughing. She couldn't help it. The hysteria grew, folding her over on the sofa, her hands crossed on her stomach and tears streaming from her eyes. He wasn't breaking up with her, and he wasn't leaving his wife. So he had her followed. His obsession with her was that strong. Vince was looking at her like a little boy who has been caught doing wrong. When he realized her laugh held no bitterness, he started laughing too. Only his was the nervous laughter of relief.

Suzanne sat up and wiped the tears from her face. She lowered her brows and frowned at him. 'Vince, I should be furious with you and throw you out of here. Instead I'm going to forgive you. But if you ever invade my privacy again, there won't be a second chance.'

'I swear, I'll never do anything like that again.'

'There is one thing about your confession that's bugging me though. What made you decide to tell me?'

'Because the police are looking for the guy I hired. Your friend Maggie gave them a phone number and they traced it to me. They have the misguided notion he might be involved in Angie's murder. I wanted to tell you about him before they did.'

'But why would Maggie have his number?' Her eyes widened as she remembered the scene in The Overhang. 'Oh, Vince, you don't think Maggie . . .'

He looked away.

'Oh my God,' was all she said.

She fell asleep quickly after their lovemaking, and Vince lay beside her in the dark still trying to catch his breath. Even in his depleted state, a ripple of excitement flowed through him. He studied her profile in the feeble light through the blinds and thought how he could never bear to be without her. For the first time in his married life, the notion of divorce occurred to him. It was amazing how fate could step in and change a life. A wrong turn. A chance encounter. A market crash. Sometimes you have to grasp an opportunity while you have it. Suzanne was an opportunity he didn't want to ever get away.

He knew it would cause his daughter a lot of pain. She too was the love of his life, but it was a different kind of love and he hoped she loved him enough to understand about this other one.

# THIRTY-NINE
## 2 Days Until

Three tough-looking punks, wearing torn T-shirts and backwards baseball caps, watched me descend the El stairs at the Fullerton stop. I glared back at them, daring them to mess with me. If they beat me up and left me for dead, they would be doing me a favor. It was nine o'clock and my day was finished. True to my promise to Marian, I'd made it across the finish line. My desk was clear, my inbox empty. The only work standing between me and the wedding was running into the office tomorrow to take care of a couple of last-minute details.

However, the easing of work pressure did nothing to ease the other pressure binding me. The horrid reality was my period still hadn't come. There was no dodging that I could be pregnant. I had actually stopped at Walgreen's and bought an early-pregnancy test, my last desperation play. Knowing might tell me what course to take.

The evening was pleasant with no humidity for a change and a mild breeze blew off the lake. Walking down the pavement beside closed stores and open diners, I took my time, trying to forestall the inevitable. I turned onto my street and walked slowly beneath the canopy of trees until I reached my building. Then I froze. Someone was sitting on the front steps in the shadow of the porch light. There was no face. Just a mass of dark frizzy hair sprouting from a pair of shoulders. My first thought was that it was a bag woman, but when the bag woman raised her head, I saw it was Carol Anne, her face so bloated and red from crying, she was barely recognizable.

I rushed to her and wrapped my arms around her. 'What is it? Did something happen to one of the kids?'

'The children are fine. It's Michael. Oh, Maggie, you're never going to believe this.' She was sobbing so hard I could barely understand her.

'It's all right. Let's go inside.' I fished my keys out of my purse and took her hand. We walked up the stairs to my apartment hand in hand. Once we got inside, I sat her on the couch and went into the kitchen to pour us each a glass of Pinot Grigio. Then I thought better of it and brought out the entire bottle.

I handed her a box of Kleenex and the wine and she blew her nose and took a blubbery sip. I waited for her to pull herself together. The glass was half-empty before she was finally able to talk.

'My life is ruined,' she moaned.

*Get in line*, I thought. She proceeded to unload a story that set me back on my heels: Michael's confession of his sexual leanings toward men, his promise to change in order to keep their marriage together. I had no words. Who would have ever suspected Michael Niebaum of being homosexual, or bisexual, or whatever the hell he was? He had always seemed to be the perfect mate. And he acted so very macho. That just shows what a person should make of appearances.

'I never wanted anyone to know – not even you – about all those years with hardly a sex life. It was too embarrassing. For the longest time I thought it was me, that I was unattractive or boring. Then, when Michael told me the truth, in a bizarre way I was happy to finally pinpoint the problem. I thought, *At least I know what I'm fighting.*'

She started crying again. 'But after all his talk about trying to change, nothing's changed. He was supposed to be home at five thirty tonight and when he hadn't shown up by seven I called his office. He said he had a late patient, but then I heard a man's voice in the background, and I flipped. You know all his patients are women.

'So I called a sitter and came to see you. I couldn't face it alone anymore. I needed to tell someone. I've been sitting here so long I was afraid you weren't coming home.' She reached into her purse and pulled out a pack of cigarettes. 'Do you mind if I smoke?'

We finished off the Pinot Grigio, Carol Anne chain-smoking the entire time, me fighting off the temptation to join her. I opened a second bottle of wine. Carol Anne waved off another glass saying she needed to sober up before driving home. That didn't put the brakes on me. I had nowhere to go. I poured another glass.

'Oh, and on top of all this,' Carol Anne sniffled, 'he's a suspect in Angie's murder.'

'Jeez, who don't those cops suspect? The guy I slept with is a suspect too.'

'Oh my God,' she said. 'I've been so wrapped up in my own problems I completely forgot about you and that guy. Did you get your period?'

I pointed to the white Walgreen's bag sitting on the table at the entry. 'Pregnancy test. The problem is a false negative can be fairly common in the week after the missed period, so if I get a negative I still can't be certain I'm not pregnant.'

'But if you get a positive?'

'Then at least I'll know for sure. Do you think I'd make a good unwed mother? That ought to go over big with my parents. Can you imagine my mother?'

'Forget about your mother. What about Flynn?'

I shook my drunken head. 'I don't know, I just don't know. I guess I'll wait till the last minute. They stopped the space shuttle once with twenty-seven seconds left to lift-off. I guess I can stop a wedding if I have to.'

The second bottle of wine was on its way to empty with Carol Anne's parting words ringing in my brain. *If you are pregnant you're not doing that kid any favors drinking all that alcohol.* I put the glass down and thought things over. I wasn't facing problems. I was facing challenges. I thought about Carol Anne's situation and came up with a drunken solution for both of us. If I had to call off my wedding and Carol Anne divorced Michael, we could live together and raise our kids as one big happy dysfunctional family like *Kate and Allie*. The telephone jarred me from my alternate reality.

'Hello,' I answered with a thick tongue.

'Maggie? Are you all right?' It was Flynn and he sounded irritated.

'Fine,' I replied, working to sound lucid. 'Carol Anne stopped over and we had a few glasses of wine, that's all.'

His silent reproach carried through the line. 'You better get some sleep. I don't have to tell you tomorrow is a big day. The Dartmouth crowd is coming in and I don't want you hung-over.'

Hang over this, I thought, raising a single finger in the air, delighted at my private rebellion. 'Don't worry about me. I'll be fine.'

He must have sensed the potential for an explosive situation, because his tone changed. 'Maggie, I know you've been under a lot of pressure. I don't mean to pick on you. I just want everything to be perfect. Now go and get a good night's sleep and I'll call you in the morning. All right?'

'OK, Flynn. Good night.'

'And, Mags. I love you.'

'Me too.'

I hung up thinking about the next day. Flynn's ten groomsmen were flying into O'Hare, and they would have to be shuttled to their hotels. My side of the wedding party was small by comparison, the one concession my mother had granted me. My only attendants were my two sisters, Flynn's sister, Nan, who was just returning from a semester abroad in Italy, and Carol Anne, who was my matron of honor.

I had emptied the last glass of wine in defiance when the phone rang again. Certain it was Flynn calling back, I snapped a gruff *hello* into the mouthpiece. The male voice was less familiar than Flynn's, but familiar, nonetheless.

'This is Steven.'

'Where did you get my number?' I demanded.

'I took it off your phone that morning,' he answered unapologetically. 'I'm leaving the state. I just wanted to let you know that.'

'Do you know the police suspect you in a murder?'

'You know it wasn't me.'

'How do I know?'

'Oh, c'mon,' he said.

'No, really. How do I know you didn't slip me something and then sneak out?' I asked, echoing Kelly's theory. 'What were you doing outside Carol Anne's that night? And why did you follow us into The Overhang and then seduce me after that?'

'It's not how it looks.' There was an extended silence, and then, 'Can I come over to explain? It's important to me that you know before I leave.'

'You can't tell me on the phone?'

'It's complicated.'

The wise thing would have been to answer an unequivocal *no* and hang up. Or just hang up. That would have been the wise thing to do. The rational thing to do. Well, no one could accuse me of being rational as of late, or even close, and having drunk myself to invulnerable, I saw no harm in letting him stop over for a few minutes. In fact, his visit might help me clear up a few questions I had within myself.

'All right, you can come over. But you better get here fast and you can't stay long.'

'I'm on my way,' he said.

I flopped down in front of the television, flicking from channel to channel in a futile search to find something to hold my attention. I was suffering through a rerun of *Cheers* when there was a gentle knock at my door.

I answered and he was there before me in the flesh, real not dreamed. He was more attractive than I remembered, his sinewy muscled arms poking from a black cotton T-shirt tucked into blue jeans. I blocked him from entering my apartment.

'Well?' I demanded.

'Can I at least come in?'

'Are you sure you're not dangerous?'

'No more dangerous than you.'

I moved aside and let him enter. 'You look nice,' he said casually, walking past me and settling into the same chair he'd sat in that morning way back when. He acted like a casual date for the evening. I wondered how he would feel if he knew my very life was poised to fall apart on his account. I perched on an arm of the sofa, working to exude an impersonal manner and keep my balance at the same time.

'I didn't invite you here to make comments on my appearance. I want some answers. You can start with your explanation of what you were doing in Kenilworth that night.'

'I was doing my job. I was hired to follow you girls around.'

I nearly fell off the sofa. While I listened in stunned silence, he told me about his boss and Suzanne being lovers and how his boss paid him to report back on Suzanne's activities. Though I was the other side of shocked to learn of Suzanne's affair, I pretended to have known about it all along.

'So were you spying on us the whole time we were at Carol Anne's house?'

'I spent most of my time in the truck. Though I did sneak around back after the stripper came and saw you handcuffed to the chair. That was the first time I noticed you, and I thought you looked pretty cute.'

My face heated up. Was it him or the wine? 'What then?'

'When you all were leaving I heard you tell Suzanne you'd meet her at The Overhang. So I stopped at a payphone to tell Vince what was going on and he told me to stick with Suzanne no matter what.'

I thought of first noticing him, sitting alone at the bar, his curls nearly in his beer. And then how my little joke of trying to pay for his drink had spelled my demise.

'So why didn't you follow Suzanne when she and Angie left? Why did you stay?'

Steven looked down and scratched the rug with the toe of his boot. I found the action endearing and couldn't help but think it was so refreshing he wasn't an MBA or an investment banker. His hands hung idly at his sides, those strong capable hands. I liked that he worked with his hands and created things that endured, things of real value, not money making money for more money's sake.

He looked up and gave me a smile that made me feel like Scarlett O'Hara with Rhett staring at her from the bottom of the stairs.

'I guess you could say, I got distracted by something a whole hell of a lot more interesting than Vince Columbo's girlfriend.'

I wanted to hate myself for the tingle that climbed my spine. *Oh, Lord, this is where I came in.* There was an inexplicable connection between us, an unspoken chemistry charging the air with desire. I thought about the possible child growing in my womb, an intimacy nothing could transcend. Before I could say anything, Steven was articulating my feelings. 'Do you believe in destiny? That we are meant to be together? Tell me you're not feeling it right now.'

Without intending it, I was leaning toward him, steel to a magnet. Every bit of decency in me told me this was immoral, but the indecent atoms kept pulling me closer. Then sanity prevailed momentarily and I drew back.

'You have to go now. I can't make this mistake again.'

Determination sparked in the coffee-colored eyes. 'Maybe it wasn't a mistake, Maggie. Maybe it was meant to be.'

And then, I put my drunken mouth in gear without engaging my drunken brain. 'Yeah, like my being pregnant was meant to be too?'

The moment the words rolled off my tongue I wanted them back, but that would be like bringing water up a drain. They could not be retracted. And though the words were intended as a slap, he took them as an invitation.

He crossed the space between us and lowered himself to the floor and buried his curly head in my lap. *You don't understand. This is all wrong.* It was the moral tug-of-war all over again. As much as I wanted to do right, my mental *nos* were giving way to *maybes*. He reached up and touched my face and I turned to gelatin, sliding from the sofa to the floor. Then I was on my back and his weight was upon me entirely, the hardness of him through his jeans a paradise just beyond reach.

My desire for him was so strong, there was nothing else. There was no Flynn, no wedding, no baby in my womb. His hands undid my bra and his mouth was at my breast. My mouth was hungry for him and I took his lips from my breast and covered them with mine. The lower hemisphere of my body was rotating, slowly at first, then faster, moving with him and then away, teasing him with delicious deprivation. Every bit of me was on fire, my face, my fingers, my toes. Even my ears throbbed with heat. I wanted so much . . . so much.

*Thump. Thump. Thump.*

The sound was disorienting. At first I thought we had knocked over a lamp, but the noise persisted, continually growing louder. With a passion-dousing gasp, I realized someone was pounding on the door. My heart stopped for a three count. Flynn had come to check on me. I could read the shock in Steven's eyes and his grip on me relinquished. I thought how pathetic it would be for Flynn to catch us like this.

Then came the voices and they sure didn't belong to Flynn.

'Police. Open the door. You have ten seconds or we break it down.'

'The bathroom,' I said to Steven, pointing down the hall. I jumped to my feet and tucked in my blouse, counting to ten before turning the knob. O'Reilly and Kozlowski burst into the room followed by two uniformed cops.

'Where's Kaufman? We have a warrant for his arrest,' O'Reilly demanded, barely giving me a look. His eyes went to the hall where a beam of light peeked out from under the closed bathroom door. 'There,' O'Reilly shouted. Kozlowski and the two uniforms positioned themselves outside my bathroom. 'Give him two seconds and then kick it in.'

'Wait,' I screamed, my compromised state only fueling the chaos. 'What are you doing?'

'We have a warrant for his arrest,' said O'Reilly.

'But he didn't kill Angie. He was with me,' I argued, tugging at his arm.

'This warrant's not for Angie's murder. It's an existing from the State of New Hampshire. For sexual assault and bigamy.' And then without any further notice, O'Reilly yelled to Kozlowski, 'Long enough. Get him out of there.'

I closed my eyes and waited to hear the door splinter into pieces. Seconds passed without a sound. When I opened my eyes the two uniformed cops were walking out of the bathroom guns drawn, shaking their heads. Inside, a fan ran for no one's benefit.

Swearing beneath his breath, O'Reilly ran into my bedroom followed by the others. The room was empty, the blinds blowing back and forth in the shadows. O'Reilly stuck his head out of my now screenless window and found himself looking at the fire escape.

As the circus played out before my eyes, I was oblivious to everything except O'Reilly's words reverberating in my ears like a bomb blast. Sexual assault was bad enough, but bigamy? *Bigamy!* To think I had almost thrown my life away for a son of a bitch who was not only married to one other person, but two.

# FORTY

## Kelly

Kelly checked her watch impatiently as she sat on a park bench across from Water Tower Place waiting for Detective O'Reilly. Surrounding her were neighborhood children letting off steam under the watchful eyes of nannies catching up on the morning's gossip in Polish and Spanish. Free of their condominium confinement, the children were the essence of unbridled energy, urban monkeys tackling jungle gyms, tornados spinning destruction in the play lot sand.

She checked her watch again. O'Reilly was already fifteen minutes late and Kelly was beginning to wonder if he was going to show at all. She just hoped he hadn't stopped in a bar on the way. He had sounded none-too-pleased to hear her voice this morning and less pleased when she insisted he meet her once again. Well, he could eat shit and die for all she cared. He was a public servant and she was a tax-paying citizen. She had to know if he had followed up on her tip about Maggie sleeping with the guy from New Hampshire. One thing was for certain, if she were on the force, the nightly news would never report that a suspect slipped away. Take for example that poor Asian kid killed at the hands of Jeffrey Dahmer. If she'd been one of the cops interviewing Dahmer, she would have smelled a rat for sure.

And she smelled a rat in New Hampshire. It confounded her that O'Reilly wasn't all over finding that guy. Though her opinion of the bleary-eyed cop was far more generous than it had been before learning about his childhood and his mother's premature death, she still questioned how much of his job performance was compromised by drinking.

Another ten minutes passed before she saw him coming across the street in front of the Ritz, his gait cocksure, his barrel chest assuring his arms never quite touched his sides. Though his shirtsleeves were rolled up, the heat and humidity had already drawn rings of perspiration in his armpits. When he got to the park, he picked his way through the dervish-like children and plunked down beside her. A missed ball rolled over and stopped at his feet. He picked it up and tossed it gently back to the little boy chasing it.

'You're late.' Kelly pointedly looked at her watch. 'I need to leave for work soon.'

'I'm a busy man. You're not the only case in my file. I mean, Angie's isn't the only case in my file. Nothing personal, Ms Delaney, but you're like the Chinese water torture. Drip, drip, drip, until a person thinks their head's going to explode. Now what is it today?'

She tried not to glare. 'Have you talked to Maggie yet about that guy?'

'Oh, have I ever,' said O'Reilly, suppressing ironic laughter. 'But before I tell you about it, let me ask you something first. You ever think about becoming a cop?'

'Furthest thing from my mind.' For the most part, her encounters with cops had been unsavory. 'But maybe after I get my psych degree I'll get a job as a police psychologist. God knows you guys could use it.'

He let the comment die. 'Well, I gotta admit you were right about something not being kosher with the New Hampshire guy. We ran his prints and found outstandings on him including sexual assault and bigamy.'

Kelly nearly flipped off the bench. 'I told you he was dangerous. Do you think he killed Angie? Thank God he didn't hurt Maggie. She told you what happened then? I'm sure he slipped her something that night.'

'Yeah, well, he sure didn't slip her anything *last* night.'

'What's that supposed to mean?'

O'Reilly was actually enjoying this. It was nice to have the upper hand for a change. He looked at her waiting impatiently for him to explain. She was tanned and freckled, her blue eyes as transparent as marbles. And then, as if seeing her for the first time, the notion occurred to him that she was actually quite attractive. For a moment, he lost his train of thought.

'What do you mean he didn't slip her anything last night?' Kelly repeated.

'Oh. Yeah,' he answered, his thought process back on track. 'Seriously, you should really talk to your friend about her judgment. Kaufman was in her apartment last night. A squad spotted his truck on her street and called it in. We went running in, swords drawn, but it appears his sword had been drawn first. Metaphorically speaking, that is.'

'That bastard was in Maggie's apartment!' Kelly couldn't believe what he was telling her. 'What, did he break in? Did you get the son of a bitch?'

O'Reilly's face fell slack in embarrassed defeat. 'He climbed out the window and got away. In light of his marital status, I should've known he'd be good at speedy exits.'

Kelly's mind raced through what she'd just learned. Did Maggie have shit for brains? Worse yet, how did the dipshit cops bumble catching him? When she looked back at O'Reilly, his face wore a contrite look. She felt bad for him for screwing this up after coming so close. Maybe they had more to talk about than finding the guy from New Hampshire.

'Do you live alone?' she surprised herself by asking.

'That's kind of personal.'

'I bet you don't eat real well.'

'What cop does?'

'Well, I was thinking you might like a good home-cooked meal some time. Italian with an Irish flair.' *Where were these words coming from?*

O'Reilly flushed and his already red face turned redder. It wasn't so much over this sudden display of interest in him, but because she was the one making the overtures. In his neighborhood, it didn't work that way. The man always made the first move. Even worse, he didn't understand how his absolute disdain for this woman could flip so randomly. His next words made him think he needed to take a few psych classes himself. 'Or maybe you wanna go out and have someone wait on you for a change?'

'When were you thinking of?'

'How about tomorrow night?'

'Can't. Tomorrow's Maggie's wedding.' She reflected a moment before adding, 'At least I think it is.'

O'Reilly couldn't stop from rolling his eyes. 'If that wedding takes place, that marriage sure ain't off to a good start. How about if I call you tomorrow, just in case?'

'Sounds like a plan.'

They left it at that and went in opposite directions, he back to the Ritz where the valet watched his car gratis, she towards Chicago Avenue and her lunch shift. She turned briefly and watched him go. He seemed to be walking straighter than before. Her stomach fluttered in an unfamiliar manner. *Don't go there. This is just an act of friendship.* She wasn't ready for anyone in her life other than her cat. Especially a cop with a drinking problem.

'Damn Irish curse,' she muttered aloud.

But the Irish suffer curses besides the drink, and Kelly was falling victim to that other Irish curse: martyrdom. In Detective O'Reilly she had found a cause, and far be it from her to abandon him. He needed her whether he knew it or not.

# FORTY-ONE
## One Day Until

My desk was perfectly clean, not a scrap of paper, not an empty coffee cup. Even the trash was empty. Against all odds, I had accomplished the impossible. I pushed my chair out and stood in the window, looking down enviously on the world below me. The cars on Michigan Avenue weaved from lane to lane like beetles scavenging for food. Little bodies scurried along the pavement, moving in concert alongside other bodies, each occupying his or her own world. Lives. Each untouchable stranger had a unique life with its bounty of happiness and sadness, success and failure, love and loss.

I would have traded places with any one of them. My Waterloo was upon me, and I was facing it with yet another hangover. The blinding pain in my head was an almost welcome distraction compared to the mental anguish centered beneath it.

How could the carpenter have fooled me so completely? What kind of person could do that? For that matter what kind of person was I, ready to give myself over to him again, completely blocking out all thought of the consequences. What was his hold on me? Even now, knowing who he was and what he was, the image of his head lying in my lap haunted me, like he was trying to connect to the possible – no, probable – life growing inside me. A maternal pang of conscience struck me for drinking so much. If my hangover was making me feel so lousy, I couldn't imagine the effect it was having on the little critter inside.

How I wanted to be away from this moment, to go back! I wished there was a time machine I could set pre-Steven Kaufman, pre-Flynn, pre-*Chicagoan*, pre-college. I wanted to be young again, before being caught in bed with Barry Metter, before the abortion I could never forget, before gaining all the weight that isolated me for so long. I wanted to go back and make the right choices, go back to college again and study theatre or creative writing or something with soul, even if I had to pay for it myself. I wanted to go back to that tight-knit circle of friends so close they were never more than a phone call away. I wanted to look forward to the future instead of dreading it. I missed summer vacations and part-time jobs. I hated looking in the mirror and seeing fine lines forming at the corners of my eyes and mouth. Not so much out of vanity, but because they were more proof of time rocketing past. I was middle-aged and had never done anything exciting or outrageous. My entire life had been about going along with the flow.

Well, the flow was about to turn upstream. My decision had been made. It had been made before the first of Flynn's two calls this morning when he was heading out to the airport for one of the Dartmouth shuttles. It had been made before talking to my mother for the third time today about the rehearsal details. It had been made before I snapped at Sandi for disturbing me, when the receptionist only wanted to know what time I planned on leaving. My decision had been made last night in the emptiness of my apartment after the police had gone, listening to Laura Nyro in the dark.

The earth had cracked, the waters were receding and a five-story tsunami was barreling in.

There was a knock, and Marian stuck her head into my office. Her prepared smile disappeared when she saw me standing in the window. My employer held her thoughts back on most occasions, but this was not one of them.

'Are you all right? You look like hell.'

I was certain I looked worse than hell. The fear, the indecision, the long hours of work, and the excessive boozing had taken their toll. My skin was the color of the pavement below and a pair of dark circles had taken up residence under my eyes. Even my hair was flat.

I tried telling her I was fine, but the words never made it from my mouth. My throat tightened around them, turning them into a pathetic squeak. Though I was too embarrassed to cry in front of my boss, I was too far gone not to. I buried my face in my hands and sobbed.

'Oh, honey, get a grip,' said Marian, showing a rare display of affection as she laid a gold-laden hand on my shoulder. 'It's only a wedding. They can be draining. I've been through a few myself. Do you want to talk about it?'

Shaking my head, I bit back the tears. There was nothing left to talk about. The cry had made me feel a little better, like a car's radiator letting off steam. Marian's presence was actually reassuring. She was a survivor of the first magnitude, living proof that being alone didn't necessarily mean death.

'I have to warn you,' Marian said. 'You might want to freshen yourself up a bit. There's a little crowd gathered out there waiting for you.'

So that was why Sandi kept pestering me about when I was leaving. I had answered her with rudeness. I really was the bitch of the planet. Marian stopped at the door and straightened her perfectly fitted jacket. 'I'll go out and hold them off for a few minutes. Will you be all right?'

I nodded and smiled foolishly, as I wiped my snotty nose. 'Thanks for having faith in me.'

'Why wouldn't I? Maggie, you've always done a superb job. You need a little more faith in you.'

The door closed leaving me with only a pressed-powder compact and lipstick to make myself presentable. The powder helped diminish the blotches around my eyes, and the lipstick added some color to my face, but nothing could lessen the anguish in my soul. The last thing in the world I wanted was to face a bunch of well-wishers who thought I was entering a wonderful new phase of life when I knew the opposite to be true.

I braced myself and stepped out into the hall.

'Surprise!'

My apartment felt lonelier than ever, the stacks of cardboard boxes giving silent testimony to a move. All the shelves were empty, my knickknacks and mementos, photos and books, all packed neatly away, ostensibly to be delivered to the new house while we were in St Bart's. Only the furniture remained in place, ready to be picked up by Goodwill. Though I'd lived in the same apartment for over ten years, I'd never invested much in my furniture, always assuming it was temporary, that I would be moving somewhere else soon. I put down the gifts from the office crew, next to the gifts from the lingerie shower, and wondered how long it was going to take to send everything back. On the upside, there wouldn't be any more thank-you notes to write.

It was just after two o'clock. The rehearsal at Holy Name was at six, and I was supposed to be there at 5:30. It was imperative I find Flynn before then.

I called his office and got a recording informing all callers that he was getting married and wasn't expected back for two weeks. Next I tried his townhome. Another answering machine. I left a message asking him to call me back as soon as possible. My phone rang not a minute later.

'Hello, my bride. What's up?'

'Flynn, are you alone?' A flurry of voices in the background told me the question was absurd.

'Nope. Bunch of the guys are here. And I'm on my way out the door to pick up Toady and Craig. Last trip. Last of the Sig Eps.'

'Oh. Will you call me as soon as you're alone? It's important.'

''K, babe. Gotta go. Traffic's going to be hell.'

After he hung up, I called my childhood home. I wanted to hear my mother's voice one last time while she still loved me. My older sister answered. My headache spiked as I realized Ellen and her family had flown in from New York that morning. I never thought I cared much what my sibling thought of me, but now I feared Ellen would hate me too.

'Mom's not here, but she should be back soon. She's picking up her dress. Are you excited?'

'I'm past excited,' was the best I could do. 'Don't bother to tell Mom I called. It's not important.'

'Then we'll see you at the church. And Maggie, don't be late. You know how that sets Mom off. Things go so much better when she's in a good mood. Take it from one who knows.'

I hung up feeling sorry for the legacy my sister would inherit. It was Ellen who would have her hands full dealing with my mother's mood later. I wondered how my father would react. Until now, I hadn't given much thought to the calm, loving man on the other side of the team that raised me. Would he still be so calm and loving when he realized how much money he had wasted on a wedding that was not to be?

I went into my bedroom and lay down, waiting for Flynn's call. The minutes ticked off into hours without a ring. At five o'clock, there was nothing else to do but get dressed and go to the church.

Before leaving, I threw the unopened pregnancy test into the trash. I had decided I didn't need it.

# FORTY-TWO
## Vince

Vince stared from his office window across the manicured lawn, hoping his blood pressure wouldn't push off the charts. The carpenter had flown the coop early last night, taking his truck and his tools with him, leaving an unfinished bar behind in Vince's game room. Vince was fairly certain he wouldn't see him again. Well, good riddance. Now that he had told Suzanne about having Kaufman follow her that night, the threat of her learning about him no longer loomed.

No, the thing spiking his blood pressure at the moment was the drama going on upstairs in his house. Giovanna was pitching a fit because he'd forgotten about some fundraiser they were supposed to attend tonight, and he had no intention of going. Not when the alternative was being with Suzanne.

'I told you about this months ago,' she shouted.

'Months ago is months ago. You should have reminded me. Now I'm committed to take some clients to the Sox game tonight. I have a box.' Sporting events were always convenient lies. 'How do you think we manage to afford this lifestyle we live?'

Opting for the universal feminine fallback position, she burst out crying. Now he was forced to make the unwelcome choice between cancelling his date with Suzanne and disappointing himself or keeping his date with Suzanne and disappointing his wife. Vince had always treated Giovanna well, given her just about everything she wanted, and taken care that she never learned of his affairs. It had been easy before because his previous infidelities had been short-lived, pleasurable but meaningless distractions from the tedium of marital sex.

But he hadn't recognized the hole that existed in his life before he met Suzanne. His feelings for her ran deeper than he'd ever thought possible. The day the two homicide detectives showed up at his door, he had realized he was more concerned over Suzanne's feelings than those of his wife. Even his daughter's paled in comparison. In fact, it had already occurred to him that if Giovanna found out about Suzanne, maybe she'd ask *him* for the divorce. He'd penciled out how much he was willing to give her. It was a lot more than he would have ever considered before Suzanne, but no price was too high to pay to have her in his life.

He dialed her number. The very sound of her voice turned him into a dog pining over a sirloin in the butcher's window. 'What time are you coming over? I picked up a little surprise at the lingerie shop around the corner,' she teased. 'I'm wearing it right now. Well, barely wearing it.'

His skin prickled and he fought hard not to feel cheated. 'There's a slight dilemma. I may not be able to make it tonight.' Before he could elaborate, the door opened and his daughter walked into his office. Her dark hair was piled up on her head and she wore a pair of cut-offs that he wished were several inches longer.

'Daddy, we need to talk.'

He covered the mouthpiece with his hand. 'Not now, Anna. Business.' She gave him an impatient look and flopped into a chair to wait. When he realized she wasn't going to leave, he uncovered the phone and spoke in a formal tone, 'Something's come up, Bob? Can I get back to you?'

The phone went wordlessly dead in his ear.

Vince turned back to his daughter. He wanted to be angry with her for disturbing him while he was talking to Suzanne, but it was impossible. She ruled his heart too.

'What is it, sweetheart?'

'Sorry to interrupt your *business*, Daddy.' Was it him or was that irony lacing her voice? 'Mom's upstairs crying. She says you refuse to go to the Arts Club gala with her tonight. You know how much those things mean to her. She bought a table. She'll be humiliated in front of her friends if you don't go.'

'I told your mother, I made a business commitment, sweetie.' He didn't sound very convincing – even to himself.

Anna came around behind his chair and massaged his neck.

'Daddy, please. You don't need to do business tonight. Please go with Mom. Please.'

He looked up into his daughter's pleading eyes and realized he couldn't fight both mother and daughter. He would be free someday, but it sure wasn't going to be tonight. His partial erection deflated as he realized Suzanne's surprise would have to wait.

'All right, I'll go. But under one condition. You must promise to buy the rest of the shorts next time.'

'I will, Daddy. I promise.'

Anna stopped rubbing his neck and headed toward the door. As he watched her move, soft flesh dressed in the tight shorts, her breasts pushing against her flared top, his father's heart skipped its usual beat. She was too young and trusting to be shaped that way.

'Wait,' Vince called out. She stopped and turned back toward him, 'What are you doing tonight, sweetie?' he asked, wanting to freeze the moment while they still loved each other uncon-ditionally and were still one happy family.

'I'm going out with Sal.'

His mood darkened again as he thought of the fast-talking West Sider she was seeing. He wanted to forbid her to see him, but that time was long gone. 'Well, have fun, but not too much fun,' he conceded. All Vince could hope was that she wasn't sleeping with him.

'Yes, Daddy.' She gave him an odd smile. 'I'll tell Mom to put your tux out.'

He waited until he heard her footsteps going up the stairs before calling Suzanne back. 'Sorry about cutting you short, but it was my daughter. As it turns out I'm not going to be able to see you tonight. Seems I have a command performance at a charity function. I'm so sorry.'

'Don't worry about it,' she said. 'With the new unemploy-ment figures coming out next week, I was on the phones all day and I'm beat anyhow. Guess I'll order a Canadian-bacon-and-pineapple pizza and eat it in front of the TV watching something mindless.'

It slayed him that she didn't sound disappointed that she wouldn't be seeing him. He had expected at least a little anger on her part, an indication she was as miserable without him as he was without her. But instead she seemed unperturbed. Not wanting to let her go yet, he prolonged the conversation, asking, 'A Canadian-bacon-and-pineapple pizza? Where do you get that?'

'From Parducci's.'

'Parducci's? The place on Huron? Now you're making my mouth water over food almost as much as it does over you. While you're enjoying your pizza think of me chewing a piece of overcooked beef and listening to some bore talk about why I should empty my pockets for the cause. I'll be wishing I was with you the whole time. Can I see you tomorrow?'

'You know I've got Maggie's wedding tomorrow. I'll see you on Sunday.'

Sunday. There was some conflict on Sunday, but what was it? The answer glared at him from his calendar. Brunch at the club with his wife and daughter. He had promised and he couldn't break his promise a second time. His heart sank at the thought of missing another Sunday morning in Suzanne's bed.

'I can't wait until Sunday,' he said, struck with a sudden inspiration. 'How about tomorrow morning? I'll come get you early. We can go out on my boat and look at the skyline. I promise to get you back in plenty of time to get ready for the wedding.'

'I never knew you had a boat.'

'You didn't? Yeah, it's in Belmont Harbor. Just brought it out of dry dock a couple of days ago,' he lied. The truth was the boat had been in its slip for a couple of weeks. He'd never mentioned the boat before because he never used it. It had been an anniversary gift to Giovanna because she thought they should have a boat. It turned out that neither his wife nor his daughter loved being out on the water, so it sat idle most of the time. Lately he had been thinking of selling it, as the upkeep was ridiculous, but now he was glad he hadn't. The thought of making love to Suzanne offshore was irresistible, trumping any concern over violating a family trust.

'All right. You're on my calendar for tomorrow morning, Mr Columbo. But we have to put in early . . .'

*Did she really say that?* 'That will be fine, Ms Lundgren.

Don't forget to bring that little surprise you were going to show me. And Suzanne . . .'

'Yes?'

'I . . . well, I'll tell you tomorrow.'

'I can't wait.'

'I can't wait either.' He held the phone to his ear long after she hung up as if it might help keep the connection to her. Speaking into the dead line, he added, 'Suzanne, I love you.'

He unlocked the bottom drawer and took out the strongbox where he kept the boat keys. They sat atop the pile of cash, attached to a little yellow buoy. He put them back in the strongbox and locked it back in the drawer. Then he headed reluctantly upstairs to dress for the evening of torture.

He was so distracted he didn't see his daughter huddled in the game room just outside his office, behind the unfinished bar.

'This is Parducci's on Huron. Can I help you?'

'Hi, I just ordered a pineapple-and-bacon pizza. I wondered if I gave you the right address.'

'Lundgren? 1025 Lake Shore Drive? Apartment 4025?'

'That's it. How long did you say it was going to take?'

'About an hour and a half. Sorry, we're really buried tonight.'

'You know what, just cancel my order. I'll go out for something.'

'Will do. Have a nice evening.'

Anna Columbo hung up the phone feeling very pleased with herself.

# FORTY-THREE
## Wedding Eve

The massive triple doors of Holy Name Cathedral rose before me, the church the European-style showpiece of the Chicago archdiocese. It had taken a lot of string-pulling, not to mention an obscenely generous donation on my father's behalf, to get a June wedding date on relatively short notice. Some people waited years. I took the steps one leaden foot after another. Upon reaching the top I hesitated, trying to prolong the moment in time. It was so humid the air clung to my skin like wet cheesecloth. Taking a last damp breath to fortify myself, I opened a heavy wooden door and stepped into the cool, dark vestibule.

I blessed myself with holy water and walked into the church, the echo of my heels making the empty cathedral larger than it already was. I sat down in the last pew and took in the magnificence of the sacred place where my wedding was to take place the next day. It was pure Gothic Revival with pink marble columns ascending to a vaulted ceiling inlaid with gold. Floor-to-ceiling stained-glass windows filtered the evening sun. Christ kept watch over me from a golden cross on the distant altar. I prayed to him for both strength and forgiveness.

The hollow sound of the doors opening rocked the silence, and I turned to see my mother and my two sisters come into the church. Ellen was holding the hand of her daughter, Olivia, the flower girl. Laurel was carrying a CD player, a headset hugging her ears. I finished my prayer and got up to greet them. My mother's face told me how bad I looked. 'Oh Lord, you're not sick, are you?' she demanded, her concern resounding through the empty church. 'You didn't look well the last weekend at Natasha's, but this is worse.'

My younger sister plopped into a pew and closed her eyes, moving her body to the music.

'Laurel, this is a church. Put that away,' my mother snapped. She put a hand to my forehead. 'You don't have a temperature.'

'I told you, I'm fine,' I repeated, knowing I was anything but.

'Hi, stranger,' said Ellen, touching her cheek to mine. 'We would have been here earlier, but traffic into the city was inhumane. I'll bet you everyone's going to be late.'

*Fine*, I thought. More time to contemplate my suicide.

Flynn's younger sister, Nan, was the next to arrive, her face flushed and red from the heat. She shared her brother's blonde hair and cornflower-blue eyes, but unlike Flynn, who was fit and trim, Nan was plump with a full second chin and sausage-like arms that had grown after her semester overseas. Getting her bridesmaid gown fitted from Italy had been a nightmare with her having to call in her changing measurements several times. She drew me to her in a damp hug.

'I'm so excited,' she said in a squeaky-girl voice. 'I picked up my dress today and it fits perfectly. Everything is going to be so gorgeous.'

Another pang of relentless conscience. Nan had made it abundantly clear how honored she was to be standing up in the wedding. I thought about the $700 bridesmaid's dresses of lilac silk and the cloth shoes tediously dyed to match. I thought about my own $3,000 virginal white dress hanging on a special rack in my former bedroom, awaiting its fleeting moment in the spotlight before being relegated to preservation. I thought about the $80-a-plate veal chop with wild rice and seasonal vegetables, and the $20 per glass Taittinger toast. The band. The flowers. The personalized napkins.

Most of all, I thought about Flynn.

I prayed for some disaster to deliver me from my unhappy task. Like a tornado ripping off the top of the church or an earthquake crumbling it to its very foundation. If not that, then a sniper's bullet striking me as I exited the church after the rehearsal would do quite nicely.

All such wistful thought came to an abrupt end as Flynn made a noisy arrival, flanked by his rambunctious entourage from Dartmouth, the roar of their voices threatening to dislodge the gold from the vaulted ceilings. Toady Cornwall, the best man, and Bart Pierce, one of the groomsmen, were making age-old stupid jokes about marriage being an institution and who would want to be in an institution. They came over to me en masse, leaving me feeling like I had just stepped into a frat party. Doing my best to resurrect a personality, I tried joking with them and was failing miserably when I saw Carol Anne slip into the back of the church and take a seat.

I excused myself to have a word with her. Carol Anne looked like she hadn't slept well either. I put an understanding hand on her arm and asked, 'How are you doing?'

'I'll live. Michael and I had more discussion. This time he swore he's going to get help and not just give me lip service, so I've agreed to try and work things out. How about you?'

'Let me put it this way. Don't bother paying too much attention to Father Jennings instructions,' I whispered.

'The test was positive?'

I shook my head. 'I didn't take it. I don't need to.'

'Oh, Maggie.' True friend that she was, Carol Anne shared my anguish. 'When are you going to tell him?'

'After this charade, I guess. I tried to do it today, but I couldn't get him alone.'

Tears welled in Carol Anne's eyes, but I stopped her. 'Don't go there. I'm having a hard enough time as it is.' I gave her hand a hard squeeze. 'Promise me you'll still be my friend. You may be my only one.'

'Here's my blushing bride,' said Flynn, interrupting us. His smile faded when he saw how haggard I looked, but he recovered quickly. 'We've been looking for you.'

'Always,' said Carol Anne touching my arm as Flynn led me away.

My father had arrived, tall and distinguished looking, his graying hair slightly receded, his round tortoiseshell eyeglasses pressed high up his nose. He had come from his law offices in the Loop and his navy suit and blue tie remained perfectly pressed. I thought about all the good fatherly things he had done for me over the years. Paid for my education and the abbreviated trip to Europe; quelled my mother's hysteria on that worst day of my life when I was caught in bed with Barry Metter. Well, the first worst day of my life. He didn't know about the second worst. Yet.

Father Jennings came in from the rectory, dressed in priestly black with a white collar, his bald head shiny under the glow of the church lights. The middle-aged priest had a casual attitude, making him feel more like a friend than a religious leader, and my guilt multiplied thinking of all the time he had invested in pre-cana with Flynn and me. *Have you discussed who will take care of the finances? Do you both feel the same way about children? Does Flynn expect to have a night out with the boys?*

'Here's my lucky couple,' he said, giving me a friendly kiss on the cheek and shaking Flynn's hand. 'Is everyone here?'

'If they aren't, then they're missing out on being part of the best wedding of the year,' said Flynn. My flesh grew goose bumps and I seriously feared I would barf.

The priest clapped his hands to quiet the crowd, and the inside of the church fell silent except for the sound of Toady's voice, which diminished a minute later. Acting more like a stage director than a man of God, Father Jennings called out, 'OK, people. Let's do this so everyone can go to dinner.'

For the next agonizing hour, he walked us through the mechanics of the ceremony, sorting out people by their role, best man, maid of honor, flower girl, ring bearer. I came close to losing it when we did the run through of my father walking me down the aisle. I loved my father so much, the last thing I wanted was to hurt him too. My relationship with him while growing up had been different from that of either of my sisters. I never pouted or threw temper tantrums to get my way like Ellen had. Nor had I been like Laurel, dependent on him for everything from filling out college applications to opening her checking account. I knew he always appreciated my acceptance of things as they were, my lack of neediness. We were the same in many ways. Neither of us was complainers. We just sucked things up and did them.

My mother was tracking every move of the rehearsal, filing it away in her steel-trap brain for later analysis in order to make any needed corrections. She was one of the most organized and meticulous people on the planet, her house beautifully decorated and always immaculate, her parties always perfectly orchestrated. Her entire life revolved around order. I hoped she was up to managing the disorder that was to descend upon her soon.

My eyes moved to Flynn, beaming in the combined presence of family and friends. He was such a good person, had been so good to me, that I hoped when it was all over he ended up hating me. I deserved it.

Everyone gathered in the vestibule after the rehearsal. Flynn was sorting out transportation to the Chicago Club when I took him by his arm and peeled him away.

'Flynn, I want to ride with you. Alone. I need to talk to you.'

'Sure, Mags,' he said agreeably, doing his best to cover his puzzlement.

Once the last of the guests was on their way, we crossed the street together into the church parking lot. As I climbed into Flynn's spotless Audi for what I was certain would be the last time, my heart was beating so loudly it practically muffled his voice.

'What's with all the mystery, Maggie?' he asked as he pulled out onto the street.

There was no way to evade it any longer. I was through with lies. 'Flynn, before anything else, I want you to know that I care for you deeply and this is the hardest thing I've ever had to do in my life.'

His jaw tightened in anticipation of something unpleasant, but his eyes remained fixed on the city street, a steeplechase of stop signs, stop lights and bicycles.

*Deep breaths, like in yoga. Inhale. Exhale. Inhale. Hold. Let it out.* 'I cheated on you. I had a one-nighter.'

The air inside the car turned dense. Flynn pulled across two lanes of traffic and screeched to a stop at the curb, nearly taking out a cyclist in the process. His hands gripped the steering wheel so tightly his knuckles were white peaks. He rolled down the driver's window, and the noise of the surrounding traffic filtered into the car, leaving us not so alone together. He didn't look at me at first. Then ever so slowly he turned his head in my direction. Anguish flickered like buried embers in his blue eyes.

'Why are you telling me this now?' he said quietly.

I reached out and touched his arm, wanting desperately to make contact with him for the last time, to touch the flesh that had once been my future. 'Because I think I'm pregnant.'

'Maggie, tell me I didn't hear you right.' When my only response was silence, he banged the dashboard so hard the car rocked. It was the closest I'd ever seen him come to violence. 'Maybe somehow we could reconcile cheating. But a pregnancy? I'd ask you who or why or how, but that doesn't really matter does it? Not if you're pregnant.'

'Flynn, I'm sorry. So sorry. How can I ever explain?' I fought not to cry. I didn't want him to think I had the gall to expect his sympathy. But the tears started anyway, flowing down my face and spilling onto my dress, making me sorry it was still light out so that the passersby could see inside the car. In a gesture that nearly tore me apart, Flynn rested his head on my shoulder and started crying too.

'Why, Maggie, why?'

I didn't know how to answer him. I wasn't certain of the answer myself. All I knew was that us together as a couple wasn't enough for me and never had been. That I had never really been in love with him. It wasn't that I wanted something more, but I wanted something else. The swiftly moving current of middle age had caught me up and I hadn't been brave enough to break free of its pull. Until this moment. But I could never explain this so he could understand it. The best I could do was rock my former fiancé gently back and forth, saying over and over again, 'I'm sorry. I'm so sorry.'

# FORTY-FOUR

## Suzanne

S uzanne was watching the news when the doorman called
from the lobby.

'Ms Lundgren, there's a delivery for you here.'

'Thank you, Alvin. Send it up.'

She turned off the TV and went into the foyer, surprised her
pizza had arrived so soon. When she'd placed the order,
she'd been told they were running an hour and a half for
deliveries and here it was in under an hour. Well, there was
no sense in complaining about a pizza arriving sooner than
later. She was starving.

She stood in her doorway and waited, holding enough money
in her hand for the pizza and a generous tip. The elevator doors
opened and instead of the usual green-capped Parducci's delivery
man, a voluptuous raven-haired girl stepped out carrying a
brown shopping bag.

'Suzanne?' she enquired, looking towards the doorway.

'Yes,' Suzanne replied cautiously. She'd never had a delivery
person address her by her first name, and besides where was
Parducci's signature box? The shopping bag sure didn't look
like it held a pizza. An impulse to slam the door came over her,
an impulse she failed to act on. The girl stared at her from dark,
unreadable eyes.

'I'm Anna,' she said with a broad-lipped smile. 'Vince's
daughter.' Before Suzanne had a chance to speak, Anna added,
'My father sent me to get you. He's at the boat and he wants
you to meet him there.'

Suzanne was stunned speechless. She sized up the young
woman standing at her threshold. There was something familiar
about her she couldn't pinpoint, or was that just Vince's DNA
she was seeing? More importantly, what was Vince thinking,
sending his daughter over to collect his mistress for a romantic

rendezvous? Had he lost his mind? The very notion stretched the limits of sanity. When Suzanne found her voice it was an angry one. 'Look Anna, I'm not quite sure what's going on here, but I'm not going anywhere. You can tell your father I'm in for the night.'

'You don't understand,' the girl implored. 'My mother knows all about you. She confronted him tonight just before they were supposed to go to the gala. They had a big fight over you and she threw him out of the house. He's staying on the boat.'

'So why didn't he come to get me,' Suzanne asked skeptically. 'Why would he send you?'

'Daddy thinks my mother's hired a private detective. He didn't want to come to your apartment himself in case he's being followed. He's afraid my mother is going to take him for every cent. She can be quite a vindictive bitch,' Anna added.

Suzanne felt herself boiling with anger. She couldn't believe Vince had put her on the spot like this. It was weird enough that he had her followed the night of the party, but now sending his daughter to retrieve her like she was some kind of chattel? That was over the top. Really over the top. She was having none of it.

'Anna, it was very nice of you to make the trip here to get me, but you can tell your father if he wants to see me he can call me. I'm in for the night. Goodbye, now.' Suzanne started to close the door, but the girl reached out and touched her arm.

'You don't understand,' she pleaded. 'I promised I'd bring you. Don't make me let him down. I told him we can be friends. All I care about in the world is my dad's happiness.'

Suzanne looked into Anna's strange pleading eyes. She knew how much the girl meant to Vince, and how hard the collapse of his family would be on him. And she understood only too well his concerns about his wife going after his money. Well, that was his problem and something that he would have to deal with on his own. Then her own finances crept into her mind. The penthouse was tied to him through the loan. If things went the wrong way, could Vince's wife somehow end up getting her home? Could she sue Suzanne for alienation of affection? There had just been a case in the *Tribune* where a wife won a million dollars from the girlfriend. Suzanne began to feel panicked. Maybe it was better that she and Vince talk after all.

'All right, I'll come with you,' she capitulated. It wasn't until they were riding down the elevator in silence that Suzanne remembered she'd ordered a pizza. She gave the doorman money to pay for it and told him to share it with the staff.

'My boyfriend's waiting in the car,' said Anna. She led Suzanne around the corner to a silver Buick parked in front of an expired meter. Loud music was emanating through the tinted windows. Anna opened the back door for Suzanne and then climbed in front. 'This is Sal,' she said, pointing to a dark head hunched behind the wheel.

'Yo,' he grunted without turning around as he pulled onto Lake Shore Drive. The music was so loud it was virtually impossible to think, so Suzanne asked him to lower it. This time he glanced back at her, and when she saw his face, she thought he looked familiar too. Surely she couldn't forget a face like his. Then her blood iced her veins as she noticed the heavy gold Rolex and gold bracelet wrapped around his wrist.

Angie's taunting words echoed in her brain. *I make it a policy to never dance with someone wearing more jewelry than me.*

Now she knew where she had seen him before. At The Overhang. And Anna too. Only Anna had been blonde that night. Warning bells started going off and she decided that she was going to get out of the car at the first opportunity. When they exited the Outer Drive at Belmont, she waited until they stopped for the light and then pulled on the door handle. The warning bells turned to sirens. The door refused to open. It was locked from the outside.

# FORTY-FIVE

## Vince

Vince stood in his walk-in closet working his bow tie in front of the full-length mirror. Having resigned himself to his fate, he had decided to go with the flow and make the most out of the fundraiser with its bores, bad food, and long speeches. Maybe he could do some business. He tugged at the tie until he achieved the desired result and stood back to admire himself. He really wished Suzanne could see the imposing figure he cut in the penguin suit. Then he buried the thought. It only made her seem that much farther away. He went into the master bathroom where his wife sat at her vanity putting on makeup.

'What do you think?' he asked, pointing at the tie.

'So much work,' she said, squinting as she applied eyeliner. 'I don't know why you don't just get a tie that's already done. You make things so difficult.' Giovanna was immensely relieved that her husband's earlier foul mood had dissipated. She loved getting dressed up and going to events with rich, important people. With only a high school education, she was never quite sure she fit in with this crowd, but then again, money was the great equalizer. She wanted Vince to bid on an expensive auction item tonight, to put her that much closer to acceptance in Oakbrook society. She had her eye on a lot that included a week at a villa in Tuscany and a private tour of something called the Uffizi. She wondered if it was a restaurant.

Knowing his wife would be another half hour with her makeup, Vince went down to the game room and poured himself a vodka at the unfinished bar. He took the drink outside onto the patio where the evening sun had painted the manmade lake a shimmering gold. He had just taken a bracing sip when a movement caught in his peripheral vision. He pivoted to see Kaufman crouched in the bushes, his clothes gray with dirt, his dark curls falling in greasy spirals.

'What in hell are you doing here?' Vince demanded.

'Hiding from the cops for one,' he replied, scoping out the yard like an animal checking for predators. 'You wouldn't believe what I had to do to get here. Do you mind if we go inside?'

'What the fuck?' said Vince, opening the sliding door to the game room. The moment they were inside he turned to the carpenter, and demanded, 'What the hell happened to you last night? I fuckin' put my ass on the line for you, I put you up at my house, give you money and food, and you go and pull a disappearing act. Well, don't expect to stay here anymore. I already told Suzanne the truth, so I don't give a flying fuck if the cops find you now.'

Kaufman stood at the bar, running his hand along the smooth wood. 'This was gonna be beautiful,' he lamented before turning back to Vince. 'Look, I'm not asking to stay, but I need your help. There are some outstanding warrants on me, and I've got to get out of the state. I need more money.'

'Warrants? What do you mean warrants? What kind of warrants?'

Steven shrugged and held his former employer's gaze. 'Assault and bigamy. The charges are bullshit. It's a long story.'

'Yah. Well, my wife takes forever to get dressed. I got plenty of time.' He stared at the carpenter with growing anger as he realized he had allowed a man with assault charges to eat and sleep in the same house as his wife and daughter. Vince had always considered himself a good judge of character. Had he made a mistake in Kaufman's case? He took a good look at Steven, pulled out another glass and filled it with vodka. He handed it over to the bedraggled carpenter. 'Go ahead,' said Vince, turning back to stare out the window. 'I'm all ears.'

Steven took a measured sip and started to pace. 'Like I said, those charges against me are a piece of shit. You want the short story or the long story.'

'Short story'll do. My wife's not *that* slow.'

'The short story is I married Meghan, my high school sweet-heart, right after graduation. We were way too young and thought we were in love, and I suppose we were – then – but after a few years we realized it was a mistake. We were more like brother and sister than husband and wife. So we decided to get a friendly divorce. No big deal, right? We went to this attorney who told us since we didn't have any kids it would be easy. The deal was Meghan got the house, which didn't have much equity in it anyway, and I kept my truck and all my tools. I heard about some work in Manchester, so I signed a bunch of papers, gave her the money for the lawyer and told her to take care of finalizing things. One day she calls me and says, *Congratulations. We're divorced.*

'So, now I'm in Manchester working for one of the local contractors who had this hot-looking daughter named Heather. I swear, this chick was nothing but trouble. She starts showing up wherever I'm on site, basically throwing herself at me. Her being the boss's daughter and all I did my best to avoid her. I mean, who needs that kind of trouble, right?

'Then one day she shows up when I'm alone installing some kitchen cabinets,' Steven continued, 'and next thing I know we're banging on the plywood floor. After that she starts showing up more often, and well . . . you get the picture. Next thing I know, she's telling me she's pregnant and that if her father found out he would beat her senseless and that I had to marry her. I mean, we never even had a date. Just sex at construction sites. And I seriously doubted I was the only one doing her.

'I tell you, I thought about getting in my truck and hauling ass out of there. But my guilt wouldn't let me do it. So we eloped. Her father didn't care much for that, but once it was done it was done. The asshole even gave me a raise.

'A few months go past and Heather isn't getting any fatter. Turns out she lied about being pregnant. She just wanted someone to get her out from under her father's thumb, and I ended up the stooge. When I found out there wasn't a baby, I told Heather I wanted out. So I called my ex-wife to find out who handled our divorce because it had been so easy. That's when the real nightmare began.'

Steven stopped pacing and downed the better part of the vodka. Vince's eyes turned towards him, unblinking as he sipped his own drink. 'I'm still listening,' he said. Steven resumed his pacing.

'Turns out my divorce was never finalized, because Meghan

used the money I gave her to buy a car instead of paying the lawyer. So, shit, here I am with two wives through no fault of my own. I decided to get out of Dodge and deal with the marriages later. I was almost out of Manchester when I got pulled over. Cops put me in handcuffs and threw me in the back of the patrol car.

'When we get to the station, my new father-in-law is there and next thing I know he cold cocks me so hard he nearly broke my jaw. The cops are holding him back and he's yelling that when he's through with me, I'm going to wish I looked one-tenth as good as his daughter. Then Heather walks in and if they didn't tell me it was her, I swear to God I wouldn't recognize her. Her face looked like it's been through a meat grinder. I don't know what happened, but her lip was split wide open and one of her eyes was swollen shut. And she's telling the cops and her old man I did this to her. It was like she was the guy in *Dirty Harry* who gets himself beat up and blames Clint Eastwood. Only I was Clint Eastwood.

'And her old man is not the type to listen to explanations. He's the shoot first, ask questions later type, so I know I'm as good as dead if he ever gets his hands on me. I called Meghan to make my bail, she owed me that much, and the minute I was out I blew town and didn't look back. It was either my father-in-law or prison and neither looked very appealing.

'That's the truth. I swear it. I'm not a bad guy. Just the victim of some pretty crappy circumstances. And I wouldn't be in this huge mess now if you hadn't asked me to . . .' He lowered his voice and looked up the stairs before continuing in a near whisper. '. . . if you hadn't asked me to follow your friend.'

Vince chewed over the carpenter's story. As wild as it was, he had no reason to disbelieve it. Kaufman had always been a straight shooter with him. 'I may be a fool, but I'll help you out. How much do you need?'

'Just enough to get me to Colorado and to buy some new tools. I know a guy working around Aspen who says they're starting to build like crazy around there. The cops have my truck, so I'll have to take a bus. Can you front me a couple grand?'

'That all?' said Vince almost as if he meant it. He went back into his office and brought out the strongbox. The first thing he noticed upon opening it was the boat key was no longer sitting atop the stack of hundreds. Which made no sense since it had been there not an hour ago when he made the date with Suzanne. He started opening and closing drawers thinking perhaps he'd absentmindedly put it into the wrong one.

'Everything OK?' Steven asked.

'Yeah. Just misplaced something.'

He was still riffling through his desk when his private line rang.

'Hello,' he barked.

'Hey, I got some good news, bad news, really bad news for you.' There was no mistaking the nasal voice of Charley Belchek. After telling Suzanne the truth about having her followed, Vince had almost forgotten about his deal with the ex-cop. 'The good news is I found out who did the chick in Lincoln Park. The bad is I had to spread a shitload of fertilizer around. Sixty large. You good for it?'

'Of course,' Vince replied, knowing it probably cost Belchek about half that. But a deal was a deal. And though he didn't care about getting the cops off Kaufman's ass anymore, presenting Suzanne with the person who murdered her best friend would make him golden in her eyes.

'Hold on a minute,' he said to Steven who sat anxiously waiting for the money.

'You talkin' to me?'

'No, Charley. Got somebody else here. Go ahead.'

'So like I told you,' Belchek continued, 'you throw enough fertilizer around and you can grow anything. Me, I start with the prison population first. Usually there's someone you can buy in exchange for a favor. You know, help out the felon's family or something like that. Now, I gotta tell ya, from the beginning I was sure it was some shine who did her. Or some spic. But when I wasn't hearing anything from my usual Afro-American or Latino contacts, I moved to the lighter side of the tracks.

'Turns out there's a punk named Rico in on a B and E at County. Guess he had this cellie named Joey in on a possession charge. So Joey's reading the days' old papers they get to read

– they do read, some of them – and he points to a picture and says, 'I know who did this girl.' A couple days later Joey's sprung and that's that. When Rico gets word about my little incentive, he gets in contact and puts me on to Joey. When I find this Joey, he's all clammed up until I up the incentive, and then he's willing to share. Seems he's got a bit of an H problem.

'Told you spreading the green grows things,' he added as an aside.

'Can you get to it, Charley? I've got to be somewhere within the year,' Vince nudged.

'Right. So Joey tells me he was with this guy and some broad and they picked up the girl who ended up dead outside some bar. She's all drunk and Joey smells trouble, so he decides to beat it. But he's dead certain, the guy did her. Says his buddy's done some contract work in Lake County, enforcement, debt collection and all, and so snappin' a neck wouldn't be nothing for him.'

'Gotta name?'

'Name is Salvatore Gianfortune. Goes by Sal. You know how I said there was good news and bad news and really bad news. Here comes the really bad news. He's been mouthin' off all over about . . . uh . . . spending time with your daughter.'

Vince dropped the phone and instinctively reached for the gun he kept taped beneath the drawer. The space was empty. He jumped up from his desk and ran through the game room to the foot of the stairs.

'Giovanna,' he howled. 'Is Anna still home?'

'No. She left while you were in the shower. You coming up? I'm ready to go.'

The missing boat keys. The missing gun. He turned to Steven who had followed him out of his office. He looked at his well-knuckled hands. He had seen the carpenter unload an entire truck of wood by himself and carry it around to the backyard. 'My daughter's in danger. Come with me,' he commanded.

With Steven close behind, Vince took the stairs by twos and roared into the kitchen where his wife was waiting for him in a strapless Dior evening gown, her hair piled on top of her head, clusters of diamonds around her neck and at her ears. One look at her husband's terrified face put the fear of God in her. She couldn't remember ever seeing him look so frightened. 'What is it? What's wrong?'

Vince stared at the woman he had shared the last twenty-two years with. He couldn't tell her that their daughter was in the company of an assassin, couldn't burden her with that knowledge. That was too much for any mother to know. He wouldn't tell her anything until he was certain their daughter was safe.

'Giovanna, I'm sorry. I can't go tonight. There's been an accident at one of the building sites. I'm sorry,' he repeated. He brushed her lips quickly and ran out to the garage with Steven on his heels.

Upon hearing the words *building site*, Giovanna's fear was transformed into rage. How dare he desert her when she was all dressed up and ready to go? There was always something with that business. Didn't he pay people to take care of things for him? Well, this time she wasn't going to stay home and suffer in silence. This time she would go by herself and make excuses for him. But she hoped he was prepared to pay for that trip to Tuscany, because she was not going to be outbid.

# FORTY-SIX

The stretch of Indiana Toll road was consoling in its emptiness, the high beam of my headlights the only thing to
cut the endless gray. I sped across the open country,
seldom encountering another vehicle, finding security in being
unreachable. I wasn't sure where I was going. I only knew that
for the time being, I was free of other people's opinions and
judgments.

My tears had stopped sixty miles back. They had been torren-
tial when I left Flynn alone in the Audi, worse in the taxi to
my apartment. I was crying so hard the taxi driver wouldn't let
me pay for the ride. The way my heart ached, it was a miracle
it even continued to beat. If it had stopped beating, I don't know
that I would have cared.

The moment I stepped into my apartment, I called the restaurant and asked for my father. When he picked up the phone
the concern in his voice was apparent. Where were we? Flynn
and I were expected a half hour ago. Everyone was worried
about us.

I told him right then, a cold delivery of a cold reality. *Because
of some major differences, Flynn and I have decided we can't
get married.* That was the line Flynn had come up with to save
us both the humiliation of the truth. The part about me being
pregnant could wait for later. My almost wedding would prove
enough trauma for my parents for one day. And Flynn.

My father tried to keep me on the line while he sent someone
in search of my mother. Whenever something major went wrong
in his life, his wife could always fix it. I didn't know how to
make him understand this was one thing my perfect mother
couldn't fix.

'Dad, don't get Mother. What's happened can't be changed.
There's not going to be a wedding.'

'We're coming right over,' he said.

'Dad, don't do that. I won't be here. I'm going away. I'm sorry. I'm really sorry.' I hung up thinking how much I'd used those last words in recent days. My apologies had grown tiresome in their necessity. One thing I knew for certain was I had to leave quickly. The phone was bound to start ringing at any second, so I took it off the hook. I grabbed a quick change of clothes, some of the necessary toiletries, and hurried from the apartment. I climbed into my car, determined to take the first highway I saw.

Three hours later I was halfway to Toledo. No one would ever think to look for me there. Not even myself.

So I sped across the vast Midwest unaware that while my headlights cut a path to nowhere, another drama of a far more frightening nature than mine was unfolding.

# FORTY-SEVEN
## Suzanne

B elmont Harbor was veiled in lead-colored light, the hue of an unrestored Renaissance painting. Sal pulled to the far end of the nearly empty parking lot and turned off the ignition, the blaring music replaced by ominous silence. Anna turned around and grinned at Suzanne, a raven-haired Cheshire cat.

'Here we are,' she said.

Not wanting to let them see her panic, Suzanne kept pulling on the door handle with no result. 'Excuse me, but I'm not able to get out of the car,' she said with false calm.

Sal smacked his head with the butt of his hand. '*Stupido*. It's child-locked. I had my nephews yesterday.' It was the first he'd spoken other than the grunted greeting. He got out of the car and came around to Suzanne's side. He opened the door and flicked a lever in the door panel. 'See. Childproofed.'

Suzanne's veins flooded with relief that there was an explanation. Maybe she had been a little paranoid. So what if Anna and Sal had been in The Overhang? But then an even weirder thought took root. What if Vince had sent them there to spy on her too? Would he actually put his daughter up to such a thing? A new spike of anger overrode her common sense.

'Where is your father?' she demanded.

Anna pointed to the far dock. 'He's on the boat.'

'Well, then, let's go talk to him.'

They walked through the marina parking lot past a family carrying beach towels and tote bags to their car in the dimming daylight. When they reached the pier, Anna punched in a security code at the metal gate that kept intruders from accessing the boats. The door clanged closed behind them, and the noise echoed flatly across the harbor. A sense of being trapped descended upon Suzanne again. In the deepening dusk, lights glowed from within a few boats in the harbor, but aside from a small, tired-looking cabin cruiser two slips up, the vessels lining the dock she was standing on were dark.

'Which boat is it?' she asked, holding her ground.

'There,' said Anna, pointing to an impressive cruiser moored the end of the pier.

'That boat is dark. I thought you said your father was here.'

'He must be taking a nap,' said Anna.

Suzanne recalled a seminar on safety she'd attended years ago. It was given by a retired cop who maintained fear was the body's built-in warning bell against dangerous situations. The warning bell had sounded at her apartment and again in the Buick, but she had ignored it. Well, it sure as hell was sounding now. In her eagerness to talk to Vince, she'd taken leave of common sense. If she'd paid attention to her instincts in the first place, she'd be home eating pizza instead of staring at the darkened hull of a cabin cruiser that Vince wasn't on and hadn't been on all evening.

Suzanne remembered another key point from the seminar. *Never permit yourself to be taken to a secondary location.* Things didn't get any more secondary than a dark boat in a dark harbor. Deciding she'd acted stupidly long enough, she turned to go back out the gate. Sal was blocking her way, a gun in his hand.

She'd never seen an actual gun before. Her parents didn't own one, and neither did any of her friends. At least that she knew of. She'd seen them on television and in the movies, of course, but that couldn't begin to compare to the cold reality of the forged steel pointed at her and the destructive power it held. Adrenaline flooded her system as the fight-or-flight response took hold. Fight was out of the question. The only possible alternative was flight. But fear was all too quickly tightening its grasp on her, paralyzing her ability to take action.

'Move,' Sal commanded, pushing her in the direction of the boat. Anna stood beside him grinning, holding the shopping bag she'd been carrying earlier in her hand. Suzanne decided to stand her ground.

'What do you want from me?' she said, trying to put some authority into her voice.

'Move, I said.'

Feeling there was no other option, she started walking down the pier, taking small steps to slow her progress as she assessed her situation. What *did* they want from her? Did they plan on harming her or was this just to frighten her? Was it about money? Did they want her money? And then her thoughts plunged to a darker place, the one she had been avoiding. Could she be taking her last breaths?

The lake to either side of the pier was bleak and black and beckoning. If she threw herself into the water, it would be virtually impossible for them to see her. She envisioned herself plunging headfirst into the harbor, the way she and Johnny had in the icy Minnesota lakes, and swimming frog-like underwater as far as her breath could take her.

But the gun at her back kept her moving until they stopped next to a large, sleek boat with *Giovanna Anna* stenciled in gold on the stern. 'Get on,' Sal demanded. Suzanne held her ground, refusing to move any farther. 'One shot right here,' he said, pressing the cold steel against her spine, 'and you're in a wheelchair for the rest of your life with one bag for piss and one bag for shit.'

Her fear was so strong, her mouth so dry, she could feel the sacs of her lungs stick together. It was now or never. In a last ditch effort, she pitched forward toward the gap between the boat and the pier. She was falling towards the water and promise of escape, when she felt her ankle snagged by a steel hand. Her body slammed into a piling, and she was hanging upside down and helpless over the black void. She twisted her head upwards. The starry sky came into focus behind the head of Anna who was holding onto her with hate-fueled strength.

'Stupid bitch,' she said aloud. Sal reached down and pulled her back onto the pier by the back of her jeans. Suzanne tried to scream, but Sal slammed a hand over her mouth so furiously it split her lip. He held her down while Anna unlocked the cabin and turned on the light. Then he dragged her onto the boat and threw her into the salon. Anna closed the door behind them.

'Nice boat, isn't it?' Anna spit the words at Suzanne, glaring at her with unveiled hostility. 'I bet you'd like to get your hands on this. Well, my father bought it for my mother and me. Understand?'

Splitting her face with a chilling smile, the girl reached into the shopping bag and took out a roll of duct tape. Sweat beaded Suzanne's forehead, drenched her armpits, dampened her groin. Her bowels threatened to loose. Sal forced her into a chair and held her while Anna used the duct tape to tape her legs to the chair and secure her hands behind her back.

'Please,' Suzanne implored. 'I don't know what you want, but if it's money . . .'

'How dare you, bitch.' Vince's daughter picked up the gun Sal had put on the table and hit Suzanne in the face. Suzanne's head jerked like a ragdoll, and tears of pain rolled from her eyes, as a bright red welt sprung up on her cheek. 'Money? My father has more money than you'll ever see in this lifetime.' She turned her attention to Sal. 'I can't listen to this bitch anymore. Will you shut her up?'

Sal covered Suzanne's mouth with the duct tape and rolled it around her head several times for good measure. Anna continued her rant. 'You broke into our family and changed everything. My father never acted like this with his other whores. You're not the first, you know. There have been lots before you. But ever since you he's different. He never put any of them before me and my mother. With you, it's almost like we don't exist.

'What I don't get is you're not even his type,' she hissed. 'He's never gone for skinny, titless women. He's always liked his women with curves, like your friend. Man, I was sure that bitch was the one. It all fit. Except guess what? Nothing changed after she was gone.' Anna pressed the gun to Suzanne's cheek. 'This time I know I've got the right person.'

'Anna, stop! You crazy?' Sal pried the gun from her hand and put it down on the table. 'No shooting here. The noise would echo all over the harbor.'

'Sorry, Sal. I guess I'm overexcited.' She turned her back to the table and gave him a long, promising kiss, licking his face with her tongue. He slipped a hand to her backside and pulled her close, splitting her legs with one of his.

'Let's show her how it's done,' said Anna, staring directly at

Suzanne as she rubbed herself up and down his leg. 'Is this how you do it with my father?'

Sal gave a wicked smile. Anna pulled up her shirt and bra, taking one of her massive breasts in each hand, the dark aureoles the size of silver dollars. She moaned aloud as Sal took one breast in his mouth and suckled it. Suzanne shut her eyes to block out the scene, but nothing could block out the animal sounds of sex.

'Oh, baby, baby,' Sal kept repeating. 'My dick is going to explode.'

'Does my father say that when he fucks you?' Anna taunted. Finally, after an interminable time, there were deep grunts followed by silence. Suzanne cracked her eyes open to see Sal pulling his stonewashed jeans up his long white legs, belting them high on his stomach. Anna lay on the couch, her breasts splayed to either side of her ribcage, her legs spread wide.

'You like to watch, bitch? I thought you would.'

Sal picked up the boat key and went out onto the deck. Anna put on his shirt and followed him, leaving Suzanne alone in the cabin. Her heart was pounding so hard she feared she might pass out. There was no doubt in her mind they intended to kill her. She asked herself why had she made the mistake of coming with them.

And then the harsh truth dawned on her. The mistake wasn't allowing herself to be brought to the harbor. That was an auxiliary mistake. A larger mistake had been made, and that mistake was the reason for Angie's death and would now lead to her own. The mistake of having an affair with a married man.

She should have known no good could come of it. *No married men* was the primary mantra of every advice columnist in the world. The simple fact was she had gone against all she had been taught and committed adultery. What stupidity! Instead of asking Vince for money when she got into financial trouble, she should have sold her condo. She knew all along he would lend her the money because he was attracted to her. She thought she could handle it, string him along until she could repay him. Instead she fell victim to her own selfish desires. It was too late to wish she had never gotten involved with him.

The boat's engines came on, and the chair began to vibrate,

intensifying her fear. They were going to leave the harbor and head to the open lake. She envisioned her body sinking to the murky bottom, food for the deep lake fish and other marine life. No one would even know what had become of her. Her heart pounded harder.

How much time would pass before anyone even realized she was missing? Vince would miss her tomorrow morning when he came to pick her up and she wasn't there, but what could he do? He couldn't notify the police his girlfriend was missing. The first alarm bell would sound later, at the wedding, when her place at the table sat empty. She imagined her parent's frantic phone calls and the ensuing heartbreak in the weeks to come at not knowing what had happened to their last living child.

The police would go to her building and ask questions. The doorman might remember that she left with a young dark-haired woman in a tight skirt, had given him money for a pizza, but little good that would do.

The engine stalled and there was quiet before it sputtered back to life. Gathering what wits she had left, Suzanne looked around for any possible out. The table where the gun was resting had square, sharp edges. Maybe she could shimmy over to it and use the edges to cut the duct tape holding her hands. From there the gun lay in easy reach. There was nothing to lose. Anything was better than sitting there waiting to be a victim. Using her body weight to rock the chair back and forth, she managed to move it the tiniest bit forward. Encouraged, she continued working the chair back and forth towards the table in a race against time. The engine started up again, a rhythmic churning beneath her, and soon they would be leaving the harbor. She began to work harder.

She was halfway to the table when the engine cut out again. The cabin door opened and Anna stepped in. Sal's shirt was open and her breasts hung nearly to her naval, a wisp of dark pubic hair pointed down her vulva. When she saw Suzanne had moved, her eyebrows met in a vexed frown.

'Think you're going someplace?' she asked. The girl came toward her, raised a bare foot and gave the chair a push, sending Suzanne clattering down the galley steps. She landed on her back, banging her head so hard she nearly lost consciousness. When she finally forced her eyes to open Anna was standing over her with the duct tape in her hand.

'Stupid bitch. Where did you think you were going? You're even more trouble than your friend.'

Unimaginable terror seized Suzanne as Vince's daughter cut four pieces of tape and bent over her. *Oh no oh no oh no.* Unable to move her arms or legs, she shook her head and tensed her body, flopping in the chair like a beached fish. *Oh no oh no oh no.* 'See no evil,' said Anna, pressing a piece of tape over Suzanne's eyes. 'Hear no evil,' she continued, placing a strip over each of Suzanne's ears.

'Breath no evil,' Anna shouted. She pressed the last piece of tape to Suzanne's nose and held it fast.

Suzanne tried to inhale, but the tape was blocking her nostrils. She tried to exhale and air backed up her nose. She tried working her mouth to loosen the tape to no better avail. Her mind flashed to one summer in Minnesota when she had nearly drowned and her aunt had to give her artificial respiration. She had gone to a pleasant place and come back to see her parents and Johnny circled around her, their faces carved images of worry. Maybe something like that could happen again. She lost consciousness just as the engines came back to life.

# FORTY-EIGHT

O'Reilly had just unwrapped his Subway when the Seville rocketed past them. 'Holy crap,' he said, throwing the sandwich into the back seat. He started the Crown Victoria and pulled a U-turn. 'Was that Kaufman in the passenger's seat?'

'Sure looked like him,' said his big partner, taking a leisurely bite of his own sandwich. They'd been watching the Columbo house for hours, hoping to catch sight of the elusive carpenter. Well, they'd seen him now.

'How the fuck did he get into that house without us seeing him?' O'Reilly pushed the accelerator to the car floor, praying there were no children playing outdoors as he flew down the residential street. By the time they reached subdivision exit, the Seville was a dot of red heading east.

'Man, he is moving,' said Kozlowski, calmly eating his sandwich. He saw no reason not to eat. He wasn't driving.

O'Reilly pushed the Crown Victoria into service, the speedometer passing seventy within seconds. Luckily, his hangover was mild today since he'd only drunk five or six beers the night before. He knew he was breaking about every rule in the book driving at this speed, especially outside his jurisdiction, but he didn't want to think about that.

'Do you want to call for support?' Kozlowski asked as the gap between them and the other car narrowed.

'No. Let's see where he's going first.'

The Seville pulled onto the Eisenhower and headed toward the city, moving so fast that O'Reilly had to put all his driving skills to the test. Columbo was a madman at the wheel, defying all speed limits, crossing four lanes at a time, once even driving up an exit ramp and back down on the other side to bypass slower traffic.

'This is almost like the movies,' said Kozlowski, finishing off his last bite. 'Only in the movies there'd be a dozen cops on us by now.'

'Yeah, that only happens in the movies,' O'Reilly concurred. 'This guy think he's a Nascar racer?'

'I dunno. But he sure is in some hurry.'

They reached the city in record time. The Seville left the expressway and entered the subterranean maze of lower Wacker Drive. There was construction going on with orange cones and cans confusing the lanes. They spotted the Seville in front of them and were closing in on it when a car avoiding a misplaced cone pulled out in front of them. O'Reilly slammed on the brakes, the force nearly putting both himself and Kozlowski into the windshield despite their seat belts. He let off a stream of swear words as they watched the Seville disappear down the rows of orange neon.

'What now?' asked Koz.

O'Reilly pondered the situation as the errant car moved out of the way. 'Ten'll get you twenty, they're on their way to Belmont Harbor. And somewhere in this picture, I'm seeing Dr Niebaum.' He put his foot back on the accelerator. Hard.

Ten minutes later, they screeched to a halt at Belmont Harbor. The Seville sat abandoned in the middle of the lot with its engine still running and the driver's and passenger's doors left open. They approached the car cautiously with their service revolvers unloosed.

'Sure were in a hurry,' Kozlowski repeated.

O'Reilly scanned the harbor. Lights burned in very few boats, but the *Dermabrasion* happened to be one of them. 'I just knew there was some connection between Niebaum and—' His words were cut short by the sound of pounding feet. But the pounding wasn't coming from the direction of the Niebaum boat. It was coming from the pier at the far end of the harbor. In the eerie shadows of the yellow harbor lights, they could see the figures of two running men.

*It would be the far pier*, O'Reilly thought. He hitched up his pants and gave Kozlowski a nod. They secured their weapons and took off after them.

# FORTY-NINE

Vince's hand was shaking so severely he could barely key in the security code. He could see lights glowing inside the *Giovanna Anna* and hear the smooth rumble of the cruiser's engines. Vince had never killed a man, had never even dreamt of it, but if Sal had harmed his daughter in any way, there could be a first time. The gate clanged open just as the *Giovanna Anna* started backing from its slip.

'Hurry!' he shouted at Steven. Their footsteps echoed like drumbeats across the marina as they raced down the pier. They reached the boat just as it was clearing the slip. Vince leapt onto the bow first, followed by Steven who fell noisily onto the deck. The engines went idle, and Sal's dark head appeared at the bridge.

Without waiting for Steven, Vince made a beeline to the aft deck. He tore open the cabin door with such force it nearly came off its hinges. Standing in the middle of the salon, half naked in a man's shirt, was his daughter. Upon seeing her father, she gasped and pulled the shirt closed.

'Daddy,' she cried. 'What are you doing here?'

'Has he hurt you?' Vince demanded, drilling into her with black eyes. 'Has he hurt you?' he repeated.

She gave him a pitiable look like that of a creature in pain. Flinging herself toward him, she grabbed him by the lapels and broke into tears on his tuxedoed chest. 'Oh Daddy. Thank God you're here,' she cried in a tremulous voice. 'He raped me.'

The fury within Vince brought pinpricks of red into his vision, his blood pumping with such force it was a miracle an artery didn't burst. That piece of living scum had raped his daughter. He was going to personally tear Sal to pieces with his bare hands. Embarrassed by his daughter's near nakedness, he grabbed a throw from the sofa and wrapped it around her shoulders. A loud crash came from outside. 'Stay here,' he commanded.

Vince stepped out onto the aft deck to find Steven and Sal locked in physical combat. The West Sider had the carpenter in a stranglehold and was trying to throw him over the edge. Steven turned the advantage and flipped Sal over his shoulders onto the deck. Then both men were on the ground wrestling like street fighters, crashing into deck chairs, each putting the other onto his back every few seconds.

Steven had never fought anyone so strong. Sal's strength was inhuman, and despite utilizing every bit of muscle he had, the other man was besting him. Sal fought without rules. He bit Steven's neck, barely missing the jugular. Steven arched his back with adrenaline charged strength and managed to throw Sal off, but a moment later Sal was atop him again, smashing his face with his fists.

Vince watched from the sidelines, trying to work out what to do. The positions of the two combatants changed so frequently that any attempt to intervene would be like putting a hand in a dogfight. At one point, he tried to pull Sal off Steven, but, like an enraged dog, Sal sank his teeth into the meaty part of Vince's hand, taking out a piece of flesh. Vince backed off in pain, blood pouring from his injured hand while Sal continued to pummel Steven.

Steven somehow pushed Sal off him and then the two were back in furious battle, the outline of their tensed muscles like sculpted marble as they fought hand to hand. Finally Sal got the best of the exhausted carpenter, pinning his shoulders to the deck with his knees. He wrapped his iron hands around Steven's neck and began to squeeze. The carpenter's mouth opened in mute entreaty, his hands flailing empty air as they reached for his opponent. There was no doubt in Vince's mind that if he didn't stop Sal, he would kill Steven. And perhaps Vince next. He didn't want to think about what might happen to his daughter after that.

Vince opened a storage bench and took out a wooden oar, felt its heft in his good hand. He turned back to the grappling men and drew the oar over his shoulder, readying himself to smash Sal's skull open. But before he could strike, a gunshot rang out, reverberating like a timpani across the open water. Sal gasped and crumpled to the deck. Vince looked over to see his daughter standing beside him with a gun in her hand. Her eyes were fixed on Sal who was writhing on the deck with blood spurting fountain-like from a severed artery. Vince gaped in dumbstruck horror.

'He raped me, Daddy, he raped me,' Anna sobbed, falling against him with the gun still clasped in her hand. She was near hysteria, and he tried to console her as he stared with unbridled hatred at the man bleeding out on the deck. Steven got up slowly, coughing and rubbing his throat, and gently dislodged the gun from Anna's hand. He climbed to the bridge and eased the drifting *Giovanna Anna* back into her slip. Then, he turned off the engines and returned to the deck.

Then there was silence except for the sound of Anna's crying, her dark head heaving upon her father's shoulder.

# FIFTY

O'Reilly and Kozlowski were stuck at the gate when the gunshot rang out, the sound magnified like thunder across the open water. A man in cargo shorts popped from the gangway of a dilapidated boat searching for the source of the noise. O'Reilly called to him and waved his star through the iron bars.

'Hey you! Police. We need to get in here fast.'

The cargo shorts scrambled down the dock to let them in. The two cops began running again, tightening their hold on their seldom drawn weapons, O'Reilly hoping he would make it to the end without collapsing or suffering a heart attack. When they neared the *Giovanna Anna*, they slowed and took shelter behind a nearby boat to better assess the scene on the deck. Steven Kaufman was holding a lowered gun while a girl wearing a man's shirt sobbed onto the front of a tuxedoed Vince Columbo.

'Don't move, Kaufman. Police,' O'Reilly called from the shadows. 'Put the gun down on the deck and raise your hands. You too, Columbo. And the girl. Don't anyone move.'

Steven turned toward the two detectives and weighed his options. In the background, the wail of sirens could be heard. The water below looked dark and inviting. Maybe, just maybe, he could evade them.

'Don't do it,' Vince said, sensing the carpenter's intention. 'Don't run. I will personally see to it that you'll have the best of legal help. I owe you that much for saving my daughter.'

Steven placed the gun on the deck and raised his hands over his head. Vince raised his hands too. The sobbing girl's hands remained at her side, her face hidden in her father's chest. O'Reilly and Kozlowski climbed on board.

'What the fuck,' said O'Reilly at the sight of the dark-haired figure on the deck, his life draining into an expanding pool of blood. O'Reilly picked up the gun Steven had put down and dropped it into his pocket.

With his sobbing daughter still clinging to his shirt, Vince pointed at Sal and appealed to the detectives. 'That man murdered Angie Wozniak. And he raped my daughter.'

The girl raised her tearful head from Vince's chest. 'He raped me,' she affirmed in a voice drawn from some dark place within. 'He raped me and swore if I told anyone he would do the same thing to me he did to the woman in the galley.'

'What woman in the galley?' O'Reilly asked uneasily.

Kozlowski was already on his way into the cabin. An anxious minute passed while O'Reilly kept watch over the other players on the boat. The cabin door opened and the big cop emerged carrying the limp body of a woman in his arms, a handful of duct tape in his fist. Slim lines of red glistened on her legs where he had used his pocketknife to cut her free from the chair.

'She's not breathing, but there's a pulse.' He laid the unconscious woman on the deck and got down on his knees to start CPR, pumping her chest and working feverishly to push air into her unresponsive lungs, his massive back blocking her from sight of the others. O'Reilly had already radioed for an ambulance for the man on the deck, but he radioed for another while his partner continued working on the woman. The first of the responding squad cars had pulled into the parking lot, and a couple of uniformed cops were already nearing the boat. O'Reilly stopped them and pointed to the *Dermabrasion* three docks down.

'See that boat,' he shouted. 'There's a doctor on board. Roust his ass and bring him here. We've got a dying woman.' The cops sprinted away faster than O'Reilly ever could have.

Still sheltering his weeping daughter under his arm, Vince thanked the powers that be that she was in one piece. He hoped the psychological damage wouldn't be too great. But she was a fighter like him, and he was confident she would pull through unharmed. His eyes turned to the less fortunate figure on the deck. Her face was blocked from view by the enormous cop, but he could see a white arm with a Cartier watch adorning a slim wrist. A smooth manicured hand. His heart threatened to stop beating. He knew that arm, that hand, those fingers; he'd held them to his lips time and time again. He let go of his daughter.

'Suzanne,' he cried out, moving towards the prostrate body on the deck. Someone grabbed him by his tuxedo sleeve and held him back. Thinking it was O'Reilly, he turned, ready to plead his case. But it wasn't O'Reilly holding him back. It was Anna.

'Stop, Daddy. Stop,' she shrieked, her face so malignant with hatred he barely recognized her as his daughter. Her nails clawed into his arm like a cat that had climbed too high. 'Don't go to her.'

The two uniforms came running back to the boat, followed by a shirtless Michael Niebaum carrying a first-aid kit. He climbed on board and froze upon seeing Sal lying in a puddle of blood. 'Not him,' O'Reilly shouted. 'It's too late for him.' The big cop moved aside, and the plastic surgeon drew a loud breath at the sight of Suzanne on the deck. He knelt beside her and felt her pulse. Without hesitation, he dug in the kit and pulled out the EpiPen he kept on hand because of Cara's peanut allergy. He plunged the syringe into Suzanne's chest. Almost immediately, there was a sputter and a cough followed by a wet gasp. Suzanne's body jerked as it fought to recapture life. Her breathing was erratic, a gasp and a breath, a gasp and a breath. Gradually, she began to inhale in a regular rhythm. Her eyelids fluttered open.

She looked about in confusion, her eyes traveling from Michael Niebaum to Detective Kozlowski and Detective O'Reilly, wondering why they were there, her memory empty. Vince was there, too, with Anna at his side, staring at her like he'd seen a ghost.

Then it came back in fragmented bits. Leaving her apartment with Anna. Being forced onto the boat. Being duct-taped to the chair by Sal. Anna striking her with the gun. The two of them having sex in front of her. The last thing she remembered was Anna pushing her down the galley steps. All memory stopped there.

'Vince,' she whispered, stretching out an arm. Vince pried

his daughter's fingers from his sleeve and knelt beside Suzanne. He took her hand in his and brushed it with his lips.

'I'm here, Suzanne. You don't have to worry.'

'Vince.' Her eyes closed in exhaustion.

'No, Suzanne. Don't talk. You can tell me later.'

'No, Vince. I have to tell you now.' Summoning every bit of energy her depleted body could muster, she said, 'Your daughter tried to kill me.' Then she closed her eyes and went quiet.

'That's not true. It was Sal. It was all Sal,' Anna pleaded, tugging at her father's sleeve.

The paramedics arrived, wheeling two gurneys. The police held Vince back as Suzanne was strapped to a gurney, a sheet pulled up to her shoulders. Sal was loaded on the second gurney. His sheet went over his head. Vince and Anna were escorted to two separate squad cars, Anna screaming for her father as she was loaded into the back seat, Vince's emotions torn between his daughter and his lover.

The press had arrived on scene and was there in time to film Steven Kaufman as he was loaded into a third squad car, his hands cuffed behind his back.

# FIFTY-ONE

For the first time in days, I actually had an appetite. Over the past week, I hadn't eaten more than a bite or two. I considered the seed growing in my womb and how it had been mistreated since its conception with too much booze and not enough food. I vowed to take better care of it from now on.

I was approaching the Ohio border and signs began to spring up advertising a rest stop. Soon a glow of light beckoned from the boundless darkness. I pulled off the interstate and parked my lowly VW amid an arsenal of semis and pickup trucks. The adjacent diner was filled with truckers and hunters, most wearing hats bearing heavy equipment logos. A few heads turned to check me out, a woman traveling alone was always a source of interest, but for the most part the eyes of the customers were glued to silenced televisions mounted around the room.

I took a table in the window and picked the menu out of a wire holder. A waitress came over and I ordered a chicken salad plate and a milkshake, leaning back in mindless exhaustion to watch the TV while I waited for my food. The television was tuned to WGN, and a replay of the *Nine O'Clock News* was on the screen. The mayor welcomed some dignitary followed by a series of commercials. The chicken salad arrived and I started eating like I had just been released from a prison camp. When I finally lifted my head for a breather, the news had come back on and a blonde reporter was standing in front of a dozen police cars with a subject line reading: *BELMONT HARBOR*. The screen flashed to a prerecorded tape. Steven Kaufman was being led to a police car in handcuffs. He turned his dark curly head and stared at me from the screen. His face was bruised and one of his eyes was swollen shut. Things became even more surreal when the camera panned around to show a shirtless Michael Niebaum standing in the background.

I put my fork down and went in search of the pay phone.
Carol Anne was at home, the sleepy sound of my best friend's
voice reassuring in the sea of uncertainty.

'Guess who?'

'Maggie, is that you?' Her voice shifted to wide awake. 'Are
you all right? Everyone is worried about you. Where are you?'

'Don't worry. I didn't hang myself. I'm somewhere near the
Ohio border. Sorry to call so late, but I just had to know what
happened.'

'Well, the truth is, everyone was in total shock. Your mother
cried. Flynn's mother cried. Your dad looked like he'd been
foreclosed on. And I've seen Flynn look better.'

'Flynn? He went to the restaurant?'

'Yep. He showed up and took your parents and his parents
aside and talked to them. Then he told the attendants, that would
include me, what he must have told your parents. That the two
of you came to the realization that it wasn't right for you to
get married and you had to stop before you made a mistake.
He rocked, Maggie. Handled it with a lot of class. Didn't say
a bad word about you.

'Then the Sig Ep boys rallied around him and declared that
if there wasn't going to be a wedding, there was going to be
one hell of a party. He'll be OK, Maggie. Of course, I don't
know about his sister. Nan looked really heartbroken.'

I flinched at the thought of disappointing Nan. God, I was
an evil creature. But you can't get married for other people, I
reminded myself. That was what had brought me here in the
first place. And then I got down to the real reason for the call.

'I'm at a truck stop and I just saw them arresting the father
of the child on the news. And, am I totally out of my mind, or
was Michael there?'

Carol Anne's voice changed yet again. 'There's a hell of lot
more to this story than what you just saw on the news.'

She filled me in on what she knew, of Suzanne nearly being
killed by the same guy who probably killed Angie, of Michael
saving Suzanne's life. She had no idea where Steven fit into
the picture. She only knew he was arrested. There were so many
questions, I didn't know where to start. I asked the most
important one first.

'How's Suzanne doing?'

'She's in the hospital. They had to sedate her and her parents are with her. I think she'll be OK, physically anyhow.'

'Thank God Michael was there.'

The prolonged silence told me maybe it wasn't such a good thing that Michael was there – for Carol Anne anyhow. 'He was entertaining a male friend while I was at your almost rehearsal dinner. Maggie, I've had it. We're done.'

I hung up thinking how the world as we knew it had rotated off its axis.

This time my headlights faced west. My Volkswagen and I sped through the pitch black towards Chicago, driven by an urgency I didn't quite understand myself. Despite all the misery I'd caused Flynn and others, for the first time in ages, I didn't feel trapped. I felt a sense of liberation like the caterpillar that had just sprouted wings and was able to fly.

And then the truth unveiled itself. For once I had done what I wanted. The truth was not becoming Mrs Flynn Rogers Hamilton III tomorrow sat quite well with me. During my college days in Iowa City, I was passionate about things. Theatre. Poetry. Literature. And causes like world hunger and equal rights and the environment. In the years since graduation, those passions had been muted by age, but they'd also been buried under the heavy workload of a job I'd never been passionate about. Sometimes you get so swept up in what everyone else thinks you should be doing that you aren't sure what you want anymore. And while I still wasn't really sure what I wanted, I knew it wasn't Flynn and the life he would have provided for me. Flynn was my mother's dream and the dream of a lot of other women. But he wasn't mine. And there was one other thing I knew. No matter what happened, I would not be returning to the *Chicagoan*.

As for the mysterious Steven Kaufman. I had no clue who he really was or what would become of him, but I did know one thing. If this baby in my womb caused only one-tenth the upheaval in my life that he had, then I had to put on my seat belt and get ready for the ride of my life.

It was after two a.m. when I let myself back into my

apartment. I rushed into the bathroom to relieve myself for the first time in hours. When I turned around to flush the toilet I didn't know whether to laugh or cry. The bowl was as red as a Christmas tree ornament.

I crawled into bed and slept soundly for the first time in months.


The next morning I went to the lock-up where Steven was being held while waiting extradition to New Hampshire. O'Reilly made arrangements for me to see him, leaving us alone in a small windowless room with a couple of plastic chairs. He looked tired, his curls drooping, his face speckled with cuts and bruises. The swollen eye looked better than it had on last night's news. He sat in his chair like a student awaiting a lecture.

'I just came to tell you I'm not getting married after all,' I said. 'I don't know why I felt compelled to let you know, but I figure you had enough to do with it that it seemed like the thing to do.'

Our eyes met with a shared understanding that both thrilled and frightened me. 'They're sending me back to Manchester,' he said. 'I'm not going to fight extradition. But I want you to know one thing. I'm not the man who did those things I'm charged with. Well, except for the bigamy, but that wasn't my fault. The worst thing I've ever done in my life is try to set things right by everybody else.'

'Don't I know how that goes?' I reflected.

'Maggie, I know our meeting hasn't exactly been under the best of circumstances, but if I get out of Manchester in one piece and I come back through this way, can I see you?'

'I don't see why not. That is, if I'm still here. I may head out west.'

His next words were guarded, tossed out like a fly fisherman's lure in the wrong season. 'And what you told me Thursday night about being pregnant? Was that the truth?'

'I thought it was,' I replied. 'But wouldn't it just figure. I got my period.'

# FIFTY-TWO

Kozlowksi was spending a leisurely Saturday with his wife and, with nothing to keep him in his dreary apartment, O'Reilly was tidying up his desk, his hangover so mild that he barely noticed it. He was cutting back on consumption. His phone rang.

'O'Reilly here.'

'Well, Detective.' There was no mistaking her husky voice. 'I should have known better than to second guess you.'

'Is this the intuitive and persistent Ms Delaney? Don't feel too bad. You weren't a hundred percent wrong about your man from New Hampshire. We did have a warrant out for his arrest after all. And it's a good thing we were watching him or things could have turned out pretty poorly for your friend, Suzanne.'

'I don't know. Something about that guy still bugs me. But I'm not calling to talk about Angie's murder for a change. Not entirely anyhow. I believe you offered to buy me dinner if I was free tonight.'

'Yeah, I heard the wedding is off.'

'You called that one too. But I don't know if that's a bad thing.'

'Your friend Maggie is a nice person,' he said. 'A little confused, but nice just the same.'

'We're all a little confused,' said Kelly. 'But what about dinner? Does your offer still stand or was that a bogus invitation?'

'How about seven o'clock?' he asked, running a finger beneath his already loosed collar.

'That would be great.'

'I'll pick you up.' He ended the call and watched as a group of five young skinheads were shepherded across the room for a lineup. It never stopped. But it was over for him for today. He opened his top drawer and pushed the ever present paperwork inside. Then he reached into the back of the drawer and took out the flask that lived there. He considered it for a minute and then tipped it into the trashcan.

Kelly pushed her plate away, leaving half of slab of ribs and an untouched mound of French fries. 'I can't eat another bite,' she exclaimed. 'I'll be running this off for a week as it is.' She took a sip of diet cola and opened a Wet-Nap from the pile stacked on the table. O'Reilly polished off his last rib and washed it down with a couple swallows of beer. It was only his second of the evening. She had been counting. He put the glass down, leaving five clear barbeque-sauce fingerprints.

'No trouble getting a conviction there,' Kelly teased.

He examined his sticky hands. 'Guess this isn't the smartest place for a first date, is it?'

'Is this a date?' She opened a few more Wet-Naps and tossed them to him.

'So now I'm waiting.'

'Waiting?'

'Waiting for you to fill in the blanks.'

O'Reilly drained the last of the beer. 'Well, the Columbo girl is under psychiatric observation and ten'll get you twenty she cops a loony. Her old man will see to that. If it even comes to trial. Her lawyer shut her up and no one's talking.'

'So what do you think happened?'

'In short order, she was insanely jealous of Papa's girlfriend and wanted her out of the picture. Only the first time, she didn't get it right. Then, when Papa Columbo's behavior doesn't change . . .'

'She figures out they killed the wrong person,' Kelly finished for him, 'and goes after Suzanne.'

'Told ya you should be a cop,' O'Reilly said. He was thinking about another beer and looked around in search of the waitress. Then he looked back at the woman sitting opposite him. Her pale blue eyes seemed to see right through him. Maybe he didn't need another beer after all. 'How about a movie?' he asked, surprising himself. He hadn't been to a movie in years.

'Sounds good to me,' Kelly said, pleased with herself.

\*      \*      \*

After the movie, he drove her home and walked her to the door. She had chosen some art film, and while he thought he was going to hate it, it was actually pretty good even if there were no cops, no car chases, and nothing blew up. Standing awkwardly in front of the garden apartment, he noticed how pretty she looked, half her face in the glow of the streetlight, half dappled with the shadows of the overhead trees, her transparent blue eyes as inviting as the water he'd swum in once, on his only vacation with his wife to the Caribbean. He was struck with the urge to kiss her, but the fear of failure stopped him. It had been some time since he kissed a woman. Since his wife actually. The only thing he'd kissed since his divorce was a bottle.

Kelly looked down at O'Reilly in the yellow light. Even in flat shoes, she was taller than him. She was feeling emotions she wasn't quite comfortable facing straight on. Though she knew it might spell trouble, she didn't want the night to end yet.

'Do you want to come in for a coffee?' she offered.

He shrugged and the corners of his mouth tipped upwards. 'Why not?'

Too late, she remembered Tizzy. The cat was asleep in the middle of the flowered sofa, and when they entered the room, she raised her head, giving O'Reilly a one-eyed glare. Before Kelly could stop him, O'Reilly put a thick-fingered hand to the cat's head. Kelly gasped and waited for the cat to tear into him. Tizzy looked at the hand warily and then pushed her head against his palm.

'That is the strangest thing I've ever seen,' Kelly said, watching in amazement. 'That cat hates everyone but me.'

# My Epilogue

'll talk about the others first.

Kelly and O'Reilly ended up getting married a year later. In a small civil ceremony at City Hall followed by cake and coffee. That was it. No four-course meal, no bridesmaids, no band, no flower arrangements, and definitely no champagne toast. The rummy cop had actually dried out. But he never got the promotion he was hoping for. His partner Kozlowski got it, so he quit the force and Kelly quit school and the two of them opened a private detective agency. They named it, of all things, White Truck Investigations.

I went back for the wedding, one of my last trips back east, even if it meant listening to my mother lament over Flynn's elopement to Las Vegas shortly after our non-wedding. She could barely contain her tears at the thought of another woman living in what would have been her daughter's house. It pleased me to learn Flynn had rebounded. He was a good man and I wished only the best for him. There was relief in knowing I hadn't ruined his life after all.

Carol Anne ended up divorcing Michael. She tried giving him one last chance, but after months of sex therapy, couple's therapy, regression therapy – you name it – Michael realized he couldn't practice heterosexual monogamy. The divorce was an amicable one. He left Carol Anne quite well off financially, and with a lifetime guarantee of complimentary cosmetic improvements. At first, life without Michael had been difficult for her since it was all she knew. But she started a decorating business and met a man seven years *her younger* at a seminar for small business owners. He came to Kelly's wedding with her, and I must confess, not only was he good looking, I hadn't seen Carol Anne smile like that in years.

Unfortunately, things did not turn out as well for Suzanne.

She suffered from terrible anxiety and nightmares following the experience on the boat, and was in therapy for years afterwards. She ended things with Vince right off, refusing to see him ever again except once in the presence of her attorney to settle their accounts. Since her memory of that horrible night was impaired and Sal was dead, no charges were ever filed against Vince's daughter. In fact, Anna ended up the CEO of her father's company and her name crosses the headlines from time to time. Suzanne sold nearly everything she owned to get out of debt and moved in with her parents. She ended up working at their store. She was diagnosed with breast cancer just before the millennium and died a few months later. Her parents followed her shortly thereafter.

Natasha's life ran into a major speed bump when Arthur was indicted for insider trading. He ended up doing some serious jail time and they lost the Lake Forest house. However, ever resourceful Natasha divorced the buffoon and married an even richer, more obnoxious trader. I hear she spends most of her time in France these days.

As for me, Steven stopped back in Chicago less than a month after he had been extradited to New Hampshire. I was still in my apartment, living off my savings, and planning my move out west. When I saw him standing on my threshold, it was like a ticket to the stars. You have to experience true passionate love in your life to understand how it felt to see him again, his long curls framing his face, his eyes apologetic behind the wire-rimmed glasses.

His criminal charges had been dropped when his second wife recanted her story against him. She confessed it was her own father who had given her the brutal beating after catching her on the floor of a jobsite with one of the roofers. The lawyers were still working on the bigamy charges, but that didn't matter to me. We didn't need a piece of paper to enjoy what we shared.

So we moved to the Roaring Fork Valley in Colorado, best known for the town of Aspen. There was a serious building boom going on, so Steven had no trouble finding work and I got a job writing for the local newspaper. Our life was idyllic. We hiked and camped and skied. We climbed a few mountains. We managed our lives so our work was flexible, and spent a couple of months a year traveling around places like Europe and the Far East. We trekked to Machu Picchu and snorkeled off the Great Barrier Reef. And in the times between sport and travel, we attended concerts at the Music Festival and studied the classics in Great Books.

We eventually started our own construction firm, the business grew, and our lives continued to blossom. We were deliriously happy, our passion for each other fed by the beauty and culture that surrounded us.

Even the crash, which ruined us financially along with many of our friends, didn't dull our love for each other. Though we had our challenges, the chemistry we shared kept us together. But the crash was responsible for our end in another way. After our company went bankrupt, Steven found work on one of the few jobs in the valley, the construction of a massive house up the Castle Creek Valley. While he was putting in a retaining wall, a massive boulder broke loose from the mountainside, ending his life in a matter of seconds and in so many ways mine.

So it was with mixed emotions that I learned of this brain tumor. The doctors have told me it's a fast-growing cancer, so the end won't be far off. I actually look forward to parting ways with this world now, because I am sure I will see him again in the next. And when we are back together I hope to finally get an answer to the question I never asked him, a question that has plagued me since he left my apartment after our first night together.

How did his truck end up on the other side of my street that next morning?

# Postscript to Readers from Kelly O'Reilly

This story was given to me by Maggie's younger sister, Laurel. I was totally shocked when she called to tell me of Maggie's death, and even more shocked when she and her partner, Alice, showed up on my doorstep with the manuscript. They found it in Maggie's cabin after her death, and Alice told Laurel her sister's memory would best be served by turning the manuscript over to me.

Looking at Laurel, I was reminded so much of Maggie, the red hair and impish eyes. My heart skipped a lonely beat as I thought back to how close we had once been. All those shared memories, some good, some not so good. Time and distance had moved us apart, tethered each of us in our own worlds. But it was amazing how quickly I was drawn back into our mutual world when I started reading Maggie's words. Her story was well told, and I had to laugh at how much about me she nailed on the head, especially the start of Ron's and my relationship. And in all truth, I owe my marriage and children to Maggie, either directly or indirectly. Had she not gone crazy on that last night out, I don't think Ron's and my paths would have ever crossed. Unless I started drinking again!

But more seriously, the last line of her book was an *aha* moment. Regardless of how her life played out with Steven Kaufman up until his death, I always thought there was something fishy about that guy. In fact I worried about her being with him somewhere so remote to us as Colorado, especially because we barely saw her again after she moved west. But as the years passed and our communication grew more infrequent, I forgot about my suspicions. After all, our lives were so separate, and I was working and raising my kids.

But now the matter had been reopened. After I finished reading Maggie's manuscript, I went into the living room where Ron was glued to a Bears game. I try to be sensitive to his interests and not disturb him in the middle of sports events, but this was far too important to wait even an hour.

'I have a new case,' I said. 'Or actually an old case.'

'Wha—?' His eyes stayed riveted to the television. 'Wait till a commercial.'

I sat down on the sofa and waited. Our company does basically divorce and subpoena work, and it is quite lucrative. In fact, business actually increased after the recession started. It seemed everyone was suing everybody, looking for where some spare change might be hidden, and as a result we were delivering subpoenas like they were Christmas cards.

When the game went to a commercial break, the Bears were winning 10–0. Ron muted the screen and turned his now entirely silver head towards me. I told him about Maggie's story and how Steven Kaufman's truck was somehow on the other side of her street the next morning. He rolled his eyes in exasperation as he revisited my relentless pursuit of the guy all those years back. But our marriage has endured, despite some rocky times, because we recognize what is important to the other. And without my saying another word, he knew this was important.

So we opened a new file.

Naturally, it had been so long since that last night out, that the odds of learning anything locally was slim to none. Neighbors seeing a truck at four in the morning twenty-five years ago? Right. At first, I was scratching my head at where to even start. That's when my brilliant (believe me I don't use that term often) husband suggested we head to New Hampshire and talk to Steven Kaufman's first two wives.

I started doing a little research on the Internet, and bingo, found Heather Kaufman living outside Concord where she and the carpenter had owned their home. I've always found you get better results when you confront someone in person without giving them a heads-up that you're coming. A phone call puts them on alert or gives them an opportunity to turn you down. So Ron and I got on a plane for New York and transferred to a commuter to Concord.

Since I had Heather's physical address, with GPS it didn't take us much to find where she lived. But when we pulled up to the house, I thought I must have made a mistake. For some reason I envisioned the high school sweetheart first wife to be living in some crumbling cabin or cramped apartment. After all, she hadn't changed her name, which indicated that she hadn't remarried after Steven. That translated to poverty for me. So when we saw the huge English Tudor where she lived, Ron and I were both stunned.

We were even more stunned at the woman that answered the door. I thought I was going to have to haul my husband's jaw off the ground. She was extremely pretty with shoulder-length dark hair and very large breasts. She looked to be about thirty-five even though, if you did the math, she had to be in her mid-fifties. We told her that her first husband had died within the last year and we were looking for possible heirs. (I've learned, no matter how rich the person, the possibility of more money is always a great way in the door.) Her face took on a guarded look at the mention of her ex, but luckily, New Englanders tend to be trusting and friendly, and, after giving it some thought, she threw the door wide open.

New Englanders also tend to be neighborly. She offered us coffee and donuts, which I declined and Ron readily accepted. We sat in her warm great room in front of a roaring fire.

'So now what is all this about Steven and some inheritance?'

Ron is always good at deflecting, so I let him proceed. 'I understand you were high school sweethearts,' he said, taking in the rich surroundings.

Her pretty face screwed up like there was vinegar in her mug instead of coffee. 'Where in heavens did you get that one? I met Steven when he was doing some carpentry work here in the house for my dad. Dad's dead now, rest his soul. My mother too, so the house is mine.

'Anyhow, when Steven was working here, he wasted no time in trying to get into my pants. And unfortunately he succeeded. When my father found out, he confronted Steven who agreed to marry me. So we got married and he deserted me not long after. Here one day, gone the next. No explanation. Nothing. I think my father carried his hatred for Steven to his deathbed.

'I didn't hear boo from him, and then two years later I read in the paper that he had been accused of assaulting his wife. His wife? He already had a wife, thank you, all of one hundred miles away. And get this. He did it again. His new wife was the daughter of the construction company owner. He clearly had a thing for his bosses' daughters.'

Ron gave me a long inquisitive look before asking, 'So did you ever end up getting divorced from him?'

'Yep. And she did too. About twenty-five years ago, some big-time attorney from Chicago stepped in to negotiate both deals. Gratis. I even got a cash settlement. And the charges about him assaulting his other wife? They were dropped. It was like someone waved a magic wand and all his problems went away.'

I recalled what Ron had overheard Vince Columbo say to Steven, when they were standing over Salvatore Gianfortune's body on the deck of the *Giovanna Anna*. 'I'll get you the best of attorneys.' I had no doubt it was Vince and a lot of fertilizer that made all of Steven's problems go away.

Steven's second wife didn't buy into our pretext of an inheritance and refused to see us. She had remarried and obviously wanted to distance herself from her past. Still most of New England is like a small town; people know other people's business, so it wasn't too hard to garner some more information regarding Steven's alleged assault on his second wife. Some said her father was the one who put the hurt on her face for marrying Steven in the first place. Others said she'd done it to herself to get even with him for leaving her. But most concurred he probably did it after catching her on the floor of a jobsite with another man.

Regardless, having learned basically all we could in New Hampshire, we got on a plane and headed home.

Back in Chicago, I made an appointment with Anna Columbo. We weaseled our way into her offices under the guise of doing a feature on her in a local business magazine. It was general knowledge that she was a publicity hound. Her father, who was richer than ever, had his name plastered on just about every new construction project in the city. She was still beautiful, but far thinner, and was dressing in a far subtler manner than she had those many years ago. We were admitted to her office and sat in a conversation area, looking out over the Anish Kapoor kidney doing its backbend in Grant Park. Ron was feeding her some lame BS about business conditions in the city, when she must have recognized him, and her eyes narrowed in visual dissection.

'What's this really about?' she demanded.

'Just a couple quick questions. You knew Steven Kaufman. He worked in your house.'

'That's enough,' she said standing, still unruffled. 'You can just get the hell out of my office.'

But I wasn't finished. This is how you do it. Good cop. Bad cop. This time we were both playing bad cop. Like I said before. The element of surprise doesn't give them time to prepare the safe answer.

'You were sleeping with him, weren't you?' I snuck the question in before she could show us the door. The assertiveness of her answer told me everything I needed to know.

'You're kidding, right? He was the help.'

And then she showed us the door.

That night over linguini in clam sauce, Ron and I discussed possible scenarios. We figured one of the scenarios could have gone something like this.

Of course, Kaufman was banging Vince's daughter. That was his MO and he was probably supposed to meet her on her father's boat later that night which meant she would have had the boat keys on her. But she'd gone to the Overhang first to check out her rival after hearing her father talking to Suzanne on the phone. When Kaufman saw Anna hanging with Sal, he decided to show her by going after Maggie. But when Maggie passed out before he could get lucky – yes, that was the reason she hadn't used her diaphragm that night – Kaufman decided to rethink his rendezvous with Anna, after all. So he headed for Belmont Harbor. Somehow he stumbled across Angie's body and realized that in her vitriol, Anna had killed a woman she mistakenly thought was her father's lover. Knowing full and well that he might end up associated with the murder, he sped back to Maggie's unlocked apartment and a rock solid alibi. Of course, by then his original parking space had been taken, so he was forced to park across the street.

That is just one of the many scenarios we came up with. Here is another.

Maybe, just maybe, unlike all those other *I'll call you* one-nighters who never do, he left after Maggie passed out, but had second thoughts after driving away – turning back when he realized he had left something very special behind.

I'll leave the decision of the true scenario to you.

# Acknowledgements

First and always, I must thank my agent, Helen Breitwieser of Cornerstone Literary Agency. We have been through many ups and downs together and she has always been there to support me. She's absolutely the best.

And to my editor, Holly Domney, who has helped shape *The Last Night Out*, my publisher at Severn House, Kate Lyall Grant, who has taken support to a higher level, and Jamie Byng, of Canongate, whose enthusiasm for the book is overwhelming. I couldn't hope to be supported by a better publishing team as well as one with a shared psyche. Here's to our future successes.

I can't let this book go to print without mentioning six special friends who date back to whenever – and who may or may not have provided inspiration for this novel. In alphabetical order: Alison, Carol, Iris, Jane, Rosie, and Vita. Love you girls.

And lastly, to Aspen Words, the literary branch of the Aspen Institute, which tirelessly works to bring readers to writers and vice versa. As Seneca said, and I paraphrase, 'Life is short, but art is forever.' Aspen Words work to fill that mission and hopefully people are talking about our present day art long into the future.